FOR THE LOVE OF GRACIE

For the Love of Gracie © 2016 by Amy K. McClung

This book was previously self-published by Amy K. McClung in 2013. It has since been reedited with many changes and revisions taking place and republished with Hot Tree Publishing.

Be prepared to enjoy a fresh version of the beautiful NA romance, *For the Love of Gracie.*

For the Love of Gracie is a work of fiction. All names, characters, events and places found therein are either from the author's imagination or used fictitiously. Any similarity to persons alive or dead, actual events, locations, or organizations is entirely coincidental and not intended by the author.

For information, contact the publisher, Hot Tree Publishing.
www.hottreepublishing.com

Editing: Hot Tree Editing
Cover Designer: Claire Smith
Formatting: RMGraphX

ISBN-10: 1-925448-19-3
ISBN-13: 978-1-925448-19-1

10 9 8 7 6 5 4 3 2 1

PROLOGUE

From the outside looking in, it can seem a person has everything they need to be happy. Many subconsciously ignore the age-old cliché of "don't judge a book by its cover." We don't all go through life meaning to judge people by looks or stereotypes, though inevitably we all do at some point, whether we realize it or not.

Gracie has several friends surrounding her at all times, yet she has moments where she feels utterly alone. Life isn't always perfect. Regrets are unavoidable for most, some greater than others. We live life in the hopes that it will be easy, that we will be happy and never have anything bad happen to us. For some, that is their reality, and they are the lucky few. For others, they have to fight for every ounce of happiness in their life.

Gracie and her group of friends are not lucky enough to have it easy. They've experienced loss, abuse, bullying, unimaginable grief, and betrayal. They are all due for a little happiness and love for a change. The one thing they can count on is each other. There is nothing better than true southern devotion.

Chapter One

The delicious smell of waffles drifted through the air. "Mmm," I groaned, reaching my arms above my head, and stretching my stiff muscles. Placing my feet on the hardwood floor, I flexed my toes, cringing from the cold sensation that nipped at the soles of my feet. Drawing my legs back up on reflex, I reached over to the drawer next to the bed and grabbed a pair of wool socks. When I looked down and realized I was wearing socks with panties and nothing else, I chuckled softly.

Hudson's favorite T-shirt was within reach. He had obtained a black Five Finger Death Punch T-shirt at the only concert of theirs he'd attended. They were his favorite band, and more like an obsession than anything else. It hung loosely on my body, covering me to my knees. My long auburn hair was hopeless at the moment. Bed-head? Definitely.

Hudson and I had only met a few weeks earlier and had spent most of that time in bed. Twirling my hair into a bun, I stuck a pen in it to keep it slightly contained. I checked my face in the bathroom mirror; my hazel eyes are bloodshot from lack of sleep. Underneath my lashes, eyeliner streaked my skin from overexertion. "Waterproof, my ass," I mumbled as I cleaned my face. "Gracie Walker, you're a hot mess. It's a wonder someone as sexy as Hudson James wants you."

The bedroom door creaked as I opened it. I stopped to let the smell of syrup assault my senses. Hudson James was fantastic at *everything,* and I grinned at the memory of our night spent together.

His tan, muscular back was the first thing I saw when I stepped into the kitchen, adorned by a large dragon tattoo over his left shoulder that screamed "bad boy." His dark blond hair was shaggy, and I loved nothing more than running my fingers through it. I propped myself against the doorframe, staring at him as he worked on the waffles. He was softly singing to himself.

His boxer briefs made his ass look so delicious; I just wanted to take a bite out of it. The house was warm already due to the humid temperature common with the end of summer in the south. The stove increased the heat in the kitchen, and the beads of sweat running down his back had me sucking my bottom lip between my teeth. My heart sped up, my excitement heightening as I watched him. Unconsciously, I let out a low moan. The noise alerted him to my presence.

He smiled as he licked his lips then turned the oven off and said, "Good morning, hot stuff." Sauntering over, he placed his hand on my hip, moving my shirt up. His lips slowly met mine as he teased me with his tongue, one hand working its way down my body to push against my core as his erection pressed into my belly. His other hand snaked inside my shirt, cupping my breast after sliding my panties to the floor.

He moved away long enough to reach into a kitchen drawer for something. Placing the foil wrapper between his teeth, he ripped open a condom.

"You keep condoms in the kitchen?"

He smirked. "Safety first, baby, no matter what room of the house."

He lifted me effortlessly and set me down on the table. I lay back as he clambered up on the table with me, moving up until we were face to face. He groaned, "Gracie girl, you make me crazy," right as he plunged into my heat. I moaned again as he moved, slowly at first, and then faster, as I held on to the edge of the table for support.

I kept my eyes focused on his as he rocked against me. He rolled his hips and I bit down as he continued to hit just the right spots sending me over the edge. Arching my hips upward, I allowed him deeper access and cried out as my body began to tremble.

After thrusting one final time as we both came, shuddering together, he lifted up and away from me as I turned to face him and licked my lips.

Hudson casually picked my panties off the floor and tossed them at me.

He smirked. "I need to finish breakfast now."

I smiled. "Sorry, didn't mean to distract you."

Grabbing a handful of my hair, which had slipped from the bun, he gently pulled me in for a kiss, the spot between my legs already aching for him again.

"Never apologize for what you just did there. And you look so sexy in my shirt."

Hudson and I met at a club a few weeks earlier. I had just broken up with a jerk—my go-to personality, apparently. I had never had a really romantic relationship, like the ones I saw in movies. I had begun to think those didn't exist, but this one seemed like it might be different.

Hudson had been standing across the club when our eyes had met. He'd strolled over to me and used a cheesy pick-up line to get my attention. "Hi, my name is Milk. I'll do your body good."

My response was beer coming out of my nose from laughter. Apparently, that was a turn-on for him. Two hours later, we were in my car making out, his hand was lifting my shirt, and he was quickly on his way to second base.

Since that night, I had practically been living at his place. I had my own house, but we hadn't kept our hands off each other long enough for me to go home. Each time I tried to leave, he'd sweet-talk me into staying another night. It was hard to say no when he was bribing me with compliments and waiting on me hand and foot.

Hudson pulled me from my thoughts when he brought a plate of waffles to the table. I slathered butter and syrup on them and began shoving forkfuls into my mouth. He laughed heartily. "Damn, Gracie. You hungry?"

I smiled, my mouth stuffed with food, and mumbled, "Sorry, I worked up an appetite."

He chuckled. "As long as you don't get fat, eat as much as you want."

Ouch. His words hit me like a slap in the face. The thing was, I used to be overweight and hated my body. I put the fork down and wiped my mouth. "That was rude," I said.

Hudson snickered. "What? I like your body the way it is. That's a bad thing?"

I scoffed. "Next time, say it a little nicer."

He shrugged it off as no big deal.

The song "Whip It" interrupted the moment. I reached for my phone, but Hudson grabbed it first. He glanced at the name. "Who's Cam?"

I snatched it back from him. "That's Cameron," I answered before he could say anything else. "Hey, Cam, what's up, babe?" I giggled and Hudson's jaw clenched. Strolling out of the room, I plopped myself down on his couch.

After thirty minutes of gossiping with Cam, I got off the phone. "I'm going to grab a shower," I called out to Hudson, moving toward the bedroom. Stepping out into the hallway, he grabbed my arm, yanking me back to him. "Ouch! What the hell are you doing?"

Releasing me, he looked crestfallen. "Sorry, didn't mean

to pull so hard. Who's Cameron?"

With my hands on my hips, I said, "My best friend."

He sighed with relief. "So, it's a chick?"

I shook my head. "No, he's a guy. We've been friends since we were kids. Damn, I can't believe he hasn't come up before now. He's usually the main topic of my conversations. Why are you making a big deal about it?"

"The big deal is I don't like you talking to other guys like you just did." There was a note of anger in his tone.

I laughed. "Are you jealous? After what we just did, you think you have something to worry about? That's too cute."

He grabbed my hand when I went to pat his cheek, twisting my wrist roughly. I cringed in pain as he laughed.

"Not so cute now, is it. Get a shower and we'll talk about this when you get out." Before he shoved me toward the door, he planted a kiss on my lips and winked at me. I watched him confused as hell as he walked away.

What the hell was that?

I'd only known him a few weeks, of course, but he'd always been pretty charming. He'd bought me roses twice, which already made him more romantic than most of the guys I'd been with. I trembled as I left the room, tempted to just pack up and get the hell out of there. But the kiss after, the teasing evident in his tone.... *He was just playing, right?*

I knew I was partially to blame for how he'd reacted; I should have explained who Cameron was earlier. I was sure I'd be pissed at him if he'd spent thirty minutes chatting on the phone to a girl I didn't know anything about.

Cameron and I had been friends since we were five. We met in kindergarten and hit it off right away, often getting into trouble for talking during nap time. On one occasion, he'd told the teacher that he had to protect me because I didn't have a daddy. The teacher thought it was sweet but still separated us.

In grade school, there was rarely a moment we weren't together. My mom let him sleep over every weekend until we were twelve, but then she worried about puberty and inappropriate things. Cameron "came out" to me when we were in high school. By then, I was totally in love with him. What girl didn't fall in love with her best guy friend?

It had crushed me that he wouldn't ever return my feelings, but I never felt any different about him. Deep down, I'd always known he was gay, and I was sure he knew it too. I was honored that I'd been the first person he had trusted to tell. His parents were supportive and encouraged him to be himself. The reassurance was great for family life, but when he came out at school, he was bullied by a lot of students, both girls and guys.

We had a close group of friends, and we did our best to protect him from the bullies. Unfortunately, there were a few times when they got the best of him. He had taken more than one beating during our high school years. Once we made it to college, things got a little better for him. We took turns between the gay bars and the straight bars each weekend, so everyone in our group felt included.

When I stepped out of the shower, Hudson was waiting in the room, his eyes trained on me. I grabbed a towel and covered myself, still unsettled by his odd behavior.

"What the hell?" I exclaimed, tucking the end into the top to tighten it.

He laughed, looking sheepish. "Nothing I haven't seen before. I wanted to finish our talk."

I backed away from him with my hands in the air. "A little privacy would be nice. Look, there's no reason to worry about Cam. There's nothing going on with us."

His hand shot forward, and I flinched in response.

Hudson grimaced, visibly upset at my recoil. Gently, he placed his hand on my cheek and said, "Did you think I was going to hit you? I'd never hurt you, Gracie."

I rolled my eyes. "You just hurt me a few minutes ago." I held up my wrist to show him the bruise beginning to form.

Pain flickered through his eyes when he took hold of my wrist and kissed the bruise softly. "I'm so sorry. I didn't mean to hurt you. I've had a rough week, but I shouldn't take that out on you. I'm sorry, baby."

He stepped closer and pushed my hair back, lightly pressing his lips to my shoulder before moving to my neck. He nibbled on my earlobe and whispered, "You make me so crazy, Gracie. How do you do it?"

His hand moved to loosen the towel and I let it fall from my body. We spent several hours exploring each other again, and I luxuriated in every touch and caress, the bruise on my wrist becoming a distant memory.

I knew I had to make an appearance at home.

"Will I see you tonight?" he asked as I stood at the door.

I shrugged. "Maybe. We'll see." I winked at him and, when I turned, he smacked my butt. I glanced back at him, and he openly stared at me as I walked away, a small smile playing on his lips.

Hudson James. Even his name oozed sexiness, and he was into me, Gracie Walker. I'd never believed I could land a guy so dreamy.

CHAPTER TWO

My keys were in the door when it was yanked open, my friend Angel standing there beaming at me. "Well, look who remembered where she lives!" she teased as I pushed by her into the house. "How's Hudson? Have you ever seen him standing up, or are you guys always horizontal?"

Angel and Mary Jane had been my roommates for three years, ever since we graduated high school and had started college life.

We lived in Nashville, Tennessee, where we attended college in a nearby town. Angel was originally from Florida. She was Hispanic, five-four, with long black hair, and deep brown eyes. We envied her because she had a small waist but a "badonkadonk" butt the guys went crazy for, plus enough of an accent to make her sound exotic and sexy.

Mary Jane was from Kentucky. She was five-eight, with blonde hair and pale green eyes. She was considered plus-sized because she was a size eighteen. I personally thought she was the hottest of the three of us, sometimes finding myself envious of her soft curves. She had a wonderful country twang the guys seemed to go crazy for the whole "farm girl" persona.

Angel's family moved to Tennessee when she was twelve; Mary Jane's when she was ten. The three of us had been inseparable since we met in junior high; only men seemed to interrupt our time together lately.

"Yes, I've seen him standing. We do it vertically too." I nudged her and she laughed.

She turned and yelled up the stairs, "Yo, MJ, come down and see who made an appearance!"

Mary Jane—or MJ, as we liked to call her—came stumbling down the stairs, two at a time. She grinned at me and said, "Nice bed-head."

I gave her a one-finger salute.

"What are the plans for tonight? Are we meeting Cam and the guys?" I asked, setting my purse on the counter.

"Yep, we have about three hours to get ready. Come on upstairs. I have the cutest top you *have* to wear."

Eagerly, I followed her up to her bedroom. Angel brought a red spaghetti strap shirt out of her closet with diamond studs all over the top half. "Try this one. It'll make your boobs stand out."

I laughed. "For where we're going, do I really need that?"

She nodded. "Of course. It always helps to dress up the girls."

I slid on some black jeans and pulled the shirt over my head. It really did make them stand out.

A few years ago, I had gone through a depression stage and gained a lot of weight. I had worked hard since then, losing over sixty pounds. I was proud of showing my body off now. Angel and I could share tops easily enough, but pants weren't as easy to exchange. I had curvy hips, but nothing compared to hers.

Angel pointed to a chair, demanding I sit so she could straighten my normally wavy hair. When she was finished, it hung down my back, only inches from my waist. She handed me some diamond-studded hoops to finish my look.

She ran to the closet and came back with a pair of red suede, four-inch heels.

"Those are some wicked shoes!" I exclaimed, and Angel nodded in agreement.

I slid them on, securing the strap across my foot before standing to spin in a circle.

Angel whistled. "You look sexy, chica!"

Tonight, I didn't care about towering over the guys. I wasn't looking for a date—wouldn't find one where we were going, anyway. I was dressed up simply to make myself happy.

We had used up a full three hours getting ready and were on the verge of being late to meet our other friends.

The doorbell rang. "Gracie, it's for you!" yelled Mary

Jane from the bottom of the stairs. She looked up, smiled and said, "Look at you, hot momma."

I grinned. "Thanks, babe." Standing at the door was Hudson with a dozen red roses. "Um, hi. I wasn't expecting you."

His smile faded as he looked me up and down. "Who were you expecting?" he asked, his brow raised. While he looked cute, the edge of accusation was there.

Mary Jane reached for my hand. "You want him to leave? I'll gladly slam the door."

I laughed at her overprotectiveness. "It's all good, girl. He didn't mean anything." I turned my attention to Hudson once more. "I'm going out with my friends tonight. Are those for me?"

Hudson kept a firm grip on the flowers, a scowl slipping into place. "You sure look pretty hot to be going out with just friends."

I decided to ignore his jealousy and focus on the compliment, pressing myself against him. "You think I look hot?" I pressed my mouth against his, letting my tongue snake out and lick his bottom lip. He groaned and pulled me in for a deeper kiss.

Mary Jane cleared her throat. "Get a room."

I laughed and invited Hudson to come inside. He held the flowers out to me, but I took his hand instead and led him to the kitchen.

He placed the flowers on the counter as I bent over to collect a vase from under the sink. Grabbing my waist, he pressed himself against me as he groaned.

I stood and he turned me around, pulling me into a kiss again, his excitement pressing against my stomach. *Good grief, this man is insatiable.*

My phone buzzed, and I pushed him away to answer it with a giggle. "Hey, babe. Yep, we're leaving here shortly. See you there. Love you, too." Hudson's eyebrow rose with curiosity. "That was Cameron. We're meeting him at a club." Hudson's jaw stiffened.

In an attempt to appease him, I said, "Come with us, baby."

His face softened. "I like it when you call me baby. Yeah, sure, I can do that. Am I dressed right for this club or should I go change?"

I looked him over. He was wearing a gray V-neck T-shirt with faded jeans that hung loosely on his hips. My tongue darted out and I licked my lips.

He smirked. "Guess that answers my question."

Angel walked into the kitchen and groaned when she caught us mid make-out session again. "Geez, guys, come up for air."

We chuckled together at her annoyance before I grabbed his hand and pulled him out the door with me. Hudson and I rode together in his sports car while Angel went with Mary Jane in her Mustang convertible.

When we arrived at the club, the line was wrapped around the building. Angel went up to the bouncer, Chris, and worked her magic, slipping him Cameron's name in the process. He let us right in.

The music shook the room; the beat pounded in my chest.

Hudson stiffened beside me, his eyes rolling as he listened to the non-heavy metal music playing. He was a bit of a snob that way; it was either heavy metal or it wasn't music. I found the quirk kind of cute.

Before I even saw him approach, Cameron hugged me, almost knocking me over. He yelled, "Is this Hudson?"

I nodded, and Cameron stuck his hand out in greeting. They shook, a tight smile forming on Hudson's face. Cameron waved us to follow him and we went to a back room; there was a private party going on, and the music was at a much lower decibel. The room had about twenty people in it, an even mixture of men and women. Cameron directed us to the table he occupied, where three guys were already seated. "This is Gavin."

Gavin had a blond faux-hawk, and his brown eyes danced with happiness. I could tell Cameron was interested in him; he hadn't taken his eyes off the guy. He was gorgeous, to say the least, so I could understand my friend's attraction. He smiled, showing off his perfect white teeth, and held his hand out to me. "Heard a lot about you, Gracie," he said. I returned his smile, blushing a little.

"And this is Ashton."

Ashton stood and extended his hand. "I've also heard lots about you, Gracie. Cam talks about you all the time." His voice was low and husky; hearing him say my name made my skin tingle. My eyes drifted up to his face. He was exceptionally tall. I had to lean back a little to look up for any attempt at eye contact.

His lips curved in a polite smile that made my stomach

quiver with nerves. He had a neatly trimmed beard with a hint of gray in it, and I found it extremely hot that he wasn't clean-shaven. He didn't dress in the latest fashions like Cam's other friends either, wearing a simple black button-down shirt tucked into a pair of jeans that hugged his hips.

My eyes drifted over him and, when I made eye contact again, he was smirking. The fact that I was undressing him with my eyes didn't go unnoticed, by him at least. I wondered if he noted my disappointment when he didn't do the same in return.

I was so enthralled with Ashton I almost missed the third introduction Cameron made. Xander, the dark-chocolate stud, got to his feet and extended his hand to me. One thing about Cameron was there was no shortage of hot southern gentlemen around him.

Hudson cleared his throat and I introduced him to everyone. He made it a point to interject that he was my boyfriend, and I rolled my eyes; we hadn't talked about that particular title applying to him yet. Cameron gave me a look that said, *When did this happen?*

I shook my head and mouthed, "We'll talk." Throughout the evening, I made every attempt to include Hudson in our conversation, but he would only grunt or tell me he was ready to go. He sat with his arms folded across his chest with a scowl on his face. Rather than calling him out on it, I ignored him and enjoyed the time with my friends.

I couldn't stop my eyes from periodically drifting back to Ashton. When he'd sat back down earlier, Xander had stretched his arm behind the back of Ashton's chair, and it had remained there ever since. I smiled when I watched them. My eyes then landed on his frozen pink cocktail with a purple umbrella in it. I chuckled and said, "Kind of a girlie drink, don't ya think?"

He smiled. "Really think I'm going to be judged here?" A hearty laugh erupted, and it took a moment to realize it was coming from me. I liked this guy; he reminded me of Cam. Hudson didn't seem to like the attention he gave me, however; he'd marked his territory by playing with my hair and keeping a firm grip on one of my hands, in plain view, at all times.

After a few drinks, Cameron leaned over and put his hands on my breasts. "This shirt makes these look awesome, girl."

Hudson jumped up and kicked his chair back, sending it sailing across the room. He snarled, "What the hell was that?"

I stepped between him and Cameron. "Calm down, Hudson."

Cameron butted in. "I think Gracie can tell me if she doesn't want me to do something. She's a big girl."

Hudson pushed forward, and I shoved him back. "Stop! Take a look around for a moment and realize where you are."

He glanced around with a scowl on his face. It took him a moment, but his surroundings began to sink in.

"Is this a gay bar?" he asked, a little taken aback.

I laughed. "Yep. Cameron is gay. He can touch my boobs

anytime he wants, and he's not a threat." Since the day Cameron came out to me, he's had questions about the female form and wondered what appeal it has to straight men. He could see the beauty, but was never turned on by it. He asked if he could feel my "fun bags" one day, as he called them, after hearing a jock at school refer to them by the same name. They intrigued him, and he sat there for so long, it became awkward for me at first. After a while, it became a regular thing where we'd cuddle up watching a movie, and he'd grab my breasts and fluff them like a pillow before lying against me. It's never been done in a sexual way, always humorous, and normally he doesn't do it in front of a guy I'm with, but he's a bit drunk tonight.

Hudson faced Cameron and raised his hands in the air, as if in surrender. "Sorry, man. It would have been nice if Gracie had told me that."

Cameron stood and accepted the apology, but asked, "Do you introduce your friends by saying 'This is my gay friend, Cameron?'"

Hudson nodded. "I get it. Sorry for being a jerk." He turned to me. "I'll be back. I'm going to hit the head."

As Hudson left, Cameron pulled me onto his lap. "Gracie, he's cute, and I'm sure he's a great lay, but girl, you deserve better than that. You keep falling for such asshats." He was right about the asshats in my life, though I didn't want to admit it.

"I know. Hudson's just insecure. But he's not a bad guy. Give him a chance, for me." I stood and put my hand out. "In the meantime, come dance with me, hottie."

With the beat jumping, Cameron and I went out to the main floor of the club and got our groove on. We had always loved to dance together. I had my arms wrapped around his neck, and he was grinding against me as I threw my head back, laughing at the faces he made.

Then I felt a tap on my shoulder. Turning, my laughter stopped when Hudson's angry face greeted me. His ears practically had smoke rolling out of them. He clasped my hand and dragged me outside, Cameron following close behind.

Once we were out in the street, Cameron yelled, "What is your problem, man? Take your fucking hands off her!"

Hudson turned, his jaw ticking. "A dude hit on me in the bathroom. I don't need this crap. Let's go." He grabbed my hand again but I yanked away from him.

"You should be flattered. All you have to do is say you aren't interested. Don't be such a homophobe!"

"I'm sorry, you're right. I was just freaked." Hudson stepped back. "Let's go back to my place. I wanna spend time with you, baby." He lowered his voice and stroked my cheek with the pad of his thumb, but it wasn't working this time.

"I'm staying here with my friends." I took Cam's hand in mine. "You head home, Hudson."

The skin around his eyes tightened, and it looked as though he was holding back words he wanted to spit out. I drew my brows together, confused as hell by the different versions of Hudson I'd seen. He shrugged, before turning and stomping away to his car.

Cameron put his arm around me. "Gracie, Gracie, Gracie, where do you find these assholes?"

I spent the rest of the evening with Cameron, Ashton, Xander, and Gavin. Mary Jane and Angel bolted on us around two in the morning to go home. It was the third beer after my second martini that had me feeling it was time to finally call it a night, which was around three in the morning. Whenever I drank, I always mumbled to myself, "Beer before liquor, never sicker. Liquor before beer, never fear." I lived by that rule after learning the hard way how very true it was.

Every month or so, we would get together for what we called "Loozas," and they usually had a theme. Our first looza, called Cam-is-fabpalooza, was absolutely crazy. I had to credit Cam for coming up with that fantastic name. I was triple-dog-dared to shotgun a case of Natural Ice beers. Meaning, I poked a hole in the side of the can near the bottom then popped the top and chugged.

Well, by the end of the night, I had done that with the full case, and they ended up mostly all over me, soaking my white T-shirt. Then someone handed me a shot of tequila, and before it made it all the way down, everything from the night came up. Tequila burned terribly when coming out your nose—I wouldn't recommend it, ever. Lesson learned that night, so I always followed the rule.

As for tonight, I was currently feeling no pain and was in no condition to drive, so Cameron asked his friend Ashton to give me a ride home. It seemed Xander had his own ride. When we made it to his car, it turned out to be a motorcycle instead. As sexy as they were, I hoped desperately that I wouldn't become dizzy and toss my cookies on Ashton.

The thing about Nashville weather was that it changed at the drop of a hat. The joke was, if you didn't like the weather, just wait until tomorrow, and it would be different. It was September, which was usually somewhat warm; when we had left home the previous evening, it was in the high seventies. But in the wee hours of the morning, I was left shivering in the low fifties. Ashton slipped his black leather jacket across my shoulders when he saw me quiver.

"Thanks." The great thing about the South was there were a lot of gentlemen. Unfortunately, I never seemed to date any of them.

He handed me a helmet and helped strap it to my head, and I huffed. "This must look attractive."

"You look cute." He smiled. "There's a microphone inside so we can talk." He then passed me a small earpiece. "Pop this in your ear and we're all set."

He sat on the bike and I straddled behind him, wrapping my arms around his torso. Pressing my nose against his shoulder, I inhaled his scent. He smelled fantastic, like cedar, which was odd for cologne. I rested my head on his shoulder and cursed the gay community for getting all the deliciously gorgeous, sweet men in the world.

Ashton weaving in and out of traffic was making me queasy. Speaking into the microphone in my helmet, I screamed out, "I'm going to hurl."

He pulled over quickly and lifted me off the bike in one swoop. Throwing the helmet off, I ran to the side of the road and heaved. I felt his hands lift my hair back from my face. "Wow, that's a lot of hurling you just did."

I sighed. "Gross. Sorry about that. I'm great with first impressions."

He reached into the satchel attached to the motorcycle and pulled out a bottle of water. Handing it to me, he said, "It's warm, but it will at least rinse your mouth out."

I glanced down and noticed some was on his jacket. "Oh, gosh, I'm so sorry, Ashton."

He waved it off as if it were nothing. "Don't worry about it. It can be cleaned."

We had pulled over near a small park, which the locals called Dragon Park. A large mosaic dragon sculpture weaved around the playground with benches built into it. Ashton pointed at the dragon. "Wanna sit for a minute before we go? Give you time to recover." I nodded and took his hand as he led me over there.

"So, how do you know Cameron?" I asked.

"Gavin, Xander, and I have been friends since high school. He introduced me to Cameron a few months back. Gavin has a thing for him. He didn't want to look too obvious going around him by himself all the time, so we offered to be his wingmen. I personally think they'd make a great couple."

I nodded in agreement.

He continued, "It's probably none of my business, but

you seem like a great girl, Gracie. Why would you be dating a guy like Hudson? He seems… intense."

I laughed. "It appears the general consensus on Hudson is that he's an ass." I shrugged. "He's honestly been a great guy until now. Unfortunately, no one has seen the softer side of him yet. I just think he was a bit jealous, you know?" I sighed, hoping that was all it was and that he'd get over it. "Plus, the sex is great," I joked.

He raised his brows in surprise.

"Sorry, that's how Cam and I talk. Didn't mean to give you TMI."

He waved it off. "No, it's all good. Based on what I've heard about you from Cam, I'd rather see you with a better guy, though. But if you think he's a good guy, you'd know." He paused. "So, off the subject, you just let Cam touch your breasts whenever he wants?"

I nodded and laughed, "Why not? He finds them interesting. It's funny how fascinating he finds them without being turned on." I pressed my chest forward. "You can touch them, too, if you want."

"You're drunk and I'm not Cam."

I laughed, "Come on, touch them!"

He shook his head once more. "Not going to happen, and you'll thank me one day for not taking advantage of you right now."

I laughed and bumped against him. "Don't be such a prude. They're just boobs, fun bags, bazoombas, melons, hooters, ta-tas, boobies…."

He laughed heartily. "Don't forget chesticles, knockers,

lady lumps, and, the most appropriate for you, George and Gracie."

I giggled and held my fist up. He put his fist up, bumped it, and we pulled away as though they exploded. This guy was a lot of fun.

After the laughing died down between us, there was a moment of silence. I didn't want him to bring up Hudson again, so I came up with a safer subject. "Gavin's cute. I noticed Cam checking him out too. Wonder why they haven't hooked up?"

Ashton shrugged. "Gavin can be shy about that stuff sometimes. He hasn't been out as long as Cam."

I nodded. "I can understand that. Cam came out early in high school, but even then he wasn't sure. In fact, he and I started to hook up one night. He wanted to test himself. I didn't argue because I was in love with Cameron back then. He never could perform with me, so nothing happened. It broke my heart, for a bit, but now I'm glad we didn't. I got over him when I realized we were meant to be the best of friends."

Ashton listened to me so intently, making me smile and my tummy warm. I couldn't take my eyes off his lips, thinking how soft they looked. I leaned forward, unbidden, my drunken ass egging me on. *I wonder what his lips will taste like?* In my alcohol-induced stupidity, the movement made my head spin. His hands on my arms braced me from falling.

"Let's get you home to bed."

I ran my hand along his arm, feeling his bicep flex at

the sensation. "Ashton, are you trying to seduce me?" I couldn't contain the hiccup from escaping as I finished my sentence.

His face paled and his mouth gaped slightly.

With another hiccup, I laughed and said, "It's a joke, lighten up." We hopped back on his motorcycle and I wrapped my arms around him once more. My thoughts were clearing a bit and I stayed quiet for the ride so I didn't embarrass myself further than I already had tonight. Pulling into the driveway, I saddened, wishing the drive had been a longer one.

"Thanks for the ride." I leaned forward and lightly brushed my lips against his cheek.

He smiled. "Think about what I said. You deserve better than that jerk."

Angel was waiting for me at the door. "All right! Moving on from the pain in the ass already!"

I snickered. "Whatever. That was Ashton, and he's gay. No chance there."

Angel held her hand out to me. "You left your phone here. Hudson has been blowing it up with messages."

I took the phone from her and sighed, not sure if I had the energy to deal with a jealous boyfriend.

Chapter Three

Calling Hudson back seemed pointless; instead, I crawled in bed for the night. The next morning, I was awakened by my bed sinking in and a body stealing the blankets, then curling up against me.

"Good morning, Cam."

He snickered. "Morning, hot stuff. So, Ashton got you home safely last night."

I rolled over and sat up with him. "He's a nice guy. He told me that you and Gavin have a thing?"

Cameron grabbed his chest in shock. "What? Okay, tell me everything he said! Oh, my gosh, so Gavin likes me?"

Oops, now I remember. Ashton said Gavin had a thing for Cameron, not that they had a thing together.

"Um, shoot. I'm not sure I was supposed to tell you that.

Stupid martinis." I slapped my head then winced. "Ouch."

He put his hands together in a praying fashion and begged, "Baby girl, if you love me, you'll tell me. Gavin is the *hottest* guy I know, and if he has a thing for me, it would make my lifetime!" He was giddy, to put it mildly.

He bounced on the bed next to me, as anxious as a kid on Christmas morning.

"Dude, hangover! Please stop bouncing."

He calmed himself and batted his eyelashes at me, not giving up on his quest for information.

I sighed, exasperated. "All I know is that Gavin has a thing for you and Ashton thinks you two would make a cute couple." Cameron fell back onto the bed, staring up at the ceiling, grinning like the Cheshire cat.

He was so still I thought the news had sent him into shock. That was until he sat straight up and shouted, "Woohoo!"

I placed my hand over his mouth to cover the sound, not sure if everyone was awake in the house.

Angel answered by knocking on the wall and yelling, "Zip it, Cam!"

We both snickered before Cameron wrapped his arms around my waist and tackled me back down on the bed in a hug. "Girl, I love you. You made my day!" he whispered loudly. He pressed his lips against mine fiercely, stood up and helped me out of bed.

"Let's go shopping today," he said. "I want to find a new outfit for the next time I see Gavin." Cam invaded my closet and assaulted me with one piece of clothing after the next.

"Let me get a shower first, 'k?"

He shrugged. "'K. I'll go make you my patented hangover cure—scrambled eggs."

When I stepped out of the shower, the smell of eggs made my stomach churn. Tucking the towel around me, I stepped into the bedroom, immediately focusing on Cam scrolling through my phone.

"Damn, does anyone understand privacy?" I snatched the phone from him.

He didn't laugh, his face suddenly pensive. "Check your texts. I picked your phone up to check my Facebook account and saw you had fifteen missed messages. I don't like that guy, Gracie."

I dropped my towel and slipped on black lace panties and a matching bra.

Cam whistled. "What's with the sexy unders?"

I shimmied into my blue jeans and buttoned them before answering. "I'm going to see Hudson later today. You don't know him, Cam. That's not the Hudson I know, so can you just lay off a little until I figure things out with him?"

Cameron wrapped his arms around my waist from behind. "You shouldn't be wasting your time with that asshat, Gracie. That's all I'm saying. You're smoking hot and you deserve someone better. Is this really a guy you can see yourself with forever?"

I scoffed. "Who's talking about forever? He's sweet and kind. And Jesus, the sex is good. I'm only twenty-one. I have plenty of time to find forever."

He shook his head. "Spoken like a true guy. I should be so hot for you."

I smacked him playfully.

"So, what was wrong with the texts?" I asked, sitting next to him to fix my hair.

"He sent fifteen in a span of two hours, for one thing. He also said 'sorry I offended your gay friends.' Glad I've been segregated into a group. And he said something really crude about what he'd like to do to you. If he were a decent guy, I'd be high-fiving you and telling you to 'get it, girl.' Not this guy, though. He gives me the creeps."

I sighed at his overprotectiveness. Yes, Hudson had displayed jerk-like qualities for sure, but there was more to him than that. My phone rang, interrupting the conversation. "Hello?"

"Hey, Gracie, it's Ashton."

"Hey. Um, how did you get my number?"

Ashton chuckled and responded, "You programmed it into my phone at the club and said we had to chat sometime soon."

"Oh, I did? I was a bit out of it."

"That's why I called. I wanted to see how you were feeling."

"I'm good. I have a slight hangover, but nothing major. Thanks again for giving me a ride last night. We should hang out again soon."

"I agree. I had fun with you. We'll talk soon."

"'K, bye."

Cam's eyes were alight with curiosity. "Who was that?

Was that Ash?"

I nodded.

He grinned. "Cool."

Cameron and I spent the day shopping like a couple of teenage girls. We went to Opry Mills Mall, where we could literally spend the entire day if allowed. He dragged me into one shop after another looking for the perfect outfit. Throughout the shopping trip, we played our favorite game of "name that celebrity," pointing out people who slightly resembled celebrities in some way. We always got a good laugh out of it, and several strange looks as well.

"Ooh, check it... Danny DeVito," Cameron said, pointing at a short, stout man with a receding hairline.

"I say more like Joe Pesci. He looks more *Home Alone* or *My Cousin Vinny* than he does *Twins* or the Penguin from *Batman*."

Cameron pointed at another one. "Check out DJ Jazzy Jeff and the Fresh Prince!" He began to loudly recite the *Fresh Prince* theme song until the guys glanced in our direction and we ducked out of the way laughing.

Cameron gasped when he saw Hot Topic. "Girl, we have *got* to go in here." He moved to the underwear section and squealed when he found a pair of glow-in-the-dark underwear that said, *Stay calm and call Batman*. "I'm so gonna rock these."

I laughed when he found me a Wonder Woman pair.

"I'm going to buy these for you, but you have to promise

not to waste them on Hudson. Save them for the next jerkweed you date."

I sighed heavily. "Jerkweed? Nice. Thanks for your inspiring words of wisdom. Fine, I'll save them. Check these out." I held up a pair of platform boots with rainbow shoelaces.

Cameron placed his hand over his chest and said, "Those are fabulous! Gimme! These are totally going to be my clubbin' shoes."

He grabbed a pair of black patent heels off the rack that were at least four inches tall, featuring cloth straps that had cherries on it and tied in a bow on top. "These will be *your* clubbing shoes. Some hooker shoes to go with that red top you wore the other night."

They *were* adorable, I had to admit. "That top was Angel's."

He gasped. "Then we must find you one equally as awesome." He grabbed my wrist, dragging me to the shirt rack. He found me the cutest corset-style top in black, with long sleeves and a red ribbon laced through the front.

"I don't really make enough money at the moment to spend a hundred bucks on a shirt and pair of shoes, Cam."

He waved me off. "I'm getting you these shoes, so you can get the top, okay?"

For an income, I was working at a café in a bookstore. The pay wasn't terrible, enough to help me pay rent and get a few items of necessity. My parents still sent money periodically to help with the cost of school.

Cameron, on the other hand, came from rich parents,

and they gave him all the money he ever needed. He loved to share the wealth with his friends too; he was always spoiling me rotten.

"Fine, I'll let you buy me the shoes, and I'll get the top. Thank you." He seemed satisfied by that compromise. "I want to stop at Victoria's Secret next. I have a coupon for free panties," I said, waving the coupon at him.

As soon as we stepped foot into Vickie's Secret, as Cameron called it, he was off on a mission. He lifted a pair of crotchless panties up to me. "Do these qualify for free?"

I snatched them from him, laughing. "You *would* go straight for the naughty panties."

He wagged his finger at me. "Honey, I don't go *straight* anywhere." Sticking his tongue out at me, he moved on to the next rack.

"Ooh, girl, look at this!" Cameron exclaimed, holding up a French maid outfit. There was very little material to it, considering it was basically a skimpy bra and panties with a sheer apron over it. "I got news for Victoria, ain't nothing a secret anymore with this thing." He held it up to my chest. "You should totally get it."

I laughed. "No, that's okay. I think I'll live."

After we left the store, we stopped in the food court and grabbed some Chinese for lunch. He held out his fork, feeding me a bite of his orange chicken.

"Mmm, delicious. So, what are you going to do about Gavin?"

Cameron shrugged. "We could play this like grade school, and you could tell Ash to tell Gav that I like him. Or

I could go for realistic and walk up, smack his ass, and ask him out."

I snorted. "Why not go with soap opera-style? Make a speech about what he means to you, give a dramatic pause, and then move in for a kiss."

He pointed his fork at me and smiled. "I like that one." I fed him a bite of my chicken lo mein, and he slurped the noodles loudly. "Scrumptious! What about Hudson? How are you going to break up with him?"

I rolled my eyes. "I'm not sure I'm breaking up with him. I like him. I've seen a side of him that you haven't. He's intense, but he's done more for me romantically than anyone I've dated before. When we're alone, he says some of the sweetest things. He cooks for me and brings me flowers. Give him a chance, please. If it doesn't work out, you can say I told you so."

He chuckled. "And I will, believe me."

I smiled. "I have no doubt."

Hudson hadn't texted me at all since the night before, and I felt guilty for not calling him. Back at the house, I left Cam to hang with Angel and Mary Jane and went upstairs to put away my purchases. I changed out of my jeans and T-shirt and slipped on a short jean skirt and a black shirt that was slightly sheer. Finishing the look off with a pair of cute wedge sandals, I headed back down the stairs.

In the living room sat Gavin, Cam, Ashton, Angel, and Mary Jane. Ashton smiled up at me, and it took my breath away for a moment.

When I recovered, I asked, "Are we having a Spontaneous-palooza?"

Cameron explained, "It's a Cam-palooza!"

I snickered. "Isn't every looza a Cam-palooza?"

He smiled. "Duh, why would you want it to be about anything else but something awesome?"

Mary Jane interjected, "We're having a game night. Ash and Gav brought beer. Come, join us."

Angel looked me over. "I think she has different plans."

I smiled. "Yep, I'm going to see Hudson."

Everyone groaned, except Ashton, who said, "Give her a break, guys. Maybe he was having a bad night. You could bring him over here to hang."

I bent down and kissed his cheek. "Thanks, Ashton. That'd be fun. I'll see you guys later."

At Hudson's apartment, I took a deep breath and knocked on the door. When he opened it, his eyes filled with lust before his arm snaked around my waist, pulling me inside. He smashed his lips against mine and his hands roamed over my body. Moaning into his mouth, I grabbed his hand as he latched onto the back of my thigh to lift my leg.

"Whoa. You okay?"

He licked his lips slowly. "Yeah, baby, I'm just horny." He pulled his hand from mine and squeezed the back of my thigh, making me giggle.

"I'd hoped you'd want to go with me to play games with

my friends, back at my house."

He pondered it for a moment. "Sure, after."

He pressed me against the wall, his breath hot against my skin as his mouth roamed my neck. Gripping the hem of my shirt, he lifted it over my head and tossed it aside. I ran my hands through his hair as he ripped my bra open, my breasts spilling free. Jumping up, I wrapped my legs around his waist, and he carried me to the living room. His hand delved between my legs, ripping my panties. The sound of his zipper opening made me moan and beg for him. Before dropping his pants, he retrieved a condom from the pocket and slipped it on. He slid inside me, thrusting me against the back of the couch.

After we were done, I dropped my feet to the ground and shimmied my skirt back down. "Great, that was some of the sexiest lingerie I own, and you ripped both pieces," I said, lifting the pieces of my bra and panties off the floor.

Hudson came up behind me and kissed my neck, grabbing my breasts and massaging them softly. "You know you liked it."

I giggled. "I never said I didn't."

He pulled me close for a soft, gentle kiss. "I'm glad you came over tonight. I know I let you down with the way I acted last night, and I'm sorry."

I ran my fingers through his hair. "Come home with me and hang with my friends. Give them a second chance, please?" I batted my eyelashes at him.

Hudson grinned. "Anything for you, baby girl."

Chapter Four

When we arrived back at the house, everyone was playing poker. The beer bottles were piling up, and they were all cackling so much it was clear they were mostly drunk. Cameron greeted me as usual with a kiss on the lips. My eyes darted to Hudson, expecting a jealous glare, but he seemed fine. He wrapped his arm around me, and I smiled. *See, he is a good guy.* I was tempted to do a little victory dance but held back.

Hudson sat next to Cameron. "Can I join the game?"

Cameron replied with genuine enthusiasm. "Hell yeah, man."

I bent down, wrapping my arms around Hudson's neck, and kissed his cheek. "Want a beer, baby?"

He patted my hand. "Yeah, thanks, babe."

I headed into the kitchen and spotted Ashton. Trying not to sound as excited as I felt to see him, I said, "Hey, you, I was wondering where you'd ran off to." I leaned against the counter beside him. He smiled at me then gave me an odd look, his gaze dropping to my chest before jerking back to my face. I looked down and gasped, covering my arms over my chest. "I'll be back." I grabbed a beer for Hudson and dropped it off before running upstairs.

Ashton came into my room, catching me without my shirt on. He turned away, looking embarrassed. "Sorry, I wanted to make sure you were all right. You took off kind of quick there."

I put on a tank top that had a built-in bra then slipped my skirt off and put on pajama pants instead.

"You can turn around." He looked me over for a moment and, if he weren't gay, I'd think he liked what he saw. "I realized downstairs that I didn't have a bra or underwear on anymore."

Ashton blushed, stuttering, "Um, o-oh... okay."

I giggled. "Why, Ashton, are you blushing?"

Instead of answering, he pointed to the door. "We should head downstairs."

I nodded and followed him down. Hudson was so enthralled in the game that he never knew I was gone, and I stood back to observe his interactions. Everyone seemed to be getting along better. Hudson's head eventually turned my way, and he waved me over, patting his leg for me to take a seat.

"Who's winning?"

Cameron spoke up, "Your boy here is tearing us up!"

I clapped. "Way to go, baby." He laughed and squeezed my waist.

"Can I get another beer, Gracie?" Cameron asked with puppy dog eyes.

Hudson massaged my hip. "Me too, babe?"

I bent forward in a bow. "Beer wench, at your service." Everyone cheered.

Ashton was in the kitchen again when I went in. "Is this your favorite room?"

He chuckled. "I don't play poker, so I prefer to hang out here and keep the beer company."

After delivering the beers, I went back to sit with Ashton.

"You don't have to stay with me, Gracie," he said when I appeared next to him.

I grabbed two beers from the cooler. "The beers said they wanted more company than just you. Said you were kind of boring by yourself. I tried to defend you, but they wouldn't hear it." I winked then took his hand in mine and dragged him outside, onto the deck. We had a swing out there that was my favorite thinking spot. "Swing with me for a bit?"

He motioned for me to sit first. When he took the seat next to me, I brought my feet up, leaning my back against him. I tilted my head up to him. "Am I invading your personal space too much?"

He laughed. "No, this is nice."

It was. Ashton put me at ease. He had a calming presence, something apparently I was missing in my life. Not surprising since my best friend was a whirlwind of energy. "I get cold easily, so body heat helps." I gazed up at the sky. "Isn't it pretty tonight? You can see so many stars."

Ashton and I sat and stared at the stars, not saying a word for a while. Comforted in his company, I quickly relaxed. I lifted the beer bottle to my mouth and took a long swig. "Thanks again, for last night. I had fun, you know, when I wasn't hurling. I cleaned your jacket too."

He chuckled softly. "I had fun too. You can keep the jacket. It looks better on you anyway." He offered me a small wink. "You're in college, right?" he asked.

I nodded.

"What's your major?" Before answering, I choked down the last swig of warm beer and grimaced. Warm beer always made me sick. He laughed at the way my face screwed up in disgust. "Was that a weird question?"

I snickered. "No, silly. I don't like warm beer. It tastes like piss."

His eyebrow rose curiously. "Drink piss often, do ya?"

Nudging him with my elbow, I said, "You know what I mean, smart-ass. Anyway, my major is undecided, much like everything in my life at this moment."

He nodded. "That's not uncommon for someone your age."

Now it was my turn to get some clarification. "Someone my age? How old are you, Grandpa?" He choked on the mouthful of beer he'd been attempting to swallow, and

I patted his back. "Need me to grab Cameron for the Heimlich?"

He shook his head. "Nope, I'm good." He chuckled between coughs. I grabbed another beer from a cooler and popped the top. "I'm twenty-six, but thanks for making me feel old, though. You really know how to make a man feel good with that mouth."

I was mid-drink that time and spat the beer all over his shirt. His face burned with embarrassment as he said, "I didn't mean that the way it sounded." I doubled over in laughter, and after his humiliation wore off, he joined me.

The door creaked behind us and Hudson stepped onto the deck. "Looks like you two are having fun." He smiled when our eyes met.

Ashton stood up. "I think I'll go try and get some of the beer and spit off my shirt."

I covered my mouth to stifle the laughter. "Sorry about that, Ash."

He waved his hand nonchalantly. "No worries."

"Gracie, I'm going to get out of here. You wanna stay at my place tonight?" Hudson asked.

I thought about it for a moment. "I think I'm going to stay home tonight. I'll see you tomorrow, though. You haven't had too much to drink, have you?"

Hudson shook his head. "Just two beers, I'll be fine."

We walked through the house, and I noticed Ashton was in the kitchen again. "I'm going to walk Hudson out, be right back. Keep those beers entertained." I winked at him.

The moment we stepped outside, Hudson turned and

faced me. "You're really going to stay here when we could repeat the fun we had earlier?" He pushed me against his car, firmly pressing his lips to mine as his thumbs tugged at the waistband of my pants. His mouth moved to my neck as I protested a little.

I pushed him back. "Not tonight. Absence makes the heart grow fonder, ya know."

He scoffed. "Absence, not abstinence," he said as he moved to kiss me again.

I pushed him lightly. "Sorry, not tonight."

He scowled. "Whatever. It's your loss."

I sighed. "You were in such a good mood. What happened?"

He opened the car door and said, "Goodnight, Gracie."

"Good night. Let me know that you make it home safe."

Hudson drove off, tires squealing. When I walked back inside, everyone stared at me.

"His good mood lasted all of two seconds," Angel commented.

"It's all good. He's just tired." I left them and went back to Ashton. "Hey, I'm back."

He grinned up at me. "Good, I was getting bored out here. And I think the beers were too." I plopped down beside him.

"So, tell me... who is Gracie Walker?" Ashton asked me out of the blue.

I nudged him with my elbow. "What's that supposed to mean?"

He chuckled. "It means I want to know more about you."

Color me confused. "Why?"

He chuckled again. "Really? We're becoming friends, right?"

I nodded.

"Well, I like to get to know my friends."

I shrugged. "Sorry, that was a silly question. It's been a long time since someone wanted to get to know me. Most of my friends have been my friends for years, so I'm not used to talking about myself."

His brow creased. "You and Hudson haven't been together long. Surely, he's asked you about yourself."

I went to agree but stopped myself. While Hudson had been kind and attentive—he'd even shown up at work one time with a rose for me—I realized we didn't actually talk a whole lot. I shook my head. "We don't talk much about me. And don't call me Shirley," I said as I stuck out my tongue, and he snorted.

Conversation with Ashton was so easy. It was different from my relationship with Cameron, yet it had the great similarities that there was no flirting or need to impress. "So, what do you want to know?" I finally asked.

"What's your family like? Do you have siblings? Are you close with your parents?"

I laughed at his barrage of questions; he really did want to get to know me. "I have two sisters, much younger than me. My dad died when I was three... car accident. My mom remarried when I was ten and had two children with my stepfather. They're nine and five, Alana and Yasmine. Cameron calls us the gay sisters. It's one of his favorite jokes."

Ashton thought about it for a moment then laughed. "Ah, because of the first letter of your names. That's pretty funny actually, considering the majority of your friends."

I nodded. "Cameron's face, when he put it together, was priceless. I'm sure you'll hear the story from him sometime. As for my mom, we've never really been very close. Throughout my childhood, she was depressed a lot, due to losing my dad. I don't remember him, except from pictures. My stepdad and I have been close ever since he met my mom, and he's never treated me any differently from his own children. He brought my mom out of her slump, and that made me happy, but she and I still have never really bonded. That's pretty much my story. What about you?"

He grabbed at his chest in shock. "What? Why would you want to know about me?"

I laughed and punched his arm playfully. "We'll start off easy. Do you work or go to school?"

"I work."

With a sweeping motion of my hand, I responded, "And? What do you do? Do you enjoy it?"

"I have a great boss, and it pays the bills, so yeah, I do."

"Boy, asking you for information is liking pulling teeth."

Ashton smirked and fidgeted with his beer bottle. "I work for myself. It's a family business in a way."

"Oh, yeah? Tell me about your family." I changed the focus of conversation to a more personal subject.

His index finger tapped against his lips. "Hmm, let's see. I have a younger brother, Derrick. He's around your age. He's twenty."

Before he continued, I said, "I should be hanging with him instead of your geriatric ass." I winked and he smiled, softening his features.

"My parents are great. They've been married thirty years. I have a niece, Katelyn, who I adore."

I liked watching Ashton speak because he loved to run his fingers over his beard as if he were worried it was sticking up in crazy directions, even though it was shaved pretty close to his skin. He licked his lips and I mimicked the movement as I stared at him. He lifted the beer bottle to his mouth and took a gulp, not noticing me repeating his actions.

"You'd like my brother. He's a good kid."

I snorted. "You trying to hook me up?"

He was midway through another drink when he choked a bit on it, and I patted his back just like earlier. Apparently, I was trying to kill him by asphyxiation.

He shook his head. "No, not at all." Ashton sounded so offended at the thought it stung.

"I was just teasing."

He smiled. "I know. What were we talking about again?"

I shrugged. "I think it's time to go to bed."

He frowned. "Did I say something wrong?"

"No, I'm tired, that's all." As I stood, he followed and we both swayed a bit. We grasped onto each other for support, laughing at our drunkenness.

His palm pressed against his head. "I think I had more to drink than I realized. Can I crash on your couch?"

I nodded. "Absolutely. There's no way I'd let you drive

like this. Come on, I'll get you set up nicely." I led him to the living room where we found Cameron passed out on the couch and Gavin in the only comfy chair.

Ashton sighed. "I guess the floor will do."

I grabbed his hand. "No way, come with me."

He followed me upstairs to my room. My bed was queen-sized, so there was plenty of room for two people. Ashton glanced at me, unsure of what was happening.

Pulling back the blue down comforter, I got in the bed. "Sleep with me," I said.

He stuttered. "What? Um, Gracie, what about Hudson?"

I giggled at his insecurity. "It's fine, Ashton. Lie down and share the bed with me. We're friends, right? Nothing's going to happen." A small flicker of disappointment lit in my chest at the truth of my words. I shook them away. *Hudson*, I reminded myself. I had a boyfriend. Admittedly, he was behaving bizarrely of late, but it wasn't like I'd ever cheat on him. Nor would I tell him I'd shared a bed with a guy either.

Awkwardly, he kicked his shoes off. He glanced down at himself and back at me. "Um, is it okay if I sleep in my boxers? This shirt is still pretty wet from the beer." Heat spread across his cheeks.

I nodded. "You won't offend me." He still seemed awkward; it was so adorable on him. I rolled over to set the alarm, so I wouldn't miss class the next day. When I turned back, he had his shirt off and his jeans unbuttoned. I bit my bottom lip while I stared at his muscular chest, which had a very light smattering of dark hair across his pectorals. I sucked in a breath as he turned to lay his jeans over the desk chair. He was wearing navy blue boxer briefs, which rode low on his hips, so that when he faced me, I could see the cut that led to his...

Wow. Gracie, you need to get your mind out of the gutter. Ashton slid under the covers with me and I turned on my side, facing the opposite direction. In a husky voice, he whispered, "Good night, Gracie-bug."

I smiled at the cute nickname he gave me and whispered back, "Good night."

The next morning, the alarm went off and I hit the snooze button. I rolled over to a muscular body and thought I was at Hudson's, as it had been every morning lately. My hands roamed until I found his morning happiness, and I ran my hand over the outside of his shorts. He groaned with pleasure as I palmed him for a moment. My hand moved to the waistband and slid inside as I opened my eyes, ready to please him.

My surprise equaled that present in Ashton's eyes when we realized what had happened. We both jumped up on opposite sides of the bed, my hand covering my mouth as I exclaimed, "I am *so* sorry. I didn't mean to molest you! That should *not* have happened!"

Unconsciously, my gaze dropped to his morning wood, and I bit my lip again. He glanced down and quickly covered himself, and I gasped again in my embarrassment. "Oh, sorry! I'm going to give you some privacy." I bounced around the room nervously before finally slipping out, and running downstairs, smack into Cameron's chest.

"Good morning, Gracie. Can we not do the body slam thing so early? My head is pounding. I need coffee."

I kissed him. "Sorry, Cam. Come with me." I dragged him to the kitchen, poured him a cup of coffee, and pulled him outside.

"What the hell, Gracie?" I pushed him down on the swing and sat next to him with my legs crossed.

"I pretty much molested Ashton just now." He had just taken a sip of coffee and spat it in my face in shock.

I closed my eyes, thankful it was lukewarm instead of scalding.

He gasped. "Sorry, Gracie. Don't shock me when I'm drinking!" He smacked me playfully as I lifted my shirt to wipe my face.

"I deserved that. Did the same thing with beer to Ashton last night."

"Okay, I need details. Are you dumping Hudson?" he asked, excited.

"Ugh, thanks, Cameron. No, I'm not dumping Hudson. I'm not exactly Ashton's type."

His face scrunched in confusion as he said, "Um, okay. I still think you should dump Hudson."

We were interrupted by Ashton stepping out on the porch. My face reddened when I saw him, fully dressed this time. "I'm sorry, Ash," I started.

He interrupted, "No harm, Gracie-bug. Wasn't the worst thing in the world to wake up with a beautiful woman's hand in my shorts."

Cameron gaped at me and gasped. "You're such a tramp!" I hit him, and he laughed before kissing my cheek. "I'm heading inside, Gracie-bug. I like that name."

Ashton smiled and took Cam's place beside me. For the first time, I felt awkward with him. Sex does change everything. We didn't even have sex, but it was still awkward.

"What's up?" he asked.

"Hmm?" I responded, coming out of my thought bubble.

"You're acting strange."

Out of my mouth came the strangest cackling laugh. "Sorry, I don't know what that noise was," I said. "It's a bit weird sitting next to someone you touched inappropriately."

He snorted. "It wasn't really *that* inappropriate."

My right brow rose, questioning his statement.

"Okay, so maybe a bit. Your bed's comfy, by the way." He nudged me with his elbow and grinned at me. "Come on, Gracie, don't be weird now. I like where we were going with our friendship."

I shrugged. "No, I'm fine. Come on, I'll cook breakfast for everyone. We'll find you a different shirt too, so you don't smell like beer."

He jumped up, excited. "Good, I'm starving. Being molested takes a lot out of a guy." I raised my fist to punch his arm, but he just laughed and dodged out of the way.

Chapter Five

I stepped out of the car and straightened my uniform, a white blouse and khaki pants. Once inside the bookstore café, I grabbed my hunter-green apron and slid it over my head, then tied it in the back.

One of the great things about this job was that I got to talk about books with people. They came and asked my advice while they waited on their drinks. It was when I got most of my reading time in as well. My supervisor encouraged us to read when times were slow and preferred we use books from the store so we could recommend them to customers.

A customer hit the bell, drawing me out of the fantasy world of the paranormal novel I was reading. I straightened my apron, turned around, and smiled brightly when my eyes landed on Ashton. "Are you stalking me?"

He raised his hands in the air. "I promise I had no clue you worked here. I'm here with Gavin and Xander, browsing. I came to get a cappuccino for us. Whatcha reading?"

I held up the book to show the title. "It's paranormal—you know, demons, vampires, all kinds of fun creatures. They're making a movie of it, so I thought I'd read the book first."

He nodded. "You know the movie is never as good as the book."

I shrugged. "Yeah, majority of them aren't. Every now and then, you get one that's still good, even if the book is better. So, three cappuccinos? You want extra chocolate sprinkles?"

He winked at me. "Duh." He glanced at the "tip" jar. "You get to keep all the tips?"

I nodded. "During my shift. We empty it at the end of each shift, so it starts over. Don't feel too bad that it's empty. We don't get many tippers. I'm pretty used to it." I turned to make his cappuccinos.

While the machine was running, I stepped back over to ring him up. "You planning on hanging out with us this weekend?"

"I'm free, so I'd love to."

I smiled. "Great. Word of advice, don't let Cameron trick you into challenging him to a game of pool. He's a shark."

He nodded. "Good to know, although I am too, actually."

I gasped. "Oh, hell, you *have* to challenge him now! I would love to see someone beat him! And don't worry, no money involved. He enjoys beating people for the pure pleasure of gloating."

He laughed. "It's a deal. Where do you guys play?"

I handed him his change and said, "Pool hall down on Second Ave in downtown Nashville. It's kind of pricey, but Cameron loves it there."

"What time do you get off tonight?" he asked.

I sighed. "I'm here until closing, at eleven. I normally don't work that late, but I'm covering for a friend."

He bobbed his head in understanding and said, "Be careful leaving so late by yourself."

I spun around to grab his drinks. I sprinkled extra chocolate on top and slid them over to him. "Don't worry, I always am."

He held the cups up in the tray and grinned. "Thanks, see you this weekend?" I nodded excitedly.

He dropped something in the tip jar and walked away; when I glanced over, I noticed it was a twenty-dollar bill. I smiled at his generosity and decided I would have to make sure I bought him a drink at the bar this weekend.

From behind me, I heard a "psst." I turned and saw Gavin and Xander waving at me as they stood beside Ashton across the room in the science fiction section. I gave them a big smile with a wave before resuming my reading.

For the rest of the evening, my shift was steady but not too crazy. Around ten thirty, my phone beeped. Cameron wanted me to meet him downtown where he was hanging out with Angel and Gavin. I texted him back.

Me: Leaving work in 30. Would take too long to go home and change. Rain check?

He texted back.

Cameron: Fine, but you owe me a drink tomorrow night, bitch.

I laughed.

Me: Deal, princess.

It took me longer than usual to clean up that night. By the time I was leaving, everyone else was gone except for the manager.

"Gracie, you want me to walk you out?" he asked.

"Nah, Jimmy, I'm fine. You can watch from the door if you want. That would make me feel safer."

He glanced outside then opened the door. "Can I help you, sir?"

I tensed up, wondering who was outside the door at this hour.

Jimmy stepped back inside. "He says he's waiting for you. Name is Ashton."

At that moment, Ashton moved in front of the window and waved awkwardly.

I smiled. "He's cool, Jimmy. He's a friend of mine. Thanks for looking out for me."

I slipped out the door so he could lock it, smiling when my eyes met with Ashton's. "You *are* stalking me!" I chuckled.

He grinned. "Gavin and Xander went to hang out with Cameron, and I had a few more errands to run. I was still in the neighborhood and didn't like the idea of you walking to your car alone. Is that too creepy?"

I held up my forefinger and thumb about an inch apart.

His shoulders sagged. "Sorry, trying to be gallant for my friend."

I slid my arm through his. "It's very sweet. I was going to pick up dinner on the way home. Wanna grab a bite to eat with me?"

He led me to my car, his motorcycle parked right next to it. "Where can we eat this late?"

I licked my lips. "Let's go to Steak 'n Shake."

He straddled his bike. "Wanna ride with me?"

I looked from my car to his bike. I really wanted to ride with him again, pressed against his body, but that wasn't a good idea. "I'll take my car so we don't have to come back here."

Ashton led the way. He was easy to keep up with because he drove like an old man, or maybe he did that for my sake not knowing I had a lead foot.

We grabbed a two-person booth in the back and ordered burgers and fries with milkshakes. "You're too sweet for coming to check on me tonight."

He took a sip of his shake and smiled at me. "I'm a bit of a worrier. Ask Gavin."

I pulled the straw out of my peanut butter banana shake, sucked all the liquid out of it then grabbed his cup, shoving my straw inside to taste his chocolate-covered strawberry shake. Instead of arguing, he followed my lead, stealing a taste of mine. He picked up a napkin and wiped my chin where I had dribbled from the straw.

I blushed. "Mmm, I should've gotten yours."

He slid it to me. "Wanna switch?"

We traded, and I moaned over the taste of the milkshake.

He shook his head. "Gracie, I think you're enjoying that a little too much."

I grinned sheepishly. "Sorry. I love ice cream."

The waiter brought our food.

"Holy sh... Seriously?" I exclaimed as I saw what Ashton had ordered. The burger had seven patties on it; I had no clue how he was going to get his mouth around it. He had also ordered a large skillet of chili cheese fries to go with it. "You hungry, Ash?"

He shrugged. "I got the munchies. Figured this would be a nice snack." We both started laughing, and I grabbed my fork to liberate a few fries from his skillet.

"I have to see you put your mouth around that thing," I said.

He smirked. "That's what he said."

I snorted and held my hand up for a high five. He smacked my hand as he laughed along with me.

His mouth stretched to its limit as he tried to shove the enormous burger into it. My own fell open in shock when he took the first bite. I said, "You're gonna need a bigger mouth, dude."

He started to choke as he laughed.

I gasped. "Are you okay?"

He nodded and held his finger up, asking for a moment. "Don't make me laugh when I've got that much in my mouth," he said after he was able to take a breath.

I winked. "That's what she said."

He held up his fist and I bumped it with mine. "You're a lot of fun, Gracie." There was something about the way he said my name that made me want to swoon.

"You're pretty cool yourself."

The check came and he grabbed it first.

"Let me get it," I said, continuing with, "I had a big tipper tonight."

He smiled at me. "You keep that. I needed a fun night tonight. Let me treat you."

When we stepped outside, I shivered, my light hooded sweatshirt no match for the bitter cold wind. He removed his coat, but I raised my hand in protest. "No, I'm fine. You keep that."

He tilted his head, giving me a stern look. "You know what my momma would do if she saw me walking with a jacket on, letting the woman next to me freeze? My momma raised me better than that." He slid the jacket around my shoulders and rubbed my arms, using the friction to warm me.

We stood next to my car for a moment, him in front of me as I leaned back against the door. Ashton leaned forward, his face only inches from mine as I felt his hand brush against my hip. I closed my eyes, waiting to taste his sweet lips, something I'd been thinking about, even if he *was* into guys.

Instead, he opened the car door and said, "You need to get in here and warm up, Gracie-bug."

Well, that was disappointing. His face was so close to mine that, if I just moved a few inches, I could pretend to "accidentally" kiss him. His lips were so full and delectable, especially when his tongue darted out to wet them.

My breath quickened in anticipation, but I pushed myself up and kissed his cheek instead. "Sit with me for a bit?" I asked.

He moved to let me slide in behind the wheel then ran around the car and climbed in next to me. I turned the heat on to warm us up. "You said you needed a fun night. Is something bothering you?" Ashton's face turned away to stare out the window. "I'm sorry, you probably don't want me in your business."

He placed his hand on mine. "No, it's not that. It's something I don't have an easy time talking about. Occasionally, I have rough days, and today was one. Gavin and Xander spent the day with me because they knew it was an anniversary for me. Actually, it's an anniversary for both Gavin and me and we were trying desperately to stay cheerful. The thing that finally made me smile was this really sweet barista at the bookstore I went to."

My heart warmed, as did my face when he gave the sweet compliment.

He patted my hand. "You really are a lot of fun to hang out with, and we should do it more often." The inner teenage girl in me grew nervous hearing, "we should do it" because I was thinking the same thing... only different.

We were interrupted by his phone beeping. Glancing at the clock, I noticed it was after one in the morning. "Booty call?" I asked teasingly, secretly hoping it wasn't.

He smirked. "Not exactly. Gavin and Cameron are both drunk, and they need a ride home. Not sure how he thinks the three of us will fit on my bike."

I laughed. "I'll go get them."

He shook his head. "No, I'll have them get a cab and I'll pay for it when they get to the house. You shouldn't go downtown by yourself this late."

I considered his response, then realized this was a perfect excuse to spend more time with Ashton.

"How about you drop your bike at my house and ride with me?"

It took us about an hour to get downtown to Cameron and Gavin, wasted beyond belief. Angel had left with some guy she met, leaving them behind to fend for themselves. When we pulled up, they were sitting on the bench outside making out.

"Well, looks like they're getting along," Ashton said.

I yelled out the window, "Get it, girl!"

Cameron's hand popped up long enough to flip me off.

"That's not very nice, considering I'm your ride."

Ashton and I had to load them into the car, deciding we'd all go back to my house so it would be easier. I placed Cameron on the couch and Ashton put Gavin in the chair. "You can sleep in my room again if you'd like," I said, then added, "I'll keep my hands to myself, promise!"

He laughed. "I'm not drunk, so I can make it home."

I walked him out, reluctantly. I knew he hadn't been drinking, but I selfishly wanted him to stay so we could talk more.

"Thanks again for protecting me tonight."

He straddled his bike and started it up. "Thank you for cheering me up." He leaned forward and kissed my forehead.

"We should do this again," I added, hopeful.

"Definitely. I'll see you this weekend too."

My night with Ashton had me in a fantastic mood; I hated to see it end and wasn't sure I'd be able to sleep. At first, I thought about going to see Hudson but changed my mind. I curled up with a good book instead, falling asleep soon after.

Cameron jumped on my bed in the morning. "What up, girl!"

I sat up, rubbing my eyes and yawning. "Dial it down a notch, Cam."

He snickered. "Sorry. I woke up in your house and remembered that you showed up to rescue me with Ashton. How'd that happen? Dish!"

I covered my mouth with one hand, waving him to follow me with the other. My mouth felt funky, so I headed to brush my teeth as I told him, "Ashton, Xander, and Gavin were at the bookstore yesterday."

Cameron nodded. "I know, Gavin told me, but that was earlier in the day."

I bobbed my head up and down. "Yep. Ashton asked me what time I got off work and when he realized how late I'd be there, he came back to walk me to my car. We grabbed a bite to eat after that and hung out for bit. He's a lot of fun."

Leaning over, I rinsed my mouth while Cameron continued his interrogation. "Wow. That's pretty sweet. I'm glad you guys are getting along."

I wiped my mouth and grinned. "Looks like you and Gav were getting along as well."

He jumped excitedly and clapped his hands together. "Girl, let me tell you, I think I'm in love. No joke. He is über sweet, so hysterically funny and freaking gorgeous. Not to mention a fantastic kisser. Okay, so that *should* be mentioned because he is *that* fantastic."

I wrapped my arms around his neck and kissed his cheek. "I'm glad. I like him a lot."

My phone rang and Cameron grabbed it for me then groaned, which told me it was Hudson calling. "Hello?" I answered as I snatched it away from him.

"Hey babe, do you have plans today?" Hudson asked.

"No, I'm not busy."

"I want to take you on a traditional date for a change."

"You do?" I couldn't help the surprise in my voice since most of our dates involved hooking up after eating at his house.

"It's time I spoil my girl a little. I'll be there in about an hour."

"Um, sure. I'll see you soon."

Cameron crossed his arms and glared at me. "You need to dump him, honey."

I huffed. "Just leave, Cameron. I need to get a shower so I can spend the day with my *boyfriend*."

He cringed at the term I used for him. "Don't you dare push me away for him, Gracie."

I wrapped my arms around him. "I love you, Cam. Nothing will change that, and no one will come between us, especially not Hudson James."

Hudson didn't tell me where he wanted to go, just that he wanted to take me on a real date for a change. It sounded promising, so I showered and put on a pair of jeans with a red low-cut sweater to show off the girls a bit, as if Hudson hadn't seen them before. I had just slipped on my new shoes with the cherry ribbons when I heard the doorbell.

Running down the stairs, I hollered, "I got it!" I opened the door to Hudson, smiling back at me. He was holding a single red rose.

"You look beautiful," he said as he handed it to me.

I pressed it to my nose, inhaling the sweet scent. "Thank you, for the compliment and the rose."

Hudson leaned forward and gave me a chaste kiss on the cheek.

"Is something different about you?" I wondered aloud.

He held his hand out. "Shall we go?"

I nodded and took his hand, heading toward his car, where he opened the door for me. When he climbed in the driver seat, I said, "You're being really chivalrous, and it's pretty hot."

He leaned over and kissed me, sliding his hand down over my thigh. "I'm trying to keep us from going straight home to bed. It's my goal to have a normal date with you for a change, to show you how charming I can be. You look so damn hot, though, so don't tempt me to ruin my goal." He sucked my bottom lip into his mouth.

"Mmm, but we do so good in bed," I purred.

He groaned. "You drive me so crazy, Gracie." He placed a hand around the back of my neck and pulled me toward him before he slid his tongue in my mouth. All of a sudden, there was a hand between my legs, rubbing over the top of my jeans.

I gasped at his touch then pulled back. "No. You're right. Let's do this real date. I want to see what you have planned."

Our first stop was the theater to see the latest romantic comedy, one I had wanted to see for a while. It was a total chick flick, though, and Hudson didn't seem like the type of guy who would go to one of these movies. "Are you sure you want to see this?"

He shrugged. "You want to see it, that's what matters."

All through the movie, he snored, which I actually thought was sweet; after all, he was being selfless by letting me see this, and he'd paid to take a nap. I curled up against his arm midway through the movie, and he stirred enough to slide his arm over me to cuddle. When it was over, I woke him up with a kiss.

He sat up. "That was pretty good, huh?"

I laughed. "It's okay. It was a good movie, but I know you slept through it."

He grinned guiltily. "Well, it's the thought that counts, right?"

I squeezed his hand. "Definitely."

After leaving the theater, he took me to a late lunch at one of my favorite restaurants in town. It turned out to be one of his favorites as well, proof that we did have some things in common. He held the door for me, and I stepped inside, telling the hostess we had a party of two.

We slid into the booth side by side; he insisted on sitting next to me. Hudson wrapped his arm around me and kissed my cheek. "How's the date so far?"

I took hold of his chin, pulling his face close. "It's perfect." He kissed me softly, the sweetest one he'd ever given me.

"Everything looks so good. What are you getting?" I asked.

He glanced over the menu. "I think I'll get a big steak. I figure I can work it off with you later," he said, winking at me. It wasn't surprising that the subject of sex came up with Hudson, but I wanted to get to know him better, outside the bedroom.

"Tell me about your family. We never talk about them," I said, closing the menu as we waited for the waitress to return.

"I got a mom, a dad, and a brother. What's to tell?"

I played with his hair as I asked, "Do you get along with them? What are they like?"

He swatted my hand away. "Why do you need to know?"

I crossed my arms over my chest. "I don't *need* to know. I *want* to know."

"Well, my life is a *need* to know."

I scowled at his switch in attitude. "Your girlfriend doesn't need to know about your life?"

He shrugged then sighed. "I'm sorry, babe. All right, if you must know, my mom is a bitch. She hates me and told me she wished I was never born. My dad is an ass, an abusive, arrogant dick, who I'd rather not talk about. Can we drop it now?"

I nodded. "I'm sorry, I didn't know."

He leaned over and kissed my cheek. "It's okay."

The waitress returned to take our orders and drop off our drinks. After we ordered, Hudson excused himself to run to the restroom.

I glanced around the restaurant, and my gaze fell on a table of four guys across the room. The two facing me were definitely a couple. The other two had their backs to me; one of them looked like Ashton. He slid his arm around the guy next to him and hugged him. He turned his head to say something. It *was* Ashton. It made my heart hurt. A pang of jealousy rushed through me, hating that once again I lusted after someone I had no right to.

I shook my head and thought, *Get a grip, Gracie. You're acting like a jealous girlfriend. You barely know the guy.*

Hudson returned and disappointment settled over me upon seeing him. Even after the great day he had planned, I was truly questioning if I wanted to be with this man. My lusty, pointless thoughts of Ashton aside, Hudson had shown me on far too many occasions that he wasn't the man I thought he was.

Hudson pressed against me, leaning down to kiss my neck. Even just a week ago, I would have been aching at his touch, but that desperate need for him had dwindled. I ignored his ministrations and focused on Ash's table. They received their check and stood up to leave. Ashton put his arm across the guy's shoulder, who turned out to be Xander, as they walked. My heart hurt watching the exchange. His eyes met mine, drifting to Hudson, who nibbled on my neck. Ashton's features hardened before his gaze returned to mine.

I pushed Hudson away lightly. "Hey, Ash, Xander," I said as he approached the table.

Xander smiled at me as Ashton spoke. "Hey, Gracie, it's good to see you. How's it going, Hudson?" He held his hand out to shake Hudson's.

They shook and I motioned to the other side of the booth. "You want to join us?"

He glanced back at Xander. "Nah. We were just leaving. I'll see you this weekend, though."

Hudson went back to pawing me. I was ready to leave. I pushed him away again, and he huffed, "What is it?"

I scowled. "We're in public at a restaurant, for one. I'm feeling a bit sick, though. Can you take me home?" He paid the check and grimaced as we walked outside.

"You coming back to my house?" he asked with lust in his eyes.

"I wanna go to my house... alone."

He sneered. "So I did this whole date for nothing? I can't even get laid tonight?" It seemed we were back to asshat Hudson again. If I didn't sort this out soon, I was sure I'd get whiplash.

Ashton was parked a few cars down from Hudson.

"Why don't you get a ride with your girlfriend over there?" He nodded in Ash's direction.

Ashton overheard him and yelled out, "Gracie, you need a ride?"

He was unbelievable. Admittedly, I was doubting our whole relationship, but I was trying my hardest to be polite. The last thing I wanted to do was piss him off. I crossed my arms over my chest, a steady flow of anger rising in my veins. "Thanks for ruining a nice day, Hudson." I turned to leave. Hudson grabbed my arm and pulled me against him, roughly, pressing his lips against mine. I shoved him back.

"What the hell?" I called out, shaking my head at Hudson.

Ashton's footsteps quickened as I heard him yell out, "Hey!"

I turned to him, "It's okay, Ash. See you later, Hudson." He stomped off, got in his car, and peeled out of the parking lot.

Ashton reached out to me, "You okay, Gracie? Did he hurt you?"

I waved it off. "Hudson's harmless. He kisses me like that a lot. He thinks it's a turn-on." Once more I realized I was making excuses for his behavior. I needed to put a stop to that. I'd only known him for a few weeks after all.

He slid his arm around me. "Come on, I'll take you home."

I pulled away. "What about your friends?"

Ashton shrugged. "They left a few minutes ago. I was on my way to run some errands. They can wait till tomorrow, though."

I grabbed my phone from my purse. "I don't want to intrude. I'll call Cameron to pick me up."

He took my phone from me. "You're never intrusive. Unless you don't want to hang out with me?" He stuck his bottom lip out and gave me puppy dog eyes.

I shoved on his chest. "That's playing dirty." Already my anger began to fade, my nerves calming, Hudson and his behavior becoming a frustrating memory.

He grinned. "Please, come with me? I'd like the company."

I reluctantly agreed. Yeah right, there was nothing reluctant about it. Inside I was bouncing up and down, like a giddy teenager meeting her teen idol.

He slipped the helmet over my head. "Hudson is an idiot for passing up time with you. You look beautiful."

Sweet mother of all that was holy. Don't kiss him and make a fool of yourself. Don't kiss him. Don't kiss him. My eyes glanced down. *Don't look at his pants, pervert!*

Stuttering, I said, "Thank you."

He climbed on. I straddled the bike and settled myself behind him. I wondered if it was weird that I wanted to lick the back of his neck. Thinking that it most definitely was, I moved my nose across his back, inhaling his scent instead.

His voice brought me out of my sniffing. "What are you doing back there?"

Smelling you? "Sorry, had an itch on my nose. I'm too chicken to move my hands."

He chuckled softly and patted my hand on his stomach. "Keep a firm hold on me. You'll be safer that way."

I smirked, relieved he couldn't see the crazy smile plastered across my face. *Oh, believe me, I'm keeping the firmest hold possible.*

His chest felt so defined. I ran my hand up along the front of his shirt. He moaned into the helmet and then snapped out of it.

"Are you cold or molesting me again?"

I jumped, embarrassed at my actions. I lost my grip on him for a moment, and he grabbed my hand to steady me. Quickly, he pulled over on the side of the road.

"You okay?" He repositioned himself and turned to half face me

"That scared the crap out of me." I was not kidding. My heart beat double time, rushing through my system, leaving me wide-eyed and shaken.

He exhaled loudly. "Me too." He took hold of my shoulders. "You sure you're okay?"

I nodded.

He pulled me into a hug. Welcoming the contact, I slid my arms around his back and pressed my face into his chest.

Stupid moments were plentiful in my life. I stood on my tiptoes once outside my house and pressed my lips against Ashton's. His eyes widened in shock. I pulled away, covering my mouth.

He stammered this time. "Uh, umm... Gracie..."

I covered my face. "Don't say anything. I'm mortified. I shouldn't have done that. If you care about me, Ash, don't say anything."

He didn't say another word. When I turned away from him, his hand caught my arm. I hesitated. I desperately wanted him as a friend, but I wasn't sure it was the best thing to do while crushing on him so hard. That and the fact that I hadn't quite figured out how I was going to break things off with Hudson. Or even if that was what I was going to do. I did know Hudson would at least distract me from Ashton, though.

Reluctantly, I turned but avoided eye contact. I wobbled on my feet when he pulled me into a hug.

"If you ever need anything, let me know. Don't settle for less than you deserve." He whispered in my ear, "It was nice... the thing we aren't mentioning."

Heat spread across my cheeks.

Waving good-bye, I stepped inside the doorway. Once the door was shut, I jumped up and down excitedly. Even though he hadn't kissed me back, it helped me make up my mind about Hudson. Angel came out of the kitchen at that moment.

"What are you so excited about, chica?"

I grabbed my chest. "You scared me!" I recovered from my brief heart attack and said, "I kissed Ashton."

Angel's eyes bugged out. "What? What about Hudson?"

I hung my jacket on the coat rack. "Hudson who?" I shrugged. "I'm overdoing it really. I wanted to kiss Ash, and I did. He didn't react, though. In fact, I think I scared him a little. Hudson was a jerk today, and Ash rescued me, then dropped me off."

Angel nodded. "Do you have feelings for Ash, sweetie?"

I sat on the stairs with my elbows on my knees, resting my head on my hands. I sighed deeply, "Yep. I do. Why are the good ones unattainable?"

She sat next to me, wrapping her arm around me and sighed. "I wish I knew that answer myself, girlfriend. Wanna talk about it?"

Nodding, I said, "Yeah, over ice cream?" She grabbed my hand, pulling me to the kitchen and shoved me into a seat. "Being a little pushy, aren't you?"

She cackled. "We haven't had girl talk in a long time. I'm excited!" She filled two bowls with ice cream and brought them over. "So how good of a kisser is Ash?" she asked, wiggling her eyebrows.

"Like I said, he didn't really react. It was more like I smushed my face against his."

Angel replied sarcastically, "That's hot."

I laughed and nudged her playfully. "I'm maybe just a little mortified."

She patted my shoulder. "What did Ash say?"

I smiled. "He said it was nice."

She stared at me for a moment. "It was nice? That's it?"

I nodded.

She shrugged. "That's positive at least. Better than him saying you kiss like a dead fish or that you slobbered on him."

I raised my hands up. "I get the picture." I sighed dramatically. "Angel... I really, *really* like Ash. What am I supposed to do?"

She swallowed the bite she had just taken and said, "Tell him how you feel, you never know."

I cringed. "I saw him with Xander again today. You know, his boyfriend, or at least I think they're dating." I wondered briefly why Ashton hadn't really spoken to me about Xander but shrugged it off. Our friendship was so new, we couldn't share every part of each other so quickly. "You know it's not like I can make him like women." I sighed.

She wiggled her body at me. "You can try. Work that body, girl."

I laughed and punched her arm lightly. "Please! Cameron would so kick your butt for even trying to convince me of that. You can't just make people... not gay."

She shrugged. "Well, the best way to get over a guy is to fall for another guy. Is Hudson really bad news? Are you breaking it off with him?"

Hudson wasn't what I wanted. I knew that for certain. He had shown more of his romantic side today, for like five minutes.

"He gets angry a lot," I admitted. "His attitude changes so quickly. I'm not sure what to think of him. He's been sweet in the past, but I don't think that's enough. Not when he goes all Jekyll and Hyde on me." My phone beeped. I tugged it out of my pocket and looked at the text. "Speak of the devil."

Angel peeked over my shoulder. "He's apologizing for being a jerk."

She cleared our bowls and came back over to stand beside me. She bumped me with her hip. "What are you going to do?"

I thought about it for a moment, then texted to Hudson.

Me: I need to speak to you.

He replied instantly.

Hudson: Come on over.

CHAPTER SIX

The weekend was upon us. Hudson was going out of town for the night to see his favorite band in Atlanta, which was absolutely fine by me. When I'd met up with him that night, intent on calling things off, he'd managed to sweet-talk his way back into my good graces. Well, sort of. I suggested we take some time off for a while and have some distance while we figured things out. He reluctantly agreed. It was either that or we ended it for good. So far, things were a bit better, certainly less pressured without him breathing down my neck. The jury was still out on whether I wanted him in my life or not. My problem was I was a sucker for a sweet apology, and I hated to hurt people. It was a weakness I hoped one day to grow out of.

For my weekend reprieve, the girls, Angel and Mary Jane, both had dates, so Cameron, Gavin, and I were going to play pool downtown. I had invited Ashton but hadn't heard from him since he'd dropped me off that night after the restaurant rescue.

When I showed up at Cameron's, I had hoped Ashton would be there with them. Gavin opened the door. "Hey, hot momma."

It was a chilly night, in the mid-forties. I had chosen black jeans, my black corset with long sleeves and red ribbons up the front, and my new favorite cherry ribbon shoes.

I also wore Ashton's jacket, though it was a little big on me and didn't offer as much warmth as one of my own would have. What can I say? I wanted to look cute, and I liked how it felt to wear something of his.

"Hey yourself, handsome." I gave him a kiss on the cheek as I stepped through the door.

Cameron peered up at me and whistled. "I thought you were coming alone?"

I raised my eyebrow. "Huh?"

He pointed at my highly pushed-up cleavage. "The girls are making their appearance known tonight."

Of course I wore this in hopes that Ashton would be here. Tight jeans, ample cleavage, high heels... a straight man would show if he liked it. This was my final test to figure him out. Probably would have been much easier if I asked him outright instead of trial and error. I knew this.

Deep down, the only reason I hadn't asked him outright

was because I was afraid of the answer. If he were gay, there would never be a chance for us. Then there was the possibility he wasn't gay, and he was just not that into me.

I wanted to pout when I noticed Ashton wasn't here. "Hey, Gavin, I invited Ashton. Is he still coming?"

Gavin shrugged. "Maybe. I haven't talk to him today."

Cameron poked my cleavage. "Are these for Ash?"

I scoffed. "What? No. I'm with Hudson, Cam. Ashton and I are friends, and that's all we'll ever be."

Gavin smiled. "Leave her alone, Cam. For what it's worth, Gracie, I know Ashton really enjoys hanging out with you."

We all rode together. Gavin agreed to be the designated driver for the night, and I was going to sleep over at Cameron's afterward.

We met up with a few of Gavin's friends. It was mostly me with a bunch of guys. That was fine with me, especially considering they were all gorgeous.

Cameron challenged me to a game of pool as soon as we arrived. No one else would play him, so I caved. He stepped up to break for me. Surprisingly, no balls went in on his first shot. It was my turn. My pool stick was lined up for the easiest shot I could find. I aimed for the yellow striped ball, but instead, I hit the green solid that was to the right of it.

A gently placed hand on my hip was followed by a voice that sent waves of ecstasy throughout my body. "Want some pointers?"

When I turned, Ash's face was beside mine. I smiled excitedly. "You made it!" I wrapped my arms around his neck, pulling him down in an embrace.

He chuckled in my ear. "Told you I'd be here."

Cameron took his turn next and, of course, ended up knocking in three. I stuck my tongue out at him.

"Show off."

He snickered.

"Don't be so cocky," I said, feigning annoyance.

He flicked his shirt. "It ain't bragging, mothereffer, if you back it up."

I rolled my eyes. "That only works for Kid Rock. Nice censorship by the way."

He shrugged. "I can't use the real phrase. It's too graphic and makes me think of my mother in ways I don't wanna." He shuddered with disgust and I laughed.

Ashton came up behind me again. He patted my hips, leaned closer to my ear so I could hear him over the music, and said, "Spread your legs."

I jumped, dropping the pool stick on the table, as my head bounced back, hitting him in the chin. I squeaked, "What?"

I quickly covered my mouth when I saw him rubbing his chin. "I'm sorry."

He laughed, his cheeks flushed as he cleared his throat. "Your stance needs to be wider."

That familiar tug in my stomach told me I liked the other way he'd said it better. I took his advice. His left hand rested on the pool table next to me, his arm across my back. His right hand sent electric tingles across my skin as he moved it along my arm to help me aim. His breath was on my neck as he instructed me on what to do. I had no clue what he said. All I could hope was that he didn't notice the drool on my face.

His hand tickled my stomach and I jerked back laughing. "What was that?"

He chuckled. "You zoned out. I needed to get your attention." Apparently, he *had* noticed something was off about me.

"Sorry, I was distracted by... the... balls?" I said, suddenly mortified as to how that sounded.

Cameron snickered. "Gracie gets distracted by balls pretty easily."

Ashton leaned up against the table and put his hands on my hips. "You all right, Gracie?"

His eyes dipped down briefly to my cleavage and back up. *Hmm, that was a good sign.* One more test should do it. I knocked the chalk from the table. I bent over slowly in front of him. When I turned to see if he was looking, he had turned to hug some guy who had walked up. I knew he was too good to be true for me.

Slipping away, I walked up to the bar to grab two beers. While I was up there, a man approached me.

"Hello, beautiful," he said as he drew circles with his fingers on my shoulder.

I took a step back from him. The bartender was distracted by another customer. I wished he'd hurry up with my beers.

"My name's Wes. What's yours?"

I glanced over at my friends, who hadn't noticed my

dilemma yet. "I'm seeing someone, Wes."

He glanced around. "You look alone to me."

The bartender brought me two beers. I quickly handed him a ten and told him to keep the change.

Holding up the two beers, I said, "See?"

He put his arm around my waist, pulling me against him. Before I could protest, he let go as he backed away with his hands up. An arm came around my shoulders.

"You got a problem, man?"

Wes shook his head. "No, man, I'm good."

Ashton's voice became deeper. "Well, I gotta problem with you putting your hands on my girlfriend."

The deepness of his voice, the possessive way he'd claimed me, it was all too much to handle. The image that flashed in my head was of Ashton ripping my corset open, lifting me onto the pool table and giving me some horizontal refreshment. *Snap out of it, Gracie!* I shook my head back and forth to erase the steamy thoughts.

Wes walked away.

"Your girlfriend?" I inquired.

Ashton didn't smile. He looked pissed, actually. "He had no right to put his hands all over you. I hate guys like that."

I placed my hand against his heart. "It's okay. I'm used to it." It was as true as it was wrong. There were too many jerks in this world who thought they could put their hands on a woman.

His jaw clenched. "You shouldn't have to be used to that crap, Gracie. He needs to learn to treat women with respect."

With my palm against his face, I leaned up and kissed

his cheek. "Thank you for protecting me. You're an amazing friend." I held the beer up to him. "Here, payback for the pool lessons."

He smiled, taking the beer and pressing it to his lips for a taste. I watched his moist lips wrap around the bottle. His Adam's apple bobbed as he swallowed the liquid down. I'd never been so jealous of a beer bottle before.

"Come on, you still have a shot to make."

His hand stayed against the small of my back as he led me back to the table. We resumed our positions. Ashton's hands were on my body, his lips next to my ear. I closed my eyes as his breath warmed my ear with the instructions he gave. I bit my bottom lip when his hand pressed against my hip, guiding my stance.

"You want to hit the red striped ball. It's in an odd position, so aim for the eight ball at this angle. It should ricochet off at the right angle to bump the red striped ball into the corner pocket."

Ashton moved to let me shoot. I followed his directions and watched in shock as it actually worked. I squealed, then wrapped my arms around his neck, and jumped up and down excitedly. After I jumped three times, the fourth time I came down hard on my heels and my foot turned. Ashton caught me before I fell over.

I glanced down. *Unbelievable!* "Dammit, my shoe broke." I pouted. "I love these shoes."

He helped me over to a stool and lifted me up on it. His hand gently lifted my foot as he checked out my shoe. "I think it's pretty much ruined. Stay here, I'll be back in a few."

Cameron stepped over after Ashton left. "Where'd he go?" Then he gasped. "What did you do to those heels?"

My phone beeped. Ashton had texted me.

Ashton: What size shoe do you wear?

I texted back.

Me: Size nine.

"Okay, I think Ashton is buying me new shoes... somewhere."

Cameron wrapped his arm around me. "You better hope he hurries if you expect to win this game of pool."

Ashton was gone for about forty-five minutes. When he returned, he carried a long box. His large muscular hands lifted my foot, his touch causing my heart rate to spike and goose bumps to dance across my skin. He then slid off my shoe. He opened the box and pulled out...

"Cowboy boots?"

He smiled. "It's downtown Nashville. What other shoes would I find to go with your kickin' outfit?"

They were black cowboy boots with red stitching in the shape of flowers. "These are actually pretty badass."

Ashton grinned. "Glad you like them."

They matched my outfit perfectly. Ashton had great fashion sense. *Damn it.* Ashton placed the boots on my feet for me. I paced back and forth, breaking them in a little, and grinning at how amazing he was to do this for me.

"Them's dancing shoes, Gracie," Cameron said with his best country twang. "Let's head downstairs and dance on the bar."

Cameron, Ashton, Gavin, and I left the rest of the guys to run downstairs to one of the country bars below. Cover was free for ladies, and the guys got in free too because Ashton knew the bouncer.

The music blared a fast country song. A squeal flew from my lips as Ashton lifted me up to place me on the bar to dance. I swayed my hips, tapping my boots against the bar top. One of the bartenders got up to dance with me. She put her hands on my hips and swayed with me.

She was wearing a cowboy hat that she moved to my head and yelled in my ear, "Love your corset! And those boots are smokin'!"

She twirled me around then gave me a dip. I laughed as she winked at Ashton and pushed me backward. I screamed as I fell off the bar into his arms. He looked down at me and smiled.

"Hey, beautiful."

I giggled, my heart racing as he set me on the floor. When Ashton called me beautiful, it felt true, not like a pick-up line. Being near him both excited and frightened me. The prospect of having unrequited feelings for someone was a lonely road to venture down. Every moment I spent with him, I felt more confused about what I wanted.

The loud music offered a small distraction from the awkward moment after falling into his arms. I'd been staring at him as I internalized all these thoughts. When a slow song came on next, I grabbed his wrist, pulling him against me. I had danced with Cameron like we were a couple before, so why couldn't I do that with Ash?

"Dance with me?"

Without hesitation, Ashton slipped his hands around

my waist, as mine went around his neck. Cameron and Gavin followed our lead. Ashton secured me tighter in his arms as I laid my head against his firm chest. My body had the impression that this was more than "just friends" dancing.

It was beyond my control as to how aroused I was by being so close to him. My heart skipped a beat when I felt his lips graze my forehead. The comfort of his masculine scent drew me closer to losing myself in him. Little things like the way he stroked my hair, or how he didn't complain the couple of times I stepped on his feet, gave me butterflies in my stomach. He leaned down, pressing a soft kiss to my cheek. His breath on my ear causing a light whimper to escape my lips.

With a questioning tone, he said, "Gracie?" I looked up into his eyes as he continued, "I think...." As he spoke, something caught our attention, distracting us both momentarily.

A man ambled over to Cameron. He placed his hand on his shoulder as he said something I couldn't make out. Cameron jerked his arm free of the man's hold while Gavin put his hand on his shoulder as if attempting to calm him. Cameron didn't get upset very easily.

I strolled over. "Is there a problem?"

The man replied, "I was asking these two to leave. This bar isn't for that kind of thing."

Offended, I spouted, "What kind of thing? Dancing?"

The man gave me an odd look. "Miss, you can resume dancing with your boyfriend over there."

My hands balled into fists at my sides. I could feel my face redden with the heat of my anger. I moved only inches from his face. "You didn't seem to have a problem with your female bartender grinding up against me on the bar a few minutes ago."

He stepped back slightly. "Two women dancing together is considered sexy to our male customers. This"—he pointed to Cameron and Gavin—"is not."

Ashton lifted me up and put me over his shoulder as the curse words spewed from my mouth. He pushed through the crowds, Cameron and Gavin following us out.

The bouncer stopped us. "Ash, man, leaving so soon? What's up with your girl?"

I was still so mad I was yelling obscenities.

"Your manager is a homophobe. You don't mind working for that, Bobby?"

Bobby, the bouncer, shrugged. "I got bills to pay. I don't bring my boyfriend in here because of that guy. If you hear of someone hiring, though, let me know, man."

Ashton shook his hand. "Definitely. We'll talk. I gotta get this girl home before she gets herself arrested."

Bobby chuckled. "Good luck, she looks feisty."

Ashton replied, "You have no idea."

Once outside, Ashton set me down. I promptly turned to walk back into the bar. Cameron is the most important person in my life, and nothing pushes my buttons more than someone hurting him. In that moment, I couldn't think of anything else but telling this homophobic asshole where to stick it.

Ashton grabbed my wrist to stop me. Angrily, I pointed at him. "Let go of me! No one makes my friends feel bad. I'm going back in there to give him a piece of my mind."

Ashton laughed. "I think you already did that, Gracie."

Cameron wrapped his arm around mine. "Forget about him. I love you for coming to my rescue, but he's not worth it." His embrace quelled my anger. Gripping him tightly, I choked back tears of frustration. His words were nonchalant as though it didn't affect him, but I knew better. As he held me, I felt the quiver of his muscles as he shook with anxiety. Whenever homophobia reared its ugly head, Cameron feared violence would ensue as it had in the past. I'd make whatever sacrifice needed if I could be sure no one would ever hurt him again.

I kissed his cheek. "I don't like anyone hurting you." I turned to look at Ashton and Gavin. "Any of you."

Gavin spoke up, a smile playing on his lips, "You're an awesome friend, Gracie." He kissed my cheek. "We're all lucky to have you. Let's go home. I've had enough fun for one night."

Ashton reached for my hand. "I can take you home if you'd like?"

I nodded. "Yeah, sure." I hugged Cameron and Gavin before following Ashton to his bike.

"I thought maybe Cam and Gav would want some alone time," Ashton said, mounting his bike.

"Oh, yeah, that makes sense."

He reached for my hand again, "Plus, selfishly, I wanted to spend some time with you."

The grin on my face couldn't speak louder to the joy I felt hearing those words. "Are you sleepy?"

He shook his head. "Nope. Where do you want to go?"

Pressing my body against him, I breathed, "Anywhere, as long as I'm with you." Ash's body didn't tense at my words or the emotions they insinuated. We'd shared an intimate moment tonight. Ashton not only protected me but protected Cameron as well by leading us out of a potentially hazardous situation. For that, he would forever hold a special place in my heart.

We pulled into a quiet suburban neighborhood, just north of Nashville. Ashton turned into a driveway and I stepped off the bike first. I removed my helmet and shook out my hair.

"Where are we?"

He reached for my hand, guiding me to the front door. "My house. I thought we could just hang out."

His house was red brick with blue shutters that matched a blue front door. Unlocking it, he moved aside for me to enter. The front door opened into a living room with a marble-mantled fireplace across from the couch.

"No TV?" I asked, surprised.

He laughed. "Of course I have a TV, silly. Big screen is down in the den, and I have another one in the bedroom."

I laughed. The response I really wanted to give was to ask if I could see the one in the bedroom.

Holding my hand during the whole tour of his home,

I could barely concentrate on the rooms, or anything he said. My attention was too absorbed on the feel of his warm hand in mine. When his thumb stroked circles against my skin, if I hadn't been so focused on holding myself back from throwing myself at him, I was sure my legs would have buckled. Okay, so I had it bad.

What was worse, I decided as he led me through the room, finally ending up in the impressive basement, I no longer trusted my ability to read him. This didn't help the conundrum that was Ashton.

My attention was finally re-focused when I stopped to look around the basement, and he released my hand. It was set up like a movie room with a big-screen television, a small couch, recliners, and DVDs. Lining the walls were neon beer signs, a dartboard, and in the corner, a pool table.

Oh, holy sweet love, the fantasy on the pool table started again in my head.

"You wanna hang out down here a bit? Watch a movie?" he asked. For the first time since I'd met him, he appeared nervous. He fumbled with the remote, and he cleared his throat when his voice cracked a little.

"Yeah, I'd like that." I sat on the couch and then patted the seat next to me. He sat down, and I leaned against him to watch the comedy he had chosen for us. Sliding his arm around my shoulder, he held me close. Heat spread up my neck and across my face as I stared intently at the screen, hoping he didn't look my way and wonder what was wrong. Cameron and I watched movies like this all the time, but this felt so much more personal. His fingers traced circles on my shoulder. I bit my lip trying desperately to focus on the film. My heart and mind were at war as I fought to remember Hudson and I were still officially together against the feelings struggling to break free for Ashton.

After sitting in silence for a while, a few soft chuckles escaping the both of us as we watched the movie, Ashton angled his head toward me. "I'm proud of you for standing up to that guy tonight," he said.

I glanced up at him, hoping my cheeks had cooled a little. "Like I said, I don't like people hurting my friends. Cameron acts tough about it. The truth is, every time he deals with people like that, it kills him a little more and I hate it."

Pressing his lips to the side of my head, he pulled back slightly. "I hate jerks like that. I'm glad we're friends, Gracie. I feel very protective of you myself."

If he added that he thought of me like a sister, I would seriously die of heartbreak. He left it at that though, and I wasn't quite sure if I was relieved or disappointed there was no elaboration.

I fell asleep at some point. When I woke, I was curled up against Ashton's chest with my arm around him. His head rested against the couch as he slept, snoring lightly. He looked adorable. I ran my hand along his chest, wanting to wake him up with my lips pressed to his, but I had to hold back. His body shifted slightly. His arms wrapped around me, pulling me closer.

I sighed with contentment.

He muttered, "Mmm... Gracie," and it made my heart race.

I glanced up to see if he had woken. He was still sound asleep but muttering my name.

My phone beeped, alerting me of a text. I jumped, causing Ashton to jump too.

He rubbed his eyes. "Hey, gorgeous, guess I fell asleep. What time is it?"

I cursed my phone. "It's early, a little before six. I'm sorry that woke you up. You were sleeping so peacefully."

He grinned. "Were you watching me?"

I shrugged. "Couldn't help it. You're so darned cute." I moved away from him to read my text. I rolled my eyes as I read it silently.

Hudson: When I get back in town, I'd like to talk again. I'm not happy with how we left things.

Ashton stood up, stretching his body, his shirt riding up slightly as his pants dipped a little at the same time. I licked my lips as I watched him. "Important text?"

"Nothing that can't wait," I replied.

He held his hand out to me. "Come on, I'll fix you breakfast."

"Thanks for bringing me back here. I enjoyed it," I said as we walked upstairs.

"Me too. If you want, you can grab a shower while I make breakfast."

I'd rather us grab a shower together, I thought naughtily. He showed me to the bathroom and set me up with towels and everything I'd need.

After breakfast, he drove me home. "You busy today?"

he asked as I got off the bike.

"Nope, no plans actually. Why?"

He grinned. "Go put on some comfortable clothes. Jeans, T-shirt, tennis shoes kind of thing. I'll be back in an hour, and we'll spend the day together, if you want?"

I couldn't think of a better way to spend my day than with Ashton. Being with him and watching paint dry would probably be an amazing time. I loved how comfortable I felt around him, how free I was to be myself. "Definitely! What are we going to do?"

He revved the engine on his bike. "You'll see." I was sure it was possible to see the smile on my face from space. The giddy schoolgirl in me bounced up and down with excitement, while trying to be cool on the outside. Ashton took off down the street, leaning to the right as he made his turn. When he righted the bike straight again, he waved. *Damn, he makes motorcycles even sexier.*

Ashton texted me an hour later, letting me know that he was outside waiting. I skipped down the stairs unable to wipe the huge grin off my face. Locking the front door, I turned around and discovered him sitting in a pickup truck. He jumped out and opened the passenger door for me.

"What's this?"

He laughed. "This is called a pickup truck. They're vehicles that require gas to run. They're also known to carry beautiful women in them to fun places for the day."

I smirked. "Nice. I meant whose is it?"

He smiled. "It's mine. I can't ride my motorcycle all the

time." He held his hand out to help me up into the truck and then ran around to get behind the wheel. He still refused to tell me where we were going.

It was an unseasonably warm November day in Nashville. Lately, it didn't matter what time of year it was, any temperature was possible. Today the high was in the low seventies. We drove the back roads from Smyrna, each one getting narrower until it was barely a two-lane road lined with trees on both sides. We crossed over the lake into Mount Juliet, and I watched the speedboats dancing across the water and the children playing near the shore.

As I glanced around, I realized we were in a local state park. I hadn't been there in years. I used to come and walk the trail for exercise with Cameron when we were in high school. Once we graduated, we never found the time to come anymore. It seemed our priorities changed a bit too. All our time became focused on clubbing, shopping, men, and well, that about covered it.

After parking the truck and getting out, Ashton went to the bed of the truck and pulled out two fishing poles.

"Um, what are those?"

He shook his head with a laugh. "Fishing poles. You've been fishing before, right?"

I snorted and covered my mouth, embarrassed. "Sorry. No."

He laughed again. "I'll teach you."

I crinkled my nose, looking around him, trying to find out if my fears were unnecessary. "Do I have to touch the worms or the fish?"

He smirked. "I give you permission to touch only what you want. I'll take care of the rest."

I grinned, liking the sound of that immensely. He didn't know how dangerous his statement could be.

We walked toward the nearest dock, shoulder-to-shoulder in a comfortable silence. The park was empty considering how pretty the weather was today. As we set up, he took a fisherman's hat out of his tackle box and put it on.

I snickered. "Hey, Grandpa."

He chuckled and put the hat on me instead. "It looks better on you. It'll keep the sun off your face."

I crinkled my nose again. "It'll mess up my hair." I laughed at his raised brows. "I'm playing. I'm not *that* girly."

It was a little big on me, so I twisted my hair up on top of my head and placed the hat on top. The extra hair inside tightened it and kept me cool too. He motioned for me to sit first. I eased myself down onto the edge of the dock. I slipped my socks and tennis shoes off and rolled my jeans up to my knees so they wouldn't get wet. Ashton made short work of rolling his jeans up and soon sat beside me.

He then picked up a Styrofoam cup, a smirk playing on his lips. When he opened the plastic top, I squealed. "Gross!" There were several fat, slimy worms wriggling through dirt inside the cup.

He chuckled at my girlishness "Not that girly at all," he teased, bumping his shoulder against mine. I watched on, my nose wrinkling in distaste as he baited the hook for me and handed me the pole.

"Do I just plop it in the water now?"

He smiled. "No, honey, I'll show you."

Oh-to-the-freaking-my! Chills raced up my arms, and I clenched my thighs together at his endearment, loving the sound on his lips.

Controlling my outward lusty reaction, I waited patiently while he baited the hook to his pole. He slid behind my back with his legs sitting on either side of me. Preventing myself from groaning at the contact, my muscles became rigid. I bit my lip as his arm reached for mine to show me how to handle the fishing pole. Ashton pulled my arm back and to the right gently. He instructed me on flinging the pole forward to cast my line. I did as he said and the line shot straight out across the lake.

He whispered in my ear, "Great job."

His lips grazed my ear, causing me to suck my bottom lip in with a gasp. I turned slightly and smiled when I saw his face so close to mine. He moved away from me and cast his line next. I admired his skill and concentration as he focused on the water, but I wished he'd put the fishing pole down and move closer once more. Selfishly, I wanted all of his attention.

"Do you come here often?" I asked.

He smirked. "Is that a pick-up line or small talk?"

I laughed and said, "You know what I mean."

He grinned. "I haven't been out in a while. My dad took me as a kid every weekend in the summer. He taught my brother Derrick and me. The three of us used to camp once a month, and he made us live off the land during that time."

I had an image of an old black-and-white TV show with the father and son whistling as they carried fishing poles to the lake. The thought made me smile. Everything about Ashton made me smile.

"What camping skills did he teach you?"

He shrugged. "The usual: fishing, hunting, building a fire, that kind of stuff."

I smiled. "That sounds nice. I've never been camping. I'd like to go sometime, with you." *Take it back, Gracie. Take it back.*

His head turned abruptly in my direction, and his lips turned up in a half-smile. "You would?"

I tried to fix my faux pas. "Yeah. Maybe we could get a bunch of people together and go camping. It would be fun."

He turned back to the lake. "Check out your line."

As I caught sight of my line, I bounced up and down excitedly. "I got something!"

He laughed as I tried to jerk the line back. "Wait, wait." Ashton reached for my hand and placed it on the reel. He held his hand over mine as he helped me reel the fish in. "Pull back gently as you turn this and it will ease the fish in."

When the line pulled harder, he took it from me to help. The fish came flying out of the water, straight for me. I squealed and flung myself backward.

Ashton yelled out, "Gracie, be careful!"

It was too late. I tumbled off the dock into the lake. Submersed in cold water, I gasped. My mouth filled with lake water and I struggled to fight my way back to the surface. A few moments later, I felt an arm around my stomach as I was yanked upward. My back came in contact with a hard surface. I coughed, jerking upward, and spit up a large amount of muddy lake water. *Yuck.*

Ashton appeared above me, his forehead pinched with worry, his eyes centered on me. "Gracie, are you all right?"

I nodded. "Except that I just swallowed a bunch of bug-infested lake water that probably had grosser things in it than I even want to think about." Then, I began to laugh.

He helped me sit up. "What's so funny?"

I shook my head. "I'm such a klutz. You have to admit that was funny."

His face scrunched up before he laughed with me. "Now that you're safe, yeah, it was. You should've seen your face when that fish came at you!" We were both cackling like crazy.

I looked around. "Where is it?"

He pointed out at the lake. "It took off with my pole. When you fell in, I dropped it to jump in and save you."

I covered my mouth. "I'm so sorry, Ash. I'll buy you a new pole."

He waved it off. "Nonsense, it was worth it to save you."

I placed my hand against his face and gazed at him. The moment felt right. I licked my lips and moved toward his mouth. Ashton moved closer. At the same time, I felt something on my arm, looked down, and screamed as I saw a large bug on it. I jumped up, shaking my arm and squealing, "Get it off me!"

Ashton grabbed at me as he said, "Gracie. Gracie! Stop!" I knocked into him, pushing him to the ground as I fell on top of him. Ashton groaned in pain.

"You okay?" I asked, worried.

He squeaked out, "Your knee."

I looked down and realized my knee had hit him directly in his crotch. I jumped up. "I'm sorry!"

Laughing, he sat up with a slight wince on his face. "You're lucky you're cute."

I blushed as he pulled me into a hug, still groaning slightly. "I think we should head home. We both need to get into dry clothes."

He smiled up at me. "We could do that. Or we could let our clothes dry in the sun and go swimming."

I glanced down at myself and shrugged. Without hesitation, I lifted my shirt off, and he turned his head when I did. I reached out to move his chin to face me. "It's just a bra, Ashton. Covers the same amount of skin as a bikini."

He nodded as he glanced over me briefly. I stood up and slipped my blue jeans off. That was easier said than done since they were so wet they stuck to my skin. Ashton shimmied out of his clothes and stood in boxer briefs only.

He grinned at me. "Race ya."

He took off running across the dock before I had a chance to move. He did a cannonball into the water, and I jumped in behind him. This time, I expected the cold water, but it didn't stop me from gasping. When I came up, Ashton was waiting for me on the surface.

I pushed my hair back off my face and shivered. "It's so cold."

He moved forward and wrapped his arms around me, running his hands up and down my back. "Is that better?" His face was only inches from mine.

"Uh-huh," was all I could say.

His face moved toward mine. I closed my eyes, ready to kiss him. His head landed on my shoulder in a hug.

"I'm having a lot of fun, Gracie."

I sighed with disappointment, but answered truthfully, "Me too." Though admittedly, this idea of us being just friends was taking a toll on me.

I turned my head when Ashton's hand went to my shoulder.

"Aww, it's a ladybug," I said.

He stuck his index finger out and waited for the ladybug to crawl onto his finger. "You know, when a ladybug lands on you, it's said to bring good luck and grant wishes." He held his finger out to me. "Make a wish, Gracie."

I closed my eyes and wished for the only thing I wanted. The man in front of me to love me the way I was falling in love with him. Ashton lightly blew on the ladybug. Her wings fluttered as she flew away from us.

"We should probably get out before we both get sick," he suggested.

I nodded, a new shiver racking through my body, and followed him to the dock. He lifted me up first, impressing me with his display of strength. Once on the dock, I held my hand out to him, making him laugh.

"Sweetheart, I'll end up pulling you back in. Back up, I got this."

My hands rose in mock surrender as I stepped back from the edge. I was more than happy to stand by and ogle him. His palms placed flat on the dock, and he lifted himself out of the water. My mouth fell open as I watched his massive arms flex to their fullest. Beads of water clung to his muscular chest, and his wet boxer briefs sagged on his hips allowing a nice view of his Adonis belt. He stood up, flinging his head backward to shake loose the water and smoothed his hair back. Ashton smirked at me, and I quickly reached up to make sure I hadn't been drooling.

We grabbed our clothes and headed back to his truck. "You don't happen to have towels do you?"

He nodded. "Yep. I knew our feet would at least get wet, so I stuck some behind the seat."

He handed me a towel first. My clothes were still wet, so I slipped my shirt on and wrapped the towel around my waist for the ride home.

Our hands rested next to each other on the seat during the drive. I kept inching my fingers closer to his but was too scared to close the distance completely. Fear of rejection ate away at me. A bump in the road caused his hand to touch mine briefly making me thankful for potholes for the first time ever.

When we made it back to my house, I let Ashton come inside to throw his clothes in the dryer. The house was too quiet, so I turned the radio on for a little background noise. Ashton stood in front of the dryer with a towel around his waist and threw his boxer briefs in with the clothes. I bit my lip, realizing he was practically naked in front of me. It would only take a small movement to remove the towel and see him in his full glory. My ogling had gone unnoticed which was evident by the little dance move he did around the table. Singing along to the radio, his movement was a little offbeat yet sexy as hell. The temperature in the room went up about ten degrees. I had to get away from the temptation quickly.

"I'm gonna run upstairs and get dressed." Once upstairs, I flopped on my bed and screamed into the mattress in frustration. *Come on, ladybug wish, and work already*, I thought to myself. At the end of my frustrated prayer, I froze, hearing my bedroom door open. I sat up quickly.

Ashton chuckled. "You're still wet."

Whoa. My mind went in a totally different direction than what he meant with that statement. Thinking fast, I mumbled, "Sorry, I felt a bit tired."

He sat next to me. Ashton Collins, the man I was falling head over heels for, sat naked with only a towel keeping me from seeing every glorious bit of his body. My mind raced with dirty images involving our bodies tangled together on this bed. I clenched my thighs together when I wanted to wrap them around his waist. I knew it was more than simple desire I felt for him because I could be just as happy curled up in his arms. And still, my insecurities hindered me from making a move on him.

"I smell like fish, don't I?" Where that came from, I had no idea. I clamped my mouth shut in humiliation, hoping the ground would open and swallow me whole. Instead, Ashton pressed his nose to my shoulder and breathed in.

"No, you smell like caramel and vanilla."

My body quivered as the familiar heat of desire ran over me, one I was becoming accustomed to with Ashton. I stuttered, "That's, um, that's my vanilla-bean spray."

"It smells amazing," he said as he lay back on the bed. The slit in the towel was open, showing me a perfect glimpse of his athletic thigh. He stretched his arms back and groaned. "Swimming is exhausting. I feel like I really worked out."

My breathing increased as I watched his body stretching across my bed. I reached out, without thinking, and trailed my hands along his abdomen.

He sucked in a breath and sat up. "What are you doing?"

I shook my head. "Sorry, you're in amazing shape. You must work out like an animal." I attempted to laugh away my inappropriate fondling.

He shrugged. "I lift weights in the morning, and I usually run at night when I feel like it." He stood up. "I better go check on my clothes."

I waited a few minutes before meeting him downstairs, needing the time to collect my thoughts and rein in my libido. He was fully dressed by the time I came down.

"All dry now," he said, holding his arms out to display that he was, in fact, dry. "I best be off."

I walked Ashton out to his truck and was about to kiss him good-bye when I heard a car pull up behind us.

Hudson stepped out and yelled, "Hey, baby girl."

My eyes on Ashton's, I offered him a light smile. "Thanks again, for everything."

He nodded without a word, his face grim and his eyebrows set in a frown. A moment later, he drove away.

Hudson stepped behind me, wrapping his arm around me. "Did you have fun at your concert?" I asked, pleased he couldn't see the disappointment on my face.

His mouth moved to my neck. "Yep, but I missed you so much. Let's go back to my place." His hands roamed across my stomach and slipped inside my shirt. He pulled me against him. "I missed the smell of your skin, the taste of your lips, and the way you drive me so crazy."

I smiled at his sweet words as he nipped at my skin, throwing one last look in the direction that Ashton went. "What are we waiting for? Let's go to the house."

Chapter Seven

Most of the next few weeks were swamped with shopping and preparations for the holidays. Christmas Eve was the night we always spent together as friends to exchange presents, while Christmas Day, we went to our separate family dinners. Cameron and I always went together to both his family's dinner and mine. There was never a thought in my mind to ask Hudson to go to either get-together. He brought it up, and I decided the one with friends was the only one I was comfortable with.

We gathered around the Christmas tree with our spiked eggnog and a huge pile of gifts. Cameron always liked to play Santa Claus and hand out the presents, because he always bought the most for everyone. He especially loved to spoil me. By the time I finished opening his gifts, I practically had a new wardrobe and enough movies to watch for a year or two.

"This one says to Hudson from Gracie." Cameron handed it to Hudson.

I was excited to see his reaction. He opened the small package and pulled out a CD of Five Finger Death Punch that was autographed by the members of the band. Hudson's face lit up. "Wow, this is awesome! Thanks, babe." I may have been a bit carried away with his gift, but the opportunity just sort of presented itself. While our relationship wasn't back to what it was before, the past few weeks especially, we'd been spending more time with each other, helped along by him making an effort to be a good boyfriend, with few temper tantrums. Admittedly, I pushed myself to spend time with him in an effort to move on from the crush I had on Ashton, too.

I smiled and he leaned over to kiss me.

His face fell slightly. "I didn't get you anything, though. I didn't know we were exchanging gifts."

I sat back, surprised. "It's Christmas, Hudson. I'm your girlfriend. It's traditionally something you do." I didn't want to be a drama queen, but it didn't take a genius to work out we'd be exchanging gifts during our Christmas celebration.

He shrugged, no longer seeming apologetic. "Sorry, babe. What do you want me to do about it now?"

Annoyed, I stood up. "Nothing, Hudson. Nothing at all." I headed outside to the deck, slamming the door behind me, more in embarrassment than anything else. It seemed I'd tried too damn hard with his gift, only to be left feeling humiliated by his lack of thought. A few minutes later, I sighed when I heard the door open. Without turning, I huffed out, "Just leave me alone."

Shuffling feet had me turning. My eyes landed on Ashton, whose hands rose defensively. "I wanted to check on you. I'm sorry."

He turned to leave but I reached out for his arm. "No, *you*, I want to stay."

He smiled and handed me a small gift box.

"What's this?"

He tapped his index finger against his lip. "Hmm, it's wrapped in Christmas paper. It has a bow and today is Christmas Eve... a gift maybe?"

I laughed. "Sorry, stupid question."

On the tag it read, "To Gracie-bug, from Ash." My heart melted a little at his words. We hadn't spent as much time together recently. My aim for distance not proving very effective, though, as I spent far too many hours thinking about him. I'd foolishly thought that with space, I could move on and stop fantasizing over him. Seeing him tonight for our get-together had thrown that out the window, but alone and before me, I had to try to remember why I'd bothered trying in the first place. He was perfection, plus he had a gift.

Grinning, I tore into it. Once the packaging was removed, it revealed a velvet box. I held my breath as I pried it open, revealing a silver charm bracelet with a beautiful ladybug charm dangling from it. The charm was lined in silver, and the ladybug was made of a large ruby with black stones—I wasn't sure what kind—and a large diamond for the head. I gasped at the beauty of it and hoped desperately that the precious gems were fake. If not, it was too damn much.

"Ash, this is gorgeous."

He grinned. "It's a charm bracelet for you to capture your happy moments, achievements, or just things that you enjoy. Something that you can look at when you feel down. Memories, I have discovered, really help with that." He winked. "I started it with a ladybug charm for our day at the lake. I hope that memory makes you happy at least. It's one of my favorites."

I didn't respond right away. I was too busy staring at the most thoughtful gift I'd ever received.

His hand lifted my chin until our eyes met. "Do you like it?"

I nodded ever so slightly and held it out. "Put it on me?" The silver bracelet looked so tiny against his large, masculine hands. My hand trembled as his fingers adjusted the clasp brushed against my skin.

He wrapped his hands around mine. "Are you cold? You're shaking."

I shook my head. "No, not cold at all." I turned the bracelet to look at the ladybug charm.

"You can find one to represent your friendship with Cameron, too. I know he'd want to be represented."

I nodded, unable to speak as I ran my finger over the beautiful charm and tried to hold back the joyful tears I felt ready to spill.

"I saw it and it made me think of you. The day we went fishing and the ladybug landed on you. Plus, since I call you Gracie-bug, I thought it was fitting."

And the tears began to fall. There was no turning back then. I was a goner. Despite everything—Hudson, Ashton being unavailable, hell, even the fact that I'd barely kissed the guy—I was falling deep for this man. I was officially screwed and had no idea what on earth I was going to do.

His fingers traced the charm against my wrist. Once again, I closed my eyes and relished his touch. When I opened my eyes, they met with his. His gaze was intense, unwavering, drawing me in. Moving his hand to my cheek, he stroked his thumb across my skin. Breath hitching, I didn't move, terrified of breaking the connection. As he leaned toward me, his face mere inches from my own, the moment was interrupted by the deck door opening. I jerked away from Ashton in surprise and saw Hudson standing in the open doorway, his mouth downturned. "Can I talk to you?"

Flicking my gaze to Ashton, I swallowed hard. He looked as disappointed as I felt. "I'm going to head back in." His voice was low and hard.

I watched in silence as he walked away, leaving me alone with Hudson. Turning my back to Hudson, I asked, "What do you want?"

He wrapped his arms around me from behind, and I cringed at his touch.

"I'll make it up to you, I promise. Give me a chance?" he asked. He moved my hair aside and pressed his lips against my neck. I squirmed away from his embrace.

"Right now I need some space. Go home, Hudson." Relief

swept through me when he released me and walked away without argument. That didn't stop him from slamming the door on his way out, though.

Inhaling deeply, I released a shaky breath. I was pissed at myself, so frustrated that I'd allowed this thing with Hudson to go on for so long.

"Did he hurt you? He looked pretty angry." Ashton had returned, stepping toward me.

I shook my head. "I'm fine. I told him to leave. He didn't do anything wrong." I fingered the bracelet again and smiled. As he stepped closer to me, I embraced him, pressing my face against his chest. "Thank you for my gift." I took comfort in the strength of his arms and his familiar scent. I'd missed him so much over the last few weeks. I was a fool to think not seeing him would change a thing.

He smoothed my hair, "You're welcome, bug." He moved toward the swing and I sat beside him.

I turned the topic away from Hudson and the direction the evening had taken. "I'm glad you spent today with us. Are you doing the family thing tomorrow?"

He nodded. "Yep, brother, niece, parents, we all have a tradition of going to the Opryland Hotel to look at the lights and the décor."

"I love that place, especially at Christmas. I haven't been since they remodeled from the big flood."

He glanced at his watch. "It's still early. Why don't we see if everyone wants to head over there tonight?"

I jumped up, eager to put the night back on track. There was no way I was letting Hudson ruin our Christmas. "That would be so much fun!"

I ran inside to tell everyone else, and they readily agreed. We bundled up, considering it was a cold, thirty-degree night with a brisk wind. Ashton had driven his truck, so Angel and I rode with Ashton, and the others piled in Cameron's car.

Angel sat against the door, putting me in the middle, against Ashton. It was a manual transmission, so I had to straddle the gearshift. Each time he went to shift, his hand grazed my knee. If I had been wearing something other than jeans, it would have driven me insane each time. Even with jeans on, it was causing me to practically bite my lip off.

Angel leaned over, smushing me into Ashton even more, as she played with the radio.

I glanced up at him and he smiled at me. "Sorry, Angel's a bit rude about music. She's always changing my stations too."

Angel shoved her elbow into my stomach teasingly. "Look, chica, I can't help it I have better taste in music than the two of you. Ash, you don't mind that I changed it, do you?"

He shook his head. "You ladies can listen to whatever you like."

As we neared the hotel, it seemed everyone had the same idea judging by the amount of traffic to get inside to park.

"Go over to the mall entrance. We can park for free and walk over," I suggested. Ashton moved out of line to head toward the mall around the corner.

When we stepped out, Angel looked down at her shoes. "I wish I'd worn better shoes for this walk."

Ashton walked over and stooped down. "Get on my back and we'll get you some shoes inside."

She laughed. "Seriously?"

He nodded. "Yeah, girl. Come on, you'll keep me warm too."

I laughed as Angel shrugged and wrapped her arms around his neck and her legs around his waist from behind. A tug of jealousy pulled at me. Crossing my arms over my chest, I made an effort to smile.

Once we made it inside, we found a boutique for Angel to get some better shoes. She'd never been to the hotel before and didn't realize how massive it was or that she would need more comfy shoes for the stroll.

We entered on the delta side of the hotel. It had a river that ran through, complete with boat rides.

Lights and Christmas décor draped the ceiling, making the whole place glow with Christmas feels. We all wanted to go on the boat ride, but the line was insanely long. Instead, we took the stairs up to the next level to grab ice cream for dessert. Unable to decide between the massive amounts of flavors on offer, we each bought a different flavor of gelato and passed the bowls around to try each one.

Cameron wrapped his arm around me. "This was a fun idea."

I smiled happily in agreement and pointed my thumb to the right of me. "Thank Ash, it was his idea." Immediately, my smile slipped and the ice cream sat heavily in my stomach. Ashton was feeding a bite of ice cream to Angel, who giggled as it dribbled down her chin.

He turned, an innocent grin on his face. "Did I hear my name?"

Unable to play it cool, fearing I'd say something I had no right to say, let alone feel, I stood up and grabbed my ice cream. "Yeah, you did. I'm full. I'm going to stroll some more." I rushed away, aware that Cameron was staring at me in confusion, but I just had to get out of there. I had no right to comment on Ashton's actions, but it didn't stop the green-eyed monster from raising her nasty head.

A moment later, I felt a tap on my shoulder. "What's wrong, bug?"

"Stop calling me that," I said, with more annoyance than I meant.

His face reacted as though I'd hit him. "I'm sorry, I thought you liked it." He turned to walk away and I grabbed his arm, pulling him against me.

"I'm sorry, Ash. I don't know what's wrong with me tonight. The holidays get to me sometimes." The lie eased off my tongue. He smoothed my hair and kissed my forehead. I glanced up at him. "I love when you call me bug, I promise."

He grinned. "Okay, good. The others decided to wait in line for the boat and wanted us to meet them there. I told them I'd check with you."

I sent a text to Cameron, telling him we were going to take a walk and would meet up with them. It shocked me Ashton didn't want to run away from me. My mood swings were making *me* dizzy. Seeing the hurt in his eyes a moment ago was worse than him doting on Angel. The green-eyed monster of jealousy had left me alone. "My favorite section of the hotel is the Cascades area. Can we go there?"

He smiled. "That's my favorite too." He reached for my hand, and I leaned against him as we strolled through the Delta atrium to the Cascades atrium. Cascades had a two-story waterfall that was surrounded by plants and beautiful flowers. It was like something from a tropical island.

Upstairs, it was possible to walk behind the falls through a cave-like tunnel. Ashton led me up there. We stepped up to the window, letting the soft mist of water spray us. A woman came up behind us and asked if we'd like our picture taken. We handed her our phones. Ashton wrapped his arms around me and leaned his head against mine. She snapped a picture with both of our phones.

"You're a beautiful young couple. You seem very happy."

Her comment caught me off guard. I pulled away from Ash's embrace. I was unsure what possessed me to move when all I wanted was to be with him. He pressed me against the wall, to let the group coming through pass, and touched my face. "What's wrong?"

I sucked in my bottom lip, enjoying the feeling of him pressed up against me.

Someone knocked into him, causing him to push harder against me. I bit into my lip. "Shit, that hurt."

His thumb reached forward and wiped the blood from my lip. "Sorry, bug." He leaned down and kissed the edge of my mouth, the corners of our mouths touching slightly.

"What was that for?" I asked.

"I kissed it to make it better. Did it work?"

I nodded, my heart pounding so hard I struggled to hear anything other than the heavy thuds. "Oh, yeah, I'm good now."

He chuckled and leaned forward again.

"Are we interrupting something here?" Cameron asked as he cleared his throat beside us.

"Huh?" I said as I turned to him.

"You looked like you guys were about to make out?"

I moved away from Ashton and I laughed. "What? Come on, Cameron. Stop being ridiculous." I sounded high-pitched and did this crazy laugh thing. If I didn't get it together, I was sure Cameron would have me committed. "So, did you guys ride the boat?" I changed the subject quickly.

Cameron shook his head. "Nope, got tired of waiting in line."

Ashton walked over to Angel and put his arm across her shoulders. "How are your shoes working for you?"

She smiled. "Fantastic." She bumped his hip with hers and said, "You can still give me a ride back to the car though if you want." She winked and he threw his head back laughing.

Cameron put his arm around me. "What's wrong, Gracie? You look sad."

Ashton turned to look at me. His expression fell into a frown as a tear slid down my cheek. I wiped it quickly. "Nothing, I'm tired and want to go home. We have a busy day tomorrow." Tonight had not gone how I'd hoped at all. From the moment Ashton gave me the gift to yet another moment ruined by Hudson, my hopes were crushed. I feared I'd never have the courage to reach for what I wanted.

Ashton reached for my hand, but I passed him as if he wasn't there. I had to stop doing this to myself. Everything about Ashton confused me. The hot, the cold, the flirting, the gift... I had no idea what it all meant. When we got to the car, Ashton opened the door for me without saying a word.

I yelled out to Mary Jane, "Hey, MJ, wanna switch rides?"

Frowning, she looked at me in question, but I just smiled, my grin too forced. She shrugged and said, "Sure, I guess."

Ashton reached for my arm and pulled me aside. "Did I do something wrong?" His face expressed so much sadness that I hated myself for making him feel bad.

I shook my head. "No, I just want to spend time with Cameron."

The drive home felt excruciatingly long, and I sat in the backseat and cried silently to myself. When we arrived at the house, I ran straight up to the house, hoping for a quick escape. Ashton caught up with me, though, reaching for my arm to pull me aside.

"Goodnight, guys, Merry Christmas," he called out to

the others as they went inside, leaving the two of us alone. He brushed my hair aside and tilted my chin up. "You've been crying?"

I turned my face away.

"Gracie, what's wrong? What did I do? Tell me what I did wrong so I can fix it."

"It wasn't you. I'm in a bad mood because of Hudson." I decided on the half-truth, as it was one of the reasons why I was annoyed. "My own boyfriend didn't think to give me a Christmas present. I mean, I get that isn't what it's about, but it still makes me feel like crap. It makes me feel like I don't mean anything to anyone." Sitting on the porch step, I put my hands over my face as I cried.

He sat beside me and encircled me in his arms. "You know there are a lot of people that care about you. One of them is holding you right now."

It wasn't the lack of gift that upset me. It was the fact that Ashton gave me such a thoughtful, romantic gift, and it was killing me inside.

A car pulled up. We both looked up, and Hudson was walking toward me with a gift-wrapped box. Ashton pulled away from me. I wiped my eyes clean and said the first thing that popped into my head, "Where did you get a present so late on Christmas eve?"

He smirked. "You don't want to know. I know I was a jerk, and I wanted to make it up to you. You deserve better than this, but it's all I can do for now." Knowing he'd tracked down a gift for me was sweet. The gesture didn't elicit feelings even close to what Ashton's did. Yet somehow, I still couldn't make up my mind. He held the box out to me while Ashton stayed seated beside me on the porch. I opened it and laughed at the contents.

Everything had come from a convenient store. It was full of stuff to clean my car and some of my favorite snacks and candy. Hudson grinned. "You're always saying you need to clean your car more, and I know you always want chocolate after... well you know," he said as he glanced at Ashton.

Ashton stood up. "I'm going to leave you two alone. Merry Christmas, Gracie... Hudson." He walked away. Setting the box down, I ran after Ashton. "Wait." Avoiding eye contact, I embraced him and said, "Thank you for everything tonight." He patted my back before letting me go.

Hudson pulled me into a hug. "This is awesome, thank you." At the same moment, Ashton turned and our eyes met. He smiled sadly as he held his hand up in a wave. I closed my eyes and held onto Hudson, wishing—not for the first time—it was Ashton and life was so much simpler. I was too young for so much drama.

"Come home with me tonight?" he asked.

"I can't. Tomorrow's Christmas and I am going to my family dinner."

He wrapped his arms tighter around my waist. "I could meet your parents," he said as he wiggled his eyebrows.

"I don't think it's the right time for that yet."

He nodded, though his jaw stiffened in obvious annoyance at my rejection. "Okay, I understand. I'm going to head home for the night. Merry Christmas, babe." He dropped a kiss to my lips and headed to his car, throwing me a wink before he pulled away.

Yep, I was totally screwed.

As soon as I stepped in my bedroom, I dialed Ashton on my cell phone. He picked up instantly.

"Hey, bug."

I sighed with a smile. "I'm sorry for how I acted tonight. None of that had to do with you. I'm in a weird place here lately. I feel like I don't know which way I'm going anymore. That may not make any sense—"

"Gracie, you always make sense to me. I like how close we've become and I don't want to lose that. You pulling away from me tonight scared me. I thought I did something to hurt you and I never want to do that."

I couldn't help smiling at the affection in his tone.

He continued, "I kept feeling like I was doing something wrong tonight."

I sighed. "No, Ashton, you didn't. You're perfect."

He laughed. "Not really, Gracie."

I clarified my statement, "You're perfect... to me."

He was quiet for a moment, then said, "Ditto."

That one word lit my whole face up. I glanced at the clock and noticed it was a few minutes after midnight. "Merry Christmas, Ash."

"Merry Christmas, bug. Goodnight."

As I brushed my teeth, I noticed the bracelet in the

mirror. It was so beautiful I didn't want to take it off. Tonight was the defining moment for me. I'd never be happy with Hudson as long as Ashton was in my life. Now I needed to figure out what to do about it.

Chapter Eight

The next few weeks I avoided spending time at Hudson's. I knew I was being unfair and to be honest a bit of a wuss, but Hudson had made such a huge effort, and every time I considered broaching the subject of ending our relationship, I clammed up and backed out. Nobody said being young was easy, and I was walking, living proof of that recently.

We had been together for five months, and it finally reached the point where I couldn't back out any longer. It wasn't fair on anyone. I'd just have to suck it up and deal with the fallout.

It was Hudson's whispered, "I'm falling in love with you, Gracie," as I lay in his arms that sealed the deal for me. I shouldn't have allowed it to get so far, and I was all kinds of pissed with myself for reaching this point. Luckily,

I'd been quiet for a while that night; I was able to pretend to be asleep.

I was being a coward for sure, but it was time to woman up and put the whole debacle to an end. Or at least, after I was able to sneak out the next morning and formulate a plan.

In the morning, I woke up to an empty bed. Relieved, I slipped my clothes on while Hudson was in the shower. The plan was to sneak out before he could come in and tell me that again. I would have to answer, but the thought of breaking it off while those three words were still so new made me feel even worse. I scribbled a quick note about getting to class and bolted out the door.

My text beeped, and I groaned until I looked at the name and realized it was Ashton. He wanted to meet for breakfast. Relief washed over me. Despite my painful crush on him, we had become genuinely close over the months. Being a guy, it seemed the perfect opportunity for me to ask him for advice. I really was no good at this relationship stuff.

We met for breakfast. As I walked up to the door, I heard his bike pulling in. The sound was familiar and comforting. It was funny how sounds could cause a physical reaction in the body, and his growling bike evoked many. Turning, I watched him climb off the bike, remove his helmet and run his fingers through his thick, dark hair.

My body reacted to his allure. It was so hard to be just

friends with this man. It wasn't the choice I had made, though; it was the way life was. Ashton couldn't help who he was attracted to, and I understood that and knew I couldn't change it. I tried to find peace with that. I just wasn't sure I was quite there yet. Either way, it didn't make him less attractive to me. Oh, how I wish it did, though.

He spotted me and his lips curved into that gorgeous smile of his, outlined by that sexy beard I loved so much. "Hey, bug," he said as he leaned down and kissed my cheek.

I was so glad he didn't kiss my lips like Cameron did. If he did, it would be hard not to want more. He opened the door for me with his hand resting lightly on the small of my back. I absorbed the welcome heat of the contact before sliding into a booth in the back of the diner. He always sat beside me in the booth instead of across from me.

"So, what's up? Your text sounded like you had something on your mind," he said after we ordered our food.

"I need to know how to break up with a guy."

His face seemed to light up a bit at this. I had a feeling he didn't like Hudson any more than anyone else and that he just always kept it to himself for my sake.

"I thought things were good with Hudson, mostly?" he asked.

"He told me he loves me."

Ashton squirmed a bit uncomfortably at this and asked, "And you...?"

I didn't have to think about the answer. "Don't love him. Some days I'm not sure I even like him." I sighed, heat rushing to my cheeks in embarrassment. "I don't really understand how he thinks he's in love with me anyway. He barely knows anything about me except for what I look like naked." I attempted a small laugh that fell flat, trying to make light of the ridiculous relationship I'd allowed myself to stay in.

Ashton squirmed uncomfortably again.

The waitress brought our food over, and we quickly dug in before taking a small breather. He shifted his body toward me, laying his arm across my shoulders. He smelled so good that I wanted to press myself against him. My eyes drifted upward and he smirked at me. I licked my lips slowly and could've sworn I felt him shiver when I did.

"What's going on in that head of yours, Gracie-bug?"

I stuffed a forkful of eggs into my mouth. I covered my mouth with my hand and said, "Just hungry."

He chuckled and began forking food into his own mouth. "You don't have feelings for Hudson at all?" Ashton asked, as though this was news to him.

"Not really. You seemed surprised at that."

Ash's shoulders shrugged. "I just don't understand why you're with him if you don't like him?"

My head dipped to my plate in shame, unable to face him. "Lack of options, really. No one wants to be alone, and it's nice to be wanted." Voicing it aloud, I placed down my fork in horror. I sounded desperate and pathetic. How had I become this girl? I swallowed, refusing to allow my embarrassment to turn into tears. *What if Ashton thinks so too?* I had no idea if my actions would make him see me in a different light. The possibility made my breakfast sit heavily in my stomach.

"Gracie, you're an amazing girl. You can't stay with the wrong person simply because you haven't found the right one yet. You're beautiful, funny, smart, and incredibly sweet." My heart picked up speed in reaction to his words. "Any guy would be lucky to have you. The thing is, you're the one who needs to feel lucky to have that guy as well. If you don't, then it isn't gonna make you happy."

I shrugged. "I always manage to meet jerks. What's to say the next jerk will be a better trade?"

He folded his arms over his chest. Good grief, they looked massive when he did that. His face crumpled up into a stern look that made me feel like I was being scolded by my father or a teacher.

"Gracie Walker, what has made you so cynical?"

I chuckled. "How much time you got?"

His face softened as he reached out and stroked my cheek. "All the time in the world, for you."

My heart fluttered. If only he knew how much he tortured me with his sweet words.

"Sometimes happiness is staring us right in the face and we don't even know it," Ashton said as he stared into my eyes. If only that statement was literal at this moment.

"Happiness doesn't like to make eye contact with me it seems," I replied.

Ashton smiled sadly. "I think we all feel that way at some point."

"Ash?"

"Yeah, bug?"

I giggled. "First, I totally love that you call me that. I've never had a nickname before. Cameron's always called me babe, or hottie, or something to that effect. Anyway... what I was going to ask is... would you spend the rest of the day with me?"

He held his finger up asking me to give him a moment. He picked up his phone and made a call. Faking a cough, he said, "Yeah, man, I'm not going to make it in today. I feel pretty crappy. Can we reschedule for tomorrow? Thanks."

Warmth spread in my chest as I listened in to his conversation. "You didn't have to do that. By the way, what do you do?" I asked, touched he would change his plans for me. Back when we first met, he'd said he worked for himself, and it was a family business; those were all the details he'd given.

"I'm an independent contractor. All I did was cancel a meeting with a venue to strategize over who they want to book next. I own a promotion company for entertainers. I help book a lot of the venues around town with local artists, as well as some big-time entertainers."

My mouth fell open. "Shut up!"

He laughed at my shock.

"Who have you met? I must know, now!"

The waitress interrupted again with the check. Ashton grabbed it before I could, handed her a large bill, and told her to keep the change. He slid out of the booth, pulling me with him.

"I can't tell you who I've met. It's a confidentiality thing."

I huffed. "You suck."

He let out a loud laugh.

"I thought you told me it was a family business?" I asked, genuinely curious.

"It kind of is in a way. My dad owned a nightclub when I was growing up. I helped him run it while I was in college, made a few contacts that way. When I graduated, my dad gave me a loan to get me started and it took off pretty well."

I grinned. "Well, duh. Anyone as hot as you will go far in show business."

Ashton's lip turned up slightly. "You think I'm hot?" I bit my lip as he leaned closer to my face. He kissed my cheek. "That's sweet."

You're evil, Ashton Collins, pure, sexy evil.

We left my car at the restaurant and took his bike. He placed the helmet on me as usual and then I watched his butt as he slid his leg over the bike.

Dang, Gracie, why weren't you born a man? I snickered silently to myself. That was something I didn't remember wishing for before! My hands ached to run up inside his shirt, to feel his muscles.

"Where do you want to go?" he asked into the helmet.

"Do you like art?" I asked, a plan in mind.

"Yeah, of course. Are you thinking the Frist Center?"

"Yep, let's start there."

As we rode, I glanced up at the back of his helmet. There were stickers all over it, hearts, flowers, smiley faces, all very girly and pink.

I snickered. "Um, what's with the stickers on your helmet?"

He answered, unabashedly, "Katelyn, my niece, decorated it last time she was over at my place."

I chuckled. "Did you forget to take them off?"

Still unaffected, he replied, "No. She was so proud of decorating it for me. I'm leaving them on there because it would break her heart to see them gone."

I sighed and pressed myself harder against his back. I was convinced there was no man more perfect than this one.

The Frist Center for the Visual Arts was in downtown Nashville. It was a museum with art exhibits that rotated throughout the year and was one of my favorite places to visit. The outside of the building was all white, and there were two stairwells to go inside. In front of the stairs was a row of giant black concrete balls. They were at least two-feet tall and wide.

Ashton handed me his phone with a smirk. "Take a picture of me. You'll know when."

I prepared myself to capture the moment. Taking off running, he jumped in the air, spreading his legs out over one of the balls with his hands straight down to brace him. I snapped the shot and grinned. It came out awesome, as though he were balancing on the ball.

He ran over and grabbed the camera from me and said, "Your turn."

I responded with, "Do, huh?"

He snickered. "Do something, anything. We're going to capture our day together with crazy pictures. Trust me, it's fun. Xander and I do this all the time. Now go!"

Saluting him, I walked to the giant balls. I pressed my finger to my lips, contemplating what I wanted to do. "Okay, get ready!"

He aimed the phone at me.

With my back to him, I bent forward, placing my hands on the ball. I lifted my legs up until I was doing a handstand on the top. I could only hold it briefly. Once I came back down, I ran to him to see what he captured. The first shot was me bent over looking as though I was making out with the ball or something.

"Nice, thanks for catching that shot!"

He laughed. "I kept clicking to make sure I didn't miss the big event."

The picture of my handstand was perfect. Then the ones of me coming down were priceless. I tried to delete them on his phone, but he yanked it from me and held it above his head.

"No way are you erasing those!" Ashton ran toward the entrance. I followed, yelling for him to give me the phone. When we were in front of the door, he stopped and I ran straight into him.

We were laughing loudly when a couple came out the door and quickly covered our mouths to quiet ourselves. They smiled as they passed us.

Time went quickly in the gallery. We looked over the different paintings, and I swooned a little harder when it became clear he loved art as much as I did. It was a pretty heady feeling.

All too soon, it was time to leave. As we headed outside, I dragged my feet a little, hating the perfect day being over. "You taking me home now?" His face fell at my question, so I added, "Because I'm up for more fun if you are."

His face lit up again. "Wanna grab a bite to eat? There is a great place called The Flying Saucer within walking distance."

I jumped at the opportunity to spend more time with him.

I'd had a few beers over dinner, the alcohol as easy as our conversation. Ashton, however, designated himself as the driver. I became giggly when I drank. So after my fourth, a serious case of the giggles hit me hard. Ashton shook his head in amusement and decided we should head home. Always the gentleman, he held my arm to steady me as we walked.

When we made it to the bike, I leaned against him, my words spilling from my lips without restraint. "You're so sexy, Ash."

He laughed. "You're drunk, Gracie."

I wrapped my arms around his neck. "I think you're sexy even when I'm not drunk. I told you that earlier too," I slurred. Grinning, he kissed my forehead and moved my arms. My disappointed exhale was loud, fueled on by too many beers.

Having left my phone in the satchel attached to his bike while we were in the museum, I pulled it out and checked my messages. I groaned: eight texts from Hudson and two voicemails.

Ashton looked up. "What happened to the giggles?"

I showed him the number of texts and his eyebrows lifted. "Wow, someone missed you today."

"More like someone stalked me today." I laughed it off as though it was nothing.

The texts he sent gave me the creeps, though. The first couple were of him telling me he missed me and that he hoped I came back over tonight after class. Then they began to get demanding, asking where I was and why I wasn't returning his calls. When I listened to the voicemail, I jumped in shock. Anger laced every word he hissed into the phone.

Brows drawn together, Ashton looked at me, placing his arms at my waist to steady me. "You okay? What did he say?"

I shrugged it off. The last thing I wanted to do was make him worry. "Nothing, he was just loud because he was at a club or something and it startled me."

"Want me to drop you off at his place?" he asked.

I answered quickly. "No, I wanna go home."

His face slackened, his brow furrowed, it was evident he didn't believe things were okay. He reached for my hand. "You sure you're all right, bug?"

No, I'm pretty sure my boyfriend is crazy, and I'm in love with a man I can never have. "I'm great. I'm supposed to hang with Cameron tonight."

Staring at me a moment, he seemed to debate whether or not to push. I offered him a forced smile, hoping he'd just drop it.

He did.

When we arrived at the house, the whole gang was there, ready to go out. "Ash!" they yelled as they saw us come in.

"Where's the love for me?" I said, pretending to be offended. Angel, Cameron, and Mary Jane all hugged me at once and planted kisses on my cheek. I laughed at them as they assaulted me with their love.

Cameron pulled me to the side. "I need to talk to you."

I turned and kissed Ash's cheek. "Thanks for today. It was truly awesome."

He nodded. "I agree."

I followed Cameron upstairs to my room, and we plopped on the bed together. "Gracie, you need to ditch Hudson. For good this time."

I sighed. "I know."

He lit up with excitement. "You do? That was easier than I thought. He called today while you were out and was really rude to Angel. He called her some pretty crappy things."

Angel shouldn't have to pay for my mistakes by dealing with Hudson's rudeness. It made my blood boil to think of him treating anyone I loved poorly.

I swallowed, psyching myself up to telling Cameron where my head was at. "He told me he loves me. I never thought hearing someone finally say those words to me would scare me to death. But not like a fear of commitment thing, more like a fear that I will never get him out of my life. The words actually made me feel ill when I heard them." I placed my head on Cameron's shoulder. "I'm an idiot, Cam. I stayed with Hudson for the wrong reasons and now I'm scared of what he'll do when I break up with him for real."

Cameron kissed my forehead. "Baby girl, I'll protect you. You tell me the time and place and I'll be there."

We determined tomorrow would be the day, and we would meet at Hudson's at noon.

Chapter Nine

The next morning, I woke up ready to face the day and end things with Hudson. There'd be no sweet-talking, no continuation of distancing ourselves a little. It had to be for good. I was in a surprisingly happy mood, considering what I had to do. Angel was in the kitchen and she smiled as I walked in.

"Hey, chica, you look happy?"

I shrugged, and with a smile, I made my coffee and then sat at the table with her. As I blew on my coffee to cool it down, she pointed at a gift box at the end of the table.

"That was brought over for you this morning."

I glared at it, afraid of what Hudson had sent me. "Hudson? He didn't ask to see me?"

She shook her head. "No, it wasn't Hudson. Ash dropped it off." I lifted it up, excitement thrumming through me.

I ripped it open and stared in awe; it was a painting that resembled *Starry Night*. In cursive, at the top, was written, *"When I look at the stars, I'll always think of you now."* It was one of the paintings we'd admired together the previous night. Both loving it and agreeing it was our favorite.

There was a card attached. It read, "I've seen *Starry Night* before, but it never looked more beautiful than it did yesterday. Everything is better when you're around."

A tear fell. This was how love should feel. When someone told me something good about myself, I should feel happy and filled with hope like I did at that moment. Why did I have to feel that with someone I couldn't be with?

I glanced at my watch; it was only ten o'clock. I couldn't wait two more hours to tell Hudson. I needed to get this over with so I could thank Ashton and tell him how I felt. I was going to come out and ask him point-blank if he felt anything for me. I had to get this off my chest before it drove me insane.

I texted Cameron, asking him to meet me earlier than what we had agreed on. He said he was in the middle of an errand with Gavin, and he would be there as soon as he could. He also asked me to wait for him. I pulled on some baggy jeans and a button-down blouse. I wanted to look as unwelcoming to Hudson as possible.

Ashton had brought my car by when he'd dropped off his gift this morning. I slid behind the wheel and nervously began my trip to Hudson's.

When I arrived, I sent a text to Cameron. Being just a

few minutes away, I decided to go on in. Knocking on the door, I didn't have to wait long before Hudson pulled it open. He looked me over and waved me in.

When I stepped inside, he pushed me against the wall and pressed his mouth against mine. His hand moved to my pants. I gasped, not wanting his mouth on mine, a shockwave of panic and disgust rushing through me. I pushed him back from me then wiped my mouth clean.

"I came here to talk, not have sex."

He slid his finger across my cheek. "I just missed my girl." He leaned forward, flicking his tongue against my earlobe.

It seemed like a lifetime ago when the same gesture would have driven me insane with passion. Today, it made me cringe. Once more, I shoved at him. "I'm not your girl." My voice was calm, neutral, despite my racing heartbeat.

He huffed. "What? I told you yesterday that I love you. What more do you want?"

Keeping my cool, I tried to be as kind as I could. I knew how easily he could lash out in anger. "That's the problem. I don't love you, Hudson. I'm sorry. I came here to tell you it's over."

I moved away from him. He grabbed my elbow and pulled me back roughly, slamming my head into the wall. I put my hand up in reflex to feel my head.

His face fell immediately. "I'm sorry. Shit. I didn't mean to do that."

I shoved him off me. "Stop it! I'm not falling for that crap. This is why I'm ending it now. You're an abusive asshole, and I'm tired of pretending you would never hurt me. I'm ending it before it gets worse." I really did deserve better. I just wished I'd had the courage to deal with the fallout before we'd arrived at this point.

He grabbed my arm again, harder this time. Darkness seeped into his eyes. He pulled me against him and pressed his mouth against mine, hard. His teeth bit into my lips and I screamed, panic throwing my voice out and pumping my blood through my veins painfully fast. My mouth filled with the taste of blood as he tore at my lips.

His face became unrecognizable with the sudden fury that it displayed. This was not the Hudson I had known for the past few months. This was a monster in front of me. I'd seen him get upset before, but nothing to this extent.

I shoved him away as hard as I could, but he stumbled back only a few steps. He moved forward again, his left hand making contact with my cheek, knocking me backward onto the floor. My head hit the hardwood boards with a resounding smack, and I landed in a heap on my side. Wincing, I closed my eyes and begged Cameron to hurry.

Turning my head, I saw the bracelet Ashton had given me and I let my mind drift into happy memories that I had made with him. I stared at the ladybug charm as the tears fell down my cheeks. All the while, Hudson paced the space in front of me, shouting at me, calling me names, blaming me.

I tried to speak, but it came out more of a squeak when I gasped out his name, my failed plea to reason with him.

His hard eyes paused on me.

His eyes then shifted, throwing me completely. "Baby..." His voice softened. With two large strides, he was before me, grasping my face with a too-tight grip. "I love you. Let me make this better." I shook my head and cried out as he held me down, undid my jeans and yanked them down.

His fingers were inside me an instant later, making me gasp and cry out. "No." Tears rolled down my cheeks, my voice quiet and panicked. "No!" My voice was louder this time.

"Shh," he whispered against my hair. His hand wrapped around my throat, constricting my airway. "I'm sorry, baby. I need you to remember how good this is between us. Me inside you. You want this."

My tears continued to flow, but I could no longer cry out, his hand too tight around my neck. I closed my eyes, ignoring his pants and groans and he shifted over me. Ignored the pain in my head and my heart as he took what he had no right to. His lips were bruising against mine as he grunted his release and dotted kisses over my tear-soaked face.

When he released his grip, he backed away, tucking himself back in his jeans. I gasped in a breath and dared to open my eyes.

His eyes connected with mine. "You see how hot we are together?"

I stared in wide-eyed horror. It couldn't be real. It couldn't have really happened. This couldn't be my life.

He nodded down to my bare legs and I sat, welcoming

the distraction of the pain as I quickly pulled my jeans back on. Nausea rolled in my gut. I focused on the feeling and skirted away from him, shivers racking my body.

"What?" He seemed indignant and confused.

What? How could I even begin to answer that loaded question? "You—"

"I what?" His leaned toward me, his spittle making contact with my skin, making me cringe, but I welcomed the distraction from the pain across my cheek and the agony blazing through my throat caused by his vise-like grip. It seemed like the pain would never end. He was so angry, his changing emotions whipping me hard and setting my nerves on fire.

The door flew open just as Hudson fisted my hair, my eyes immediately following the sound and movement. Cameron tore into the room and shoved Hudson away from me. Gasping in pain at the yank of my hair, I couldn't hold back my tears.

Hudson grunted at the contact before he stepped forward and threw a punch at Cam, knocking him backward.

Standing his ground, Cameron didn't even raise his hand to wipe the blood I saw trickling down his split cheek. Instead, he rushed forward again, this time ramming Hudson into the wall. I jumped at the loud thud and raced to the phone to call for help. I squinted to focus, my ears ringing from the hard smack to my head.

I risked a glance at Cameron before I picked up the phone. My eyes widening in surprise, I saw Hudson on the ground.

"Cameron," I gasped in relief just before I made the call.

He turned to me immediately while I was on the line and tentatively cupped my cheek. As soon as I ended the call, he spoke, "Damn it, Gracie. Are you okay?"

I held my right arm in front of my chest, realizing for the first time it was aching like a bitch. "My arm hurts pretty bad." I glanced down at it, confused. I didn't even remember hurting it.

He tilted my face to the side, staring at what I assumed to be redness that would no doubt turn into a bruise soon.

"Has he done this before?"

I shook my head, regretting it when pain burst through my skull. "No. You know I wouldn't have stayed with him if he had."

"Did he?" His eyes were focused on my shirt, his face turning red.

I followed his gaze. Surprise flickered through me when I noticed a rip in my shirt. "No," I answered.

His shoulders relaxed slightly, and he embraced me, paying attention not to hurt my arm.

His body felt heavy on mine as we fell to the ground a moment later. Hudson stood over us. He'd hit Cameron over the head with something. I cried out in horror and then in pain when Hudson jerked Cameron off me.

My scream was desperate when Hudson's booted foot landed hard on Cameron's side. "Leave him alone!"

I wrapped my good arm around his waist in a frantic attempt to try to pull him away. Agony sliced through me when he shoved me clear across the room and I hit the wall with an aching thud. Flicking my attention to Cameron, nothing could have stopped me from getting to him. With all my strength, I ran at Hudson and thrust him to the ground with my weight to keep him from getting to Cameron again. I landed on top of him with a pained cry and fought against his struggle, knowing I had but a few seconds before he'd throw me off him with ease.

Screeching tires had my head lifting toward the open doorway. Hudson immediately jerked me aside when my concentration slipped. "No!" I cried out.

The police rushed in a moment later, and I sagged in relief. I clambered to my feet wincing in pain. I needed to get to Cameron. In my peripheral vision, I was aware that Hudson had his arms in the air in surrender, and he was then being cuffed, his arms tugged around his back.

I fell to my knees beside Cameron. Blood covered his swollen face and he remained unresponsive.

One of the officers rushed over and checked his pulse and vitals. "He's weak, but he's still here. Hang in there, young lady. Once we get you both to the hospital, we need to know what happened here."

I remained at Cameron's side, the officer's words barely registering, too lost in the horror that had unfolded. A few moments later, I looked on numbly as the paramedics arrived and they eased me into the waiting ambulance to ride in the back with Cameron. I clutched at his hand, not daring to break our connection in fear he'd leave me. During the journey, one of the EMTs secured my injured arm in a sling until it could be examined. But the last thing

I was concerned about were my own injuries.

With a croaking voice, tight with emotion, I whispered, "Cameron sweetie. I'm so sorry. Please wake up. Please talk to me." He should've woken up already and the longer he remained unconscious, the more anxious I became about his condition.

Blame sat heavily on my heart. He couldn't know, couldn't ever find out. The thought kept me from telling the police what else had happened. Cameron discovering he'd been too late would break him. Me? I was already broken. I refused to let Cameron break with me.

At the hospital, the paramedics rushed Cameron straight to X-ray while they put me in an exam room. Being separated from him was the last thing I wanted, but I knew he needed more attention than I did. While waiting for the doctor, I texted Ashton and asked him to meet us there. When he asked what happened, I told him it was an accident, and that I'd explain it all later. I wasn't sure yet what my story to him would be. The truth seemed too much to fathom.

My arm was sprained pretty badly and had a small fracture; it wasn't broken, though. From the outside looking in, it was my worst injury. Inside, I knew there was much worse damage. The nurse wrapped my forearm in a removable splint, giving me an empathetic smile when our eyes met. She probably thought I was weak or stupid, maybe both. When asked if I needed anything else, I begged her to take me to Cameron's room.

Immediately my eyes landed on the bandage covering

his head. My heart splintered, knowing he was hurt while protecting me. Stitches on his right cheek, the skin red and swollen. Tears sprung to my eyes as I continued to gaze at his face, taking in every bruise, every swollen piece of flesh. I bit back the sob that threatened to escape, allowing the nurse's reassuring words to wash over me. He'd be okay and would be released the following day.

I slid a chair next to him and gently touched his head, whispering, "I'm so sorry." His eyes struggled to open. With a pained smile, I wiped my fallen tears. "Hey, gorgeous."

He squeezed my hand. "You're safe."

I nodded, swallowing the emotion bubbling in my throat. "Yep, thanks to you. Just a sprained arm with a small fracture, and a couple of cuts and bruises, all because of my own stupidity."

He snarled at me, the power in his voice startling me. "You're damn right, Gracie. I told you to wait on me. You could've been killed. Why do you never listen to me?" He was right. I never did and he was *always* right.

Blame sat heavily in my gut. "I'm sorry. I wanted it over with. I had no clue he would do this to either of us."

Pity washed over his bruised features. "You need to wake up, Gracie." He sighed. "You keep making really shitty choices, honey. It has to stop. Tell me something. Why did you stay with him?"

I shrugged. "I don't know."

He raised his brow before he winced and remembered his condition. "I deserve a real answer. Be honest with the both of us."

I sighed. "It was easy and convenient. I also used him to

help me forget about someone else. I allowed him to try to distract me to get over someone I couldn't have. It's stupid, I know."

Pity washed over his bruised features, enough to encourage me to go on.

"I met someone recently that I've been spending a lot of time with. I fell in love with him, without meaning to. The problem is he's gay and I knew that from day one. I allowed myself to fall for him anyway because he's everything I ever wanted in a guy. It was asinine for me to use Hudson to forget about him and I realized that, which is why I wanted to end it."

He touched my face. "Sweetie, I can't believe…. Wait, is it Ash?"

I stepped backward and the tears began to fall again. I couldn't bear his pity, not after everything he'd been through because of me.

He sighed and reached for me. "Gracie, you need to know…"

I couldn't listen. Spinning on my heels, I ran out of the room, not allowing him to finish.

Ashton walked in just as I was leaving. I didn't even spare the time to gasp as my shoulder slammed against his arm as I tore past him. Ashton called out my name, but I kept pace, needing the space to lick my wounds.

My heart hurt worse from Cameron's injuries and his pity than my injured arm or bruised face. I kept running until I reached the parking lot. My car was still at Hudson's so I didn't have anywhere to go. Defeated, I sat on a bench with my head in my hands. *How did I allow everything to spiral so out of control?* My naïvety could only fly for so long as an excuse before I had to take full responsibility of my poor choices.

I sat there ignoring the world carrying on around me, trying my hardest not to feel sorry for myself, especially considering my best friend's injuries. I failed, sniffing back my tears of heartache and guilt. I couldn't even begin to think about myself and all that had happened to me. If I allowed that, I didn't know if I'd ever recover.

Ashton's soothing voice penetrated my fog. "Come on, bug. Let's get out of here for a bit."

I kept my face turned so he couldn't see me, wishing in that instant I really were invisible. Undeterred, he took my hand and led me to his truck, offering me comfort I didn't believe I deserved.

The silence of the drive tore at me. I wasn't sure what Cam had told him. I feared his anger when he found out what Hudson had done. He pulled over to the park where we'd spent our first evening talking and parked the truck. My skin tingled when his hand touched my hair. "Talk to me, Gracie-bug."

With all the courage I could muster, I turned my head. Devastation rolled over him when his eyes roamed my face. Gently, he reached out to touch my cheek; I flinched at the pain when his finger grazed the swollen flesh. Surprise flittered through me when his eyes welled with tears.

With the back of his hand, he softly caressed the side of my face that wasn't bruised. "Did Hudson do this?" His voice choked.

I nodded.

The anger flamed in his eyes. "And Cameron?"

I nodded again. "He was protecting me. Cam's always protecting me."

His hands gripped the steering wheel, his knuckles turning white. "Where is he now?" His gaze fixed ahead.

"Jail." My voice came out barely above a whisper. "Cameron hates me now," I said, wiping the tears that fell.

Ashton shook his head. "He sent me after you. He asked me to take care of you. Thought you might need to talk, especially to me?"

Ashton's hand appeared in front of my face with a tissue. I reached up with my arm in the splint.

"What happened to your arm?"

My eyes answered his question, and he slammed his fists against the steering wheel, making me jump. Instinctively, I scooted closer to the door.

Seeing my fright, his face fell again. "I'm sorry. Don't be scared of me, Gracie-bug. I'm angry with Hudson, not you. Damn coward, that's what he is. I'd never hurt you."

I reached for his hand and held it. "I'm not afraid of you. You startled me, is all."

His face hardened. "How many times has this happened? You said Cameron always saves you. He knew this was going on?"

"No, this was the first time Hudson hit me. Cam was there for me in case the breakup went badly, because of Hudson's temper." Saying those words aloud made me wince. I knew he had a temper yet had stayed with him anyway. I wished I could go back in time and shake myself. "He got there shortly after Hudson hit me. I wouldn't have stayed in an abusive relationship all this time. Before this, it was a hard grip or a shove, nothing that I thought was too serious. The other times Cam saved me were different."

I paused, not sure how much I wanted to share, and pushed down the sickness that sat in my stomach at what Hudson had done to me. Ashton sat there patiently while I shifted through my thoughts. I knew I could trust him with anything.

"Gracie, you don't have to tell anything you don't feel comfortable talking about with me."

I squeezed his hand. "There's no one I feel more comfortable with than you... and Cameron. You two have been the best friends I could ever want."

I closed my eyes and began, "My first date when I was fifteen, I was almost raped. Cam stopped it from happening, well mostly." I choked back tears. "He felt terrible that he hadn't gotten there before Chris violated me at all. It was the first time I saw him cry. He had nothing to feel bad about as far as I was concerned. Chris was the only person to blame."

Ashton's jaw clenched tightly as he said, "I'd have killed him." The look on his face told me he wasn't kidding.

"Like I said, Cam's been my ongoing hero. He's never been hurt before, though. Seeing him in that hospital bed...."

Ashton's features softened. He opened the door and

stepped out without another word. I watched as he walked around the front of the truck, and then opened my door. His hand reached forward, palm upward. I placed my hand in his and stepped out. Ashton gently cupped my head in his hand and pulled me into his embrace. He cradled my head against his chest allowing me to release my sobs. As the anger over the events in my life spilled out of me, I shook violently.

Ashton's chest jumped as though he had hiccups.

My head tilted back as my eyes rolled up to meet his. He didn't have hiccups. Tears trickled down his cheeks silently, fighting the anger I knew pulsed through his limbs.

Ashton let go of me to wipe his face with his sleeve before he reached inside the truck again. He turned the ignition, played with the radio for a moment, until he said, "Perfect." Garth Brooks's "To Make You Feel My Love" played. He extended his hand and said, "Dance with me."

I took his hand, resting my splinted arm around his back. He placed my free hand over his shoulder, pulling me close. This song had always been one of my favorites. The words encompassed everything I felt for Ashton.

My eyes lifted upward to meet his. "What are we doing?"

He pressed his mouth against my ear, his voice low and husky when he said, "Taking our mind off things."

His warm breath brushed my ear making me shiver. When his hand rested at the small of my back, I absorbed his warmth, soaking in the beauty that was Ashton, and goose bumps broke out over my skin. I needed this, needed him. He could wipe away everything that had happened, replace my horror with something pure and beautiful.

He peered down at me, "Are you cold, sweetheart?"

I shook my head.

"You're so beautiful, my Gracie-bug," he whispered softly as he caressed my undamaged cheek. He'd never called me "his" before. The song, the dance, the way he looked at me, it was too much, it sent me over the edge. I broke our embrace and placed an unsteady hand to my mouth, shaking my head.

"I can't do this anymore." It was all too much. I was at the point of telling him that Hudson had raped me, but I couldn't. I didn't want it to be real.

Ashton's brow creased. "I wasn't trying to push. I only wanted to take your mind off everything." He didn't understand. But how did I explain without changing everything. Instead, I focused on what else held me back.

"No, you're sweet. You're *so* sweet. And you're funny, gorgeous, a true gentleman, an amazing friend." My rambling words sprung free. "We can't be friends like this, though. You're everything I want. It isn't fair and it's breaking my heart."

Still confused, he asked, "What isn't fair? You aren't making sense."

Ashton followed me as I moved around the truck. "I'm falling for you, Ash," I offered a half-truth, holding back the fact that my heart already belonged to him. "I have been for a while now. I've tried to fight these feelings, but I can't anymore. Every moment I'm with you, my heart breaks a little more because being friends is not enough for me."

His hand touched my shoulder, turning me to face him. A smile lifted his lips. "Why is that bad?"

I sighed with exasperation, heat spreading across my cheeks. "Because you're gay!"

He spouted, "What? I've never told you that!"

I paused, allowing his words to sink in, thinking back to every conversation we ever had. Frustrated, I continued, "Come on, your best friend is gay."

He nodded. "So is yours."

Undeterred, I added, "You like hanging out at gay bars."

He nodded again. "As do you."

Confusion swirled in my already befuddled brain. I threw my hands up. "You're a guy!"

His face twitched. "Okay, now you lost me. What does that mean?"

I sighed. "Guys don't hang out at gay bars unless they're gay."

He laughed. "Wow, nice assumption you made there! Has Cam never had a straight guy friend?" I shook my head and he responded, "Oh, well, I guess I can see how you came to that conclusion."

My brows furrowed. I'd heard every word he'd said, both before and in the present. Nothing made sense. I opened my mouth to speak, still unsure what to say or how to respond, but clamped it shut when heavy raindrops bounced on my skin. I backed away and ran for the nearest pavilion, my fog of confusion preventing me from simply stepping into the truck.

He ran after me, gently grasping my shoulders before

I reached cover. Ignoring the heavy rain that drenched us both, he turned me to face him.

"What would you say if I told you I don't want to be friends anymore either?" He pulled me close and moved my soaked hair from my face. Leaning down, his lips softly pressed against mine. Ashton tightened his grip around my waist, lifted me off the ground and moved us to stand under the pavilion we were merely a few feet from.

His lips alone made me feel things I'd never felt, diluting the bruised kisses from Hudson and the nightmare he'd left me with. I ran my tongue along the seam of his mouth, desperate to allow Ashton to make me forget and make it all better. His tongue slid into my mouth in response. I moaned as the heat from the kiss warmed my body all the way to my toes. His body reacted to my moan and he tugged me even closer. Our hearts raced, his beating against my chest at the same pace as mine. This kiss was what I had been dreaming of, and I didn't want it to stop.

Lifting me to sit on a picnic table so that I was closer to his level, Ashton's right hand cradled my head while his left hand moved inside the hem of my shirt. His gentle fingers caressed my bare skin, sending chills all over my body. In my head, I was begging for him to go higher, but he stopped short of my bra line.

When we came up for air, he placed his palm against my face, gazing at me as though it was the first time he'd seen me. It hurt because it was what I had always wanted and it wouldn't last. I leaned back, pressing my hand against my mouth. Fear and the possibility of rejection burned in my veins, heating my cold skin.

"I can't. We can't." I hated every syllable I spoke. "I can't be… your science project."

He cringed, hurt passing over his kind eyes. "What the hell does that mean?"

I eased off the table and walked toward him, unsure exactly what I felt: hurt, fear, concern. My words were low when I spoke. "I'm not here for you to test your attraction for girls on. I told you that I have feelings for you. Instead of letting me down gently, you lead me on?"

"I'm not gay, Gracie. I never have been," he said.

Confusion swam in my already foggy brain, and my heart stuttered with possibility. "What? How can that be? If that's true, why didn't you tell me before today?"

"I had no clue you thought that!" he cried out.

I bit down on my lip, trying not to laugh. It was the best reaction I could go with. This whole confusing, misunderstanding had the power to make me cry, scream and urged me to smack the both of us. His grin told me that he could see it was hard for me to hold back.

Courage bubbled to the surface. "Why didn't you hit on me or tell me you were interested?" At any other time, there was no way I'd be so forward, but this was Ashton, and hell, after the kiss we'd just shared....

He stepped closer. "You were with Hudson. I'm not the guy who goes after girls who are taken. I held back until yesterday. When you told me that you weren't in love with him and were going to end things, I made my move. After we spent yesterday together, I knew more than ever that

I wanted you. That's why I painted the portrait for you."

The memory of his gift warmed me, and I hadn't thanked him for it. "You always give me the most thoughtful presents." His words finally registered and my eyes grew wide. "Wait, you painted it?"

He nodded.

It was time to ask the big question, the one that could break my heart for good. "Do you have feelings for me?" Even as I said the words, I gave an internal eye-roll. Considering all he'd told me, and the kiss that had left my body thrumming with need, I was sure I knew the answer already, but after all of the confusion and misunderstanding, there were simply things I needed spelled out to me. This was one of them.

He tilted his head, his piercing gaze intense. "Part of you has to know the answer to that. I gave you a cutesy nickname. You're the first person I call for anything, and we talk all the time. I'm falling in love with you, Gracie. I have been since the moment I first saw you."

"What about Xander?"

Ashton's brows furrowed. "What do you mean?"

"You were always with him. At the restaurant, you had your arm around him. He's not your boyfriend?"

Ashton shook his head. "No. He's one of my closest friends, which is why we're always together."

I coughed, choking on a sob as I said, "Why didn't you tell me before? If you had told me sooner, I'd have left him. I didn't know... I didn't know anyone else wanted me. I thought I had to get you out of my system."

As soon as I said the words, I wanted to retract them. The way they came out sounded as though I blamed him for Hudson's actions.

Ashton closed the distance between us, his palm touching my bruised cheek. He whispered, "If I'd known he would do this,"—he kissed my forehead, his soft beard tickling my skin—"I've always wanted you. Every time we were together, it took everything I had not to kiss you. Several times, I tried to kiss you and we were interrupted. I assumed it was a sign that it was for the best."

He leaned forward, slid his tongue across my bottom lip, and then said, "That morning when you forgot it was me next to you, I wanted to make love to you right then and there. The day I saw you at the restaurant and Hudson was all over you, it made me sick. I wanted to pull him off you. When I drove you home from the restaurant, when you kissed me, I wanted to kiss you back so badly. I thought you were trying to get back at Hudson or something, and I wanted our first kiss to be special. I couldn't be that guy."

Warmth swept through my body, causing me to gasp softly at his confession.

"How could you not know I was into you? I practically undressed you with my eyes every time we were together," I admitted, heat creeping up my neck.

He frowned. "I noticed the first night we met. After that, you were always telling me about your intimate moments with Hudson. I didn't think you would tell me that stuff if you were into me."

I covered my mouth. "I'm sorry, that probably wasn't

easy to hear."

He shook his head. "No, it wasn't."

"I've wanted you ever since we first met too, Ash. I've had fantasies about us, lots of them, not all dirty either." The last words burst free in a rushed whisper.

With a wicked grin, he answered, "Well, I'd like to hear about the naughty ones first," he said in a husky whisper. My blush earned me a laugh. The sound was light and brushed across my skin, leaving behind a happy trail of goose bumps. He lifted me up in a bear hug, careful to not squeeze my sore arm.

He then set me down, stepped back, and gave a loud, "Woohoo!" and jumped up and down.

His dorky display was as endearing as it was crazy. I laughed. "What was that?"

He replied, "That was me cheering at finally telling you how I feel!" An instant later, his lips pressed against mine.

"Your beard tickles." I reveled in the simplicity of the moment, loving the sweet distraction.

He grinned. "I'll shave it."

I gasped. "Don't you dare!" He lifted me, spinning me around. I ignored my aches and the pounding of the rain; instead, I rejoiced in the perfectness of the moment. He would help me fight the darkness Hudson left behind. I had no doubt Ashton had the power to do that. As he spun, I was unsure if it was the twirling or my happiness that left me giddy. I didn't mind either way. With his hands on my body and the truth of his words, I welcomed the comfort and rightness.

"I can't believe you thought I was gay all this time," he

said with a laugh.

"You must have thought I was such a tramp!" I exclaimed.

He lifted his index finger and thumb an inch apart, signifying a little. My mouth gaped open in shock. He roared with laughter and lifted me up again. I gasped as pain shot up my arm and he quickly lowered me to the ground.

"Baby, I'm so sorry. I should've been gentler."

"I'm fine. I'm better than fine. Call me that again."

He stared at me curiously. "Call you what?"

I smiled. "Baby."

He caressed my face. "I'll call you baby from now on if it elicits that smile."

My smile widened, and if it weren't for my recent gasp of pain, I would have pinched myself just to be sure this was all real. I sighed contently against his chest when he wrapped his arms around me. "Do you mind taking me back to see Cameron? I need to make things right with him."

After placing a kiss on my head, he said, "Sure, let's go."

As we approached Cameron's room, my squeeze on Ashton's hand became tighter. We stopped just outside the room. He turned to me and asked, "You sure you're ready?" I gave his hand a squeeze and nodded.

As we walked in, Cam and Gavin looked up at the two of us, quickly noticing our fingers entwined. Cameron gave me a sly grin. "You're such a tramp!"

I knew, at that moment, that we'd be fine. I wanted to throw myself on him, but I was gentle with my embrace. "I love you, Cam."

He patted my hair. "I love you too, girl. You just make me so crazy, Gracie." I cringed at the words Hudson would say, my body tensing. "I didn't mean it in a bad way."

I sat up. "It's not that. Hudson used to say that all the time."

Cameron's face hardened. "If I ever see that bastard—"

Before he could finish, Ashton wrapped his arm around my waist, kissed my hair and said, "Don't worry. I'll take care of him if that ever happens."

Cameron smiled as he watched me relax against Ashton. He exclaimed, "It is about damn time you two got together."

Confusion filtered through me. My brows dipped, and I bit the inside of my cheek before I spoke. "You knew I thought he was gay, and you never said anything. Why?" The truth of my words spilled out, and I clenched my jaw, trying to contain my frustration.

Cameron patted my hand. "Gracie, I know you too well. You thought Ashton was gay so you were comfortable with him. You opened yourself up to him and gave him a chance. If I had told you he was straight, you'd have frozen up and never had an opportunity for anything real. He's a good guy and for some reason, you always fall for the scum or the unattainable. I had to step in this time and hoped that it worked. Don't be angry with me. If I'd known what Hudson would do...." Sadness filled his words.

I glanced at Ashton, then back to Cameron and said, "I'm not mad. Everything you said is true. I'd never have opened up to him otherwise."

Ashton sat patiently, talking to Gavin, while I reunited myself with Cameron. After a solid twenty minutes of talking, Cameron grew tired. I offered him a kiss on the forehead and said good-bye before Ashton drove me home.

He walked me to my door and gave me a light kiss on the lips. "Goodnight, call me later?"

I shook my head. "Nope, not a chance." I grabbed a fistful of his T-shirt, pulling him inside. Urgency to be close to him rushed through me, sparked by the horror of the past twenty-four hours.

He grinned and then stopped short. "We can wait, Gracie. I've waited so long to be with you. I don't want to rush things now."

Relieved by his words, I smiled. There was no way I could cope with anything beyond a kiss and the comfort of his safe embrace. He placed an innocent kiss on my cheek and turned to leave. "Ashton?"

He stopped. "Yeah, bug?" His hand rested on the door, muscles flexed.

"Can you stay with me and just hold me, please?"

He stepped forward, motioning for me to lead the way, a soft smile lighting his face. He waited patiently as I went to my closet to grab some pajamas to change into. I set them on the bed and looked at him for help. He helped to unbutton my shirt as I stumbled a few times with the awkwardness of my cast and my shaky hands. When my bra came into view, he sucked in a breath and stopped momentarily. I peered up at him, my breath seizing when I noted the passion in his eyes.

He used one hand to keep the shirt closed and the other to continue unbuttoning it. At the last button, he gently spun me around, putting my back to him. He then slipped the shirt off my shoulders. Reaching up, I moved my hair, exposing my neck to him. Warm breath against my skin caused an outbreak of goose bumps, and I bit my bottom lip, caught between desire and amusement when his fingers fumbled with my bra.

I welcomed his innocent touch, knowing that while heat sparked between us, his actions were about caring for me.

He turned me around. His eyes widened when they roamed over my neck. "Baby," he whispered. The simple term of endearment sounded heartbreaking at that moment as he reabsorbed the sight of my injuries. I swallowed, hoping desperately he wouldn't ask specifics. He kissed my cheek and then sighed again in defeat as his arms moved around my back, and he unhooked my bra. He slid the straps down slowly, never taking his eyes away from mine.

"You're so beautiful."

My breath caught in my throat at the sincerity in his voice. He was the first man who made me believe those words. Low self-esteem had always been one of my biggest flaws. With Ashton, I saw myself through his eyes and finally loved what I saw. His hands moved to my jeans as he kissed my uninjured cheek, not wanting to push my vulnerable position. He worked to unbutton them, and then he stepped back, gently tugging my pants to the ground.

His face lifted. "You're beautiful, Gracie-bug."

A smile lifted my mouth with ease and warmth suffused my chest, despite the coolness in the room. As he stood, he softly traced my collarbones and then moved down my arms. His chest rose and fell as his breathing increased again. When his mouth touched my skin, I gasped.

Ashton's lips moved gently over my chest, leaving a soft trail of kisses. He then lifted me off the floor and laid me on the bed. My heart wanted more, wanted to feel more of his touch, wanted to be closer to him in every way. My mind couldn't erase the images of Hudson violating me.

He exposed his beautifully sculpted chest when he'd removed his shirt. Unable to resist the pull, I ran my hands through the light covering of hair over his stomach. Muscles tightened under my fingertips, and I lifted my eyes to his when I heard his quick intake of breath.

His body moved, and my gaze traveled to his hands as he slid off his jeans and lay beside me with his sexy black boxers still on. I felt Ashton's heat immediately as his skin brushed mine. A small sigh of contentment escaped my lips when he pulled a blanket over us and encouraged me to curl against him. "We can just lie here together. I want to be with you any way I can." It was exactly what I needed and wanted.

Soft fingers glided over my hair as he spoke. "Can I ask

you something?"

"Anything you want."

His fingers entwined with mine as he asked, "So, that night at the Opryland Hotel, what was really up?"

I tensed at the memory, thinking about how it would sound if I told him what was wrong with me that night. "Nothing, it's stupid really."

He seemed unsure about his next words. "Was it really about... Hudson?"

I shook my head. "No. I never cared enough about him to cry over something like him not getting me a present."

His eyes saddened. "So, what was it?"

I glanced at the charm bracelet dangling from my wrist. "It was this."

Ashton sounded confused. "But I thought you liked it. Those definitely weren't tears of joy that night when I dropped you off."

I shook my head. "I didn't like it, I absolutely loved it. It was the sweetest gift anyone ever gave me and it made me feel special."

Still confused, he said, "I'm sorry. I'm still not following you."

I sat up facing him "That night you made me feel important, like I was someone special, and that what we had was unique. It was the night I realized I had fallen in love with you and, for the first time, thought that maybe you felt the same. Then you spent the evening doting on Angel, and I thought it meant that we really were just friends and nothing more. I cried because I felt like all my hopes crashed down around me. It seemed impossible that you'd ever be more to me than just a friend."

Ashton's face made me wish I could take back the last few moments and rephrase what I had said. He cupped my face in his hands. "Bug, I'm so sorry. I wish you'd told me that night. I knew that I had hurt you, no matter what excuse you came up with to say I didn't. I hated myself. It was our first Christmas together and I ruined it. I haven't stopped thinking about it.

"We almost kissed that night, before Hudson interrupted us. It was the perfect moment, but once he came out, and you looked so hurt, I thought it was all for him."

I shook my head. "No. I wasn't hurt. I was angry with him for ruining *our* moment. That was for us. We should've had that moment on Christmas. Everything would have changed right then."

My emotions betrayed me as the tears fell.

Ashton pulled me into his warm embrace. "We have many more moments ahead of us. We're not going to let anyone take that away from us again." I moved to crush my mouth to his. He growled deeply in his throat. There was no better sound than that low growl of passion.

He put his hands on my shoulders, pushing back slightly. "Really, Gracie. We can wait. I want it to be special... for both of us."

I closed my eyes in relief. Nothing would make me happier than being intimate with Ashton, but I wanted it to be right too. I didn't want it tainted by fear. Curling up against his chest, I drifted off to sleep.

Chapter Ten

Lips grazed my neck, moving my hair to the side. I rolled over and my eyes met Ashton's.

"Am I dreaming?" I asked, afraid that it was really a dream. He smiled as he leaned in to kiss me. He rolled over on top of me as his mouth continued to explore mine. All at once, suffocation weighed me down. Panic rolled through my body and his weight felt impossible to move.

Ashton's mouth moved to my neck. I tried to breathe deeply and let the panic roll off. It didn't work. Instead, my heart raced as the room closed in on me.

I needed to break free.

I shoved at him, yelling, "Get off me!"

Ashton rolled off me instantly, and I fled. "Gracie?" Panic laced those two syllables.

Words escaped me as the fear swallowed me whole.

Cowering in the corner of the room, I curled up in a ball trying to cover myself. My skin crawled with the memory of Hudson's touch. My body ached from the bruising on my skin and the force of the rape. Scratching my nails across my skin, I tried to tear away the dirt and shame. It seemed impossible to ever move forward.

"Are you in pain? Do you need to go back to the hospital?"

I shook my head. "I need clothes, please." Too much skin was exposed; too much of me could be seen. The thoughts were jumbled and crazy, but I desperately wanted to cover myself. He dug through my drawers for loose pants and a shirt. All I could do was cry and curse myself. I was going to have to tell him the truth.

"I can't go to the hospital. I'm not hurt. Cam can't find out," I cried out in fear, my words not really making any sense in my panic.

His brow creased and he asked, "Cam can't find out what? Talk to me, Gracie."

"Cameron can never find out." My words played on repeat, the only ones I was able to form in my blinding panic. Short gasps of air filled my ears, my repetitive mumbling barely cutting through the sound.

He knelt beside me and smoothed my hair. I flinched before allowing his gentle hands to caress me. "Baby, talk to me. Does something hurt?"

Ashton's brow furrowed, his mouth opened as though he wanted to speak but didn't know what to say. "Promise me you won't tell, Cam, please."

Ashton sighed with frustration, gritting his teeth to

keep his cool. "Dammit, Gracie, tell me."

My hands shook as I tried to put my thoughts into words. How could I share this without the words breaking and ruining me? "Hudson... before... I didn't want you to know, didn't want anyone to know."

Ashton touched my cheek and I jumped up, hating the hurt that shimmered in his concerned eyes.

I whispered my confession.

Ashton's eyes closed and I knew he heard me. Still, he asked, "What?"

I wanted tonight to be a new start with Ashton. I wanted tonight to be a new beginning for us. This confession would push back any happiness we could have.

I gave him the full story this time.

Silence.

I braced myself for an outburst from him.

Nothing. I opened my eyes to see Ashton staring at the window.

"Ashton?"

He turned slowly, his face unrecognizable with the grief it displayed. In a soft voice, he said, "Get dressed. You need to be checked out. I'm taking you to the hospital." He didn't ask or give me a chance to argue.

Tension washed away from my body and mind at his words and his care. I hadn't realized I'd needed them so much. A sob broke free. This time, the emotion and sadness was completely my own, for me and all I had been through, what I had lost.

Ashton didn't hesitate as he wrapped me in his arms,

allowing my tears, my anger, and my pain to pour out. My soul felt a little lighter, and the first remnant of healing light of hope sparked to life. I'd previously thought that Ashton could help to mend my fractured soul, and as his strength transferred into me, I realized it could actually happen.

I just had to get through the next grueling task at the hospital and then the police.

When the doctor came in to ask what I was being seen for, I couldn't bring myself to admit the rape again. It was hard enough to tell Ashton; I wasn't ready to tell a stranger.

"My ex-boyfriend did this to me," I said, holding up my arm and motioning to my bruised face. "This was the first time he was violent toward me and we've been together for months. As a precaution, I wanted to be checked out for any possible diseases he may have given me. I know I could see my regular doctor, but I don't want to wait until they can schedule me in."

She nodded and began making notes on a tablet. "Did you have unprotected sex?"

I nodded, "Once or twice. I know how bad that is, and I regret it now, believe me."

Asking me to lie back on the exam table, I scooted down to the edge, placing my legs in the stirrups at the end. This exam had always felt humiliating under normal circumstances. Unsurprisingly, this time, it felt even worse. I took a deep breath and tried to remain calm. She placed her hands on the inside of my thighs, telling me to relax.

The moment she made contact, I flinched and sat forward, pulling my legs together.

Concern crossed her features. "Did he rape you, Gracie?" she asked.

"No. I'm sorry. I wasn't ready and you startled me."

The doctor began the examination again, and I bit my lip as the tears fell from my eyes. She took tests to check for STDs and pregnancy and said the results would be back in a few days. She gave me pamphlets for abuse counseling.

The entire visit took a little over an hour. When I stepped from the exam room, Ashton was sitting on a bench down the hall. His head was in his hands, tugging at his hair as if trying to yank out the thoughts in his head. He'd never looked so destroyed.

Gracie Walker, you break everything you touch.

I knew it was too good to be true to find Ashton. I didn't deserve him; he was too good and deserved better than this shell of a person I'd become.

As I approached him, he looked up at me. "You should go home. I'll go visit Cam and call Angel for a ride."

He reacted as though I slapped him, his face flinching in pain. "Don't do that, Gracie. Don't push me away, not after everything that happened today."

Sickness swirled in my gut. The last thing I wanted to do was hurt him, but I continued anyway. "I don't know how you can look at me. I can barely look at myself. I'm giving you an easy way out."

Reaching for me, he grabbed my wrist. With a hitched breath, I recoiled in fear. It shattered him. His shoulders slumped as he let out a ragged breath of defeat before he stood, shoved his hands in his pockets and walked out of the hospital.

As I watched him leave, my chest ached, a lump formed in my throat, and I choked back the tears as my heart broke. I sat down for a moment to collect myself so that I wouldn't have to explain what was wrong to Cameron. He knew me well enough though that he would wonder why I wasn't with Ashton.

"Hey, gorgeous!" he said as I walked in. I put on my best fake smile and gave him a hug. I leaned down and kissed Gavin's cheek.

"Thanks for keeping him company, Gavin."

Gavin took Cam's hand. "He's my guy. Don't want to be anywhere else."

Cameron was happy, truly happy. It was the first time he had feelings for someone, and I loved seeing him so elated. I wasn't going to burst his happy bubble with my problems.

"Where's Ashton? I thought you two would be humping like rabbits by now."

Ashton's voice answered from the door, making me jump. I thought he'd left. "Yeah, we would be except she wanted to see your ugly mug."

Cameron laughed. "This face is fucking flawless, and you know it."

Ashton stepped up beside me and gently pressed his hand against the small of my back.

When I forced myself to look up at him, he was focused

on Cameron. His mouth was smiling, but his eyes were full of sadness. I slid my arm around his waist, and it surprised him, almost as much as it surprised me. But nothing about this whole situation was normal or rational. His head turned toward me and he smiled. This time it met his eyes. He leaned down and kissed my forehead softly.

I sighed against the contact, allowing myself to experience the comfort his touch offered.

Cameron let out a squeak that sounded like a low squeal. He sat with his hands together and the biggest smile on his face. "Gracie girl, you have no idea how you have made my whole existence today. I've been waiting for you to find a good guy, and you found the best. But sista, you don't have to start dressing all sloppy now. What is up with the metal T-shirt and baggy sweats?"

In my haste to get dressed, I had put on a T-shirt without paying attention. I was wearing Hudson's Five Finger Death Punch shirt.

As soon as I realized it, panic set in. The room began to spin and dizziness threatened to buckle my knees. There were people speaking, but everyone sounded so far away. The very bare contents of my stomach threatened to release. I ran to the nearest trash can and threw up. Hands grabbed my hair, pulling it away from my face, and a cool washcloth appeared on my neck a few moments later. Standing upright, I ripped the shirt off, shoving it into the trash can where it belonged.

In my bra and baggy sweatpants, shakes racked my body. When I turned, all eyes focused on me, concern and confusion at war on their faces. Without a word, Ashton pulled his shirt over his head. Lifting my arms, he slipped it over me. I inhaled deeply, welcoming the scent of Ashton's cologne. I had never truly realized the power of a familiar scent until that point. My eyes connected with his and I managed a faint smile.

"What the hell, Gracie?" Cameron's face was pale with worry.

I laughed. "I hear those words a lot here lately."

"I didn't mean for you to destroy the shirt," he said as if I were going crazy.

"I got dressed quickly and didn't realize what I'd put on. It's Hudson's favorite shirt."

Tension took hold of Cameron's expression. "Then it's where it belongs." The mood eased when Cameron looked over at Ashton. "Whew, honey! Check out that six-pack. Kind of makes me wish you were gay now."

Gavin playfully swatted his hand. "Watch it." They shared a loving look and once more, warmth spread through my system.

Ashton interrupted with a small amount of amusement lacing his words, "It's a bit cold in here. I think I'll ask the nurse for a scrub shirt."

I touched his chest before he could move. Shivers danced down my spine on contact and pulled at my stomach. "I'll get it."

When the nurse brought in the scrub top, she molested Ashton with her eyes. Jealousy erupted in me and I snapped, "Thanks for that. We can take it from here." My emotions were already frayed. I couldn't handle any more upset.

The guys laughed and I scowled.

Smirking, Cameron said, "Take her home and bang her already, Ash. I'm good here, babe," he then directed at me. "Go home and relax... or not." He winked at me.

Nodding, I bent down and gave him a kiss. It was best if I headed home and tried to give myself the time needed to start processing everything. "Love you, Cam."

He patted my cheek. "Love you more, baby girl."

Taking my hand, Ashton led me out of the hospital in silence. "I'll take you home and we can talk," he said.

I cringed, but there was nothing more that I wanted than to feel him against me and I couldn't do that at home. "Take me for a ride on your bike first? Help me pretend things never changed."

With a light kiss against my forehead, he agreed. I straddled the bike behind him and heard him sigh as my hands slid around his waist. He adjusted his helmet and started the bike up.

I wasn't sure how long we rode. At first, I watched the city surroundings fly by, trying not to think about things. It was getting colder, so I moved my hands inside his shirt. The bike swerved slightly and then righted itself. In my headset, I heard his intake of breath as my cool hands rubbed his chest. Even with my tense state, the sound eased my heart. Ashton slowed the bike and pulled over on the side of the road. I had no clue where we were, somewhere in the country.

He stepped off the bike and pressed his palms against my cheeks, holding my face. Slowly, as if unsure of my reaction, his head lowered to mine, allowing me the time to break away should I need to. I didn't move, could hardly even breathe with each slow millisecond of movement. He sucked my bottom lip into his mouth. Closing my eyes, I opened my mouth to invite him in. His tongue slipped past my lips and slid against mine.

His hands moved from my face and his mouth left mine wanting more.

"My feelings for you haven't changed, Gracie. When you told me what he did, my stomach turned. I had feelings that I've never had before. I want to rip his throat out for touching you. I understand you couldn't tell me at first. But why did you let me take things so far? Why didn't you stop me?"

I swallowed before I answered, needing a moment to sort my thoughts. "I wanted you, that's why. I wanted you to make me stop feeling so dirty and disgusting. You make me feel beautiful, Ash. You made me feel wanted and special and I needed that to take away the disgust that I feel. You're the only person whose touch has made me feel special."

His arms encompassed me and he kissed the top of my head. "You can't imagine the pain I felt hurting you though. Tell me what the doctor said."

I peered up at him.

"Tell me why you came back to the hospital first."

He exhaled. "I knew you were going to see Cam and

he would ask why you weren't with me. You don't want him to know what happened, so I came to keep you from having to tell him. Plus, I didn't like how we left things. You thought I couldn't look at you. Gracie, all I see is you, a strong, beautiful woman, who never should have had to deal with what you did. If anything, I can't look at myself in the mirror. I'm not that guy who makes everything about sex and I felt like that. I mean, don't get me wrong, I'd love nothing more than to hump like rabbits, as Cam said. But I refuse to put you in jeopardy to do so."

I didn't want to admit that I left out the part about being raped when at the hospital. Instead, I told him a white lie, though I hated lying to him.

"The doctor said I should abstain for a week or so to heal. She said that the roughness of the attack may have caused tears which could make sex painful. She ran tests and I should get the results in a couple of days."

He took the news in, nodding. I needed things to be light again, needed a semblance of normal to keep going. "When I'm all better though, we're going to hump like rabbits... for days." A timetable for when I'd be able to keep that promise was impossible to determine. I wanted to consider the possibilities of a normal relationship with him. The more I looked toward our future, the sooner I could put my terrible feelings behind me.

He chuckled softly. "As long as you're ready for it. I won't push. I'll wait forever for you, Gracie." Trusting Ashton came easily; he would never hurt me physically. Love has never come easy to me outside of friendship, and no one had ever stirred emotions in me of this intensity. With Ashton, it seemed there was no choice but to love him. My heart belonged to him alone. Thinking about my past relationships made me wonder about Ashton's.

The next question, I wasn't sure I wanted an answer to. "Have you been in love before, Ash?"

He nodded. "Just once. A few years ago. Her name was Addison. I called her Addy."

He paused a moment, so I asked, "What happened between you two?"

Avoiding my gaze, he said, "She died. She was killed in a convenience store robbery."

His eyes closed and his face scrunched up in pain. It was evident this was not something he spoke about easily. "We were at a casino for a weekend getaway. I was stuck on a machine, refusing to leave. She'd left to go get us some cigarettes as they cost twice as much in the casino machine and the convenience store was close. I should've gone with her, but I knew the machine was going to hit soon. Everyone in the casino heard the sirens and one of the ushers told the manager there had been a robbery at the shop next door. I dropped what I was doing and ran to check on her. The paramedics were loading her into the ambulance when I arrived on the scene. I followed closely behind them watching them work on her through the back window. The sirens turned off just before reaching the emergency entrance. She had passed away moments after being loaded on...."

I gasped. "I'm so sorry, Ash."

"I wasn't there for her, Gracie. I haven't gambled or smoked since that day. I went through hell. It aged me," he said as he fingered the gray spots in his beard. "I never thought I'd love again, and then you came along. What I feel for you, it may sound dramatic, but if I lost you... I'd never survive it."

Chapter Eleven

After Ashton drove me home, he made sure Angel was in before he left with Mary Jane to go get my car from Hudson's. Angel came into my bedroom as I was changing into pajamas.

"Hey, sweetie," she said cautiously. I waved her inside and we sat on the bed together.

"Cameron called me after everything happened. I kept missing you at the hospital, and I've been worried sick about you." I leaned against her as she stroked my hair. "Girl, I want to get my hands on that man and claw his eyes out, cut pieces off... anything to make him suffer."

I chuckled softly. "I appreciate it. I'm going to be okay, though. It'll take time, but I have Ash."

"So, are you two a thang now?" she asked, adding a little country twang to her question.

I smiled up at her and she squealed.

"Good. He's a great guy. Damn, if I'd known he was straight all this time, I'd have made a play for him!"

I sat up. "See! It wasn't just me!" She laughed and I added quickly, "You stay away from him now, though. He's taken."

She smirked. "Yes, ma'am. Seriously, Gracie, there's no way I'd come between you two. You've spent too much time with scumbags. You deserve a Prince Charming on a Harley."

I smiled at her words before I yawned. "I'm feeling a bit sleepy. I'm going to take a nap. You aren't leaving the house, right?" I asked, panicked to be alone.

She patted my hand. "No way. I promised Ash I'd be here until he gets back. Relax, take a nap. I'll check in on you periodically." She kissed my forehead, turned the light off, and quietly closed the door. I curled up in the bed, missing Ashton. My body was exhausted from the last few days and I just needed some sleep.

When I woke up, terror immediately encompassed me. I could hear Hudson singing "Far from Home" by Five Finger Death Punch. He wasn't in the room, yet I needed to hide. I searched the room frantically for something sharp, but all I had were keys. I put them in between my fingers.

I slipped into my closet and hid in the back, behind some clothes. I closed my eyes tightly and started to pray. Praying wasn't something I did every day; it wasn't something I did, ever. But I would have done anything to keep that man from finding me.

My bedroom door creaked open. The bed groaned as he sat on it. I covered my mouth to keep from screaming. I prayed that Angel was safe. Please don't let him hurt her because of me. His voice called out my name, no doubt realizing I wasn't in the bed, and that it was just pillows under the covers.

Light spilled through the crack under the door as the room illuminated. The shadow in front of the closet door told me he was standing there waiting to come in. I covered my head and begged that he didn't open the door.

The door opened. My arms covered my face as a scream escaped my lips. I felt hands grab at me. My eyes remained closed as I screamed for help. Someone had to hear me. He hadn't hit me yet, and so far, I was safe. His hand touched my leg and I scooted in tighter, curling myself toward the wall.

Next, I felt his hand on my shirt as he shook me and said my name. He wrapped his arms around me, and I began to cry uncontrollably, begging him not to touch me again.

"Get your hands off me!" I screamed as I swiped my fist across his face with the keys. I knew they made contact somewhere on his skin. He moved away from me as he shouted out, "Shit, Gracie."

Ashton's soothing voice reached my ear. "Bug, it's me. You're safe." The words calm and quiet.

Prizing my eyes open, I wiped away the tears. Ashton's face was in front of mine, his hands to his side, not making contact. A sharp exhale of relief, followed by nervous laughter before I threw my arms around him. He nestled his face into my neck and smoothed my hair.

"It's okay, baby. You're safe."

I needed to know that was true. "Where's Hudson? Did you get him?"

He pulled away. "He's in jail, baby."

Trepidation rocked through my body. "He was just here. He touched me."

Ashton moved aside to show me the person who was in the closet with us. "Cameron came up to surprise you. He wanted to see if you were okay. It was Cam, sweetie."

Worried eyes stared back at me when my gaze flicked to Cameron's. There were fresh gashes on his neck from where I scratched him. He stared at me with questions in his eyes. "Gracie, what the hell was that?" he asked with concern, not anger.

Ashton whispered to me, "He needs to know. It isn't his fault any more than it is yours. Hudson is to blame. Cam loves you."

I shook my head. "I can't tell him."

Ashton whispered back, "Do you want me to tell him?"

I shook my head no, but answered, "Yes."

His eyebrow rose in confusion.

I clarified, "Yes. Tell him."

Anxiety filled Cameron's words when he asked, "Tell me what?"

Ashton told Cameron every disgusting detail of what Hudson had done to me. Cameron's face was exactly what

I had expected, absolute desolation. His eyes met mine and I watched as he broke inside. I hated myself for letting him find out.

He sobbed, "I'm sorry, Gracie. I'm so sorry." His hands moved and then stopped. I knew he was afraid to touch me again.

I kissed his head and whispered, "You can hug me."

He pulled me into an embrace.

"I love you, Cam."

I was unsure how long we sat there and cried. At one point, I sat against the wall with Cameron's head in my lap.

Looking up at me, he said, "I'm an asshat." He sat up. "I shouldn't be lying here like a little bitch. I should be taking care of you."

I laughed. "You always take care of me. It's my turn."

He stood, helped me up, and pulled me into a tight hug. "I'm so sorry that I didn't get there in time, Gracie."

I sighed. "Stop it. I didn't want to tell you because I knew you'd blame yourself. Ash is right. It's Hudson who's to blame, not you or me."

He nodded in agreement.

I touched the scratches on his neck that had dried; luckily, they were superficial. "I'm sorry I scratched you. As if your poor face isn't battered enough."

He waved it off. "I plan on saying it was a sex injury."

Chuckling, I shook my head.

A little while later, we headed downstairs. Ashton

was in the kitchen cooking. Whatever it was, it smelled amazing. My stomach growled loudly.

Cameron looked over and said, "When was the last time you ate?"

I shrugged. I honestly couldn't remember. Cameron sighed. "You need to take better care of yourself. Go in there and let that man take care of you. I'm going to rest on your couch for a few minutes if you don't mind."

I kissed him. "Of course, go rest."

Ashton stood over the stove, stirring a pot of something. I wound my arms around him, from behind, and felt his hand touch mine. "What are you cooking?"

"Chicken Alfredo and garlic bread. I also made cherry cobbler for dessert."

Moving, I leaned my back against the counter, so I could see his face. "Is there anything you can't do?"

His eyes drifted over to mine and his lips turned up in a grin. He smiled and said, "Nope, not really."

Leaving him to the cooking, I reached into the cabinet pulling down plates for the table. "Cameron said he would eat in a bit. He wanted to give us some alone time."

Nodding, Ashton fixed a huge plate of pasta and set it in front of me. I looked up and asked, "This is your plate, right?"

He chuckled. "No. You haven't eaten in forever. I know you're starving, so eat up."

With wide-eyes, I glanced down at the pasta. "I'll never eat all of this. Besides, I don't want to get fat."

Ash's eyebrows scrunched up. "Gracie, you don't strike

me as someone who worries about their weight. You've never been one to worry about eating in front of me either."

The truth of his words filtered through me, and though the food smelled amazing, all I could think about was Hudson telling me he didn't want me to get fat. I didn't want to lose Ashton because of that either.

"I just want to remain attractive for you. Things are different now that we're dating."

He set his plate down and sighed heavily. "Why would you gaining weight change how I feel? And I don't want things to be different. I like how we are together."

I rolled my eyes. "It's fine, Ash. I used to be overweight. I know how guys looked at me." I hated being this insecure, being this girl, but my emotions were still in turmoil for me to get a grip on reality. He set his fork down and leaned to the side. From his back pocket, he pulled out his wallet. "I'm not like those guys. I don't know what I have to do to make you see that, but maybe this will help."

His hand covered something on the table as he slid it forward.

When he moved his hand, there was a picture underneath. It was Ashton, with his arms around a woman. She had golden blonde hair with tight curls. Her hips were wide, her thighs thick. She had a soft stomach that protruded slightly over the top of her jeans.

Ashton's hand was on her face, and the look he was giving her made my stomach clench with jealousy. He had such love in his eyes. She was the most beautiful woman he'd ever seen. It was transparent in his gaze.

Her face was round, her body plump, at least a size twenty because this was the shape my body was a few years earlier. Through his eyes I could see how extremely gorgeous she was.

"Is this Addy?" I asked.

He nodded. "Yep, that's my Addy. I hope it doesn't offend you that I carry her picture around."

I placed my hand on his. "No, of course not. I'd never ask you to forget about her."

He relaxed. "As you can see, she was beautiful. I never cared what size she was. When I met her, that's how she looked and that is how she stayed. I'm attracted to women, any size, shape, or color."

I smiled. "You said you fell in love with me at first sight. Wouldn't that mean it was my body that attracted you?"

He smirked. "I fell in love with Addy at first sight too."

He placed his hand on mine. "Love at first sight isn't really about someone's looks. It's more of a connection you feel to that person, instantly. An attraction doesn't always have to be physical."

"I didn't mean to insinuate.... Sorry. Will you tell me about meeting her?" I asked.

He shoved a forkful of pasta in his mouth as he shook his head.

"Please, Ash?"

He set his fork down again. "Why?" he asked, his voice choking a bit.

"I'm interested in knowing more about her."

"I haven't talked about her. Not like that. Not since—"

Guilt washed over me. I was so selfish. I wanted to soothe myself by forcing him to talk about his pain and that wasn't fair. "It's okay. You don't have to."

We ate the rest of our food in silence. Ashton stood up and cleared his plate. He then walked to the deck door and went outside, shutting the door behind him. For a moment, I considered running after him and begging for forgiveness. Pushing him to talk about something he wasn't ready for, though, was hypocritical of me. It was my turn to be the understanding one, to be the respectful, patient person.

I headed to the living room, my gaze landing on a sleeping Cameron. The swelling had gone down on his face while his eye was a deep purple color. It hurt seeing him like this.

I sat beside him and rested my hand on his chest. He jerked awake, rubbing his eyes. "Gracie?" He shifted to lie on his side and patted the couch. I curled up in front of him and he wrapped his arms around me. "What's wrong?"

I shrugged. "I wanted to check on you, that's all."

He squeezed me gently. "I'm good, baby girl. I'll be back to my sexy self in no time, don't worry."

I smiled. Cameron always made me feel good.

"Why are you here when you should be with that hot hunk of man?"

I didn't answer him.

His voice grew stern. "Gracie, tell me you didn't screw this up."

Ashton answered for me, "She didn't."

I looked up to see he was propped against the entryway. He smiled at me. "Come join me on the porch. I have a story to tell you."

He put his hand out. I placed my hand in his and let him lead me outside.

"I'm sorry I flipped out a bit, but I want you to know about her. She's a big part of my history," he said.

I leaned up against him as he told me their story.

"Addison and I met in high school. She was my high school sweetheart. It was the first day of junior year. She walked into my math class. I didn't notice her at first. Then she sat down in the seat in front of me. She smelled like sugar cookies. I told her that and her face scrunched in pain. She assumed I was making comments about her weight, I discovered later. I hadn't even noticed it. She ignored me after she called me a jerk under her breath.

"I saw her later crying under the stairwell. Handing her a tissue, I sat beside her. After refusing to take it from me, she'd turned and told me that she didn't need more comments to make her feel bad about herself. I genuinely didn't have a clue what she meant. I glanced over her body and asked what there is to feel bad about." He laughed lightly. "She'd been so pissed. I was sure she was going to lay into me. I'd never had a girl so angry with me before. When I told her, 'I like the way you smell. It may not have been the best line, but pretty girls make me nervous.' She smiled and asked, 'You think I'm pretty?' In my gawky youth, I'd just nodded. When she'd blushed though, rather than punching me, I knew she was the girl for me. I'd asked her to go to the first school dance with me that year so I could make it up to her."

Watching him talk about her made my heart ache as his face lit up with every memory. Ashton had loved this woman with everything he was. I'd never felt love like that before I met him.

He closed his eyes and smiled.

"When I went to pick her up for the dance, she looked amazing. She had a black dress on that dipped somewhat low in the front, with a flowing skirt. She wore tall black heels that made her legs look so sexy. Her hair was pushed back off her face with a glittery headband. When she saw me look her over, it made her eyes light up. I couldn't help myself, I leaned forward and kissed her before she even invited me inside. It was my first real kiss and it was fantastic."

Opening his eyes, he turned to face me. "Sorry. I seemed to have gotten lost in my thoughts."

I moved my arm to the back of the swing. "I can see how much you still love her."

Ashton's hand reached for my face; I closed my eyes at the contact. "I love you, Gracie. Addy will always be a part of me though. She was my first everything. I can't change that part of my past."

That was when something hit me. "Is she the only person you've been with?"

He exhaled. "She died three years ago. We had been together for six years, and I thought I'd spend my life with her. I had a lot of things to deal with other than dating.

Besides, no one interested me after she died, until the night I met you."

He lifted a strand of my hair, letting it slide between his fingers. "She would approve of me moving on with you. I've never forgiven myself for what happened to her, and I have moments where I break down. You can't let that make you feel as though my feelings for you don't matter."

"I understand." Even though my voice was quiet, I meant the words. "That night that you picked me up from work?" I didn't have to clarify my question.

He answered with, "That was the anniversary of her death."

His eyes left mine when he asked, "Why did you think Cam was Hudson earlier? What caused you to hide in the closet?"

I squirmed in my seat. "I thought I heard Hudson singing."

Ashton turned to me. "Singing what?"

My hand moved a piece of hair behind my ear, a nervous habit I had. "Far from Home." It was a heavy metal song that he used to sing all the time."

Ashton's face paled. "Damn, Gracie."

He pinched the bridge of his nose with his index finger and thumb. "I had no clue. That was me. The song was playing in the car. I walked upstairs to let Angel know I was back. I was singing that song when I passed by your room."

He moved closer to me. "I wanted to fix you something to eat and asked Cameron to check on you. A few minutes later, I heard you screaming. I made it to you just in time to see you scratch the hell out of Cam. He didn't have a clue what he had done or what was wrong with you."

He placed his arm on the back of the swing. I moved myself into the crook of his arm, reached up, and pulled it around me. He relaxed as he kissed my forehead.

"Did people make fun of Addison for her weight?" I asked, wanting to get away from the subject of me.

"They did before we started dating." His hand ran up and down my arm.

"Were you Mr. Popular or something?"

He chuckled. "Not exactly. I wasn't very outgoing in high school. I had hit my growth spurt by the time we met though. Would you say anything negative to someone when they were walking down the hall with me?"

He had a point. He was a bit intimidating to look at. "I'm glad you and Addison were together. She was lucky to have found a guy like you who was good to her and helped her confidence, instead of tearing it down."

He placed his palm against my cheek. "I'm not trying to push, but damn, Gracie, I want to kiss you so bad right now."

I stood up.

He added, "I'm sorry, I—"

Interrupting his train of thought, I straddled his waist on the swing. If I took control of the moment, I could take things as far as my comfort zone would allow. His hands moved to my hips as I lowered my head to meet his mouth. He kissed me softly, letting me tell him with the actions of my lips how far I wanted to go. Fingers massaged my sides, not straying too far too soon. Each move would need to be advanced by me; he was letting me lead.

My tongue slipped through the seam of his lips and I moaned when his tongue moved against mine. His hands tightened around my waist, pulling me against him. Welcoming the closeness, I kept my hands pressed to his face as our mouths did what our bodies couldn't.

Chapter Twelve

"Now *that* was a hot kiss. Damn, I think *I* got turned on!" Cameron drawled, interrupting the moment.

Ashton stood up, with me still straddling his hips, and set me on the ground with a kiss on the forehead.

"I take it back. That, right there, you standing up like she weighed nothing at all, that was hot! Are you sure you like chicks?"

Ashton laughed. "If I didn't, you'd definitely be my type, Cam."

A cute red blush spread across Cameron's cheeks, much to my amusement. It was a rare sight.

"Did you need something, Cam?" I asked.

"Oh yeah. I wanted to talk to Ashton for a second."

Smiling, I left them alone. While they had their guy talk, I cleaned the kitchen. The table was cleared and the dishwasher was loaded. Just when I had started it up to wash, my phone rang. Before I could get to it, Ashton tore through the door, frantic, grabbing my cell phone before I could pick it up.

He glanced down and handed it to me, relieved. "It's Angel."

"Hey, girl. What's up?" I said, uncertain of why Ashton looked so panicked. "No, I'm fine. Ash has gone bat-shit crazy for some reason, but I'm good."

Cameron stepped in beside Ashton where they exchanged a look that made me uneasy.

"Angel, I'm going to call you back in a bit. My two guys are up to something and I need to find out what."

I set my phone on the counter. "What's going on, you two?"

Cameron bit his lip, which told me he was trying to come up with a lie.

I called him out on it. "Don't lie to me, Cam."

He cursed as he turned to Ashton for help.

Ashton said, "Sit down."

Those words weren't usually followed by good news. Matching expressions of concern didn't reassure me.

Cameron slid a chair out for me. I eased myself onto the seat and prepared for the worst. Cameron then placed his hands on my shoulders while Ashton took my hand in his, stroking my palm with his thumb. They were catering to me too much, I felt suffocated and began to sweat as the anxiety tugged at me.

"Cameron got a phone call from the police station.

Hudson has a clean record. They let him out on bail because they didn't feel he posed a threat."

Tightness gripped my chest; I could barely catch my breath. Deep breaths, counting to ten, I tried every calming quirk I could think of until I could choke out words once more. "Why? He beat me and put Cameron in the hospital."

Ashton nodded and tightened his grip on my hand. "He made a statement that said he was provoked by the two of you. That you were trespassing, and that Cameron attacked him first. You were on his property, so it's basically your word against his on that part."

He paused and glanced up at Cameron. "There is a way for him to go back to jail. It's something you have to do."

Relief washed over me; I'd do anything to keep that monster away from Cameron and me. "Done. Whatever it is, I'll do it."

Cameron sat down next to me. Ashton scooted closer at the same time.

"There is one thing that Hudson did that would make him a definite threat to society. You have to release your medical records and report the rape."

Before he finished speaking I stood up, my chair scraping the floor and falling behind me. Reaching for me simultaneously, I backed away not letting either touch me. I edged away from them to move to the living room.

"I can't face him, Cameron. If I release those records, I have to testify. I can't tell all those people what happened to me. They'll call me a whore and say I deserved it for all the months I slept with him."

Cameron's jaw clenched, his hands balled into fists, and his eyes hardened. "The hell they will. I won't let them."

Ashton came around the corner, keeping his distance. He stood with his arms crossed over his chest and said, "Neither will I."

"I can't testify, Ash. I'm not strong enough."

Ashton lifted my chin until our eyes met. "You're one of the strongest people I know, bug."

With a trembling voice, Cameron whispered, "Gracie?"

Turning to face him, I waved him over and he laid his head against my shoulder.

"He's right. You're stronger than you know. I have faith in you and we'll both be there every step of the way. Right, Ash?"

Ashton nodded as he sat. "Absolutely."

I pulled myself onto Ashton's lap hugging his neck. His hand rubbed my back as he held onto me.

Cameron broke the silence. "Can I just say that you two are cute as shit! I should've introduced you a long time ago. I'm going to go see Gavin for a bit, give you guys some time."

"Thanks, Cam." Ashton said, then turned to me, "Give me a minute. I'm going to walk him out."

I nodded. Standing with me in his arms, he then turned and sat me back on the couch.

Grabbing his chest, Cam swooned. "Sweet love of all things good, you are one strong man." He then grabbed Ash's flexed bicep and he exclaimed, "Holy bulging biceps, Ashman. Just give me one fantasy and carry me out the door?"

Cameron smiled and batted his eyes. I glanced at Ash, waiting for him to let him down easy. Instead, he lifted Cam over his shoulder and carried him out.

Cam yelled, "I've died and gone to gay heaven, and it's fabulous."

Then he pointed at Ash's butt and his mouth dropped open before he mouthed, "OMG."

It was impossible to hold my amusement back. I burst out laughing. The sound caused Ashton to turn with Cam in his arms. Smiles lit both of their faces, and Ashton threw me a wink.

One thing was for sure, Cameron always had great taste in men and he was right. Ashton's butt was amazing.

A few moments later, Ashton came back in, shaking his head.

"What?" I asked.

"Cameron smacked me on the ass before he ran to the car."

I laughed again.

He sat on the couch next to me. Carefully, he touched my hair, moving it off my shoulder. "I love hearing you laugh again."

His hand started to pull away but I grasped it and tugged as a hint to come closer. He slid next to me. I grabbed a fistful of his shirt, pulling him forward for a kiss. At first, he gave in, leaning closer, but then he stopped short of our lips meeting. "Don't do more than you can handle. I'm not going anywhere."

Tears filled my eyes. This man of mine was as sweet as

he was perfect. He also had the ability to make me smile and laugh when for the most part, all I wanted to do was curl up and cry.

I closed the distance between us. My lips met his, gently at first. I nipped at his bottom lip with my teeth, and he responded with a moan. Tentatively, I placed my hand on his thigh as I slid my tongue across his bottom lip. Moving on instinct, I pushed myself up on my knees, then slid a leg across his lap, straddling him.

Hands moved to my hips as he held me in place while I nipped at his earlobe. Sliding under the hem of my shirt, his thumbs rubbed across my skin. Again, my heart and mind were at war with one another. Love for Ashton had me aching for intimacy with him. Pushing the bad memories from my mind, I tried to focus on making new ones. My hips ground against him as I felt his desire for me growing. Cupping my breast through my bra, I whimpered in pleasure as his thumb traced back and forth across the now hard nub of my nipple.

Tasting a path from my lips to my neck, his tongue trailed along my collarbone, followed by kisses up to my ear. Sliding my hand down, I rubbed my palm over his pants eliciting a moan.

"Gracie, we need to stop."

Avoiding reality, I covered his mouth again with my own. Anxiety crawled across my skin as I continued to push myself too far. In my mind, if Ashton continued to touch me, it would lessen the effect of Hudson's touch. Our love could heal all my pain. His hands were still on my skin, inside my shirt. I stood and took it off.

He protested, "Gracie, seriously. This can wait, baby."

The warning sent a tiny alarm bell ringing, but I was drunk with the feel of him. I needed him to help make all of the hurt and pain go away. Ashton had the power to do that. I glanced down at his pants, biting my lip.

He sucked in a breath. "That lip-biting you do is so sexy."

Holding my waist, he turned to lay me on the couch. He hovered above me, slowly lowering himself on top of me. He had unhooked my bra sometime when he was laying me down.

Damn, he's good.

He slid the straps down and his tongue flicked out over my nipple. I gasped in ecstasy. *Yes, this is what I need.* It was the closest I'd ever been to an orgasm from foreplay. His hand slid down my side, and when I felt his palm press between my legs, I froze.

Noticing immediately, Ashton pulled back. Concern etched his face as his gaze roamed my face looking for an answer. I shoved at him and shook my head. I only had to wordlessly ask once and he jumped away. My chest heaved as I sat up, covering my naked breasts. Ashton said my name, but I didn't answer.

When his hand softly touched my shoulder, I whimpered. "Please, Ash. I can't."

He stepped back and set my T-shirt on the couch next to me.

"I'll go in the other room while you dress." Despair laced his words, hitting me hard.

Laying my head back, I closed my eyes, took a few calming breaths, and tried to clear my mind.

Every muscle was taut as though ready to pop as Ashton stood rigid in the kitchen.

"Ash?" Cautiously, I approached him in the kitchen.

I wrapped my arms around his waist and he softened at my touch.

"It's my fault. You were right. We shouldn't have gone so far. Please hold me."

A small, sad sigh escaped his lips when he leaned down and hugged me close. As he placed a gentle kiss on my head, his phone disrupted our moment. Keeping one arm around me, he answered it, "Um, I don't know, man. I need to check and see if that's possible. Can I call you back? 'K. Give me twenty minutes."

He kissed my forehead. "Sweetie, that was a friend of mine. He asked if I could cover his security duty at a club tonight. His daughter is sick and his wife is a night shift nurse. I'll call the guys first and see if anyone can fill in, but if not, I'll have to go."

Dread threatens to crush me, but I offer a light smile of understanding and make my way to the table while he spends the next fifteen minutes making calls. With each call that ends, my anxiety worsens.

Finally, he sighs. I drag my attention away from my wringing hands to look at him.

"I'm sorry, baby. There's no one. I need to call Cameron

and see if he can stay with you while I'm gone."

Fear of being without him crept up inside, but I wanted him to be able to help his friend. "Angel and MJ will be around tonight. Even if they aren't, I'll be fine by myself."

Ashton stood firm. "No. Not with him out of jail. I'm not leaving you alone. You could come with me."

I thought about that, but a crowded club didn't sound so great. The one thing I didn't need was to have someone accidentally bump into me throwing me into a panic attack.

Angel came to my rescue when she strolled into the kitchen. "Hey, guys, what's up? Ooh, looks kind of serious in here. Everything, okay?"

"You gonna be home tonight, Angel?"

She nodded.

I held my hand out and said, "See, I'm in good hands."

Brows dipping in confusion, Angel asked, "What's that about?"

Ashton spoke up, "I'm going to do security at a club tonight and don't want to leave Gracie alone."

Angel beamed. "Yeah, no problem. I'm glad to spend time with my girl. I didn't know you were a security guard, Ash."

Ashton replied, "I'm not. I'm a promoter. Most of the bouncers know me from the clubs I promote. Occasionally they call me to take a shift for extra money. My size kind of screams bouncer, ya know."

Angel looked him over. "Yes, it does."

I narrowed my eyes. "Watch yourself there, Angel." Laughing, Angel's hands came up in surrender.

Chapter Thirteen

Ashton made sure to fill Angel in on certain orders to keep me safe. We finally had to push him out the door, though he promised to call every hour to check in. The moment he left, I wanted him to come back.

Angel put her arm around me and said, "How about we have a good old-fashioned movie night? We haven't done that in a long time."

We looked at each other for a moment and said in unison, "80's night?"

We grabbed every John Hughes, Brat Pack movie we could. We popped popcorn and made fruity frozen drinks.

"Oh, my gosh, we should call Cameron over because he absolutely would *kill* us for having piña coladas and Judd Nelson without him," Angel exclaimed.

"He definitely would. I'll call him and see what he's up to."

Cameron answered on the first ring and said, "Everything okay?"

I replied, "Yeah. I'm with Angel and we have piña coladas and Judd Nelson. I thought we'd see what you were up to."

He gasped. "Oh, you scamps! I'm out with Gavin. Girl, this must be love because normally I would ditch my date for some quality time with John Bender. Damn this man for being so perfect."

I chuckled at his frustration. "Come over later if you want."

He scoffed, "Please! You think I'm calling it an early night with him? Whatev! Love you, girl, gotta go."

I shook my head and said, "Love you, too, babe."

"Well, he's busy with Gavin," I said.

Angel grabbed her chest. "That must be serious for him to turn this down!"

I laughed. "I know, right? Too bad Mary Jane isn't here. The three of us could use a good girls' night together. Where is she anyway?"

Angel slurped a bit of her drink before responding, "Studying at the actual library. You know she is trying to get into that big engineering program. For some reason, she thinks we are too loud here so she has to go someplace quiet."

She shrugged like she truly didn't understand, and we both laughed. On a normal night, this place was filled with music and laughter. It was one thing I loved about living together.

Four drinks and two movies later, Angel's eyes drooped and she began to snore. I covered her with a blanket as my phone buzzed. It was Ash's fourth call of the night.

"Hey, Ash," I answered.

"Hey, bug, everything all right there?" I could hear the relief in his voice.

I glanced at Angel to be sure I hadn't disturbed her then moved to the kitchen to continue. "I miss you. Other than that, everything's great. Angel fell asleep a few minutes ago. I thought I'd curl up on the couch with her. Are you coming back here tonight to sleep?"

He answered with a note of surprise, "You want me to?"

I laughed. "Duh, of course. I want to sleep in your arms. If that's all right?"

Ashton replied sweetly, "I'd love that, Gracie."

After we hung up, I tried to lie down for the night but Angel's snoring made it impossible to sleep downstairs with her. I moved to my room and found sleeping was equally impossible because I jumped with every creak and moan of the house.

Through my restless state, my mind wondered over current events. I couldn't live my life in constant terror of Hudson showing up again, which was exactly what would happen if the charges weren't filed against him. Did I have the courage to go to the police and put everything out there about the rape? It was hard enough to admit it to the two most important people in my life. How could I expect telling strangers to be any easier? And what if I went through it all for nothing because there wasn't enough evidence to convict him? In the end, I realized that if I did nothing, he walked away free, but if I reported it, then there was a chance to get justice for what happened. After my grueling thoughts, I made a decision: tomorrow I would ask Ashton to take me to the police station. It may be the hardest thing I'd ever do, but with him by my side, I felt almost invincible.

Around four in the morning, I got a text from Ashton saying he was standing at the front door. Anxiously, I ran downstairs to let him in. Before swinging the door open, I peeked through the peephole to double check. He looked nervous and tired. I opened the door and when his eyes met mine, they brightened, concern fell from his face, and his gleaming smile lit up the entryway. I waved him in.

"How was your night?"

He had a backpack over his shoulder that he sat down before hugging me. "It was fine. I wanted to be here though. Let's head upstairs. We both need sleep."

"What's in the bag?" I asked.

He smiled. "A surprise for another time, plus, a change of clothes for in the morning."

He stood there, waiting on me to make the next move. Taking his hand, I released a content sigh at the contact and tugged him up the stairs. Once in my room, I plopped onto the bed, held the covers open for him and said, "Sleep with me, Ash."

He chuckled. "Wow, talk about déjà vu."

I giggled.

Ashton dropped his backpack in the corner and kicked his boots off. Mesmerized, I watched him undress. With his back turned to me, I spent time absorbing the Celtic cross tattoo on his back. As he stretched, making the muscles in his back flex, I bit my lip. Even in my raw state it was impossible not to react to just how gorgeous he was. When I heard his belt buckle open, I sucked in a breath.

He turned around. "Are you okay?" he asked.

Before I answered, he recognized the look I was giving him and he offered a sexy smile. "Are you watching me undress?"

I nodded slowly. "Oh, yeah."

He turned to face me and slowly slid his belt off. He started to move his hips, gyrating them slowly forward and back as though he were stripping for me. A big grin quickly spread on my lips as he teased me by slowly lowering his zipper. Despite laughter bubbling in my chest at his antics, my eyes were fastened to his hands. He was so damn sexy even when playing the fool.

Turning his back to me, he swayed his hips as he lowered the jeans down over his firm ass. His pants were off and he threw them aside, turning back to face me again. His thumbs moved to the waistband of his boxer briefs. He tugged them down, only slightly, giving me a view of his incredibly defined V then stopped. "That's enough for tonight."

Pouting, I said, "You don't want to be all bound in those

while you sleep do you?"

He laughed. "It's how I always sleep."

Crawling into bed next to me, he hesitated before lying on his back. I moved over and put my head against his chest, wrapped my arm around his waist and slid my leg over his. His hand moved to caress my skin with his fingers lightly tracing circles. He kissed my forehead.

"I love you, Gracie. Goodnight, bug."

Smiling, I allowed my eyes to droop closed. I knew this would be a good night's sleep for me.

In the morning, I woke up with Ashton spooning me. When I rolled to face him, he groaned sleepily and moved to his back. The comforter rested just below his waist. Staring at his muscular form, I watched his chest rise and fall with each breath. Even though I was not ready to completely give myself to him, I wanted to be intimate in some way. As long as I remained in control of what happened, I could handle the closeness. I slid my arm across his chest and down to his boxer briefs. He didn't awake.

Slowly, my hand eased inside his shorts as I found his morning erection waiting for me. Smooth, warm skin greeted me. Unable to resist the urge to make him wake up with a smile, I pumped him unhurriedly with my hand. With a soft moan, his breathing sped up, though he remained asleep. He breathed out, "Gracie," which touched my heart, and other parts of me, knowing that he was thinking of me in his aroused, yet unconscious state.

I moved down the bed, the action causing his eyes to pop open. Determined, I looked up at him without stopping. The passion in his eyes was heady, as was the need for control scorching my veins. His head fell back to the pillow in bliss as I ran my free hand up his chest and he entwined his fingers with mine.

When my mouth touched his silky hardness, rightness settled in me. I wanted this, him, so badly. I lapped, sucked, and caressed allowing the euphoria of control to sweep over me. This was on my terms, as such it was so damn hot I was on the edge of combusting with no more than a touch of his hand in mine, and my mouth wrapped around him. My eyes rolled upward to watch his face contort in pleasure. Our eyes met, and his hand gripped mine tighter as his body tensed just before his release.

Curling up next to him, he kissed me and said, "Good morning to you too."

I chuckled, loving the response I was able to pull from him. "Did you sleep well?" I asked.

"Best sleep I've had in years. Best wake-up call ever too." He grinned as he pulled me closer.

"Something told me you'd like that."

He grinned. "Oh yeah, but you didn't have to do that. I—"

I covered his mouth with my lips. "I like taking care of you. It was so hot that you called my name, even in your sleep."

His hand stroked my cheek, his expression sincere. "You've been in my dreams since the day we met."

I sighed. "Sweet, romantic, and gorgeous. I've died and gone to heaven."

With a gentle brush of his finger across my cheek, his eyes roamed my face. "You have no idea how many times I fantasized about waking up next to you this way. If you knew how hard it was for me to keep from kissing you *every* time we were together.... I'm such an idiot for not telling you sooner how much I wanted you."

His words washed over me eliciting goose bumps on my skin. All this time he'd felt the same way about me that I did for him. How could we have both been so stupid not to say anything?

"I want to spend the day with you if you don't have any plans," he said, grinning as if he were up to something.

"Yes, definitely," I replied with genuine enthusiasm.

"What would you like to do? We'll do whatever you want for the first part of the day, and then I have a surprise."

It took every ounce of courage I had to say, "Go to the police station."

His face was a mixture of emotions, the most evident being fear. "Are you sure about this?"

I nodded, though I wasn't 100 percent sure. "As long as you'll come with me."

He squeezed my hand. "I won't leave your side."

CHAPTER FOURTEEN

Ashton made breakfast while I dressed. I picked out a pair of dark blue jeans with a teal blouse and pulled my hair up into a simple ponytail.

The door opened and Angel's face appeared. "Breakfast is ready."

I walked downstairs with her. On the last step, she headed to the kitchen while I stopped beside the door to grab something from my purse.

There was a knock on the door. Without thought, I opened it to find Hudson standing there. His slumped posture, sad eyes, and drooped mouth pleaded for sympathy. Though his appearance wasn't threatening, terror choked me when his hand reached forward to touch me. I tried to slam the door but he stuck his foot in it.

"Please, just listen to me," he said.

Releasing a shrill scream, panic lurched in my chest. Ashton was at my side in an instant. He grabbed my shoulders, pulling me back from Hudson and took a protective stance in front of me. Anger shook his body. I didn't even need to see his face to know he struggled to rein it in.

"What the hell are you doing here? You need to stay away from Gracie or I swear to you..."

Hudson interrupted him. "You gonna threaten me? After what I did to your boyfriend?"

I pushed forward and Ashton's arm stopped me.

Angel came in the room with her phone in her hand. "Yes, I need an officer at the house now. We have an intruder."

Hudson threw his hands in the air. "I'm leaving!" He turned one last time and pointed to me. His eyes darkened like a man possessed. A snarl raised on his lips as he growled, "I'll be back for you, baby. You're mine. Don't you forget it."

After slamming the door on Hudson, Ashton embraced me. "Calm down, bug. I won't let him hurt you."

Angel stepped closer after ending the call and letting the police know they weren't needed. "Is she all right?"

He nodded. "She's pretty shaken up, but she'll be fine." He bent to look me in the eyes. "Right, Gracie?"

I bobbed my head, still shaking. With every bit of strength in me, I held on to Ashton. In a way, Hudson's appearance was a good thing because I was more determined than ever to go to the police station. I refused to live my life in fear every time there was someone at the door. "Angel, I'm going to take her out for a bit. You guys enjoy breakfast."

Patting my back, Angel's voice was surprisingly gentle since her anger vibrated off her in pulsing waves. "Take care of my girl, Ash. Call me if you guys need anything."

Wrapping my arms around Ashton from the backseat of his motorcycle, I pressed my face against his back, closing my eyes to imagine that I'd never met Hudson. Each time fear tried to creep back in, I took a deep breath and hugged Ashton tighter, losing myself in the comfort of him. He didn't say where we were going. I just assumed it was to the station.

Instead, he drove us into downtown Nashville. He passed by Centennial Park, pulling into a parking spot on the street in front of a meter. He dropped a few coins in as I fixed my helmet hair.

"What about the station?"

He took my hand in his and said, "We'll go after this stop. Let's enjoy the first part of our day."

It was barely eleven in the morning as he guided me across the street to the back of a brick building. A neon sign indicated Rotier's Restaurant. At first, I thought it was the back door to a fancy restaurant, by the name of it.

Opening the door for me, Ashton motioned me inside. We were greeted with a smile from a pleasant woman behind the cash register.

"Y'all can sit anywhere you'd like."

Passing the cash register, we headed to the back room where there were more tables away from the door. Ashton chose a booth in the back left-hand corner that was near the kitchen.

I loved the interior. The walls were full of neon beer signs and pictures of news clippings regarding the owners, as well as articles about the "Best Burger in Town." The booths were dark green vinyl and old fashioned. Growing up in Nashville, it seemed odd that I'd never come across this place.

"Have you been here before?" I asked, glancing around.

"You haven't?" he asked, genuinely shocked.

I shook my head.

"I've been coming here since high school. Best food in town, hands down. You ever had fried zucchini?"

I wrinkled my nose. "Not a big fan of zucchini."

Closing his eyes, he moaned a little. "Mmm... you will be. I'll get you the best meal if you trust me to order for you."

I handed the menu back to him. "Go for it." The waitress came over, and Ashton ordered us both a sweet tea, an order of fried zucchini, and a grilled cheeseburger with fries.

The waitress returned with our teas.

"So, why did you bring me here?" I inquired as we waited on our food.

"It's my favorite place and I wanted to share it with you."

He leaned down to whisper in my ear, "I also plan on giving you an orgasm today, without sex."

A surprised snort escaped my lips, and I covered my mouth embarrassed. "Sorry. And you already did that this morning."

His left eyebrow rose in curiosity. "How?"

I whispered, "Moaning my name while I was pleasing you."

A small blush colored his cheeks and he shivered at those words. It was the same shiver he always had when I would bring up topics like this, making me wish I had known how significant it was before.

He grinned proudly. "Wow. Well, this will just be another way I can please you."

It didn't take long for our orders to come out. The grilled cheeseburger was on buttery toasted white bread. One small bite was all it took to convince me. My eyes rolled back in my head as the delicious buttery goodness invaded my mouth. This was definitely the best burger I'd ever tasted.

Ashton watched me intently as I enjoyed the first tasting. "Good, right?" he asked, grinning.

I nodded and slowly licked my lips.

He grunted. "Geez, Gracie... I think watching you eat is even more of a turn-on than watching what you did this morning."

I chuckled and grabbed a piece of the zucchini. I cringed.

"I'm going to try this... for you. Pray I don't regurgitate."

He pushed my hand closer to my mouth. Taking a small bite, the flavor erupted in my mouth. It was greasy and delicious. The best food always was in the South.

Soon, our plates were empty. I leaned back, my hands holding my stomach. "Ugh, I'm so full. This was amazing."

Turning my face toward him, Ashton's hand pressed against my cheek. He leaned down and his tongue slid across the corner of my mouth before he kissed me. Electric tingles rushed all the way to my toes. For a moment, my eyes stayed closed as I delighted in the emotions flooding me.

He snickered. "Ketchup, on the corner of your mouth."

In a daze, I said, "Wow. I like that better than using a napkin any day."

He slid out of the booth and placed his palm in mine to help me out.

"Let me get this," I said as we approached the register.

He caught my hand before I could pull my wallet out. "Absolutely not. This is our first official date. I'm not letting you pay."

I smiled and offered my thanks at his sweetness. "Where to now?"

He held the door again, and I stepped out onto the sidewalk. Taking my hand in his, he then tugged me toward the park. In the park, there was a concrete platform shaped liked the front end of a boat. An older couple sat on a bench in front of it. Ashton handed them his phone and dragged me up on top of the "boat."

"What are they doing with your phone?"

He snickered suspiciously. We ran up the stairs to stand and look out at the park. Ashton dragged me to the edge and placed me in front of him. He grabbed my arms and raised them, using caution with my sore arm. I stood there, confused, with my arms held out to the side. He put his arms around my waist first and kissed my cheek. The woman below was either taking pictures or videoing this, I couldn't tell.

He raised his arms, in the same fashion as mine, and screamed, "I'm the king of the world."

Once I realized that he was mimicking Leonardo DiCaprio's line in *Titanic*, I bent forward in a fit of laughter. His grabbed my waist to keep me from falling, and I heard his laughter echo in my ears as he held me.

"I've always wanted to do that," he said.

Ashton helped me back down, grinning the whole way, and we took his phone back. Today was better than I had expected. As silly as those moments were, it was Ashton's way of taking my mind off what I had to do later, and I loved him all the more for it.

When the woman handed it to us, she smiled. "You two make the sweetest couple. When's the big day?"

I looked to Ashton for comprehension.

He pulled me close, kissing my cheek. "No date yet, but soon, we hope."

She grinned and pointed at her husband. "You remind me of how we were at your age. My Arthur and I have been married for sixty years. I hope you two are as happy as we were back then, and as we are now."

Ashton took her hand and kissed it. "Thank you again for the video."

She nodded and went back to her husband while I stood bemused.

It hit me what she was asking us. "She thought we were engaged?" He nodded as he slid his arms around my waist. I pressed on for a more specific answer. "You didn't correct her. Why?"

He lowered his head, pressing his lips to mine softly. Then dropping to one knee, he gazed at me. My breath caught in my throat, and I panicked. As much as I wanted Ashton in my life forever, I had a lot to work out and our relationship was still very new.

"Ash... we... I...."

He burst into laughter and said, "Gotcha!" He took off running leaving me in his dust, grinning like a fool. I chased him clear across the park, or as much as I could with my achy bones. His legs were so much longer than mine that he was never within reach. I caught up to him when he sat waiting on a swing.

Looking at his watch, he winked. "'Bout time you caught up!"

I flopped down on his lap. "You're a shameless tease." I kissed his cheek and leaned down to whisper in his ear, "I'd have said yes, if you meant it." My words were intended to be playful, but I barely recognized the husk of my voice. My heart picked up speed when I struggled to decipher how he felt about my confession. His face was unreadable.

He reached into his pocket and his hand came out closed over something. My heart stopped. Honest to God stopped at the gesture as I stared on wide-eyed.

"Nothing would make me happier than to marry you, Gracie."

I held my breath as I tried to grasp his words and the seriousness of them.

"I don't have a ring, but I do have something for you." He placed his fist out and turned it over unclenching his fingers. In his grasp was a silver charm of a cowboy boot.

"This is for your bracelet. It's to represent our night playing pool. That was one of my favorite memories. It was the first night you slept in my arms. You fell asleep shortly after the movie started and you curled up against my chest. I was pretty stunned at first and thought about moving you so that you didn't wake up embarrassed. Then you ran your hands up my chest and said my name and I couldn't move. It felt too homey."

I laughed. "Sheesh, all I do is molest you in my sleep."

With a sexy smirk, he replied, "You won't hear me complain about that."

I leaned in and said, "You whispered my name in your sleep that night."

He grinned. "I remember the dream too. I'll just say that my pool table had never seen so much action." Pressing against my back, Ashton pulled me nearer. Willingly, I eased in closer, resting my palm against his cheek, pressing my lips to his. The warmth of his mouth sent a current through my body.

My phone rang, interrupting the moment. I didn't recognize the number. "Give me one second. Hello?"

The voice on the other line asked, "Gracie Walker?"

"Yes, that's me."

"I'm calling from Baptist Hospital. We have your test results."

The next words stopped my heart completely. "Your tests came back clean." Knowing there would be no lasting physical effects from the rape such as a disease, or worse, a child, put me at ease.

With a sigh of relief, I replied, "Thanks," and hung up the phone.

Ashton moved to my side. "What is it, Gracie?"

I took a deep breath. "Take me to the police station. I need to put him away."

CHAPTER FIFTEEN

When we arrived at the police station after changing vehicles, I was directed to a room to speak with an officer to give my statement, relieved when I was able to have Ashton with me. They recorded the details of what happened urging me to be concise.

When I got to the really rough parts, Ashton squeezed my hand. I watched the pain roll over his face when I retold the attack blow for blow.

The officer stopped at one point with tears in her eyes. She reached out to shake my hand. "You're very brave for coming in here."

Ashton placed his hand on my shoulder. "She definitely is."

Not long after, we were able to leave once a few photographs and me signing a release for the medical reports from the attack. As we left, the officer explained that she would file the report and they would call me to follow up.

Outside the car, I exhaled deeply and welcomed the warm hug from Ashton. We remained silent while I took the time to process all that had happened. I was terrified, but I was absolutely confident I'd done the right thing.

Pulling out my cell once in the car, three texts greeted me. Cameron had sent two, asking where I was, and the other was from Angel asking if everything was okay. I texted them both back that things were fine while Ashton drove us back to the house. When we arrived, everyone was waiting in the living room.

Cameron rushed to me, but he stopped before touching me. Normally, he would wrap me in a hug and give me a kiss. I didn't like that our routine was changed. To lighten the moment, I held my arms out and said, "Where's the love, Cam?"

He grinned and lifted me in a hug. I cringed a bit at the touch, but held the emotion deep. Cameron turned to Ashton and held his arms out. "I'll be glad to give you some loving too, big man."

Ashton chuckled. "I'm good."

The knock on the door made me jump, and I backed myself into the corner. *What if it's him?* Swallowing the bile that crawled up my throat, I watched on as Ashton went to answer it. Before he opened it, he pointed at Cameron. "Go to her, please."

Flicking his gaze in my direction, Cameron's face

dropped before moving closer to me. My anxiety and fear wasn't only affecting my life. I hated knowing how much my friends were suffering with me. In almost military formation, Angel, and Mary Jane flanked Cameron, standing around me in a protective stance.

Ashton took a deep breath and opened the door. I wasn't the only one expecting problems. He exhaled at once. "Shit, man. I'm glad to see you." Gavin stepped inside and hugged him.

Heat flooded my cheeks. *Is this going to be my life, cowering in a corner at the smallest of things?* The thought made me blanch. Offering my friends and Ashton a light smile, I excused myself to go upstairs. Ashton followed, but I turned and said, "I need to be alone for a bit."

He nodded, sadness flooding his features.

When I reached the top of the stairs, he remained at the bottom watching my every move. I blew him a kiss, hating the concern on his face, and he relaxed, smiling up at me. There were many things I needed to mull over in my mind. I ached to have Ashton with me, though these decisions were ones I needed to make on my own.

My body didn't feel like my own anymore. Normal movements felt forced. I didn't know how I would react to things like a simple knock on the door. The powerlessness sweeping through me shocked me to my core. I hated this, the vulnerability, the helplessness. I didn't want to be this person.

My bed calling to me, I changed into shorts and a tank top, then slid under the covers. Burying my face in the pillow, I allowed my tears to fall. For two hours I cried, only stopping when I couldn't cry anymore.

Music and laughter drifted from downstairs. I wanted to stop hurting. I wanted to have fun, escape. The comfort of my friends would make everything disappear for a while. Washing my face, I brushed my hair and searched for a T-shirt to cover myself. Spotting Ashton's backpack by the door, I rifled through it and found one of his. I slid it on, bringing it to my nose and inhaling the scent of him. I pulled on pajama pants and opened the door to face my friends.

"Ash?" I asked as I stepped into the hall.

He sat with his back against the wall, his knees pulled up to his chest. His arms were crossed over his knees while his head rested on his arms. He glanced up at me.

"How long have you been out here?" I asked.

Standing, he stretched. "Since you first came up."

My mouth gaped open briefly. "That was two hours ago."

He shrugged. "I wanted to be here in case you needed me."

I stepped forward, slid my hand behind his neck, pulling his mouth down to mine. When he slid his tongue between my lips, I moaned low in my throat. His hands moved to my waist pulling me closer.

The moment his lips left mine, I sighed dreamily from the memory of the kiss.

"You make my shirt look so sexy." He ran his thumb back and forth across my bottom lip.

Rolling up onto my tiptoes, I moved my face as close to his as I could. "You don't mind me wearing it?"

He closed the distance, nibbling lightly on my bottom lip. "No, it's as though I'm wrapped around your body. I love it."

Tingles raced through me at the thought of Ashton wrapped around my body.

"Let's go downstairs. I need a distraction before we get carried away," Ashton said as he took my hand.

Downstairs, it was clear I'd missed more nonsense that went hand-in-hand with my crazy friends. Angel was giving Cameron hell over something. With a grin, she yelled, "You're such a queen, Cameron!"

He stood up and shook his finger at her. Together, he and I said, "Nuh uh, my momma is still alive. I'm a Princess. Get it right, girl."

Cameron heard my voice echo his and he beamed up at me from his chair. He leaned his head against mine as I wrapped my arms around his neck and kissed his cheek.

Angel stood. "We need more drinks!"

Cameron held his beer bottle up and said, "Beer me!"

Ashton disappeared into the kitchen with Angel while I joined my friends for a card game.

The game was called Apples to Apples. The simple explanation was that the green cards contained a descriptive word with a definition while the red cards contained a noun. Each player received seven red cards. There was a judge for each round, who chose the green card and flipped it over. It was then up to the other players to decide what red card in their hand was the best match to the green card. Whoever the judge chose, kept the green card, and once someone reached a certain number of green cards, they won.

It sounded boring to explain, but we had so much fun with it. It was Mary Jane's turn to judge the cards. The green card drawn was the word "Spunky." She shuffled through the red cards from each of us. She burst out laughing. "Gross, Cameron! I know which one is yours!"

He grinned suspiciously.

She laid the cards out, one at a time. The first card read, "Hannah Montana," the second, "fireworks." The third card, which she placed strategically, slowly as she stared up at Cameron read, "My bedroom." It took me a moment to make the connection, and when I did, I burst out laughing and smacked Cameron's shoulder.

"Gross!"

He shrugged. "Don't hate the player. Hate the game."

Angel and Ashton returned with drinks for all of us. She handed Cameron a beer, Mary Jane a strawberry daiquiri and Ashton handed me a piña colada.

He leaned down to kiss my cheek. His lips lingered next to my ear as he whispered, "I added an extra shot of rum to calm your nerves."

Cameron smacked Ashton's butt. "Enough whispering naughty nothings to each other. Sit down and play."

We played Apples to Apples until we were all too drunk to concentrate. Ashton was tipsier than I had ever seen him. Next, everyone wanted to play a game of quarters. I had to draw the line.

"You bitches are all too drunk for quarters."

Everyone groaned. "Ah, Mom, come on now!"

I laughed but stood firm. "Nope. Everyone to bed. Cameron, Gavin, and Ash, you're all staying here tonight."

Ashton grabbed me around the waist, pulling me down onto his lap. His mouth met mine with a ferocity I hadn't felt from him before. My heart picked up speed, both fear and desire at war with each other. I pushed him away gently.

I helped Cameron to the couch and Gavin lay with him while Angel and Mary Jane helped each other upstairs. Heading to the door to lock it, arms wrapped around me from behind.

Panic and fear consumed me at once. I screamed, throwing my elbow back. Making contact, Ashton cursed. I turned to see Ashton staggering to the floor holding his nose.

"Ash!" I exclaimed as I bent to help him. I struggled to pull him into a seated position. Pulling his hand away, he revealed a bloody face. "I'm so sorry."

Quickly locking the door, I ran to grab a towel, returning swiftly and holding it to his face.

When he mumbled something incoherent, I removed the towel. He repeated, "I'm going to be sick."

I put his arm around my shoulder in an attempt to lift him. Ashton was heavier than I could handle. He was all muscle and I could barely budge him. Thinking fast, I ran to the kitchen and grabbed a bucket. I made it back just in time to toss it in his lap before the contents of this evening's party reappeared.

While he got rid of all the alcohol in his system, I wet a rag, and then wiped his mouth clean.

He leaned against me and sighed. "Addy."

The one word crushed me. I wished it didn't as she was gone. It was not like competing with an ex-girlfriend who was capable of stealing him away. But still, it was that one word that bounced around my soul. Ashton deserved someone like Addy, someone who wasn't broken in the way I was.

Cameron stumbled over to me dragging my attention away from Ashton and thoughts of Addy. "You need help getting him upstairs?"

I glanced up at him. "No, just help me get him to the chair. I'll get him a blanket. You're in no shape to carry him either."

I covered Ashton with a fleece blanket and kissed his head. He looked adorable, snoring all slumped in the chair. Cameron took his place with Gavin on the couch. Once he lay down, Gavin's arm pulled him in to snuggle.

They made an adorable couple and I envied their snuggling ability tonight. I almost wanted to see if they would go take my room and let me get to the couch with Ashton. There was no way I'd be able to move him again though. I sighed and went up to bed alone.

Chapter Sixteen

A few hours passed. Restless, I tossed and turned. The dark was no longer a friend of mine. Too many shadows played tricks on my eyes. I wanted Ashton with me offering me the comfort my overactive imagination craved. Alone, I felt vulnerable and frightened. I had never been someone to be afraid of the dark. But everything had changed.

The door creaked open, and my anxiety heightened. A large shadow filled the doorway making me react. Reaching for the light on the nightstand, I switched it on, blinding Ashton in the process.

With a raised hand, he shielded his eyes from the light. "Gracie?"

"Ash?" Relief whooshed out of me with an unsteady breath. "What are you doing up here?"

Squinting slightly, no doubt his eyes adjusting to the

light, hurt flickered on his face. "You don't want me up here?"

I pulled back the covers to invite him in. "Of course, I do. I couldn't carry you up the stairs by myself though. I thought you'd be passed out by now."

Offering an apologetic smile, he slid under the covers with me. Curling up against him, I embraced his warmth and smiled when he kissed my head and whispered, "I love you, bug, so much."

Hearing those words gave me courage like nothing else. Lying in his arms, I thought about life with Ashton and how our future would turn out. I'd waited what seemed my whole young life for a love like this to let anyone ruin it for me. Hudson had taken something from me before, my security. I wouldn't let him take this away from me too.

The next morning, I opened my eyes to see Ashton staring down at me as he played with my hair. Propped up on his elbow, an adorable grin lit up his face.

"Good Morning, sunshine," he said as I rubbed my eyes to wake up.

"Morning. How do you feel?"

His nose was bruised slightly, but not broken, while his breath smelled minty fresh from mouthwash. He cringed. "A little rough. I don't usually let myself get so drunk. I'm sorry. What happened to my nose?" he asked as he rubbed it with his thumb.

"That's my fault. I was locking up and you came up behind me. I panicked."

He frowned. "I'm so sorry, Gracie."

I leaned forward and kissed his nose gently. "Why are you apologizing to me when I elbowed your nose?"

He shrugged. "I don't like making you feel unsafe." He lifted my hand to his mouth and kissed it.

"I wish you hadn't been so drunk you couldn't walk last night. I was hoping to take advantage of you up here."

His eyes filled with lust as I licked my lips.

"Ash, I'm ready." As long as I took control of the situation, my strength would pull me through. Ashton and I were meant to be together, and I didn't want to wait any longer. My fingernails skimmed down his chest as I pulled on his boxers, tugging him closer to me. Ashton took the hint and edged closer, shortening the space between us. His hand caressed my cheek before he licked his lips then pressed them against mine as he pulled me closer still. With my palms on his back, I massaged his muscles as our mouths melded together.

As his fingers traced the strap of my tank top, his mouth moved to my neck while he planted soft kisses on my skin.

"Your skin tastes like caramel." He groaned. His tongue darted out making tiny circles along my neck as he sucked gently, causing me to whimper. Soft lips caressed my skin, leading a trail to my earlobe. Flicking it with his tongue, he whispered, "Tell me if you want me to stop."

His mouth moved along my shoulder, trailing kisses down my arm. When I lifted my hand to his lips, his tongue sampled the sensitive skin of my wrist, an erogenous zone I never knew I had, causing my ache for him to increase. No one had ever teased that part of me. The way he gazed into my eyes as his mouth moved, and the heat it caused from such a simple act, was almost unbearable. A groan escaped my lips.

Keeping his eyes focused on mine, his hands slid inside my top. He lifted the hem of my shirt exposing my skin, inch by inch. Moving his body down the bed, his mouth explored my body. At times, the fear came back, but I pushed the thoughts away, letting myself get lost in Ashton instead.

The moisture of his lips pressed against my stomach and I bit my lip at the contact. While he tasted my skin as he moved the shirt further up, I arched at the sensations coursing through my body as his thumbs gently rubbed the underside of my breasts. Lifting the top over my head, he tossed it across the room. His eyes filled with desire as he memorized my body. Rough, masculine hands against my soft skin sent a jolt of need to my core.

Dipping his head, his tongue flicked at my nipple making me squirm with pleasure. Ashton's hand trailed down my stomach and plunged into the waistband of my pants. I whimpered as his fingers snaked under the edge of my panties. He pulled away, looking at me for an answer of what to do.

"Don't stop, please," I begged. Nothing but pure desire for Ashton filled me. All the bad thoughts floated away. Aching need replaced anxiety and undeniable love overshadowed any fear.

Continuing below my panty line, his fingers found the spot that let him know instantly how much I wanted him.

He kept his hand moving at a steady pace to my breathing. Our mouths met. His tongue delved between my lips at the same time his fingers slipped inside me.

I gasped.

He pulled back. "Too much?"

I shook my head in answer. With a seductive breath, I said, "I want to feel you inside me, Ash."

He stopped and glanced into my eyes. "We shouldn't. I don't want to hurt you."

I couldn't wait. Didn't want to hold back anymore. Everything about this moment was right. Without words, I stood and slid my pants off, panties too. I was fully exposed to him as his eyes danced over my body with yearning.

I begged him, "Please. I want you. Go slow. I'll tell you if it's too much." I needed the reassurance for myself as much as him. I reached into the nightstand beside the bed and handed him a condom. Watching as he tore open the package and slipped it on, I braced myself for the moment I'd been waiting for and hoped I had the strength to get through for my sake as well as Ashton's.

When he positioned himself between my legs, I wrapped them around his waist as he slid inside me, slowly. I gasped at the pain that immediately hit.

He whimpered, "Gracie, I'll stop."

I wrapped my arms around him. "No! Slow...."

His rhythm was precise. The more he moved, the less it hurt. Our bodies joined like a perfect mold.

This was more ecstasy than I had ever known. Electricity, passion, intensity and love. Ashton was making this new for me.

He was giving me the experience I needed to make this act completely separable from anything I'd had before. Without telling him I needed that, he was recreating what should have been my first sexual experience by making this incomparable, so that it would stand out above any of the painful memories with Hudson. Sex hadn't always been bad for me. In fact, there were many times I'd say it had been great. With Ashton it was different in some way. My feelings for him seemed to intensify every touch.

Groaning my name against my ear, Ashton then moved his arm around my back, lifting me as he knelt on the bed. I straddled his waist, my arms draped over his shoulders. He held my hips as I moved with him while his mouth explored my neck, venturing to my breasts as I writhed against him.

I tossed my head back, moaning, "Ashton."

Our bodies trembled together in bliss as he thrust inside me one last time and breathed out, "I love you, Gracie." I shivered, my hips involuntarily grinding into him as my heart raced, and I cried out.

Exhausted, we collapsed on the bed. He kissed my forehead lightly as he pulled me against him, moments after removing the used condom. "You're okay? I didn't hurt you?"

I glanced up at him and smiled. "That was amazing. I've never felt anything like it."

His face lit up with relief and excitement. "Neither have I."

I said the first thing that came to mind, which was stupid.

"Even with Addy?"

Before he answered, I attempted to take back the question. "Sorry, I don't know why I asked that. You don't have to answer."

"I know why you asked. I called you Addy last night," he said nonchalantly. A wave of irritation shot through me.

"You remember?"

He scratched his forehead. "Vaguely. I recalled it this morning hoping it was part of a dream. Your face when you asked that question told me it wasn't."

His thumb trailed up and down my naked back. My body reacted to his touch in a way that told me we needed a better topic. When his mouth opened to speak, I covered it with my own, sliding my tongue out, gliding it across his bottom lip. He growled deep in his throat, his tongue then sliding against mine. Positioning my leg across his thigh, I felt his excitement growing. I swiftly grabbed another condom and rolled it on him. He groaned. I moved my leg across his body, hovering over him briefly, watching in wonder when his head fell back to the pillow as I lowered myself on him. He moaned my name as his hips rose slightly to push deeper.

Leaning forward, I dragged my nails lightly against his chest until I reached his face. Avoiding his mouth, I continued to tease him. His hands reached up to touch me, but I grabbed them and pulled them away. I pushed them above his head and he grinned up at me. I waved a finger.

"No touching. Just lie there." Continuing to take control helped keep me from going to a dark place and made things about Ashton. After everything he'd done for me, I wanted to do something for him. I wanted to show him pleasure.

He watched intently as I sat back up, still straddling his hips. I glided my body up and down slowly, occasionally letting him ease out of me so I could guide him back in. Exquisitely tantalizing, the raw desire was mind-altering. I leaned forward, my hair tickling his chest as I licked my way up his body. I kissed him from his neck up to his jaw. His mouth moved toward me, and I grinned, moving away from him.

He whimpered, "Gracie, kiss me please." I loved the way he played along, letting me take control when I knew how much he wanted the power.

I leaned down and whispered, "I love when you beg."

He smiled seductively. "Please, I want your lips on mine."

I leaned forward, my lips close to his and breathed, "Not yet."

Sitting upright, I rode him harder. Hands gripped my waist massaging my hips. Biting my lip, I held back the urge to scream out. My breathing raced, making it difficult to stay quiet, unsure who was home. Truthfully, I didn't care who heard us. It wouldn't stop me from giving in to the desire. Occasionally, I glanced down at Ashton and his eyes were always watching me. It pulled at my core to see such passion and love staring back at me. The rest of the world be damned. I wanted to stay in this moment for as long as possible. Each thrust drew me closer to leaving utopia. I held on as long as possible. His muscles became taut, ready to explode. I dipped my head down, crashing our lips together as we both reached the height of ecstasy. When I sat up again, I screamed in pleasure as our bodies trembled.

I didn't realize how loud I had been until the door flew open.

Cameron shrieked out, "Gracie, are you... holy hell, I'm so sorry." He turned to leave, but not before sticking his head back in. "Get it girl!"

I rolled off Ashton, covering my reddening face with my hands. Cameron and I shared a lot but that was the first time he'd walked in on me with someone. He laughed so heartily that I giggled at his reaction.

"Well, that was embarrassing," I said.

His fingers pushed hair back from my face. "You're so stunning, Gracie. To answer your question, that was different than anything I'd felt before, and that's the honest truth." And I believed him without question. Before I could respond, he said, "I loved that distraction, but I still want to tell you why I said that last night."

I grabbed a sheet to cover myself, suddenly feeling self-conscious as the subject of Addy came up again. She wasn't a threat to our relationship, deep down I knew that, but it wasn't easy to hear of the late great love of Ashton's life. We sat up together.

"Addy used to take care of me when I was drunk. Gambling, drinking, they kind of go together as addictions. I used to get drunk like that every couple of days and she was always cleaning up after my binges. Last night, I wasn't wanting to be with Addy instead of you, or anything like that. We spent too much time with her cleaning up my messes and catering to my needs."

I slid away from him, turning my back. Ashton's days were spent catering to *my* needs, cleaning up *my* messes. At least those were the thoughts in my head. Deep down, I knew what he was saying, though it still stung, hitting close to home. It didn't take him long to realize what his words might have meant to me.

"Baby, no, I didn't mean anything by that. I want to take care of you. What happened to you is not your fault. Addison took care of me because I couldn't control an addiction. I should have been strong enough to fight it. Dammit." He smacked his head in frustration.

He was adorable when he fumbled over his feelings. Turning to him I couldn't help the grin on my face.

His head tilted to the side confused.

"It's okay, Ash. I understand what you're trying to say."

Standing up, I slipped his T-shirt over my head, letting the sheet fall from my body. I turned to go to his side of the bed and bumped into his chest. "What the...? For a big guy, you move like a ninja," I laughed, though his face was very serious. "What's wrong?"

With a tone of sadness, he asked, "You mad at me?"

I stepped back to look up at him. "What? No. Why?"

He didn't seem convinced. "You were about to leave," he said sadly.

"No. I was going to kiss you and try to convince you to

fix me something delicious to eat. I've been up for a few hours and you just worked me up a mad appetite."

"Oh, so you're not mad about the Addy thing last night or me putting my foot in my mouth repeatedly just now? You understand I want to be with you and am ready for whatever that entails?" Ashton's pleading puppy dog eyes tugged at my emotions.

Perhaps I needed his reassurance after all. Suddenly, I felt a huge weight lift from my shoulders. "I'm not mad. Addy is your past, and I want to be your future. In the present though, I'm starving." I winked before lifting up on my toes to give him a peck on the lips.

CHAPTER SEVENTEEN

Ashton bent over to let me jump on his back and carried me down the stairs. One afternoon, while still in the friend zone, I'd seen a couple and told him I'd always thought it was cute when guys let girls ride on their backs. It amazes me how he remembers all the romantic ideas I'd mentioned. When we came into the living room, "You Shook Me All Night Long" by AC/DC pumped through the radio, our friends making lewd gestures and bumping up against each other. The room erupted in laughter.

"Save a horse, ride a cowboy! Right, Gracie?" Cameron winked.

I grinned and tapped Ashton on the shoulder to let me down. Once my feet were on the ground, I sprinted over to hug Cameron. He pulled me close and whispered, "Seriously, I'm so happy for you." Unable to hold back the smile spreading widely across my face, I could genuinely admit I was happy too. Deep down though, the fear of failure, disappointment, losing Ashton, it was still there. I just needed to keep it from bubbling up and controlling my life.

Ashton's arm came around my stomach before he lifted me off the ground. I squealed, laughter ripping through me. "You want me to cook or you wanna go out?" he asked as he set me back on the ground.

Cameron spoke up, "Let's go out!"

I bumped my hip against his and teased, "I don't know that you were included."

Ashton laughed. "We can all go out. Angel, MJ, Gav... you in?" They readily agreed.

Smiling, I went upstairs to get ready, finally feeling as though I'd found my footing again. I was feeling like me.

Ever since the rape, I'd been hiding away beneath oversized clothes, not daring to feel comfortable in my own skin. As I pulled my favorite knee-length sundress from the closet, I palmed the flowery print, a grin forming on my lips. This dress was me. I held it to my body and looked in the mirror recalling Ashton's tender touch as I stood there. My cheeks heated at the memory, my smile becoming impossibly large. This morning was perfect. Despite the speed of everything happening, the contact so soon after a moment that forever changed my world, the impact of his caring touch had been exactly what I'd needed.

Placing the dress down, I slipped off his T-shirt and

removed my splint before stepping into the warm stream of the shower. Tingles spread over my cool skin under the hot water.

The door to the bathroom opened and Ashton called out, "Gracie, I brought some fresh towels up."

My naked body responded to his voice telling me I couldn't let him just drop the towels and leave. I called, "Oh, Ash, I have soap in my eyes. I need a towel please. Hurry!" I sucked my teeth between my lips to hold back my giggle as I heard him shuffle back over to the towels.

He slid the shower curtain open. I stood there with one arm against the shower wall, one hip cocked to the side, with water dripping over my body. His alarm turned to longing. I smiled as he licked his lips.

"Join me?"

I'd never seen him move so fast. He threw his clothes off in a fury and jumped into the shower with me. I giggled when he cursed, looking down at his soaked socks. I pulled him to me. "Forget about them. We don't have much time."

Moving his hands to my butt, he lifted me up. Ashton paused. "I didn't bring a condom in with me."

"My tests were all clean and I have only been with you since they were taken. I'm also on the pill. You haven't been with anyone but Addy in several years. I think we're safe."

I wrapped my legs around his body. Our mouths met in a fury as he pressed me against the wall and entered me.

We had made love only an hour ago, yet it felt as though it had been forever since we'd touched. As he held me against him the water cascaded down my chest. Each thrust pushed me into the wall harder as he grunted. Ashton's lips crashed against mine once more as our bodies released together.

"Want me to wash your back before we get out?"

I nipped at his chin with my teeth and turned my back to him. "I'd like that." Gently moving my hair to the side, Ashton kissed my shoulder as his hands moved over my back in a foamy massage. Everything about this moment was like a dream. Gorgeous man naked in my shower, using gentle loving hands to care for me. If I could have written a recipe for the perfect man, it would include everything about Ashton.

Slipping his socks off, Ashton wrung them out before we stepped out of the shower. I laughed at him again for having been so anxious and forgetting to remove them.

After kissing my cheek, he climbed out of the shower and patted himself dry. "I'm going to give you some privacy to get ready."

As he stepped out into the bedroom, I heard Cameron shout, "Hot damn, look at you!"

Ashton ran back into the bathroom, and grabbed a towel to cover himself. I bent over in hysterics watching him fumble to cover up. Ashton had been taken off guard by Cameron, but he had a good laugh at his own expense. Once I calmed, I dried off and slipped on my dress, pleased with my appearance and choice. It was a brand new day and there was no way I would allow it to be ruined by my insecurities.

I stepped out into the bedroom expecting Ashton.

Cameron was sitting there instead. He whistled. "Baby girl, you look hot. You haven't worn that dress in forever."

I nodded. "I hadn't really felt like being cute lately. I'm feeling better though." He grinned, and then ran over to my closet. He pulled out some strap-tastic sandals. They were white fabric sandals with a wedge heel and straps that crisscrossed up my calves. "Wear these to show off those fabulous legs."

I sat next to him and wrapped my arm across his shoulder. "What about Ash? Is he hot or what?"

His mouth fell open as he said, "Honey girl, Gracie, if you mess this up with that *fine*-looking hunk of godliness, I'll disown you."

I snorted. "I wouldn't blame you." I held my wrist out to show him the bracelet.

After explaining the sentiment behind it, he gasped. "Prince Charming on a Harley for real. I love that man."

I smiled. "Me too."

Cameron jumped up and hugged a confused Ashton. "Welcome to the family, man. We are dysfunctional, unpredictable, crazy-fun and most of all..."

I chimed in with him, "Fabulous."

Ashton smiled. "I can handle it."

Cameron's eyes drifted over him. "Oh, I bet you can, big boy. I'll leave you two alone if you promise me you will actually come downstairs in like two minutes. I'm freaking starving!" He then left us alone.

Ashton looked me over. His thumb and forefinger smoothed his beard while he slid his tongue across his lips slowly. It drove me nuts. He sighed. "You look gorgeous, bug."

Everyone piled into cars. Ashton went to his motorcycle and handed me a helmet.

"Um, let's go in my car. If I ride this, I'll have to pull my dress up to my hips."

He grinned. "And that's a problem?" He winked.

"Do you want to show the world my goodies? If so...." I started to shimmy the dress up my thighs.

My neighbor next door whistled at me and yelled for me to take it all off. Panicked, my laughter faded and I pushed my dress back down, wrapping my arms around myself defensively. "I'm going to run inside and change. I'll be down in five minutes."

He reached to stop me. I recoiled, shaking my head.

In an instant, my world came crashing down around me. I ran upstairs and quickly removed my dress, replacing it with a T-shirt and jeans. My heart pounded against my chest. I could barely breathe. Body trembling in fear, the room closed in around me, suffocating me.

Footsteps sounded from the hall. Running, I closed and locked it. Anxiety strangled me as I searched for an escape from whoever had followed me. Wrapping my arms around my waist, I tried to cover myself, feeling too exposed even in the new clothes. As I backed away from the door, my knees hit the mattress and I fell onto my bed. My eyes closed briefly as I felt Hudson's weight on top of me. I felt him shoving against me, felt his hands pulling at my hair, my clothes. I scrambled off the bed just as there was a knock on the door. Without pause, I ran to the closet and crouched in the corner.

As the anxiety built, my stomach cramped. My head was spinning out of control with thoughts of what was about to happen. Something then brushed my shoulder. Releasing a shriek of terror, I didn't recognize the sound of my own scream. Someone was beating on the bedroom door.

I covered my ears, trying to cut off my silent screams of "No," as they resounded in my head.

A figure stood at the door and instinctively I knew the pain was coming again. Curling into a ball on the floor, I hid my face. As his hands touched me, my skin crawled in disgust.

"Don't touch me!" I whimpered. "Please don't hurt me," I begged. I couldn't stand for him to take away the comfort Ashton had given me. If Hudson hurts me again I could lose my chance at happiness forever.

"Gracie. Bug, it's Ashton, sweetheart." Sadness laced every word, puncturing the scream in my head.

Slowly, I moved my hands from my eyes and looked up at him.

He held his arms out to me, but I couldn't go to him. I backed away until I bumped into the wall behind me. His face exhibited the worst expression of sadness. "Gracie-bug. I'd never hurt you."

I stifled a sob. "I know. I'm broken, Ash.... I'm so broken."

His voice choked. "No, you're not broken. Gracie, let me hold you?"

I shook my head. "I can't, not right now. It's too much.

I can't stand for anyone to touch me right now." Needing to escape and desperately needing to breathe, I stood and ran out the door. He was close behind me, yelling for me to stop. It broke my heart to hear the fear in his voice. Warring emotions kept him from reaching me. His legs were long enough he'd have caught up with me, but instead, he knew I needed the time to think so he lagged behind.

Once in my car, I turned the ignition and drove without thought of a destination.

After driving for a while, thinking over everything in immense detail, I needed a break. Pulling over to get a drink, my body froze in terror as I spotted someone through the window. Hudson sat inside the café and I watched as he met with an older man. Seeing him brought back every emotion I'd tried to quell; fear, anxiety, anger, and hatred. How could he be allowed to even be out in public acting as though he'd never ripped my life apart? Did this man know what his lunch companion had done? Was it a scumbag attorney advising him of ways to damage my reputation so Hudson ended up the victim?

Before having what appeared to be a very serious conversation, the two men shared a hug, which was unusual for Hudson, piquing my curiosity more.

As they stood to leave, I drove away before Hudson could spot me. I didn't know where I wanted to go. Ashton's face, the fear and rejection he felt, haunted me and I couldn't face him at home yet.

As soon as I had left the house, I had turned my phone on silent. It sat in my cup holder turned away from me.

Without looking at it, I knew there would be missed messages. I'd been gone for three hours.

With a shaky hand, I picked up my phone. Fifteen missed calls as well as ten texts. Most of the missed calls were Ashton and Cameron; a couple were from Angel. The texts started out from Ashton begging me to let him know I was safe.

Then came Cameron's texts, which started out with worry then turned to him being pissed.

Cameron: Dammit, Gracie, you better let me know your ass is safe! I'm freaking out here!

Me: I'm safe. I love you.

He replied instantly.

Cameron: Tell me where you are. I need to see for myself. I'll come alone if you don't want to see Ash right now.

My heart hurt thinking about Ashton worrying about me.

Me: I don't want to see anyone right now.

The next text told me that Ashton and Cameron were together.

Ashton: I'll be at home. Come over when you're ready to talk. I love you, bug.

The last text clinched my chest with absolute fear.

Hudson: You looked hot sitting there watching me from your car today as you followed me. I'll be coming for you soon. You'll never get me out of your life.

My skin crawled as my nausea grew. I knew he wasn't lying; I would never get Hudson out of my life. Perhaps

Ashton and I had moved too quickly. Coming to terms with the attack and taking control of these conflicting emotions may take longer than I originally thought.

Chapter Eighteen

Needing a quiet place to think, I checked into a hotel for the night. It didn't have all the comforts of home, but it was affordable and quiet. If I had gone back to the house, it would be inevitable that I'd run into either Angel or Mary Jane. It seemed selfish of me, but I had to see if I could do this on my own instead of relying on everyone else to brace me. My mom and I weren't close. We never had been, but if I called her, perhaps she'd let me stay with her for a while. She didn't know what had happened so I could use the excuse that I was taking the next semester off to consider my options. After the attack, I chose not to register for next semester so my grades weren't affected by my emotional healing.

My hands shook as I wrote a note to Cameron, letting him know that he was my world for so long and that none of this was his fault. I encouraged him to stay with Gavin as I'd never seen him happier. He was the best friend I'd ever had in life. I left messages in his letter to give to Angel and Mary Jane for me, explaining how they were like sisters to me and that I loved them dearly.

Cameron would be angry with me for a long time. It wouldn't be easy for him to understand why I did this, nor would it be easy for him to forgive me.

My comfort came knowing that Gavin would be there for him. The hardest part came when I had to say good-bye to Ashton. My mind drifted to this morning, the memory of our first time together. He'd been so gentle, so sweet to me. At least I could leave him with that memory. The memory made my skin tingle; I ached for him.

In his letter, my words pleaded with him to move on quickly, to not feel the pain he felt in losing Addy. He deserved to be happy; he deserved someone whole, not the broken shell of a person I had become. He didn't deserve what wrath Hudson might have in mind for the two of us.

I expressed how sorry I was to cause him any pain and that it was never my intention. My only intention was to give him the very best of me. I couldn't find anything good inside me anymore. I'd pretended for a while, and led myself to believe I could have it all. It was all lies. My hope was that our short time together would make it easier for him to move on. He'd had six years with Addy. We had barely a few months together.

Sealing the envelopes, I placed them by the bed before slipping under the covers.

I tried not to hate people because that was how I was raised. For the first time in my life, I could truly say I hated Hudson James. None of the amazing things Ashton had said to me could erase the negativity planted in my head by Hudson. No longer did I feel beautiful or special. Most days I could barely look in the mirror without cringing. His words cut so deep that they obliterated any chance I had to be truly happy.

Leaving wasn't what I wanted, but it seemed the only logical solution. Distancing myself from the town, the reminders around every corner, the chance of running into Hudson in person, could possibly save my sanity.

The sound of a text coming through caught me off guard.

It was after two in the morning.

Ash: Unable to sleep. Wherever you are, I wish I were there with you. I need you, Gracie-bug. You paint a portrait of happiness in my life like no one else can. Without you, paintings are just drawings. With you, they're masterpieces. You have my heart always. Don't shut me out.

Me: I love you, Ashton, with my whole heart.

I hoped that would be enough to make him feel better.

Ashton's text played over in my mind. As the words sank in, a barrier of sadness and despair was broken down, allowing me to feel happiness again. It felt as though someone else had been controlling my body, and they released it back to my control. I loved my life here and didn't want to let Hudson take anything else from me. Nashville was my home, and I wouldn't run away to let Hudson have it. I showered and dressed. Lacing up my tennis shoes, I took a deep breath to prepare to face Ashton.

As soon as I checked out of the hotel, I drove straight to Ashton's house. I didn't call as I didn't know what to say. I knocked on the door and it swung open quickly.

Bags darkened his eyes. With the hair along his jaw, and his disheveled hair, Ashton looked exhausted. Once he focused on me, his face lit up with relief. He closed his eyes and sighed. "Thank God, you're in one piece." He motioned for me to come in.

We sat on the couch. He kept his distance, but never took his eyes off me.

"First, you need to know you did nothing wrong. I was ready to make love to you and I don't regret any of that. In fact, it was the most amazing thing I've experienced and it's what has kept me going."

His face paled. "Where were you?"

I stopped him. "I planned to leave town until your text changed my mind."

Standing, he paced back and forth in front of me. He rubbed at his beard in silence. With his thumb and forefinger, he pinched the bridge of his nose as he choked out, "Tell me you meant for a short trip."

I pulled his letter from my purse and held it out to him. He opened it, realized what it was and collapsed into the closest chair. His head fell to his hands. He dropped the letter and looked up at me. I'd never seen someone so distraught.

"Are you all right, Ash?"

"Are you kidding me? You disappear yesterday without telling me where you're going. Then you come here and tell me that you were going to leave? I'm not all right, Gracie. Not at all."

Feeling guilty for hurting him, I moved toward him and reached out. Standing up he moved back from me for a change. His actions stung and gave me a sense of guilt over how often I'd done that to him. Though I knew he understood why I kept my distance, I knew it hurt him.

"How could you be so selfish?" he asked wounded.

"I didn't mean to hurt you, Ash."

He stepped closer. "Not just me. What about Cameron? He's called me every hour to see if I've heard from you."

His phone rang then as if on cue. He glanced at it. "It's been an hour exactly since he last called." Answering, he said, "She's here, Cam. She's safe. Yeah, you can come over. I think you *should* come over." He kept his eyes on me the entire time.

Cameron would be so mad when he found out about what I almost did. As selfish as my actions appeared, I knew they would understand once they had time to think it over.

"Have you eaten?"

I shook my head. "Not in two days."

He stalked away to the kitchen. I followed. "What are you doing?"

He grumbled, "Fixing you something to eat." He set out ham, cheese, and bread to make a sandwich. As he reached to open the bread, I laid my hand on his to stop him. When I touched him, he sucked in a breath. Waiting for me to speak, he remained silent and still.

"Ash, please. I promise I'll eat. I need something from you first."

Crossing his massive arms over his chest, he seemed unsure if he'd like my request.

"Hold me, please."

His arms dropped to his sides and his features softened. "Are you sure?" he asked as he stepped forward.

I nodded and held my arms out, needing him to feel close and wanting the comfort of his embrace.

Slowly walking over, he slid his arms around my waist and pulled me close. I tightened my arms around him. At the same time I tightened my hold, he sighed against my ear.

He kissed my hair and whispered, "Please don't ever leave me like that, Gracie." With his plea, I knew I'd made the right decision to stay. Ashton, Cameron, my friends, they were my sanity. If I walked away from them, I'd lose everything important to me.

I pulled back from him. "I'm so sorry." Pushing myself up on my tiptoes, my lips met his. He leaned down, softly moving his lips with mine. His hand moved up my back to press me against him. I slid my hands inside his shirt. He groaned, his lips vibrating against mine.

Incessant banging on the door interrupted us. He smiled.

No sight had ever made me happier than that smile.

"You better answer that."

I walked to the door, inhaled deeply and opened it, ready to face Cameron's tirade. He stood there, looking worse than Ashton did.

Cameron never went without shaving, nor did he leave the house in any sort of disarray. He stood in front of me with his hair a mess, stubble on his cheeks, wearing jeans and a baggy shirt.

He threw his arms around me, almost knocking me backwards. "I don't care if you don't want me touching you right now. I'm sorry. Baby girl, you *ever* do that to me again and I'll never forgive you."

Hugging me tighter, I felt his body shake. "Cameron?" He didn't speak. He just held me.

Letting go of me all of a sudden, he seemed distracted by something. He bent over and picked up a piece of paper off the floor. My stomach dropped as his eyes scanned Ashton's letter. He peered up at me and I averted my eyes in shame. Strong heaves of breath rose and fell in his chest.

Ashton put his hand on his shoulder and said, "She's safe now, Cameron. Remember that."

Plopping onto the couch, staring forward, Cameron's eyes were red. A single tear fell from each eye and it tore through me, causing an ache in my chest.

"Cameron, talk to me."

Cam faced straight forward. "You were going to leave me, Gracie? You're the most important person in my life. Did you think about me?"

I knelt in front of him, making eye contact. "Of course I did. I have a letter for you too."

Jaws tightening, his eyes narrowed. "You wrote me a damn letter? You thought about me enough to tell me how important I was to you, but didn't think leaving would matter?" I knew Cameron well enough to expect this reaction, but didn't realize the impact it would have on my heart. As he vented, I tried to stay calm and remind myself he would be fine in the end, but the guilt ate away at me.

"The only thing I thought about was the two of you. You're my family. I didn't want you to have to spend your life tiptoeing around me wondering when I would break down again. You both deserve better than that." I said, exasperated. Saying the words aloud made me wonder once more why I didn't stick to my plan of leaving.

Cameron's face paled. "I'd rather spend my life taking care of you than live without you!"

Ashton nodded. "I agree, a million times over." And their admissions of unconditional love brightened my hope once again.

Cameron moved next to Ashton. They both stood with their arms crossed.

"Are you two going to gang up on me now?"

Cameron yelled, "Gracie! I have grunge stubble. I'm wearing baggy clothes. My hair is a mess *and* I turned down sex to look for you! What does that tell you?"

He looked so serious it took me a moment. Then I let out a loud laugh accompanied by a snort. They remained staring at me as I bent over in laughter. I fell to the couch in hysterics. It would be okay. His response alone told me he forgave me. There was no doubt he'd make me work for it still, but it was Cameron. He knew me as well as I knew myself, sometimes better.

Cameron walked over. "Gracie, have you gone bat-shit crazy?"

I yanked on his neck pulling him down to me and we rolled off the couch onto the floor together.

His head lay against my chest as I hugged him to me. "I never want to leave you, Cameron."

The mood grew serious when he asked, "Tell me why you chose to stay."

I reached into my pocket for my cell phone. I opened it to show him the text from Ashton.

Cameron moved off me and we both glanced up at Ashton, who stood with tears in his eyes. Immediately, Cameron went to Ashton and hugged him. Actually, they hugged each other, and I heard them both sniffle.

"Thank you, Ash."

He pulled away, while both wiped at their eyes. Cameron glanced over at a mirror and scowled. "I should totally have my gay card taken away for being out in public like this! Can I shower and shave, maybe borrow some clothes that look better?"

Ashton laughed. "Yes, of course. I wouldn't want to jeopardize your gay card." While Cameron changed, Ashton disappeared for a moment, returning with my sandwich. "Eat this, please."

One bite made my stomach growl in hunger making

Ashton chuckle softly. "I'll get some chips and a Coke."

He turned to leave, grabbing something off the couch. I didn't see what it was, too lost in my sandwich. After a few more bites, he still wasn't back so I ventured into the kitchen.

On my way in, I asked something that had been on my mind, "What made you text me last night?" I stopped as I watched him reading the letter I wrote.

He glanced up from the letter. "You know, if this were just a letter you wrote me, it would be the best thing I'd ever read in my life. The fact that it is a good-bye letter kills me each time I even see it. You need to talk to someone, Gracie."

I nodded. "I know. I promise I will talk to you and Cameron from now on."

He placed his hands on my shoulders. "No, Gracie. You need to talk to a professional, a rape counselor or a therapist."

Cameron's voice sounded behind me, "He's right, Gracie. You're beyond what the two of us can do."

I turned and smiled when I saw his freshly shaven face. I ran my hand along his smooth cheek. "I love your face."

With an egotistical smirk, he said, "Everybody does." I threw my arms around his neck and he patted my back. "I'm going to give you two some alone time." He moved to the door and then turned back to me. "Can I have my letter?"

I pulled it from my purse. "If you're sure...?"

Reaching out, Cameron took the letter from my hand.

He heaved a sigh and said, "You listen to me, Gracie Walker. You ever contemplate leaving me again...." He choked up before he could finish his sentence. I didn't need him to say anything. Instead, I wrapped my arms around him and hugged tightly.

Kissing my head, he said, "I love you. Even when you're an asshat who wants to break my heart into a million pieces, I love you. So don't ever feel as though you're alone. Besides one amazingly hot best friend,"—he pointed at himself—"moi, you have that man over there, Prince Charming on a Harley, who was completely destroyed last night when he couldn't find you. If you'd seen how devastated he was... well, don't do that to either of us again... *ever*."

He grabbed my face with both hands, pulling me forward to kiss me. I glanced at Ashton, who leaned against the wall watching our exchange. He patted Cameron on the back. "Call me later, man."

Ashton walked him out. They were gone for a few minutes, and I could only imagine what they were saying. Peeking out the window, I saw the two of them hug.

Chapter Nineteen

This was one of the first times I'd really looked around Ashton's house. He had paintings on the wall and each one had his signature on them. On the table next to the couch was a picture of me from the day at the Frist Center. It was of me laughing. Though, I didn't remember him taking it.

On the fireplace mantel were more pictures of me. It was the series of pictures of me getting ready for the handstand on top of the concrete ball. It surprised me that all his pictures were of me or of us together. I guessed I expected there to be a shrine to Addy, but I couldn't find a single picture of her.

The next picture was on the coffee table. Ashton and I were making goofy faces at the camera with our heads pressed together. I laughed loudly.

Ashton came in at that moment. "I love that picture of us.

It's one of my favorites."

"Let's sit down, I need to tell you something," Ashton said solemnly.

I followed him to the couch and sat. He took my hand and held it. "You and I, Gracie, we're forever. I know that in my heart. If you're not ready for this, right now, I'll let you go, because I know we'll be back together soon. Don't shut me out completely though. If all we can be is friends, I'll accept that and I won't push. You mean too much to me. I don't want to live each day without you being a part of my life, in some way. I'll be the best friend you've ever had if that's all you want from me."

I squeezed his hand in mine. "No one has ever said anything that means more to me than that." After all we'd shared, I couldn't imagine going back to being just friends with Ashton. Just knowing he wanted to put my needs above all else showed me how incredibly strong his love was for me.

His face scrunched up in sadness, and he dropped his gaze from mine. I lifted his chin to face me; his eyes were glossy with tears.

"Being friends with you is amazing in itself, but it about destroyed my heart. I know what I want in life…. It's you, Ash. You're all I've ever wanted. I knew that before I met you." I was sure I wasn't making much sense, but I carried on, hoping he'd realize the significance of my words. "When I met you, I thought it was life's cruel joke. The perfect man, everything I ever wanted, who would never want me. Instead, it was fate making my dreams come true. Who am

I to argue with fate? With you, nothing seems impossible anymore. I'd be an idiot to turn away from you. I've been an idiot for too long, Ash. This is what I need, what I want, what I desire, more than anything else in life."

He exhaled. "Good, 'cause I'm not sure I could let you go."

I smiled and kissed him softly. "Me either." He leaned down and kissed the top of my head. "You look tired." I said to him.

He yawned. "Yeah, I haven't slept in two days. I'll be fine though. I want to spend time with you." Ashton put his arms around me, holding me close to him. Feeling responsible for his lack of sleep, I needed to make sure he rested now. It was my turn to put his needs first.

"We have all the time in the world, Ash. I'll lie down with you if you don't mind."

He chuckled. "I can't sleep anymore without you there."

Taking my hand, he led me to the bedroom. He turned his back to me and lifted his shirt off. Unable to resist, I placed my palms against his skin. His body relaxed at my touch. Trailing my fingers across his shoulder blades, I pressed my lips against his back as I moved my hands to the front of his chest.

"Gracie," he protested.

I shushed him. "I discovered that as long as I lead, I can stay calm."

My splayed fingers rested on his chest as I continued planting kisses on his back. He didn't move. I could feel his breathing increase. My palms glided down his front, caressing his skin. Wrapping my fingers around his belt, I unfastened it, unbuttoned his jeans, and slid his zipper down. Letting me have control, without pushing, was one of the many reasons I loved him.

I gazed at the reflection of him in the mirror to the right of us. His eyes were closed and his lips were turned up slightly. Lines of worry had left his face, replaced by a grin of contentment. It eased the heavy load of guilt from my shoulders. I slid his jeans down to the floor with steady hands. Kissing the back of his strong muscular calves, I then ran my hands up the front of his legs. When I stood again, my palms were resting on the front of his hips. In nothing but boxer briefs, he turned to face me. Instinctively, my lips moved to his chest while his fingers ran through my hair.

Our eyes met as I stood back from him and unbuttoned my blouse. Sucking in a breath, he bit his bottom lip, watching the shirt slide off my shoulders. Moving down to my jeans, I unfastened them as he watched me intently.

In just my underwear, I stepped closer to him, feeling the heat from his skin. His hands moved to my hips before he dipped down, his mouth inches from mine. "Are you sure?"

I breathed out, "Yes, please."

Ashton's lips met mine as his hands slid up my back. Unhooking my bra, he slid it off my arms. Closing my eyes, I enjoyed the slow graze of silk against my skin. Strong arms enveloped me, carrying me to the bed. Falling into a cloud of fresh cotton scent with a hint of Ashton's musk, I sighed. Gentle hands moved along my skin, creating a trail of warmth. As his fingers grabbed the waistband of my panties I arched my back aching for him. Sliding them off slowly, I whimpered as the cold air brushed against my core. Standing to remove his shorts, I relished the view of Ashton in all his glory. A sprinkling of hair across his chest, the light trail of hair below his belly button, the sexy curve of his ass as he turned to the side.

Ashton lay next to me, pressing his mouth against my cheek. "I'll stop anytime you want. Tell me if it's too much."

He moved his body over mine, propping himself up on his arms above me. There was no fear, no trepidation. My body didn't tense at his touch. This moment was full of bliss and nothing else. There was no pain this time. I leaned my head back as he dipped his mouth to taste my skin.

After hours of pleasure, we collapsed to the bed exhausted. Ashton curled up against my back. He pulled the blanket up over me, kissed my shoulder and said, "Goodnight, bug, I love you."

When I finally woke up, I realized we had slept for over ten hours. Ashton lay on his stomach beside me. The sheet draped low on his hips. He looked beautiful lying there so peacefully. Still sound asleep, he never stirred as I kissed his lower back.

Sliding out of bed, I slipped on his T-shirt. My stomach growled loudly, urging me to create a nice meal for the two of us.

In his kitchen, I found all the ingredients I needed to make lasagna. Once it was prepared and in the oven, I gathered the ingredients for a salad. Being carefree wasn't a familiar feeling lately. It was refreshing to think about proper seasoning and tasteful dishes rather than police reports and anxiety attacks.

I turned on the stereo on a low volume as I worked. While preparing the salad, I danced to John Mayer and snacked on cherry tomatoes. Using a wooden spoon as a microphone, I sang along, quietly performing for my nonexistent audience.

I couldn't wait for Ashton to wake up. Even though he was just in the other room, I missed him. The timer showed ten minutes left on the lasagna. I popped a few croutons in my mouth as I finished the salad.

Quietly sneaking into the bedroom, I checked on Ashton. The blanket had fallen down further, giving me a glimpse of his beautifully toned ass. Sitting next to him, the bed sank slightly. I ran my hands over his back, tracing the tattoo there. Unable to control myself, I bent down and lightly nipped the side of his hip.

His deep husky voice sounded muffled against the mattress as he said, "Did you just bite my ass?"

I giggled. "Um, maybe."

He rolled over, smiling. My leg was pulled up on the bed. His hand moved up my thigh, massaging his way up as he spoke. "Why are you out of bed?"

I gasped as he grabbed my waist and flipped me over, his body hovering over me. Hair sticking up in all directions, I ran my fingers through it to smooth it back. Ashton brought my wrist to his mouth, teeth nibbling at the sensitive skin.

Heart racing, heat rushed over me, and I gasped. "Why does that feel so good?"

He grinned. "Because I'm doing it and I am that awesome."

I burst out laughing. "You've been hanging around Cameron too much. He's rubbing off on you."

He rolled to lie next to me. "You give the best wake-up calls," he said with a smile.

I laughed again as his lips brushed against mine.

The oven beeping had him raising his eyebrow. "Are you cooking?"

I nodded and smiled. "I woke up starving. You looked so peaceful I didn't want to disturb you."

He breathed in deeply. "It smells delicious."

We went to the kitchen. I was about to open the stove when I glanced over at him and laughed.

"What?" he asked.

"You might want to put something on."

Glancing down, he realized he was completely naked. He laughed. "Oops, be right back."

Shaking my head in amusement, I slid on oven mitts to retrieve the lasagna from the stove. When he came out of the bedroom again, he was wearing shorts and a T-shirt.

"Wow, everything looks great." He kissed my cheek. "Especially you." Crimson filled my cheeks with heat from his compliment.

I motioned to the table. "Sit, I'll get our drinks and salads." He took a seat and I brought in a bottle of wine. Holding it up, I asked, "Is it okay to open this?"

He nodded. "Yeah, of course." We sat down to eat.

"Can I ask again, what made you text me last night?"

Ashton's face hardened. "I felt something... a pull in my chest. It felt a lot like the grief I felt when they told me Addy had died." He set his fork down and placed his hand on top of mine on the table. "I had been thinking of you nonstop. Something told me you may be in a place, mentally, where you felt alone. I wanted to remind you of my feelings for you. I wanted you to know that I was available if you needed me."

He stopped talking and shook his head. "Gracie, I've never been so happy for texting in my life."

I took a calming breath before I spoke, his words giving me courage. "I'm going to find a doctor to talk to. I don't want to go to that dark place again. This morning, our reunion, that's the life I want. I know that now. I want to wake up next to you each morning, and make love to you each night."

He grinned. "I like the sound of that life. So, when do you want to move in?"

I choked on my bite of food. "What?"

He reached for my hand. "I don't want to go to sleep another night without you. Move in with me?"

The truth was, I hadn't thought about anything other than staying with him. The last thing I wanted to do was go home and be away from him. The commitment of moving my things here had not occurred to me before, for some reason.

My phone kept me from answering.

"Hey, gorgeous."

"How are you this morning?" Cameron asked with concern in his voice as though he thought I might have changed my mind again.

"I'm fantastic." It was the most honest response I'd given in a long time about my feelings.

"Good. Now, did you make it up to Ashton in some proper way?" His voice filled with innuendo. I could imagine the obscene gesture he'd be making if he stood in front of me.

I burst out laughing. "Yes, Cameron, I made it up to him good and proper with some naked happy fun time."

Ashton snickered.

"Hold on a sec." I whispered to Ash, "Can I invite them over to eat?"

He nodded. "Of course."

Back on the phone, I said, "I made some lasagna if you and Gavin want to come over and eat."

"You know I never turn down food or hot men and that includes both. So we'll be there in a few. Love you, girl."

"Great, that sounds perfect. Love you, too."

I turned to Ashton. "Does it bother you the way I talk to Cameron? Or the fact that he kisses me on the lips?"

Ash's face scrunched up, confused. "No, of course not. He's your best friend and that's the way your relationship has always been. I'd never ask you to change that part of your life. Why would it bother me?"

I shrugged. "No reason."

He leaned over, checking me out under the table. "You might want to get dressed." Glancing down at my bare legs, I agreed with a sheepish grin.

He cleared the table while I put my jeans back on. I twisted my hair into a bun and stuck a pen in it. When I turned, Ashton was propped against the door watching me. His face was clean-shaven, except for the soft trace of beard that I loved so much on him. His lips turned up in a beautiful, gleaming white smile.

"Hello sexy," he said.

I smiled as I sauntered over to him. "Funny, I was thinking the same thing."

Chapter Twenty

Ashton answered the knock at the door while I grabbed the food. Boisterous voices resounded from the living room announcing Cameron's arrival. As I entered the living room, with hands full, three men rushed to help me. Southern gentlemen, there was nothing better. Ashton had warmed up a plate for Cameron and Gavin, so we sat down to chat while they ate.

It seemed as good a time as any to bring up a tough conversation. With Gavin here, he could help me rein in Ashton and Cameron if they freaked out a little. At a lull in the conversation, I announced, "Guys, there's sort of a bigger reason I asked you over here. I wanted Gavin here too since he is important to both of you. And he's becoming an important part of my life because of his connection to my two guys."

Cameron smiled at Gavin, squeezing his hand.

"I saw Hudson yesterday."

The moment the words left my mouth, Cameron and Ashton stood up, slamming their hands on the table yelling, "What?"

Gavin put his hand on each of their shoulders. "Calm down and let Gracie explain. The last thing she needs is to see you two so angry."

I mouthed "thanks" to him. He nodded and indicated for me to continue.

Cameron got in first though, mumbling, "Gracie Walker, I swear you're going to kill me one day."

Ashton remained quiet, patiently waiting for an explanation.

"It was an accident. I saw him at a café." I watched Ashton's fist clench harder with each sentence. "He wasn't alone. A man walked in and gave him a hug before sitting to talk with him."

Cameron exclaimed, "Well, we all know it wasn't his boyfriend. He's a freaking homophobe. So who was it?"

Gavin interjected again, "Will you let the woman finish, please?"

Cameron threw his hands up in mock surrender.

I replied, "I'm not sure who he was, but they looked pretty chummy."

I choked back tears. "There's more."

I pulled the text up on my phone and passed it to Ashton. Cameron leaned over to see what it was. Ashton clenched his fists tightly. With his teeth clamped together, he said,

"We need to go to the police station and report this, today."

"How will that help? They aren't going to believe me any more than they did when he beat me."

Ashton's face was red with anger. "We can use this text to get a restraining order or something against Hudson. He threatened you!"

I nodded. "After he stated that I was following him around town. He isn't stupid. He knew it would sound bad. He can spin the story to make it sound as though I followed him. It would add to his accusation that we were harassing him that day."

Ashton and Cameron both yelled, "Shit!" They seemed to be answering in unison a lot.

I pointed from one to the other and said, "You two have hung out too much lately." Neither of them laughed.

Ashton stood up and paced the room. He tugged on his earlobe alerting me he was deep in thought. Pressing his hands against the mantel of the fireplace, his back bent, he leaned his head down in defeat. Cameron nodded toward Ashton and whispered, "Go to him."

Silently striding across the room, I offered the only comfort I could at the moment. Ashton sighed as I wrapped my arms around him, resting my head against his back. He placed his hand over mine. "My ladybug." He moved to face me and kissed my hair. "We'll get through this, together, somehow." Though I knew neither of us had answers, I believed him.

"I need a few moments to talk to Cameron, if you don't mind?" Ashton requested.

"Of course. Gavin can keep me company," I assured him.

Cameron and Ashton stepped outside, leaving Gavin and me to clean up. "Ashton is pretty crazy about you, you know?" Gavin said, taking a dirty dish from me to load the dishwasher.

I smiled. "I'm pretty crazy about him, too. How long have you two been friends?"

Gavin turned the water on in the sink to rinse some of the dishes off first. "We met in high school."

"That's right. He told me that once. So, you knew Addison then?"

He stopped and glanced at me a little confused. "Ashton didn't tell you that?"

I shrugged. "All I know is how they met and how she died." His face became grief-stricken. "I'm sorry, Gavin. Were you good friends with her too?"

His eyes glistened with fresh tears ready to spill. He turned away before he spoke. "Addison was my sister."

The plate in my hand dropped to the floor shattering into several pieces. I gasped. "I'm so sorry."

He grabbed a broom to help me sweep it up. "Sweetie, you're fine. You didn't know." It seemed odd Ashton would leave out an important detail such as this one. If I'd known Addy was his sister, I'd have brought the topic up in a gentler way.

We dumped the broken plate in the trash.

Leaning against the counter with his arms folded across his chest, he explained, "Addison started dating Ashton junior year. I was a sophomore. The year they became seniors was the year I came out to my parents. They went crazy, spouting off religious mumbo jumbo about going straight to hell, etc. Addison protected me. She was worried that Ashton would react the same as my parents. The next day, she prepared to break up with him. She told him about me and how my parents had reacted, expecting that he would end things with her over it. He asked if he could talk to me about it, instead. My dad had never met Ashton. When he saw us together, he flipped.

"He ran at me, calling us both abominations. Ashton shoved him away from me and told him that he should be ashamed of himself. Ashton told him that it was his job as a father to love me, unconditionally. My father threw me out, told me to never come back. Ashton's family welcomed me with open arms. They are my family now. He was the best thing that ever happened to Addison."

I smiled, adding, "And vice versa."

Gavin patted my arm. "No, you're the best thing that ever happened to Ashton. You're his saving grace."

We both snickered.

"Sorry, no pun intended. What I mean is, Ashton was destroyed after Addy died. I didn't think he'd ever find anyone to fill that void. Then he met you. He has talked about you nonstop ever since."

Feeling self-conscious, I wrapped my arms across myself. "Really? And it doesn't bother you to see him with me? As though it's offensive to her memory or something?"

His brows lifted in surprise. "What? No, of course not. You and Addison would have been great friends if she were still here. She'd love knowing that you're making Ashton happy now." Somehow knowing Addy would approve of me relieved some of the tightness in my chest. I wrapped my arms around his neck and he squeezed me tightly.

Cameron voiced from behind me, "Get your hands off my man!"

I turned to him, leaving my arm around Gavin. "This man is fan-fucking-tastic." I kissed Gavin's cheek. Turning back to Cameron, I narrowed my eyes and pointed a finger in his face. "Don't screw it up."

His lips turned up in the most genuine of smiles. "Never."

Ashton came in the kitchen, his eyes immediately landing on the broken plate in the trash. "Everything all right?"

I nodded. "Yep, Gavin just shocked me when he told me he's Addison's brother."

Cameron was confused. "Who's Addison?"

Gavin replied as Ashton looked at me sadly. "My sister. She passed away a few years ago."

Cameron was still confused. "I'm sorry, sweetie. I remember you mentioning your sister briefly before. What I don't understand is why is it so shocking to Gracie that you're her brother?"

Ashton walked over, lifted my hand and said, "I wasn't keeping it from you. We just haven't talked about her much."

I kissed his lips softly. "I'm not mad, just surprised."

Ashton glanced at Gavin. "How did it come up?"

Gavin responded, "Gracie wanted to know how we met.

I told her what you did for me."

Smiling up at Ashton, I added, "Makes me love you even more." His face softened from worry into a smile.

Cameron whistled. "Um, hello! Can someone fill me in on why we love Ashton even more?"

Gavin pulled him aside to tell him. While we had a moment alone, Ashton stepped in front of me and pressed me against the sink. His hand stroked my cheek as he lowered his mouth to mine. His soft lips glided against mine as his beard tickled my face. I giggled.

Smiling, he pulled away. "What are you giggling about?"

I ran my fingers over his beard. "It tickles my cheeks."

He grinned. "You sure you don't want me to shave it for you?"

My mouth fell open. "I'm positive. I love it." As we were about to resume kissing, we were interrupted.

Cameron stepped back in the kitchen raising his hands defensively. "I don't want to know what you want to shave for her. Sculpt it, brush it, trim it, shave it, hell, tattoo a lawn mower on it and die it green with a sign that says 'Keep off the grass,' just don't tell me about it. I wanted to thank you guys for dinner. We're heading home. Ash, we'll talk?"

Ashton nodded. "I'll walk you guys out."

I burst out laughing. "Keep off the grass, Cam?"

He shrugged. "You laugh, but I've seen it done." Cameron faked a shiver as if creeped out.

While Ashton walked the guys out, I had an idea. I wrote a note stating to meet me downstairs. I ran to the bedroom and slipped off everything but my panties. I slid on a button-down shirt of Ashton's, leaving the top few buttons open.

I ran down the steps. Leaning forward, I shook my hair out, giving it that sexy messy look. Boosting myself up onto the pool table, sitting on the edge with my legs crossed, I leaned back and waited for him. The door opened. I fixed my shirt to show a little cleavage and a whole lot of leg. "Gracie?"

I smiled and said, "Down here, Ash."

His feet came into view and I prepared to seduce him, leaning forward so that he could see straight down my shirt. Ashton stopped when he saw me. "Wow. Um...." He glanced up the stairs, and then I saw a man peer down at me.

I sat and covered up quickly. "Hi?" Ashton pushed him back up the stairs. He came down a few minutes later with pants for me. "I'm mortified. Who is that?"

He smiled. "My little brother has perfect timing as always. Baby, I want you back here after he leaves. You have no idea how many fantasies I've had of you on this pool table, especially since that night we played pool together."

I smiled. "Probably as many as I've had."

He grabbed my collar and pulled me in for a kiss that made my body ache for him. His hands were on my naked thighs as I wrapped my legs around his waist, tugging him closer. His arousal pressed against me, causing me to whimper against his mouth.

My hands tugged at his belt, but he stopped me.

He groaned. "Damn it, Derrick. Why did you show up now?" He moved away and tossed my jeans to me.

I smiled. "You sure we can't have a quickie?"

He grinned. "Don't tempt me."

Once I was wearing pants again, I followed Ashton up the stairs. I kept his shirt on and just tied it in the front to keep it from being so long on me. Derrick sat on the couch, playing on his phone. He stood up when he saw me enter behind Ashton.

He held his hand out. "You must be Gracie. I'm Derrick."

I took his hand, shaking it firmly. "I'm so sorry about what happened downstairs." Derrick grinned, looking exactly like Ashton when he did. "It's not the worst thing I've ever walked into. Actually, it wasn't bad at all." He winked at me.

Ashton's palm landed on Derrick's chest. "Watch it, kid."

Derrick laughed. "Not trying to offend you, Gracie. I like giving my brother here a hard time."

Derrick was very attractive. Of course he was; he looked like Ashton. His hair was longer than Ashton's, and his face was clean-shaven. He was slightly shorter, same build though, which was rock-hard sexy goodness, at least from what I could tell.

"I've heard a lot of great things about you, Gracie. This guy hasn't shut up about you."

Ashton spoke next, saving me from having to lie and tell him I've heard tons about him. "What brings you by, Derrick?" I took a seat on the couch and Ashton sat next to me.

"Katelyn's birthday is this weekend. She asked me to deliver this personally."

He handed Ashton an invitation that had a giant four on the front. Ashton took my hand. "Gracie, Katelyn is my niece. She is the other special woman in my life."

I nodded. "I remember, you mentioned her before."

He turned to Derrick. "You tell my Katie that I'll be there. You don't mind if I bring Gracie, right?"

Derrick grinned. "No, not at all. Gracie, you like kids?"

I nodded. "Yeah, of course."

Anxiety crept in trying to take over my emotional state. Unsure if it was meeting someone new or the idea of a party that stirred up my nerves but it felt as though the room was closing in on me. Ashton and Derrick were talking, but their voices sounded muffled in my head.

I stood up abruptly. "I don't feel so good. I'm going to go lie down."

Ashton stood up with me. He put his hand on my shoulder, causing me to flinch slightly. "You all right, bug?"

"Just tired. You two visit. It was nice meeting you, Derrick. I'll see you at the party."

Derrick nodded. "I hope you feel better." I smiled as I passed by him, keeping my distance.

When I got to the bedroom, I closed the door behind me. My phone rang. It was an unlisted number, which probably meant it was a telemarketer. I'd had a lot of unlisted calls lately so I decided to answer it and find out.

"Hello?"

There was silence for a moment, then I heard, "Baby,

have you missed me?"

Hudson's voice sounded taunting. I sat straight up in the bed, feeling instantly sick to my stomach.

"I miss that sexy body of yours, having my hands all over it. I miss the way your skin tastes."

I was frozen, unable to move or speak.

"I want to come see you. Put on something sexy for me, and I'll be at your house within the hour." He hung up. Tears ran down my face; I held my breath in agony.

Once I was able to breathe again, I screamed for Ashton. He burst into the room with Derrick behind him. Derrick looked around frantically as Ashton ran to my side.

Derrick asked, "What happened? Is she hurt?"

Ashton sat beside me on the bed. He spoke softly to me, "Gracie, what happened?"

I gasped for air. The words wouldn't form for me to explain what was happening. "Angel...."

Ashton responded, "Did Angel call you?"

I shook my head. "MJ... my house...."

Derrick called out to Ashton, "What's wrong with her?"

Ashton shushed him. "I'm trying to find out." He turned back to me. "Baby, tell me what happened."

I handed him my phone. He looked and saw that the call had ended. He looked at the number.

"It shows an unlisted number. Who was it?" he asked, being more patient than I would have been.

I croaked out, "Hudson."

Ashton jumped up. "What?"

Derrick moved toward Ashton. "Who's Hudson?"

Ashton knelt in front of me. "Tell me what he said."

I reached for his shoulders and pressed into them with so much force, my fingertips were white. "He said he's coming to see me at my house. He wants... he wants to..." I gasped for air. "...touch me."

Ashton stood up quickly turning to Derrick. "Call 911. Have them send an officer to her house, now. Here's my phone. Her address is in it."

Derrick was still confused. "Tell me again why I'm sending the police to her house?"

Ashton turned angrily. "Because the man who raped her and beat her to a pulp is headed there now."

Derrick's eyes moved to mine and I saw the sadness envelope him. "Oh, God. I... I'm sorry."

Ashton shoved him. "Go call now!"

Ashton reached toward me; I flinched before he made contact. "I'm sorry, Ashton. I didn't mean to jump. You can touch me."

Ashton moved his arms around me, and I held on for dear life. He smoothed my hair. "Calm down, baby. Breathe. I won't let him hurt you."

I panicked. "Call Angel and MJ. Make them get out of the house."

Ashton called and was able to reach Angel who said Mary Jane wasn't home. She told Ashton that she was leaving right then and would go to Cameron's. "I'm going to go to your house."

Before he could finish, I screamed, "No! Please, I can't lose you."

Ashton embraced me again. "Gracie, calm down. You won't lose me. I need to go to your house to meet the police and fill them in. I'm taking you to Cam's. You'll be safe there."

I cried, "Please let me go with you," as I clawed at him, pulling him closer.

It panicked me to think about sitting at Cameron's house worrying about if he was safe or if I'd have to see him in a hospital bed next. I knew Ashton could take care of himself, but I didn't trust Hudson to not play dirty.

Chapter Twenty-One

Reluctantly, he let me go with him. When we arrived at the house, the police were not there, nor was Hudson's car.

Ashton pulled over. From the moment I stepped off the bike, Ashton held my hand tightly. He had his phone ready. He made a call and stated angrily, "Yeah, we called and reported that we needed a police officer and there's no one here."

I'd never heard him raise his voice or be rude to anyone before.

I saw Mary Jane's car in the driveway, and my stomach clenched. I broke free of Ashton's grasp and ran to the door, fumbling with my keys.

He caught up and took them from me. "Gracie, you're not going in there!"

"Mary Jane is here. He could have been here already

and hurt her!"

I moved inside and immediately found Mary Jane sitting on the bottom of the stairs. Her face was a mask of fury.

"You're okay." A relieved breath rushed out of me. "Thank god."

"He was here. He's such a dick. Tried sweet-talking me into the house, but I threatened him with a phone call to the police and he hightailed it out of here."

I sat next to Mary Jane and hugged her, happy she was safe and Hudson had left quietly. I didn't know what that actually meant though. He wasn't one to make idle threats.

Standing in the doorway, Ashton's gaze roamed to the two of us. Relief washed over his features. "Everything okay here?"

I nodded. I didn't like the games Hudson was playing, but I'd take the breaks where I could get them. Ashton called the police to let them know the threat was over. He asked me to consider filing a restraining order against Hudson in case there was a next time. Since he wasn't being held accountable for his actions so far, I wasn't sure it would do any good, but I promised I'd consider it.

"Gracie?" Ashton asked as we pulled into the driveway of his house.

"Hmm?" I replied. "

"You ready to go in?"

I nodded.

He led the way. Once inside, I wanted some time alone

to think. Emotionally drained from the panic of Hudson's threat, my mind buzzed. "I'm a little tired. Do you mind if I lie down?"

"Sure, bug. Do you want me to come with you?"

I thought about it for a second. "No. I mean, I do. Right now, I need a little time alone. I have a bit of a headache after everything today."

He nodded in understanding, though his face displayed the rejection he felt.

"Tuck me in?" I asked with a smile.

He followed me to the bedroom. I removed my jeans and untied Ash's shirt that I was wearing. He came up behind me and kissed my neck, sliding his arms around my waist and placing his chin on my shoulder.

"I love you, bug."

Reaching up to caress his face gently, he sighed at my touch. His mouth met mine with a soft caress while his tongue slid into my welcoming mouth. Gentle hands moved to my waist, lifting me off the ground. Placing me on the bed, he reached for the blanket to cover me. With a seductive half grin, he promised, "We'll pick that up later." I fell asleep shortly after he closed the door.

Chapter Twenty-Two

When I woke up, my head was feeling better. After throwing on a T-shirt and shorts, I padded against the hardwood floor as I walked to the living room to check for Ashton. Cameron sat on the couch. When his eyes landed on me, he snickered and pointed. "Nice bed head."

I reached up to smooth my hair down. "Where's Ash?"

He acted offended. "Nice to see you too, sunshine."

I rolled my eyes. "You know I'm always glad to see you. Would you like something to eat?"

With an Old English accent, he stated, "Yes, fair maiden, fetch me food!"

I turned away from him. "Wanna guess how many fingers I'm holding up?" I strolled to the kitchen, whistling.

Cameron followed like a lost puppy. I turned almost bumping into him. "Personal space, man."

He stepped back from me, "Sorry. What are we going to make?"

I opened the fridge. "Hmm. Eggs, bacon and French toast... how does that sound?"

His stomach growled in response. He pointed to his stomach. "Little Cam says that sounds delish."

I cocked an eyebrow at him. "So that's what you call Little Cam?"

He stuck his hand on his hip and said, "Yep, 'cause ain't nothing else little." I snorted with laughter.

"Seriously, where is Ash?" I asked again.

"He said he had to run an errand and asked if I'd sit with you until he got back."

I wrapped my arms around Cameron. He squeezed me close and kissed my head. "Wanna go downstairs and watch a movie?"

He shrugged. "Sure, why not. Let's bypass breakfast and make snacks." We loaded our arms with snacks and drinks, and then headed to the basement.

In the middle of the movie, Cameron tossed a handful of popcorn at me. My mouth fell open in shock.

"You are so in for it."

I grabbed a handful and threw it back at him, hitting him directly in the face. He spat out the popcorn that landed in his mouth. He tackled me on the couch tickling me.

I screamed, "Uncle."

We were laughing so hard that we almost missed the phone ringing. I felt a pang of dread wash over me. I glanced at the number; it was unknown. "It's unknown,

Cameron. That's what it said when Hudson called."

He took the phone from me, answering it gruffly. "Who is this?" he demanded. "Oh. Yes, she's right here." He held the phone out to me. "It's the police station."

I took the phone from him. "Hello. Yes, this is Gracie Walker."

"Ms. Walker, I was asked to contact you by an Ashton Collins. He's been in an accident."

"I'm sorry, can you repeat that?" Panic filled my tone.

"Mr. Collins was in a motor vehicle accident," the police officer reiterated.

I immediately started trembling, my voice becoming higher with each word. "Is he okay?" Cameron's face paled with worry, and I closed my eyes.

"As a precaution he was taken to the emergency room. I can tell you he was conscious and aware of his surroundings since he asked me to call you. Is there someone else I should call or can you meet him there?"

"I'm heading there now. Thank you."

As soon as I hung up, Cameron burst out, "What happened?"

I grabbed his hand leading him upstairs as I said, "Ash wrecked his bike."

Cameron tugged on my arm. "Slow down, Gracie. You're shaking like a leaf."

I shook my head, my mind going at full speed. "He needs me. We have to get there."

Cameron grabbed my face. "Stop. You'll do him no good like this. Calm down. I'm driving." He pulled his phone out and began to text.

"What are you doing?" Gradually becoming impatient I snapped a little harder than intended.

He sighed. "Telling Gavin to meet us at the hospital. Ash is his family you know."

I hugged him. "I'm sorry. I'm just freaked."

He nodded. "I know, Gracie."

When we arrived at the hospital, Cameron went to the information desk. He came back angry. "What's the matter?"

He scoffed, "They won't give us any information because we aren't family."

I whimpered, "I'm his girlfriend."

He nodded. "I told them that. They said it would only count if you were married or listed in his chart as acceptable to give personal information to."

I pushed him aside and went to the desk. I remained as calm as I could. "Please help us. My boyfriend doesn't have any...." Then it dawned on me, Derrick. "Oh, my gosh." I turned to Cameron. "We need to call Derrick." Cameron gave Gavin a quick call to get Derrick's number for me.

Derrick answered. "Hello?"

"Derrick, it's Gracie."

His voice became panicked. "What's wrong? Is everything okay?"

My voice choked so Cameron took the phone. Derrick told Cameron he would call to get Ashton's condition for us and that he would be up as soon as he found someone to watch Katelyn.

Gavin walked through the lobby doors as Cameron hung up. He bypassed Cameron and wrapped his arms around me. Immediately, I sobbed against his chest. Gavin pulled away and wiped my face with a tissue. "How is he?" he asked.

I pointed at the desk. "They won't tell me any more than they did on the phone because I'm not family."

His jaw clenched. "The hell you aren't. Come on."

He tugged me to the desk with him. "I have all Ashton Collins' information to prove I am family. I'm his brother. You should find my name on his PHI release as well."

He proceeded to give her Ashton's social security number and birth date, to which she was satisfied enough to tell us he was in with the doctor. Gavin wrapped his arm around me and led me to a chair. He pulled me close as he rocked me.

"What's PHI?"

He kissed my forehead. "Protected health information. You have to sign a release and name anyone allowed to know your medical information. Ashton, Derrick and I all have each other listed for emergencies, like this one."

Cameron sat beside us, holding my hand. Occasionally giving my hand a comforting squeeze, he calmed my nerves as I waited for news. My phone rang; he answered and handed it to me. "Hey, Derrick. Gavin's here and was able to get an update on Ash for us."

Derrick replied, "That's good. Gracie, will you keep

me posted on how he's doing? I can't find a babysitter. Dammit, I want to be there right now. I can't bring Katelyn up there and scare her."

I had an idea. "Let me call my friend Mary Jane. She's great with kids. As long as you're okay with that?"

Derrick responded, relieved, "Any friend of yours, Gracie."

When I explained everything to Mary Jane, she was happy to help. She agreed to meet Derrick at a park, near the hospital, so Katelyn wouldn't know where he was going.

Cameron told me he'd watch for Derrick. "Just describe him for me."

I sniffed. "Ash with shaggy hair, clean shaven and a few inches shorter."

Cameron tsked. "What a gene pool."

About an hour later, Cameron walked in with Derrick. I greeted him with a hug. It made me ache for Ashton. My arms tightened around him as I tried to hold back the tears.

He patted my hair. "Bad time for me to resemble him I guess."

I smiled sadly as his words rang true while Derrick embraced Gavin before taking a seat. Before Gavin could sit again, the nurse called out to him to inform us Ashton was in radiology and should be out shortly.

Cameron and Gavin offered to get us all some coffee, but before he left he transferred my hand to Derrick's. "Keep her calm, please." Derrick agreed to Cameron's request with no hesitation.

"Talk about something to get my mind off things, please," I begged. "Did Katelyn do well with MJ?"

He replied, "I was pretty shocked when I saw Mary Jane. That friend of yours, she's..."

As he was speaking, I thought he was going to make a comment about her weight and I was going to have to kick his ass.

He finished with, "...beautiful and so sweet. Katelyn took to her right away, which is unusual for her with strangers." I smiled at the realization that he was just like his brother in personality too.

"Where's Katelyn's mom?" He shifted uncomfortably in his chair. "I'm sorry, that was rude to ask. This is the second time you've met me and I have no right to ask such a personal thing."

He waved it off. "No, it wasn't rude. We're practically family now. It was a logical question. We had Katie very young, and she wasn't ready. I wasn't either, but she's my kid. I couldn't turn my back on her. Her mother didn't feel that way though. I had to beg her to have Katie and then pay her to let me have total custody. Since I was going through all the trouble, I had her sign away all rights. She's never even seen her. Didn't even hold her at the hospital."

I sighed. "Good grief. Is your family full of amazing guys like you and Ash? It has to be in the genes."

Derrick chuckled softly. "Nothing spectacular about taking responsibility for your actions."

I patted his hand. "Yeah, there is. Are you seeing anyone?"

He shook his head. "Been on a few dates, nothing special, why?"

I replied, "How about when Ashton's better, I set you and Mary Jane up?"

He smiled. "She's single? Awesome. Yeah, that'd be great." Mary Jane's luck with men had been no better than mine. If Derrick was anything like Ashton, I knew he would be great for her.

After three hours in the emergency waiting room, the nurse finally called me up to let me know I could go back and sit with Ashton if I wanted. In fact, he'd been asking them to allow it because he knew how worried I'd be. "He has been pleading with every nurse to bring you back. He's been more worried about you then he has himself. You're a lucky girl," the nurse said as she led me through the double doors. "Go straight down the hall and make a left. He should be sitting around the corner when you get there."

Chapter Twenty-Three

As I walked the long hallway to where Ashton waited, I prepared myself for whatever he may look like. My hands went straight to my face, covering my mouth, and I gasped when I saw him. His muscular arms were both littered with scrapes and bruises. The handsome face that I couldn't get enough of was covered in abrasions and his right cheek was swollen. Gently I embraced him. "Anything broken?"

"Nope, just a few bumps and bruises and a sore leg from the concrete attacking me back when I hit it."

Carefully, I palmed his face as I studied his injuries. I leaned in close and kissed his cheek cautiously. I reached for his hand, stroking it with my thumb. "Thank goodness it wasn't more serious."

"No worries, sweetheart. I'm fine. The doctor gave me the all clear and I'm ready to go home."

When we approached the waiting room, the guys stood up. Once everyone knew Ashton was released, Derrick asked for a moment alone with him.

Cameron put his arm around me. "There's something you should know, babe."

I faced him. "What?"

Cameron grimaced. "This wasn't an accident. Apparently, someone literally ran him off the road, on purpose."

"How do you know that?"

He jerked his head to the side to an older woman in the corner. "That woman was a witness. She's here because she was run off the road too, and her husband is being checked out. She said there was a car behind Ash's bike that sped up and clipped his back tire to send him spinning off the road. She told the cops she thought it was a road rage incident. I think it was something else."

I covered my mouth with my hands. "Who would do that?" I asked the question and realized the answer at the same time. "Hudson?"

Cameron shrugged. "That'd be my guess."

Ashton returned then and held his hand out to me. I leaned forward touching his lips with mine, very gently. He put his hand behind my neck and pulled me in for a deeper kiss.

I chuckled, pulling back from him. "Easy there, tiger."

He grinned. "I missed you."

I smiled. "You're on some good drugs, aren't you?" He smiled and nodded.

"I wanted to see your beautiful face." His palm glided along my cheek over and over, as though he was petting me.

The doctor called out to Ashton, "Mr. Collins, here is the prescription to help with the pain. There are a few precautions I want to go over with you before you leave."

I kissed his hand. "I'm going to check on Derrick."

Derrick met me halfway down the hall. "Hey, I was coming to say good-bye to Ashton. I'm going to meet Mary Jane to get Katelyn home. She's down the road about a mile. "

"Maybe we could both go with you? Cameron left me his car and got a ride home with Gavin."

Derrick thought about it a moment. "I think it'd be all right, since he doesn't look too rough."

After Ashton finished with the doctor, we followed Derrick to pick up Katelyn. She and Mary Jane seemed to be getting along great. Katelyn sat at the picnic table rambling on about something while Mary Jane braided her hair as she listened intently.

Katelyn was a beautiful little girl with starry blue eyes and long dark hair, both the same shade as her father's. I walked over to meet her.

Kneeling down to her level, I held my hand out and said, "Katelyn, I'm Gracie. I'm a friend of your Uncle Ash's."

She smiled and held her arms out for a hug. I wrapped my arms around her. For a little girl, she had a strong embrace. It was easy to see why Mary Jane couldn't stop smiling around her.

Katelyn grinned. "You're Uncle Ash's girlfriend."

I smiled. "Yes, I am. And you're beautiful."

She grinned. "Thank you."

I lifted Katelyn on my hip and carried her to see Ashton, who waited for us in the car.

He looked up and grinned widely. "My two favorite girls." Easing out of the car he cringed a bit as the discomfort hit him.

Katelyn's face dropped. She turned her head, resting it on my shoulder. "What's the matter, sweetie?"

Her arms held my neck tightly as she whispered, "Is he okay?"

I patted her hair. "He's fine. He's a bit sore, but he's just fine."

"Hey, Boo, it's going to take more than a motorcycle to take down your Uncle Ash, ya know."

He tickled her and she giggled. She reached out for Ashton and he took her in his arms.

He whispered, "Be easy on the love. Gracie gets jealous." She giggled again.

She threw her arms around his neck and he winced in pain. I reached to pull her off him, but he waved his hand to tell me it was fine.

He rubbed Katelyn's back with his good arm—the right one was worse from scraping the road—as he smiled at whatever she was telling him. He was great with her. I could tell she meant the world to him. Every now and then, Ashton flinched when Katelyn hit a sore spot. He refused to let her see it though, or complain.

Derrick came over a few minutes later. Concerned, he said, "Katie, you need to be careful—"

Ashton held his hand up to stop him. Derrick quieted the same as I had.

Katelyn sat up and looked at Ashton. "Did I hurt you?" She sounded so worried at the thought.

Ashton smiled. "No way, Boo. You always make me feel better." She giggled and kissed his cheek.

Derrick lifted her from Ashton's arms. "We need to get home and grab some dinner." Ashton glanced at Mary Jane, who stood next to me quietly.

"Hi, MJ. Come on over, sweetheart," Ashton said.

She smiled timidly and walked to him. "I'm glad you're okay."

He smiled. "Thanks."

Katelyn beamed up at Mary Jane. "She played at the park with me today. Mary Jane's my friend."

Ashton smiled. "Wow, you don't usually make friends so quickly, Boo. Mary Jane is pretty special though. She's my friend too."

"I like her," Katelyn admitted with a shy smile.

Derrick stared at Mary Jane, his eyes dancing with admiration, a soft grin lifting his cheeks.

Ashton noticed and said, "You're not the only one it seems."

With subtlety, Derrick reached back and flicked Ashton's arm. Ashton chuckled at Derrick's blushing cheeks.

"I want Mary Jane to come to my birthday party."

Derrick's eyes met with Mary Jane's. Blushing, she said,

"I'd love to if your dad doesn't mind." Each look they exchanged made the glimmer of hope brighter for a love connection. It was adorable watching them behave like school children who were afraid to let the other know they liked them.

Derrick spoke up before she finished her sentence, "Yes. Of course." Throwing a wink at Ashton, I tried to hide the goofy grin coming on and hold back my giddy cheer of excitement for Mary Jane.

He turned back to Ashton. "I need to get Katelyn something to eat so we're going to head home. You need to get some rest."

When he turned back, he looked at Mary Jane and said, "I'd love to treat you to a bite to eat as a thank you for earlier. If you're not busy?"

Mary Jane grinned. "That'd be great. I'm free."

She gave me a hug and I whispered, "He told me he thinks you're beautiful and sweet. Go get him, girl."

Mary Jane gasped and whispered, "Really?" I pulled away and nodded. She mouthed, "Do I look all right?"

I laughed. "Gorgeous. Go, have fun." Ashton eased back into the passenger side and closed the door. Waving good-bye, we drove off in different directions.

"Do we need to stop at the pharmacy, or did the doctor give you something for later?"

Ashton smiled at me. "You're the only medicine I need, you know?"

"I think Katelyn was your cure. She adores you," I said.

He smiled lovingly. "She's an angel. I love that kid. I

thought my brother was crazy when he decided to take on that responsibility when he was just a kid himself. He was only sixteen. One look at that sweet face though, and I couldn't blame him."

"You're more amazing all the time."

He grinned knowingly. "You're pretty amazing yourself. So, did you set up Mary Jane and Derrick?"

I shook my head. "Not really. I offered her up to watch Katelyn. While we were waiting for you, Derrick told me he thought she was beautiful and sweet. I told him I'd hook them up when you were well again. I guess he took matters into his own hands tonight. I hope they hit it off. I think they'd be cute together."

Chapter Twenty-Four

Cameron knocked as he walked into the house. "Hey, I came to check on Ash. Is he up for visitors?"

Placing my finger to my lips, I whispered, "He's asleep on the couch. His entire right side is sore so it helps to keep him from rolling onto it. You're welcome to hang out with me a little while though. We've been home long enough for me to get him settled in. He took a shower to get some of the gravel and dirt off him and we changed his dressings. I was about to go upstairs, change, and relax with a movie."

"Sounds like a good plan."

Cameron followed me up to my bedroom. "Can I get on your computer?"

As I changed into more comfortable clothes, I said, "Uh huh." I slipped into a T-shirt and curled up under my down comforter.

Cameron sat down at the computer to play games. He knew I couldn't rest lately without someone nearby.

I heard him mutter, "What is this?" Then he turned to me and said, "Gracie, you FREAK! Is that Ash's bedroom?"

I sat up to see what he was laughing about.

There was a screen open on the desktop that showed a view of a bedroom with a smaller box that showed a view of the back of Cameron's head currently.

"What is that?"

He smirked. "As if you didn't know, you harlot! You need to turn the webcam off once in a while, so it doesn't make your computer run so slow. How often do you and Ashton have webcam sex? Girl you're giving me a run for my freak of the year award!"

I walked over to look closer. "Cam, I've never used the webcam in my life...." I peered closer and froze. "If that's on, that means the person over there can see me? Anytime they want?"

He nodded. "Basically, if you have it on. It was minimized on the desktop but it's still on."

I freaked out loudly. "Turn it off!"

His face paled. "What is up with you?"

I pointed at the screen. "That's Hudson's room!" Cameron turned back to look and immediately closed the program. "Is there any way to tell how long that has been active?"

Cameron began fiddling with the computer again. He went into properties for the webcam and found that the last access date had been months ago. "I don't understand.

He's never been in my room." In the few months we dated, it always seemed easier to spend the night at Hudson's since he didn't have roommates. The few times he'd been at my house, he'd stayed downstairs with my friends or waiting while I grabbed something from my room.

Cameron seemed deep in thought. Suddenly, he smacked his head. "That night that we played cards. You were on the porch with Ashton. Hudson went upstairs to use the bathroom."

My chest tightened. My lungs constricted when I couldn't find the air I needed to breathe.

"That was ages ago, Cam!" I paced the room, my arms crossed over my chest.

Cameron continued to fiddle with the computer. "That son of a bitch has probably been taping you. Dammit. That's probably why he went after Ash. He may have seen you two on this recently and realized he isn't gay. Probably assumed you were playing him this entire time."

Cameron left after making sure I had calmed down. Placing a pillow in the recliner, I curled up in a blanket and sat in the chair watching Ashton sleep. The idea of Hudson watching me on the webcam made me never want to go back upstairs again. I wanted to burn my computer as assurance that it wasn't still on.

How could I have been with Hudson for so long and not known what a sick person he was? My mind went over the past few months and everything he might have seen, all the intimate moments with Ashton and the simple things like getting dressed.

I shuddered from the creep factor of it all and decided I needed to take my mind off things. Pulling my Kindle out of my purse, I decided to lose myself in a good book.

After a while, I fell asleep. Ashton's voice woke me up. "Gracie?"

I opened my eyes and stretched. "Good... um... what time is it? Morning... afternoon?"

He glanced at his watch on the table next to him. "Late evening. Did you sleep well?"

"Not really." Standing up, I stretched my body fully and moved next to the couch. "Cameron discovered something. I need you to be calm. Can you promise me that?"

He shifted. "That makes me nervous."

Grasping his hand, I said, "Cameron was playing on my computer and found my webcam was on. He thought you and I were doing naughty things on it."

He grinned. "Doesn't sound like the worst idea." I would've laughed if I hadn't been so scared. He noticed my anxiety. "Bug, what is it?"

I squeezed his hand. "The other end of the webcam looked into Hudson's room."

He shot straight up and cringed in pain from the sudden movement. I pressed his shoulders down and begged, "Please, calm down, baby."

His head fell back to the pillow. "Damn him! I want you to pack your bags and move in with me."

I shook my head. "Mary Jane and Angel are here with me.

I can't intrude on your home."

"You wouldn't be intruding, Gracie. Also, it would make me feel better if Derrick taught you how to use a gun. With this new webcam issue and the calls, I want you to get a restraining order too."

I cringed. "I'm terrified of guns, Ash. I'm not sure I want to touch one."

Ashton replied, "Derrick can teach you to not be afraid of them. He has a license to carry for when he works armed security. My dad taught him gun safety from the time he was ten. He taught both of us actually. It's been a while since I touched a gun, and there's no one I'd trust more with you. You need to learn to protect yourself, Gracie. Hudson is dangerous."

I kissed his cheek. "I'll do it, for you. I'm going to move to the chair though so we can sleep." His lip jutted out in a pout, so I leaned down to kiss it. "I'll be right over there." I pointed to the chair across the room.

He sighed. "Not close enough. Hopefully we'll be in our own bed tomorrow night."

I smiled. "Our bed, I like how that sounds."

Ashton fell asleep first. I could sleep anywhere, but my mind was racing.

Cameron texted to check in on me.

Cam: Did you talk to Ash?

Me: Yep, he's worried about me. Wants me to get protection.

Cam: He's thinking about condoms at a time like this???

I laughed quietly.

Me: Is sex the only thing you think about?

Cam: Uh, yeah!

I snickered.

Me: Don't forget, come see me in the morning.

Cam: Definitely. Goodnight, Gracie.

I was not sure when I drifted off, but a gentle shake woke me the next morning. My eyes were fuzzy at first when I glanced up to Ashton's face over me. "Ash? What are you doing up?"

He chuckled as I rubbed my eyes and yawned. When my vision cleared, I realized it was Derrick. "Oh, sorry, Derrick. Good morning."

His head jerked toward Ashton. "Mary Jane let me in. How's he doing?"

I moved to sit on the edge of the couch with Ashton to give Derrick a seat. "He's good." I motioned to the seat for him and he nodded in acceptance. With Ashton asleep, I wanted to get the scoop on the date, plus it would be nice to talk about something pleasant for a change.

"Tell me how your dinner with Mary Jane went," I said.

He grinned, pink filling his cheeks. "It was great. I let Katelyn pick the place, so we ended up at Chuck E. Cheese's. Mary Jane played with Katie the entire time. When she wanted to play in the ball pit, I talked to MJ a bit while we watched. She's such a sweetheart. I'd like to take her on a real date."

I cheered quietly. "I'm so glad you hit it off. When you decide the night, let Ash and me babysit for you. I'd love to get to know Katelyn."

He nodded. "It's a deal."

I jumped when I felt a hand graze my hip. Ashton snickered. "Sorry, bug. Good morning."

I leaned down to give him a kiss. "Good morning. Derrick's here. I'll give you two a few minutes alone. I'm going to get some coffee," I said as I yawned again.

As I turned to leave, the front door swung open, and I exclaimed, "Cameron! Just in time. Come with me to get coffee, babe." Gavin had dropped him off to retrieve his car from the night before, giving us the perfect opportunity to chat. Before leaving, Derrick offered to bring Ashton to meet us shortly.

We drove to a small diner down the street from the house. Grabbing two mocha latte cappuccinos, we sat at a corner table in the back of the room. Cameron wiggled his eyebrows and said, "I heard Derrick and MJ went out?"

"Well, they ate together. Not a date yet. Katelyn was there, Derrick's daughter. He did say he wants to ask her out though." Cameron turned his hand and patted himself on the back. "What the heck was that?" I asked.

"Patting myself on the back for bringing Ashton into your life, which in turn brought Derrick into MJ's." Puffing out his chest, he appeared quite proud of himself. I couldn't argue with his reasoning.

"Do we have a few minutes?" Cameron asked.

"Yeah, sure. What's up?"

He sighed heavily. "I have missed our talks so much, Gracie."

"Me too. I'm sorry things have been hectic lately."

Cameron squeezed my hand. "You've been trying to get your life together with Ash. I'm happy for you. I wish that ass, Hudson, hadn't made your life hell."

Regretfully, I stated, "You and me both. I'm to blame for most of that, I know."

Cameron's mouth opened to argue.

I continued, "I don't mean the rape. I knew something was off with Hudson and I ignored it. I knew that I didn't care for him and he was possessive and jealous all the time. I should've broken it off with him sooner." Talking about Hudson was like hearing a broken record skipping over the same tired tune.

"Enough about me. What did you want to talk about, Cameron?"

His face lit up. "Oh yeah! I need advice. Gavin wants to move in together."

I clapped excitedly. "Duh, say yes!"

He sighed. "I want to, Gracie."

I waited, but he said nothing. After a moment, I inquired, "But?"

He shook his head. "But... I'm not sure I'm ready for that kind of commitment."

I switched to his side of the table and put my arm around his shoulders. I tipped his chin upward with my index finger.

"Cam, Gavin makes you happier than I've ever seen you.

What could be wrong with moving in with him?"

He sighed. "Me. I'm afraid I'll ruin everything."

I kissed his cheek. "You're amazing, Cameron. Don't wait if Gavin is what you want. Grab your man and the life you want. Not only are you lucky to have Gavin, but he is lucky to land someone as wonderful as you."

He pulled me into a hug. "Now will you help me move?"

I hissed. "Ooh, sorry, I'm busy that day." I winked at him causing him to smile and pull me into a hug.

"Anything else you want to talk about before we go back?" I asked.

Cameron smiled. "When are you going to move in with Ashton?"

I shrugged. "I'm not sure. He wants me to move in right away after the webcam discovery. I'm worried about Angel and Mary Jane living there though."

Cameron gave me a stern look. "Gracie Walker, you better not even think about not moving in with that man. He's freaking amazing, in every way."

I laughed. "I know that. I'm not planning on letting him go. I'd be an idiot to do that. We both know I've been an idiot in the past. I'd like to think I've grown and matured."

He snickered. "I don't know about matured." I shoved him playfully and leaned into another hug.

While Cameron was telling me about his latest shopping spree, Derrick walked up to the booth and slid in the opposite side from us. I sat up with worry. "Is Ash okay?"

Derrick patted my hand. "Yeah, honey, he's fine. He'll be inside shortly. He had a work call he was finishing up.

Look, Ash filled me in on Hudson. I'd like to help. When would you like to go to the gun range with me?"

Cameron turned abruptly. "Gracie, guns?"

I nodded. "Ashton wants me to be able to protect myself. I don't like it either. He has my best interest at heart though."

Cameron turned to Derrick. "She's highly terrified of guns."

Derrick nodded with understanding. "Once she learns how to handle it, she should feel better about them."

The thought of even looking at a gun made my chest hurt. Moments like this made me sure of my love for Ash; the last thing I wanted to do was go against my word. "I told Ash I would give it a try. I'm not going to break my promise."

I looked up, my eyes meeting with Ashton's.

Carefully, I put my arms around him. "I'm so glad to see you up and about."

His hand rested at the small of my back and he kissed my cheek. "Me too, bug." With his mouth against my ear, he whispered, "Now I want you to take me home, to bed."

The warmth of his breath against my ear sent chills down my entire body. After his statement, he lightly nibbled my ear and it caused me to moan slightly. He chuckled softly when I pulled away blushing.

"I'll give you two a ride home," offered Cameron.

I wrapped my arm around Ash's waist and glanced at Derrick. "Are you on your way home?"

He smiled. "Yep. Before I leave, I wanted to ask if you

two would mind watching Katelyn tomorrow night so I can take Mary Jane out."

I squealed. "Yes, we'd love to!"

Ashton laughed and kissed the top of my head. "That's the most excitement I've seen out of her in a long time."

Cameron wiggled his keys from his pocket. "Oh hell, if that's the case, we need to get you home so you can rectify that. And you two feel free to talk dirty to each other all the way home. You will not offend me in the least."

Derrick waved good-bye as we loaded Ashton into the backseat. I buckled us in and snuggled up under his arm. Cameron glanced in the rearview mirror and smiled at us.

Ashton leaned down, pressing his soft lips to mine. With my palm against his cheek, I slid my tongue along his bottom lip, teasing him. He growled low in his throat.

From the front seat, Cameron exclaimed, "Ooh, honey, don't make that noise with me in the car, please."

Ashton's face turned a light shade of pink and he replied, "Cameron, turn on some music."

Cameron obliged and turned on the radio. Ashton leaned down to my ear and whispered, "I'm thinking a game of pool when we get home is in order." He nibbled on my ear and moved his hand to my thigh.

My breath sped up. Putting my hand on his, I said, "You need to rest."

He bent to kiss my neck. "I've had plenty of rest. The medicine I need right now is the kind only you can administer."

CHAPTER TWENTY-FIVE

Cameron helped us inside and then scurried out the door as though the house was on fire. I was guessing he felt the heat building between us.

I tugged Ashton toward the bedroom. He stopped me at the basement door. "I'm serious, let's go downstairs."

Gliding my hand along his cheek, I said, "I'd love nothing more than to go live out our mutual fantasy on that pool table. You need more time to heal your sore muscles." Trailing my fingers across his chest, I kissed his cheek and whispered, "Once you're all better, you can have me in every way possible on that table."

His arm snaked around my waist, pulling me against him. "Something to look forward to." He leaned down and captured my mouth with his.

I pulled away and led him to the bedroom. "I'm going

to take care of you for a bit right now. Do you trust me to trim your beard?"

He nodded. "Of course. It is getting a little scraggly." I slipped my jeans off and threw on a long T-shirt that I didn't mind getting wet or dirty. And by wet and dirty, I meant with water and shaving cream, of course.

Leading him to the bathroom, I grabbed the shaving cream and a razor. At first, I stood in front of him and began to slather his face with the cream. Ashton wrapped his arm around my waist and lifted me up onto the vanity. I squealed because I wasn't expecting it.

He chuckled. "I love that little squeak you do when you're startled."

"This is much easier to reach you," I said. I opened my legs and pulled him closer.

"I was thinking it was easier to reach you actually," he said as his hands moved up my thighs.

"You be good," I said teasingly, pointing my finger at him as if scolding him.

"Being bad is much more fun." He winked and nipped at my finger. Pulling it back, I squeaked, and received a hearty burst of laughter from him.

Once his face was slathered, I took the razor and rinsed it before holding it up to him. "Ready?"

He nodded and puffed his cheeks out to make his skin taut. My tongue rested between my lips as I trailed the razor across his face. When I paused to rinse the razor, his cheeks deflated.

"You look so cute all focused," he said. His hand slid

further up my thigh causing me to bite my lip. He smirked. "You're voracious, Gracie."

I laughed. "Why do you say that?"

He leaned forward. "Because you bite your lip when you're turned on. If I'd known that from the day we first met, I'd have picked up your signals better."

Heat crept up my face and I grinned.

The left side of his face was done with just a few spots of cream left on his cheek. I turned to rinse the razor and felt his thumb press against my panties and I gasped. He traced his thumb back and forth across my wet spot. "Your face is only half done."

He shrugged. "What's your point?"

As I went back to the other side of his face, his thumb slid inside my panties. I bit my lip harder as my breathing increased. My hand needed to be steady so I wouldn't cut him or shave the beard completely off; I was just smoothing out the edges. I breathed out. "Ash, you're making this hard for me."

He leaned forward with a wicked sexy grin. "It's pretty hard for me too."

My eyes drifted down to see the bulge in his pants; at the same time, his thumb found my swollen nub and his motion increased. I dropped the razor in the sink and leaned back against the mirror.

I pressed my palms on the mirror behind me as my back arched against his touch. He leaned over me, pressing his mouth against my neck. Beads of sweat dotted my skin at the building desire coiling in my stomach. Ashton's tongue made circles against my skin.

"I love the taste of you." Ashton's voice, his warm breath against my skin, heightened my arousal. His thumb continued to massage as he slipped two fingers inside me.

I moaned. "Ash, I'm getting close."

His hand cupped my chin as he said, "I want to see your eyes."

That was all I needed. My body trembled. He pulled me against him, staring into my eyes as the tremors took over. Shockwaves of pleasure coursed beneath my skin. Heat pulsated in my core as I bucked my hips into his.

When my body finally calmed, I reached for his belt. His hands stopped me. "That was for you. I owed you one."

I reached down and palmed him. "But what about this, doesn't it hurt?"

He pressed against my hand and sighed. "I'll be all right. I liked pleasing you. It was amazing to watch." His lips pressed lightly against mine as he said, "You're the sexiest woman in the world."

As he pulled away, I grinned. "Even with shaving cream all over me?"

His lips turned up in a sinful way. "It's only on the T-shirt. We can remedy that right now."

He lifted the shirt off me and his mouth found my nipple, causing a low moan to leave my throat. He growled my name, sending vibrations over my breast. My fingers wound in his hair, pulling him closer. I wrapped my legs around him and tugged his body against me. His arousal pressed up against mine; I pushed myself forward and he moaned against my chest.

I whispered, "Still just want to please me?"

Keeping his lips on my breast, he reached between our bodies and unzipped his pants. My back arched again as he entered me. Ashton was so wound up that he hit his peak at the same time my body shuddered with my second release.

The next evening, Mary Jane came over to get ready for her date with Derrick. We closed ourselves into the bedroom to get her ready. "I'm so nervous, Gracie," she said as I brushed her hair.

"If he's anything like Ash, you'll be comfortable with him in no time. How did it go the other night?"

She grinned. "Fantastic. He's a great dad, which is amazing for someone his age. He's funny, smart and un-freaking-believably gorgeous."

I laughed. "Un-freaking-believably? That's pretty hot."

We were laughing when Ashton poked his head in the room. "Ladies, Derrick and Katelyn are here."

My hand was on Mary Jane's shoulder and I felt her tense. I put my finger up to Ashton asking for a minute. He nodded as he closed the door to give us privacy.

"Still nervous?" I asked.

"A little," she said. "You know me, Gracie. Guys like Derrick don't ask me out often. The ones who do, I usually don't trust that they actually find me attractive. The only reason I'm not more nervous about this is that he's

Ashton's brother. What if I'm boring?"

I laughed. "MJ, I've known you for several years and you've never been boring. And don't lump Derrick into a group of other guys. We both know he's special."

"I've never... you know," she said nervously.

"There is nothing wrong with being a virgin, MJ. In fact, if I had waited a few more months, Ash would have been the only guy I'd been with and I wish that were the case."

Her mouth fell open in surprise. "Hudson was your first?"

I nodded. "Unfortunately. I had fooled around with guys, but never did more than that before Hudson."

She glanced down and asked quietly, "Why him? Did you feel like he was special?"

I sighed. "No. I wish I could take it back now. I had come to the conclusion that sex was no big deal and I should just do it already. It's now a huge regret for me. Don't let that happen to you."

Mary Jane fidgeted. "I don't want to run him off though."

I put my hand on her shoulder. "Sweetie, Derrick is a good guy. He'd never push you to do something you aren't ready for. I'm confident of that."

She grinned. "I wish I was more like you, G."

I shook my head. "No, you don't. I'm a mess. If I hadn't thought Ashton was gay, I'd still be dating jerks. I'm so screwed up in the head."

Mary Jane nudged me playfully and said, "Who isn't?"

She had no clue how messed up I was since she didn't know about the rape. One day I would need to confide in

Angel and Mary Jane. I was hoping that therapy would allow me to talk about it with my friends a little more.

"Come on, let's not keep him waiting."

"Give me one second?"

It was a simple request, so I stepped out of the bedroom. Derrick looked up with excitement and then disappointment when he saw me. "Wow. Way to make a girl feel good," I stated sarcastically.

He grinned. "Sorry, nothing personal, Gracie. Is something wrong with MJ?"

I shook my head. "She needed a minute, that's all." His pearly whites glistened as his smile illuminated the room. I followed his gaze to see Mary Jane stepping out of the bedroom.

Derrick stepped forward with a single flower, a pink carnation. "You look amazing. I picked this one because you said your favorite color is pink and roses seem cliché."

She smiled. "I love it. I can't believe you remembered my favorite color."

"Pink isn't exactly a stretch for favorite color when it comes to women," Ashton said teasingly.

When I nudged him with my elbow, he chuckled in response. Derrick discreetly scratched his head with his middle finger sticking up toward Ashton.

Ashton snickered. "Mature, man."

Derrick knelt down. "Katelyn, can I have a hug, baby girl?"

Katelyn ran to hug his neck and gave him a kiss on the cheek. Next she went to Mary Jane who bent to meet her embrace as Katelyn whispered, "You look pretty."

Mary Jane whispered back, "Thanks, sweetie." Derrick held his hand out. She took it and turned to me with a wink. I smiled and gave her a thumbs-up for luck.

Once Katelyn was comfortably on Ashton's lap on the couch, I sat next to them. "What would you like to do, Miss Katie?"

She shied away from me, pressing her face against Ashton's neck. Ashton kissed her cheek. "Are you going to be shy for Gracie?"

She nodded.

"You talked to her at the park the other day, don't you remember?" Katelyn rolled her eyes upward in thought and shrugged. He chuckled and tickled her stomach causing her to have a fit of giggles.

Ashton nodded for me to scoot closer. "Katelyn, you know how your daddy is your favorite person in the world?"

She nodded excitedly.

"Well, Gracie is my favorite person in the world."

There is nothing he could have said that would have warmed my heart more than that.

Katelyn's eyes became large. "She is?" She leaned down and whispered, "She's very pretty."

He replied in a whisper, "I think so too."

I blushed as he turned and winked at me. While he kept her entertained, I rounded us up some snacks and drinks from the kitchen. Ashton's phone rang with an ordinary ringtone yet he smiled as though he instantly knew who it was.

"You answer that, Boo. You know it's your dad checking in."

Katelyn answered and it was, in fact, Derrick. Ashton laughed. "He calls to check on her every hour when he's gone. He's so whipped."

I smiled. "That's sweet."

He nodded in agreement. "He's a good dad. I'm proud of him."

"Let's head downstairs and watch a movie," Ashton suggested once the phone call ended.

Katelyn looked up and said, "Can we watch *Brave*?"

He scrunched up his nose in thought and said, "Well... I guess so."

She cheered and he carried her downstairs while I made popcorn and drinks. My phone beeped with a text from Angel.

I sent a text to Ashton letting him know I'd be a few minutes. "Hey, Angel, what's up sweets?"

She sounded slightly relieved. "I called to check on you. Cameron told me about the webcam. Are you all right?"

Plopping down on the couch, I pulled my legs up underneath myself. "I'm fine, sweetie. I'm at Ash's. We're babysitting his niece right now. Look, I want you and MJ to stay with us at his house for a bit."

Angel protested, "You know I like my own space."

"I know. I'm worried about Hudson coming there for me, though, and I don't want you or MJ getting hurt. Please, Angel."

She sighed. "What about if Cameron and Gavin come

stay here, in your room?"

I thought about it a moment. "I guess there is something to be said for safety in numbers. Fine. Promise me, though, if you hear anything out of Hudson, you'll call me."

Angel agreed to let me know immediately if there was trouble. While I had her on the phone, I sent a text to Cameron to work out him moving in. He decided to use it as practice to see if he could live with Gavin.

After hanging up with Angel, I skipped down the stairs to join Ashton and Katelyn. Peering into the room, I smiled watching them. She lay against his chest with her head resting on his shoulder. They were both sound asleep. I bent down next to the couch and stared at the adorable sight in front of me.

Ashton stirred slightly. His eyes opened and he smiled at me.

"You look so cute I didn't want to disturb you." He shifted to lay her on the couch and waved me over. "Aww, I liked seeing her in your arms."

He grinned. "I love when she falls asleep like that. She snores quietly in my ear and it's the cutest thing. The downside is she's warm and it gets sweaty."

His arm wrapped around me as I leaned against him, pulling my knees up to my chest. He kissed my head. "What took you so long up there?"

I chuckled. "Did you miss me?"

He rubbed my arm. "Always."

"Angel called. She wanted me to thank you for offering to let them move in, but came up with a plan to have

Cameron and Gavin stay there for a bit just in case."

He responded, "Do you think that's a good idea? Hudson gave Cameron a pretty good beating before."

"Safety in numbers, I believe. She made a valid point. If Hudson is watching the house and sees that I'm not there, most likely he'll leave them alone."

Katelyn rolled over, rubbing her eyes and shifting her body on the couch. Her mouth fell open as she began to snore again.

I smiled. "She is so beautiful."

Ashton reached for my hand, "So, we haven't talked about our future much. Do you want kids?" Before meeting Ashton, I never imagined a life with children. Even marriage seemed an odd concept to me. It never fit my personality before. Things have changed though. I've changed.

Turning to face him, I draped my legs over his and pressed my hand against his heart. "I'd love to have kids *with you.*"

"You didn't want them before?" he asked.

I shook my head. "It's not that. I've always loved children. It never seemed like marriage or a family was in my future though. I've dated *a lot* of jerks, none that I saw the possibility of a future with."

He smiled. "I can't wait to see you pregnant. I know you will be even more radiant than you are now. Not that I am rushing us to have kids. I'd like to have a few years to travel, do things we want to do, you know?"

"Sounds amazing," I said sincerely.

He took my hand, running his thumb across my ring finger.

"What about getting married? Did you mean it that day at the park? If I proposed, you'd say yes?"

Katelyn whimpered in her sleep and it turned into a sob. I moved to allow Ashton to get up and check on her.

His phone rang and he laughed. "That's Derrick. Somehow he always knows when she is in distress. I swear he has surveillance on this kid."

"Hey, Derrick," I answered.

"Gracie, is my girl all right?"

I glanced over to see Katelyn snuggled in Ash's arms as he sang softly to her. His voice was soft and low. She had stopped crying and was falling asleep again. Her tiny arms were gripping his neck as he placed kisses in her hair.

"She had a bad dream it seems. Ashton has her almost asleep again."

"We'll be back shortly. Give her a kiss for me," he said.

"I will. It's going well, right?"

He sighed. "Yeah, definitely. MJ is in the restroom right now. I gotta tell you, Gracie, I've never had so much in common with someone. She's amazing. She's so funny too. Hopefully she's enjoying her time with me as well. She gets a little quiet at times."

"Be patient with her. She's been very nervous about this date. I know she's really into you. She's been hurt a lot, so she is pretty cautious."

He cleared his throat. "She's on her way back. Thanks, Gracie, that made me feel better."

Chapter Twenty-Six

An hour later, we heard the car pull up into the driveway. We had moved upstairs to the living room with a still sleeping Katelyn. After a few minutes, they still hadn't made it to the door. "Maybe that wasn't them?"

"It sounded too close to be anyone else. I'll look outside." Ashton gently placed Katelyn on the couch, careful not to disturb her sleep.

Through the window we saw the motion lights come on so we knew they were on the porch now. When he opened the door, I saw the back of Mary Jane's head, with Derrick's hand pressed against it as they shared what looked to be a passionate kiss. When I squealed excitedly, Ashton motioned for me to quiet down, laughing at my giddiness. As he was shutting the door, they came up for air. Derrick peered around Mary Jane's head and blushed when he saw us watching.

I waved. "Sorry, I didn't mean to interrupt."

Mary Jane turned and was blushing as well.

"Katelyn is asleep on the couch."

Derrick stepped by me to go inside while I slipped outside. I shut the door to speak to Mary Jane. "So? How did it go?"

The humongous smile on her face was enough answer for me. We both squealed with delight. I hugged her. "I'm so excited for you! So dish, how was the kiss?"

Mary Jane beamed even more. "I'm surprised I can still stand. It was so good!"

Derrick stepped outside once more. He smiled at Mary Jane and turned to me. "Thanks for babysitting tonight. I'll be back in the morning to take you to the range, 'k?"

I nodded. "Sure."

He glanced at Mary Jane again and I took the hint. "I'll go inside so you two can say goodnight."

Derrick stopped by the next morning to take me to the range. Ashton wanted to go with us, so Derrick asked Mary Jane to go as well and make it sort of a double date. They dropped Katelyn off at his parents' for the day, before picking us up.

Ashton had the bright idea that afterward, we could go with them to get Katelyn, so he could introduce me to his parents.

Thanks, Ash. I was already nervous enough with adding meeting the parents to my never-been-done-before list.

My stomach was in knots as we pulled into the parking lot of the gun range. Ashton reached out for my hand when we stepped out of the car. I squeezed it tightly.

He stepped off to the side of the walkway, pulling me to a stop with him. "You sure you want to do this, bug? I won't make you."

I nodded. "I know you wouldn't. I'm nervous, but I'm going to face my fear and see how it goes."

When we stepped inside, it was like a normal shop. There were several counters with guns and other weapons displayed inside. The man at the counter welcomed us. Ashton and Derrick paid for three of us to shoot after we handed over IDs and signed the check-in sheet. We didn't have to rent guns because Derrick had quite a collection of his own. He brought along three different calibers to practice with and one on his hip in a holster. Derrick was going to teach Mary Jane as well. She was a bit more enthusiastic about it than me. They instructed us to go down the stairs and follow the instructions listed on the wall.

Before we went inside, we had to put our eye and ear protection on. Ashton had bought Mary Jane and I pink headsets. He placed mine over my ears and tested how much I could hear. I could still make out his voice. It was as if he were standing outside a closed window speaking to me. Next, he handed me goggles. He motioned for me to remove the headphones for a moment.

"Yeah?" I said as my ears readjusted to the white noise around me again.

"When we go in, Derrick is going to show you how to hold it and to shoot. If you're uncomfortable in any way, you can stop. I'll be right there for you."

I nodded and glanced at Derrick, who was going over the information with Mary Jane.

We secured our headphones again. Derrick led the way through the first door. Once we were all in, he opened the next door and we stepped through.

The range was a long hallway with an exit door at the other end. There were stalls divided by short walls all along the hallway. Each stall was only about three-by-four feet at the most. There was a wooden plank across the front for setting the guns and ammunition.

Ashton stood with Mary Jane while Derrick loaded the weapon for me. I asked him to load only one bullet for my first time, in case I dropped it out of fear. After loading it, he handed it to me.

My chest tightened as the panic set in. Each panicked breath came out quicker than the last. I closed my eyes and took one final deep breath. He placed my hands on the gun, instructing me to make sure my finger jutted straight along the side of it and not on the trigger.

I set it down while Derrick prepared the target and placed it a few feet ahead of me. There was something about the shape of a man standing that close that made me even more nervous.

I motioned for him to move it back further. Once it was

at a comfortable distance, he pointed at the gun and gave me a questioning thumbs-up. It was sitting on the plank in front of me.

I stepped forward, placed both my hands on the plank to steady myself for a moment, and hoped that my hands would stop shaking. I lifted the gun, still unfamiliar with the heaviness. I wrapped my hands around it, careful to place my finger alongside the barrel and not on the trigger itself. The green silhouette of a man was about six feet from me. With one last deep breath, I closed my eyes and pulled the trigger.

The recoil of the gun was more than I had expected. It snapped back, hurting the space between my thumb and forefinger. As it went off, I screamed at the sound, the recoil, and the feeling in my chest. I sat the gun down and backed away, bumping into Ashton's chest. I whipped around, his face showing deep concern at my reaction.

"You okay, Gracie?" he mouthed. The gunshot repeated in my head as the fear choked me. I couldn't seem to calm myself down. Anxiety filled me as though I had used a gun on a human being.

I shook my head and began to cry. Part of me felt silly for breaking down. Though I trusted Ashton completely, guns still scared me and I didn't feel as though I was ready to wield such power. Pulling me into his arms, he waved Derrick and Mary Jane to go on without us. Ashton took my hand and led me back out to the lobby area.

He removed my headset and protective eyewear and wiped my tears with his thumb. "Gracie, talk to me."

"I feel like I killed someone just now. I don't like that feeling. You know that green silhouette man might have a family."

Ashton chuckled. "If he does, Derrick and MJ are taking care of them now so they won't have to grieve him."

I smacked his chest playfully. "That isn't funny!" He laughed as he pulled me against his chest and kissed my hair.

"I'll sit out here and we'll let them finish up," he said.

I shook my head. "Let me try one more time."

With our hearing and eye protection in place, he led me back in. Derrick smiled when he saw us return. He patted my shoulder to show his support. Ashton stood behind me this time. The gun lay on the plank again. He stepped behind me, wrapped his arms around me tightly and kissed my neck.

He yelled out, "You can do this, bug. I believe in you."

Lifting the gun again, I resumed the position I had before, aimed for the green silhouette of a man and fired. Again, it felt all too real and the thought of using this weapon on a person made me sick to my stomach. I'd never been a violent person and Hudson had already changed me too much. I set it down and turned to Ashton, shaking my head in defeat. He kissed my forehead and told Derrick we'd be outside.

Ashton waited in the lobby while I went to wash the gunpowder off my hands. The small bathroom felt as though there was no air circulating. Glancing in the mirror, I noticed my face was pale and clammy. My hands shook while my chest heaved and I began to sob, uncontrollably.

With my back pressed against the wall, I slid down to the floor and pulled my knees into my chest.

A few minutes later, there was a knock on the door and a woman's voice called out, "Ma'am?"

I sniffed back the tears and cleared my throat. "I'll be out in a second."

I scrambled to get up off the floor. I grabbed a paper towel and wet it to clean my face.

The woman smiled sympathetically at me when I stepped from the restroom. "Are you all right?"

I nodded and searched the room for Ashton. He had his back turned and was examining a gun with the man behind the counter. His head twisted in my direction and his brow furrowed. He apologized to the man and sprinted over to me.

"Baby, what's wrong?" he asked as he stroked my cheek with his thumb.

"Had a bit of a breakdown for a second." His arms wrapped around me and as soon as they did, a hundred pounds of stress lifted from my shoulders. I pressed my face against his chest. "You make everything better, Ash."

He sighed. "I feel the same about you."

"Gracie?" I turned and Mary Jane headed toward me. "What happened?"

I shook my head. "I had a moment, that's all. I'm good now."

Derrick smiled. "You did well for your first time, Gracie. Be proud. It's not for everyone. If you don't want to do it again I understand. Whatever you need to feel safe, that's what matters."

"Right now a gun makes me feel more unsafe than anything."

Derrick placed his hand on my shoulder, "Fair enough. You let me know if you change your mind. For now, what do you say I treat everyone to lunch?"

Ashton spoke up first, "If you're paying, I'm in. Who wants a big steak?"

Derrick punched his arm. "Thanks, bro." They laughed as we headed to the parking lot.

Chapter Twenty-Seven

Standing at the car, I was relaxed in Ashton's arms as we gazed into each other's eyes, smiling.

The next few moments happened in slow motion. His eyes drifted upward, his face paled, shock engulfing him.

His mouth opened and he shouted, "Derrick!"

In the next moment, I heard the rapid pops and was pushed to the ground.

Ashton lay on top of me while screams echoed around us. My eyes slammed shut, afraid of what was happening. Before I fell, I had heard Mary Jane scream Derrick's name in unison with Ashton. Dread washed over me as panic built in my chest. Ashton wasn't moving on top of me. My eyes flew open as I pushed against his weight. I was pinned to the ground and it was suffocating me.

He tightened his grip around me and whispered, "Stay

down, Gracie. Don't move."

"Are you hurt?" I whimpered.

He moved to look me in the eyes as he responded, "No. I'm fine, but I have to check on Derrick."

I grabbed his arms. "Don't leave me."

His face scrunched in pain. "Baby, I don't want to, but I don't know who's hurt."

I nodded. "Were those gunshots?"

He nodded slightly.

"Did you see who was shooting?"

His eyes grew fierce with anger. "All I saw was Hudson with a gun."

"What?"

He quickly covered my mouth, sending me into panic as I quivered from being held down. I struggled against his hold. This was all too familiar of a feeling. I had to remember it was Ashton and he'd never hurt me that way.

He whispered in my ear, "Baby, I'm sorry. I know you're scared. I know you don't like being restrained. I need you to be quiet so he doesn't know where you are. I'll be nearby. I need to see about my brother. Do you trust me?"

I nodded and he moved his hand. When he stood up, I slid closer to the car for protection. The rape, the webcam, the stalking, and now this made me wonder why I'd never seen this coming. How could I have spent so many months with this man and not seen this potential? I'd seen news stories of women who said they never believed a significant other would hurt them and I often wondered how someone could be so dense. Standing in the shoes of a woman who remained completely unaware, I was empathetic to their plight. Still cowering next to the car, I tried to seek out Hudson's location. He was nowhere to be seen. Frantically glancing around, I sought out my friends to make sure they were safe.

As I searched for what happened, my eyes fell upon Mary Jane's shirt, now streaked in blood. She seemed devastated and scared. Ashton put his arms around her as she cried. He turned and pointed at me. She relaxed and ran to be by my side.

Ashton bent over Derrick. He came back up with blood on his shirt. Covering my mouth with my hands, I gasped in shock. Poking my head up higher, I tried to determine the extent of Derrick's injury. *Please don't let him be dead.* These words repeated in my head. I turned to Mary Jane. "Is Derrick all right?"

She wrapped her arms around my neck and cried. My eyes found Ashton again; he was sitting with Derrick's head in his lap. One of the bystanders was on the phone, hopefully calling 911. I still saw no sign of Hudson. The last few moments were surreal. Emotions warred inside me while I tried to stay calm for Mary Jane.

Patting her back gently, I attempted to soothe her while trying to figure out what was going on. "Tell me what happened."

She sat back. "It all happened so fast. Derrick was about to kiss me. The next thing I know, he knocked me to the ground and I heard the gunshots. He's been shot, Gracie."

All the air left my body and I struggled to get it back.

Heaving, panicked breaths racked my body.

She added, "He's alive. We have to get him to a hospital."

Ashton waved us over.

Running to him, I knelt down to help. "Is he all right?" In the background, I heard the familiar sounds of sirens, a noise I'd heard too much of in my life lately.

Ashton applied pressure to the wound. His eyes were misty. "I think he'll be fine. We have to get him to the hospital soon."

My eyes drifted to the crowd standing nearby. I looked to see what they were staring at. Ashton's hand brushed my cheek. "It's all over, baby." The words didn't make sense to me because I still hadn't seen where Hudson was. How could Ashton be sure he wouldn't shoot again? Had the police captured him without me seeing it somehow? His body blocked my view as though he needed to shield me. If it's over, why is he still being overprotective?

My eyebrows scrunched in confusion. "What do you mean?"

He pointed at the crowd. I could see something on the ground, a body. Stepping closer, I felt Ashton's hand close around my wrist trying to stop me. Peering back at him, his eyes pleaded with me to come back. Instead, I ventured closer only stopping when I recognized the body of Hudson.

"Hudson's dead. Derrick was able to get a shot off and kill him before he could hurt anyone else. Luckily for us, he has a carry permit and had his gun in a holster on his hip. If he'd placed his in the bag with the rest of ours, well,

I don't want to think about how different things could be."

I had never been someone to be happy when a person was hurt or killed, but my whole body relaxed in relief. Finally, I had closure to this horrible situation. It didn't come in the way I hoped, but I no longer had to fear seeing him around every corner. Perhaps I could have a decent night of sleep for a change with no nightmares or fear of shadows.

The EMTs ran over to take care of Derrick. Giving them space, Ashton stepped back and pulled me into a tight embrace. Sobs broke free from me as he smoothed my hair. "It's over, baby. It's going to be fine."

I looked up into his eyes. "I know. I feel happy that Hudson is dead. I know that is wrong but...."

He shook his head. "It's not wrong for you. It's normal, sweetheart. After all the pain and suffering he caused you, no one would blame you for feeling that way."

The EMT tapped Ashton on the shoulder. "Do you want to ride with your brother in the ambulance?"

Somberly, he replied, "No. I'll meet you there."

I grabbed his arm. "Go with him. Mary Jane and I will meet you at the hospital. We're safe now. He needs you."

Ashton kissed my forehead. "You be careful, bug. I love you."

"I love you, Ash."

Mary Jane was still sitting against the car with a vacant expression. "We're going to meet Derrick and Ash at the hospital. You ready to go?" Without a word she slid into the passenger seat, fastening her seatbelt and staring out the window.

She kept quiet for most of the ride. At one point she scared me by gasping aloud. I slammed on the brakes. "What?"

She grabbed at her chest. "I'm sorry, Gracie. I didn't mean to scare you."

I pulled to the side of the road. Placing the car in Park I gave her the chance to explain. Her eyes glazed over with tears, her voice cracking with each word she spoke.

"What are we going to do about Katelyn?"

I sighed. "Let me call, Ashton."

He picked up with panic in his voice. "What's wrong?"

I sighed. "We're fine, baby. Stop worrying about me."

He chuckled. "I told you I'm a worrier. What's up?"

"First of all, how is Derrick?"

"The doctors are working on him now, that's all I know." It stung to hear the worry in his voice and not be able to be there with him.

"Did you call your parents and tell them what happened?"

He cursed. "Not yet. I don't want to worry Katie."

I agreed. "Mary Jane thought of that too. Would you like us to go by there and talk to them?"

He was quiet for a moment and said, "No, I'll call them. Let me call you back. I may need your help finding a babysitter."

When I hung up the phone, I turned to Mary Jane once more. She was staring out the window.

I brushed her hair off her face. "You okay, sweets?" She nodded without looking at me. "Talk to me, MJ."

She turned and sighed. "Gracie, why is it that we have to struggle so much to find happiness?"

That was a question I didn't have an answer to.

She explained further, "Look at what you had to go through to find Ashton. Look at what you're still going through. Sometimes I don't feel as though it's worth all of this."

That sounded ominous. "What isn't worth it?"

She turned back to the window. "Life."

"MJ, that sounds like suicide talk."

She turned to me and shook her head. "No, I'd never commit suicide. It's just that it seems like we go through so much pain to get to happiness sometimes."

I grabbed her hand. "I know what you mean. But let's stop talking about this and go be with our guys. I know you're worried about Derrick."

She smiled sadly. "I like that, 'our guys.' I really like Derrick a lot, Gracie."

I pulled back on the road to head toward the hospital. "I can tell. I'm sure he's going to be fine."

Chapter Twenty-Eight

When we arrived at the hospital, I spotted Ashton waiting outside. I saw his shoulders relax when he spotted us. "Uh-oh. We took too long. He was worried."

Ashton's protective streak was strong. He met us halfway up the walk, his long legs catching up to us quickly.

He wrapped his arms around me tightly. "Where've you been? I was freaking out."

Mary Jane, still tightly wound, stepped forward. "How is Derrick?"

He smiled reassuringly. "The doctors said he should be fine. The bullet passed straight through. The last update they gave me was that it didn't hit any organs, which is great news. He should be in recovery shortly and out before you know it." He offered Mary Jane a wink. "Hell, you know how desperate they are for beds."

Mary Jane relaxed for the first time since the shooting. You could see her whole body deflate of the tension. Ashton moved to hug her and smoothed her hair. "Derrick wouldn't go anywhere right now. He's too crazy about you."

Mary Jane gazed up at him, desperately trying to hold back tears. "Really?"

Ashton nodded. "He told me himself. Don't tell him I told you. I'm sure there is some bro code that says I shouldn't have told you that."

Though she tried to smile at his attempt to cheer her up, it didn't reach her eyes.

"Come on, ladies, there's nothing we can do until he's out of recovery. Let me treat you to something to drink and eat even if it's just a small snack."

We each took his hand as we walked down the hallway to the cafeteria. He took a seat and I scooted into the booth next to him where he moved his arm around me, pulling me closer.

Mary Jane smiled. "You two make the cutest couple."

I grinned up at Ashton and he leaned down to lightly kiss me. "So, tell us about you and Derrick. How is that going?"

Before she could answer, a woman said, "Ash, sweetie?"

Ashton stood and hugged the woman tightly; she began to cry.

"He's going to be fine. The doctor said so himself."

The woman looked up and Mary Jane waved and offered an empathetic smile.

When Ashton let go, Mary Jane stepped forward to hug her. "Mary Jane, it's nice to see you again, dear."

When they pulled out of the hug, Ashton took her hand and said, "Mom, this is Gracie." Though I'd been dating Ashton longer, Mary Jane met his parents first when they stopped this morning to drop Katelyn off at their house. At least she had the pleasure of meeting them under better circumstances.

I slid out of the booth extending my hand to her.

She laughed and pulled me into a hug. "Handshakes are for meeting acquaintances. We're family."

I tightened my grip around her. She made me feel so warm and welcome, calling me family.

"I know everything about you, Gracie. My son has been talking about you for months."

Ashton laughed. "Don't embarrass me, Mom." Ashton winked at me.

"I'm honored to meet the woman who gave me such an amazing man. You should be so proud. He is the most wonderful man I've ever known, and I know that comes from great parents."

Ashton blushed. "Is this embarrass Ash day? Can Derrick have a turn next please?" We laughed and went to sit down together.

"Why don't you sit beside Ash," I said to his mother.

She waved her hand in dismissal. "No way, you two looked adorable when I walked up."

I reclaimed my seat next to Ashton, his arm around my shoulder. He kissed my hair and hugged me close.

"I've heard a lot of wonderful things about you, Gracie. Ashton is a lucky man for finding such a wonderful woman," she said.

Considering the reason we were sitting there, I didn't feel so wonderful. Wanting to be honest and forthcoming, I respectfully stated, "I'm sorry, Mrs. Collins. What happened to Derrick is my fault."

She glanced at Ashton and he nodded. It stung that he felt this was my fault. I edged away from him, feeling dejected.

Forehead crinkled with concern, he reached out for me and I shied away. "Bug, I'm sorry. I know it's hard for you to talk about. I only told my mom because she's a nurse. She's seen this before and I needed advice."

I closed my eyes. "What? I'm confused. You nodded at her agreeing that this is my fault...."

Before I could finish, he sputtered, "No. That's not what I nodded for. She looked at me as a way of asking if she could let you know she knew what Hudson did, right, Mom?" He turned to his mother and she confirmed his assumption. He reached out for my hand as I teared up. "Baby, I don't blame you for what happened to Derrick. None of us do."

I glanced at his mother and Mary Jane and they were both shaking their heads in agreement with Ashton.

"MJ, will you come with me to get an update on Derrick?" his mother asked. Mary Jane agreed and they left Ashton alone with me. He reached out to me again.

"I'm sorry, Ashton."

He frowned. "For what, bug?"

I sighed. "For making a terrible first impression on your mom."

He laughed. "Sweetie, she loves you already. She wasn't kidding, I talk about you nonstop. She has been bugging me to bring you around since the day we met. I didn't want to introduce you to her as my friend though. I always knew, eventually, we'd be more than that. After everything that happened with Hudson, I was devastated and felt helpless as to what to do for you. I talked to my mom about it for advice. She told me to give you all the space and time you needed. I was worried you would be mad that I talked to her."

Pressing my hand against his cheek, I brought my mouth up to his. His body relaxed as his lips moved against mine. His hand pressed to the back of my neck, pulling me closer.

"Get a room. Damn horny youngins." I turned to see Cameron smirking at us. I jumped up and squeezed him tightly.

"I'm so thankful you weren't hurt today, baby girl."

Ashton stood up and Cameron hugged him next. "Ooh, lordy, you're strong. Angel sends her love to both of you. She's going to come by after work."

Ashton laughed. "Did you see MJ?"

Cameron nodded. "Yep, and I met your mother. I love that woman. One, she gave birth to you, and two, she's one of the reasons I have Gavin. She's the reigning queen in my book. Oh, and there is a police officer up front who asked to speak with you."

"Ash, why don't you go and Cameron will keep me company," I suggested.

"I'll be back shortly."

I watched him as he walked out. "Mmm, hate to see him go, but love to watch him leave, right?" Cameron said as he sat beside me in the booth. He leaned his head against my shoulder. "You all right, punkin?"

I nodded. "I'm fantastic. Is it wrong that I feel happy now that Hudson is dead?" It's not his death that made me happy, more the feeling of freedom knowing he could no longer hurt me.

He sat up. "No. After what that man did to you, you can feel as happy as you want. In fact, I'm throwing a party for all of us. Not to celebrate his death. That would be wrong. We're going to celebrate Mary Jane and Derrick, you and Ash, Gavin and me, life in general. We deserve it. We'll pick a night as soon as Derrick is out of the hospital."

I beamed. "You're awesome, Cam."

He shrugged. "I know."

"Come on, you're starting to lose that smile. I'm taking you to your happy place."

I was confused. "Where is that?"

He winked. "Beside Ash."

I smiled. "It feels good to finally have a happy place."

Cameron kissed my temple. "I agree."

In the waiting room, we found Mary Jane and Mrs.

Collins in tears. Ashton spotted me and his face lit up with joy. Well, the scene was most definitely a bit unbalanced. "What happened?"

Ashton smirked. "Derrick's out of surgery. He's fine. You women cry when you're happy or sad. That's why we get so confused sometimes."

He grinned as he kissed me before I punched him playfully in the stomach.

Ashton wrapped his arm around me and walked me over to the others. "Mom, since Derrick will be out for a while, I'm going to get Gracie out of here. We'll be back in the morning though, okay?"

She nodded and turned to hug me. "I'm so happy to have finally met you, Gracie."

I smiled. "Me too, Mrs. Collins."

She patted my shoulder. "You call me Maria. I want you and Ash to come to dinner one night, so we can talk more."

I smiled. "Absolutely."

Ashton took my hand, leading me out to the car and hit the unlock button. Before we got inside, he pressed me against the door. His mouth grazed mine gently at first. His hand slipped behind my neck as he delved into my mouth with his tongue. I moaned at the sensuality of the kiss.

His other hand slipped around my waist, pulling me against his body. My hands moved up his chest and around his neck as his tongue explored my mouth.

When he pulled away, I missed him instantly. "I promised we'd stop by the police station on the way home to give our statements. After that, we'll do anything you want tonight," he said as he trailed his thumb across my swollen lips. I nipped at his finger and he chuckled softly.

"Let's go home." He motioned for me to get in the car. Despite the relief I felt, it still seemed unreal that it's over. At any moment, it felt like I could be shaken awake to leave this crazy nightmare of a day.

On the drive home, after we'd spent an hour at the police station making statements at the request of the officers at the hospital, he said, "So, meeting my mom wasn't so bad, was it?"

I smiled. "No, she's amazing. Not that I expected anything else. Your entire family is wonderful it seems."

He laughed. "Nothing special about us. We're just good southern folk," he said, adding a country twang to his voice.

I bit my lip. "That was pretty sexy sounding."

He smirked. "You like that country twang in my voice?" he said, still emphasizing the twang.

"Mmhmm. With your deep voice, it sounds so yummy."

He laughed. "Yummy, huh?"

I nodded, biting the corner of my bottom lip. Ashton reached over and caressed my face.

I reached for his hand and kissed his palm. "I love you, Ash. You have no idea how much."

He smiled. "Probably not nearly as much as I love you."

I kissed his knuckles. "Seriously, I can't even tell you what you mean to me."

The house was empty when we arrived. Angel was out, and of course, Mary Jane was at the hospital. When we stepped inside the house, it was quiet and dark.

Ashton stopped my hand as I reached to turn on the light. He pulled me into his embrace. I didn't flinch at the sudden touch. It was the first time I hadn't reacted negatively to being touched unexpectedly. His hand swept across my cheek, pushing my hair behind my ear.

Leaning down, he whispered, "I want to make love to you."

That familiar tug in my stomach told me that I wanted that too. I pushed myself up on my tiptoes and pressed my lips against his. Leading him to the couch, I sat down watching as he removed his shirt.

Running my hands across his bare chest, I moaned. "I love the feel of your body." Closing his eyes, he savored the feel of my hands against his skin. Lifting my shirt over my head, he brushed the hair from my shoulder and nipped at the bare skin.

"You're so beautiful, Gracie. Are you sure...?"

Covering his mouth with my hand, I said with confidence, "I want you more than I've ever wanted anything." The moment my hand moved his lips crashed against mine with desperation. No longer did I feel the pull of anxiety trying to rip me from the passionate moment. Instead of fighting my inner demons, I could give in to the pleasure. Like a prisoner freed from their shackles, I bathed in the ecstasy of the moment. With a flick of his wrist, he unlatched my bra, baring my breasts, and proceeded to show me just how beautiful he thought I was.

After making love, we lay curled up on the couch. Ashton was pressed against the back of the couch, holding me against him. He flung a blanket over us to give us a little warmth. "This is going to be our life now. No worries, no cares, right?"

I nodded. "I hope so."

He smoothed my hair aside, gazing at me. I leaned up to kiss him.

"I have fallen asleep on that couch!" Angel exclaimed from behind us.

I turned, holding the blanket against my chest using my body to keep Ashton covered. "Sorry, Angel," I said with a smile.

She sat next to us. "Everyone's safe, I assume?"

Sitting up, keeping the cover tightly against my chest, I said, "Yes. Mary Jane's at the hospital waiting for Derrick to wake up. We wanted some time alone."

Angel nodded. "Say no more. I'll leave for a bit to give you guys some time."

I grabbed her hand. "No, I didn't mean it that way. We stopped here to get some clothes and well...."

Angel chuckled. "You decided to take clothes off instead?"

I laughed. "Apparently."

Ashton kissed my shoulder. "Bug, I'm going to call and

check on Derrick. Angel, do you mind?"

She glanced at him. "No, I don't mind you standing up totally naked. Won't offend me."

Ashton laughed. "Gracie, as long as you don't mind."

I pointed at the door. "Angel, get out."

We giggled and she ran upstairs to give us a moment. I moved, letting Ashton stand to dress.

First thing the next morning, Ashton called the hospital and they said Derrick was recovering really well. He was on antibiotics, was stitched up and would be looking at a quick release since there was no significant damage. He wanted to check for himself though. "I'm going to run to the hospital for a bit. It'll give you time to pack some stuff up."

"I'll come with you."

He shook his head. "It's fine. I won't be long. Hang with Angel for a bit." With a deep sigh, he added, "With Hudson gone, I can actually breathe a little easier knowing you're safe."

A quick kiss good-bye and I watched as he drove away. Alone in the room for the first time, I noticed the fear was gone. Before today, I'd have searched the room for anything strange, turned on every light in the house, and cowered at each creak and moan of the house. My life was becoming mine again. I felt like letting loose, so I searched my iPod for the appropriate song to do so.

"Stronger" by Kelly Clarkson. It was the perfect song

for how I felt. I turned the stereo up loud and began to sing with the music. Freedom pounded through my veins in time with the beat while I bounced up and down on my toes. My arms were in the air as I spun in circles. Angel came in from behind and danced with me. We laughed and flailed our arms around, dancing around each other. When the song was over, we fell to the couch together.

"Chica, I'm so glad to see you laughing!" Angel exclaimed, once she caught her breath.

"I feel guilty being in such a good mood when someone died today, but I can't help feeling relieved. I never wished him dead though. I wished I'd never met him a million times."

Angel hugged me. "No need to explain to me. It doesn't make you a bad person to feel good today. The man stalked you, Gracie. He hurt you and Cameron."

"He raped me too, Angel." She sat up and pressed her hand against her mouth, tears falling from her eyes.

"Gracie... when?"

It came out without me even realizing I was ready to tell her. It caught me by surprise that I had said it, as much as it did for her to have heard it. I proceeded to tell her all that had happened.

By the end, her eyes were red and pain etched her face. She then pulled me into her arms. "Chica, I'm so sorry."

I rubbed her back. "I'm fine, or at least I will be. Ash has been amazing."

She leaned back and wiped her face. "I've been there too," she said.

"What? When?"

She replied, "High school. It was junior year. I went on a date and the guy wouldn't take no for an answer. That was my first sexual experience."

I covered my mouth in shock. "Angel, you never told any of us?"

She shook her head. "I understand why you didn't say anything. It makes you feel dirty, ashamed... ruined. I felt like no one would believe me because of the way I dressed. I knew they would say I was asking for it. I don't blame you for not telling anyone." We both knew her fears were as real as they were ridiculous. Women should be able to wear whatever and behave however they chose without fear of being raped. Unfortunately, the rest of the world didn't always think that way.

I moved to hug her. "It feels good to know I'm not alone."

Angel smoothed my hair, and said, "It happens more often than it should, unfortunately."

Not long ago, I had promised Ashton and Cameron I would see a counselor. So far I hadn't made the call. Hearing Angel's story not only gave me courage, but gave me an idea of how to make it easier to handle. I reached for her hand. "I need to ask you something and if this is totally inappropriate, you can tell me." I paused briefly and then asked, "Would you want to go to a group counseling session with me?"

Angel took a moment to think about it. "Sure. I'd do that for you. It would be helpful for me too. It's been a long time, but the fear sticks with you long after. There are still moments when I'm with a guy that I panic. If he is too aggressive, if he takes the lead or lingers on top for too long, I begin to feel weighed down and trapped. I hate feeling helpless. I've done my share of freaking out on guys. The difference between us is that mine never stick around to make me feel better or to help. They call me a tease or worse and move on. You're lucky you have Ash. Hang onto him." Wiping away tears, she added, "Enough of this talk. We need a girls' day out."

I laughed. "That sounds like the perfect thing, but maybe we should wait until Derrick is out of the woods so MJ can join us."

She agreed.

A moment later, my phone rang. It was Ashton. I held it up to show Angel; she grinned and left me to take the call.

"Hey, baby, how's Derrick?" I asked.

Ashton sounded upbeat. "He's great. He's already pleading with the doctors to be released. Mom and Mary Jane are in there with him. He asked about you as soon as he woke up. He was worried that he didn't get the shot out quick enough. You mind coming by to see him so he can be reassured?"

"Of course. I'll have Angel drive me over now. See you soon." I hung up the phone and Angel was already at the door with her keys.

"I heard you say you needed a ride. Let's boogie."

When we arrived at the hospital, Cameron and Gavin

were walking out as we made our way to the door. "Hey, bitches," Cameron greeted.

"Hello, ladies," Gavin stated at the same time.

Angel rolled her eyes as she addressed Gavin. "Can you rub off on him some more and get him to call us ladies as well?"

Cameron stepped forward embracing Angel. "Girlfriend, you know I mean bitches in the sweetest way possible."

Angel laughed. "Somehow you make that sound believable."

Cameron and Gavin were on their way home. We waved them good-bye and headed to see Derrick. His room was full when we stepped inside. Their mom, Mary Jane, Ashton and an older man filled the space. Derrick's eyes met mine and he looked as though ten years fell off his life with the relief that washed over.

Ashton took my hand, leading me over to sit where he'd been previously. I leaned down, kissing Derrick on the cheek. "You Collins men are my personal heroes. You know that?"

Derrick smiled up at me as he took my hand in his. "I'm glad you weren't hurt."

"Since no one is going to introduce me, I'm going to assume you're Gracie," the older man stated, holding his hand forward.

Ashton's hand found the small of my back as he stood next to me. I reached for the man's hand.

"Gracie, this is my father."

"It's nice to meet you, Mr. Collins."

He had a firm handshake. "Please, call me Craig. She is gorgeous, son."

My cheeks heated from the compliment.

Grinning, Ashton bent to press his lips to my temple. "I know." Ashton then turned to Angel. "You mind going with me to grab some coffee?"

Angel seemed as surprised as I felt. "Uh... sure?"

Ashton leaned down and whispered, "Take a few moments to talk to my parents and Derrick. Help Mary Jane feel a little more comfortable too." He winked at me as he escorted Angel out of the room. Meeting parents wasn't exactly a normal occurrence for me. Ashton wanted me to make Mary Jane feel more comfortable, but who was going to help me?

Chapter Twenty-Nine

Mary Jane and I took turns answering questions about ourselves the rest of that morning. Derrick piped in every once and a while to stop the interrogation. Though, interrogation wasn't the best word; it was actually a nice talk we all had. They asked about our families and what we were studying in school.

When Angel and Ashton returned, he asked me to step outside for a moment. He slipped his hand in mine as we strolled down the hallway.

"I want to take you out this evening. I talked to Angel about it. I'd like you to go shopping for a new dress, my treat, and meet me tonight. Angel suggested you get your 'hair did.'" He held his fingers up to make air quotes.

I snickered. "Okay, sounds fun. What time do you want me to meet you?"

He glanced at his watch. "Have her bring you back here in five hours."

Angel and I left the hospital alone. We were unable to convince Mary Jane to come with us. She felt she needed to be there for Derrick. We didn't argue with her.

It was almost spring in Nashville, which meant a range of freezing to sweaty temperatures. It was currently in the seventies so when we drove to town, Angel took her car roof down.

After a light lunch, she pulled into a dress shop. We spent the next couple of hours trying on dresses, trying to find the perfect one for dinner.

"Hey, remember when we were younger and we used to love going into the stores to try on prom dresses for fun?" Angel asked as she thumbed through the rack of clothes.

"Yes! Of course. Cameron even tried on a few with us once!"

We both laughed at the memory of Cameron in a hot pink formal gown. He came to the conclusion pretty quickly that drag was not his forte.

"They have wedding dresses here. Why not try a couple on, for fun?"

I wrinkled my nose. "I don't know about that."

She grabbed my hand, tugging me toward the brilliantly white side of the store.

Dresses in opal, pearl, ivory, cream, basically every shade of white or almost-white you could dream up. I'd never imagined what kind of dress I'd want.

"Close your eyes for a moment. Imagine walking down

the aisle to Ashton. What dress are you wearing?"

With my eyes closed, I pictured every moment of my fictional wedding. When I opened my eyes to glance around, I found the perfect dress. It was a strapless mermaid style, with the bottom sprinkled with jewels.

Angel saw my eyes light up as they landed on the dress. She went to find my size and carried it to the dressing room for me.

When I slipped the dress on, I took a deep breath as I turned to look in the mirror. I'd never felt more beautiful. I opened the door to show Angel.

She gasped and said, "That's the one. You look amazing, Gracie."

I glanced at the tag and realized I'd never be able to afford it.

"Take a picture. Maybe one day I can find one close to it that I can afford."

I posed for her to take the picture. She held the phone up to show me and it took my breath away. I'd never thought I'd looked beautiful before until I saw myself in this dress. I wanted to marry Ashton in it, one day.

Angel and I continued our search for a nice dress for dinner. She helped me finally decide on a red dress with short flowing sleeves. It dipped into a V-neck in the front and had a flowing skirt that fell to a few inches above my knee. The red material matched my ladybug charm perfectly.

Angel then took me to get my hair done. We couldn't get the full works because we were running short on time, but the hairdresser did a great job with the little time we gave her. Before we left, Angel purchased a beautiful diamond studded comb for my hair. "Angel, this is too much."

She waved it off. "Whatever. Your man deserves to see you all gussied up."

We bought some black heels to match, and I was ready to go.

When we left the store, Angel said she had an errand to run before she dropped me off to meet Ashton. We pulled into the parking lot of the nightclub where Cameron liked to hang out, the one where I met Ashton for the first time. "What are we doing here?"

Angel replied, "Cameron needed me to pick something up for him. He left it in the back room the other night. Come on in with me and say hi to some of the guys. They ask about you all the time."

I took a deep breath. "It looks kind of empty."

Angel nodded. "Yeah, Cameron said there's a private party here tonight. We're just going to run in and out though."

When we stepped in the door, the bouncer, Chris, came up to us. "Gracie! Long time no see, girl! You look gorgeous as always!"

He kissed my cheek as he said, "Right this way, ladies. Cameron told me you were coming by." With my new dress on, I couldn't wait to see Ashton's reaction. I felt like a princess.

When he opened the back room, my heart stopped as the people inside called, "Surprise, Gracie!" The room was decorated in beautiful white lights hanging from the ceiling.

My friends were all standing around, including Derrick who must have been released early. My eyes widened in surprise when I saw him. In the middle of the room was Ashton, in a suit. My breath caught in my throat at how handsome he looked. He stepped forward and motioned me inside. "What's going on?"

Ashton moved closer. My heart caught in my throat as the emotions bubbled up. "Gracie Walker, this is the spot where we first met. The spot that I first laid eyes on my happily ever after." In my mind I drifted back to that night, remembering his subtle flirting, which I never picked up on until much later.

Tears of joy filled my eyes as I listened to his sweet words. "Since that evening, you've been in my thoughts, my dreams, my heart." Even though we were surrounded by people, it was so quiet it felt like we had the room to ourselves. "There are no words to express the full worth of your love. There is only one thing you can do to make me even happier than I am right now."

As he knelt down, and took my hand in his, the room erupted in gasps. Struggling to fight the tears, not wanting to have raccoon eyes when I responded, I breathed through my nose. "Will you make me the happiest man on earth and marry me?" And the tears spilled forth.

Cameron snapped, "Girlfriend do not mess up that flawless face with tears!"

I laughed and bent down, cupping Ashton's face in my

palms. "There is nothing I want more in this life than to be your wife."

The ring he slipped on my finger was white gold with a princess cut diamond. It was elegant but simple.

"This was my mother's engagement ring. She gave it to me to pass on to the woman I wanted to spend forever with."

He swept me up into his arms and spun me around. I held my arm straight out, gazing at my hand as we spun.

Ashton sat me down and said, "You look amazing tonight, Gracie. You always look amazing."

Music began to play. Cameron cleared his throat and motioned to the speakers so we understood our cue.

Ashton took me to the middle of the room and wrapped his arms around me. The song "To Make You Feel My Love" played. "This is the song we danced to that day." In the rain, at the park, the day we admitted our feelings for each other, it was as though the song was written for us. Nothing could make this moment more perfect.

With his head leaning against mine, we swayed to the music. Ashton moved his hand to the middle of my back and slowly dipped me backward. He leaned forward, trailing his lips along my skin as he pulled me back to him. I bit my lip and smiled when our eyes met. His mouth moved to mine, kissing me softly. A round of applause brought us back to reality and our waiting audience.

My arms tightened around his neck, pulling him into

an embrace. He rested his head on my shoulder. I glanced over at Gavin and Cameron as they danced together.

I loved seeing them dancing together, without fear of being judged. That was why I especially enjoyed hanging out in this club; everyone was accepted here regardless of his or her sexual orientation.

After the dance, our close-knit group sat down to chat while the party continued behind us. "How long have you planned this day?" I asked Ashton.

"Cameron and I planned it a few nights ago. Then everything happened and we thought we would have to postpone. Since Derrick didn't have serious injuries, they agreed to release him as long as he takes it easy and there's no sign of infection. As you can see, MJ has kept him seated the entire time." Ashton threw Mary Jane a wink before continuing, "There is something else we wanted to talk to you about."

Ashton and Cameron exchanged a brief look.

Cameron took my hand. "This is a good thing. I see that you have your freaked-out face on, so I wanted to start with that."

I laughed. "I was freaked out. Go on." With his free hand, Cameron reached for Gavin.

"I agreed to move in with Gavin."

I squealed as Cameron finished his sentence. "That is fantastic!" I hugged him excitedly.

"That isn't the best part. Gavin swayed my decision by proposing to me."

I gasped. "You mean?"

He nodded. "Yep, we're going to New York next month to get married."

I flung myself over both of them hugging them enthusiastically. "You guys! I'm so happy for you!"

"We want you and Ash to come with us, as our witnesses."

I began to cry.

Cameron scoffed, "Gracie, you're gonna ruin your makeup on my big moment!"

I laughed. "Oh, shut up!" I pulled his face to mine and kissed him.

Ashton spoke up next. "So, Gracie, what would you think about getting married in New York as well?"

Cameron smiled. "Wouldn't it be great? We could have a double wedding." It did sound amazing, but also expensive.

"A trip to New York will be expensive enough, but—"

Cameron covered my mouth. "My treat. No argument. Ashton and I have discussed this already. Even though it's legal now to get married in this state, being the bible belt will make it a little more difficult to find an officiant for our wedding. And you and I have talked about going to New York one day. What better reason than our weddings?" Angel walked in a few minutes later with a dress bag. She handed a card over to Ashton.

"What is that?" I asked.

Angel smiled. "Your dress."

I looked at Ashton who was putting his credit card away. "You bought me a dress?"

Angel laughed. "Not just *a* dress... *the* dress. Gracie, this man is the best guy I've ever met. He set it up for me to take you shopping today so you'd find a dress you love. He gave me his credit card and said to buy it, no matter what it cost." Using the thumb and index finger of my right hand, I pinched my left arm. It had to be a dream. If it was, I didn't want to wake up from it. Cameron described Ashton perfectly when he called him Prince Charming on a Harley.

I moved to sit in Ashton's lap. "You... I have no words." I pressed my lips against his, his hands slid around my waist.

He said, "I like that better than words. Are you happy?"

I nodded. "Happy? No. I'm on top of the world."

CHAPTER THIRTY

The next few weeks were full of revelations and announcements that would mean even more changes coming in the lives of my friends and myself.

The first announcement came during a girls' day out with Mary Jane and Angel. When I arrived at the restaurant, the girls were seated and sipping from frozen two-for-one margaritas. "Hey, bitches, where's mine?"

They smiled as the waitress came over. "I just need your ID and I will bring them right out for you." She glanced at my driver's license. Satisfied that I was of age, she brought my two-for-one drinks within a few minutes.

I took a long sip of my drink and sat back with a sigh. "Mmm, delish. So, ladies, we haven't done one of these days in a while!" They exchanged a glance. My bottom lip came out as I exhaled a large puff of air. "This isn't just a fun day, is it?"

Mary Jane shook her head. "I have an announcement." She handed me a letter.

After skimming the details, I exclaimed, "MJ, this is awesome! It says you've been accepted into the engineering program for Disney. That is amazing! This is what you wanted!"

She nodded and sniffed. "Yep, it is. I move to Florida in two weeks to get started."

I felt a pang in my chest at those words. "Two weeks?"

She nodded again. "I know it's fast. I'll be there for two years."

Tears stung my eyes. I swiped at my cheeks. "Well, we'll just have to come visit a lot." She smiled sadly, and then it hit me. "Derrick?"

I placed my hand over hers on the table. "What happened when you told Derrick? Are you guys going to try the long distance thing?"

She shook her head. "No. I won't ask him to wait for me. I broke things off."

I glanced at Angel who nodded slightly. "What did he say?"

She shrugged. "I didn't give him time to respond. I called him, broke the news, broke up with him, and came here."

I sat back. "I see. Two weeks, I can't believe it. Wait...."

Mary Jane knew the realization I had come to before I finished. "I won't be at your wedding. My orientation is that week. Cameron promised he would have it videoed and sent to me though. I hate that I will miss your weddings."

I slumped in my chair. "Me too. I'm happy for you, I really am. I'm going to miss you so very much, sweetie."

Turning to Angel, I said, "I guess that means you and I will need to plan trips to Florida! Hanging out on the beach, sipping margaritas. I can handle that."

Angel exchanged a look with Mary Jane. I sighed again. "Now what was that look about?"

Angel spoke up this time. "With Mary Jane moving away and you moving in with Ash, I can't afford the house on my own. MJ and I were talking, and I've decided to move to Florida with her. It's where I grew up. I kind of miss it, and I can use a change of scenery."

I rested my elbows on the table and put my head in my hands as I sighed sadly. "What am I gonna do without my girls?"

Angel smiled and patted my hand. "You still have Cameron. He's a better girlfriend than MJ and me combined!" We all laughed.

"So you won't be at the wedding either?" I asked.

Angel smiled. "Sweetie, of course I will. Mary Jane has work. I'm going to drive down with MJ and then meet you in New York."

My phone beeped with a text from Ashton.

Ashton: Derrick is here. Can you bring MJ by after lunch without being obvious? He really wants to see her, but she won't return his calls.

I glanced at Mary Jane as I thought about it a moment.

Me: Yeah, I'll figure out something.

"So how are you two going to get along down there

without me?" I said teasingly. I meant for the statement to make us laugh; instead, the three of us began to tear up.

Mary Jane and Angel scooted toward me and put their arms around me. We sat there for a few minutes and cried together.

"Looks like I got here just in time. You girls need some serious cheering up!" Cameron said as he bent to join the hug. He took the seat across from me and put his hand in the air, snapping for the waitress as he shouted, "*Garçon!*"

I laughed and said, "That is French for a male waiter. Ours is female."

"You say hash rounds, I say tater tots," Cameron said with a nonchalant wave of his hand. He noticed my look of confusion and clarified, "It's the same thing."

Still confused, I said, "Like po-tay-to, po-tah-to?"

He scoffed, "Yeah, but really who says po-tah-to? Can I have a baked po-tah-to? Would you like gravy on your mashed po-tah-tos? What kind of pretentious shit says that?" Cameron shrugged. "So, *Garçona*?"

I shook my head. "Try calling her by her name."

The waitress stepped over to Cameron. "Hey, sweetie, I'm Cara. What can I get you?"

Cameron turned to her and said, "So, bring me two piña coladas, please."

Immediately following his response, the four of us chimed in with the lyrics to the country song it reminded us of.

The waitress shook her head laughing at us. Most people in Nashville recognized a Garth Brooks song when it was referenced.

"How did you bitches think you were going to have a girls' day without me?" Cameron asked.

"Ridiculous idea. I don't know what we were thinking," I replied sardonically.

He turned to Mary Jane. "So what is this mess I hear about you dumping that hot hunk of man?" Mary Jane's face drooped, tears filling her eyes once more.

Cameron put his arm around her. "Oh, baby girl, I'm sorry." He kissed her forehead.

Angel chided, "Way to go, Cam." Cameron lifted his hand long enough to flip her off. Angel chuckled. "Enough of this crying! I want to plan something fun for us to do for our last few weeks together."

Cameron chimed in. "A Camloozafantastico?"

"Everything cannot be about Cam!" I said. His hand pressed to his chest as his mouth fell open in shock.

"What? That is sacrilege! Off with your head!" he shouted as he gave a wave of his arm.

When the waitress returned at the end of our meal, she asked, "Is this all separate?"

We all pointed to Cameron. "He's buying."

He spouted, "What a bunch of cunning stunts you are! Feel free to rearrange the letters for what I really think of you. You're lucky I like you ladies."

On the way out, I pulled Mary Jane aside. "Throughout the meal, I was trying to figure out a sneaky way to get you to come back to my house with me, but I can't trick you into something that could be potentially devastating for you. Derrick wants to see you." Mary Jane fidgeted with her purse as she thought about my request.

"I'll go. Thanks for the heads-up though. I don't think I could handle that kind of surprise right now." If I hadn't told Mary Jane, she'd have fled out of fear the moment she saw Derrick. Warning her gave her time to think about what she needed to do. We'd been friends long enough for me to know she doesn't do well in surprise situations.

Cameron plunked his arms around our shoulders. Thankfully he didn't drop a moving bomb on me today or I'd have lost it. Without Ashton and Cameron both by my side, I don't know where I'd be right now. My life would certainly be boring without Cameron around to liven things up. "Ladies, I am escorting you home. MJ, you mind coming to Ash and Gracie's for a bit to hang out?"

Mary Jane smiled. "Nice job, Cam. Gracie told me Derrick wants to talk." Shrugging, I gave a sheepish grin. Telling her was the right thing. I didn't regret it.

Cameron glanced at me. "Smooth, Gracie, real smooth."

Mary Jane interjected, "I'm coming, don't worry."

Cameron kissed her cheek. "All right then, way to go, Gracie!" He never could stay mad at me for long, even pretend mad.

"Angel, you wanna come back to the house with us? We can play pool, have a few drinks... um... a few more drinks." The four of us loaded ourselves into a cab to head to the home I shared with Ashton. Not sure when I would get used to calling his place mine, perhaps once all my stuff was officially moved in. Or after we were married, something else I had to wrap my head around.

Chapter Thirty-One

When we arrived at the house, Mary Jane lagged behind a moment. I stopped to check on her. "You don't have to do this. No one will force you to talk to him if you don't want to."

Mary Jane took a deep breath. "He deserves to have his say. I didn't give him that opportunity before."

The door opened behind us. Derrick's voice sounded low and sad when he spoke, "Mary Jane... can we talk?" Her face lit up when she saw him.

It broke my heart. It was easy to see, she was crazy about him and I hated that they couldn't see this thing through.

"I'm going to head inside."

As I passed Derrick, I whispered, "Be easy on her. This is tearing her up inside to have to choose."

He nodded slightly, never taking his eyes off Mary Jane. As I went inside, I turned and watched as he embraced her.

Once inside, I heard the commotion from downstairs. I approached the door to the basement. A hand covered my mouth, an arm went around my waist and I was pulled away from the door to be pressed against the wall. No fear came in this moment, only trust as I smelled the familiar musk of Ashton's cologne.

I smiled as my eyes focused on Ashton. His lips captured mine in a scorching kiss. One hand moved through my hair while the other hand reached under my knee and lifted my leg around his waist.

His mouth moved to my neck while I said, "As much as I'm enjoying this, our friends are all downstairs waiting on us."

He mumbled, "I know." Instead of stopping, he lifted my other leg around his waist and moved us to the bedroom, kicking the door shut with his foot.

As he laid me on the bed, I started chuckling. "Baby, we can't do this right now."

He lifted my hand to his mouth. "You're right, we can't do this." His tongue made circles along the sensitive spot of my wrist. "We can't do this either." He moved the hem of my shirt up and kissed my stomach softly.

"You're so bad, Ashton Collins."

There was a banging on the door. "Get out here and hang with us, you big horn-dogs! You'll have plenty of time for that later. Now is the time for you to be with friends. So, zip it up, tell Ash Junior he'll get his moment later, and get the hell out here!"

Cameron had such a way with words. Ashton laughed as he helped me up. "You knew he'd be up here shortly."

Ashton nodded. "I was hopeful that we'd have a second."

I gasped. "Oooh, a second. I'm really sorry I'm missing that!"

He growled low in my ear and said, "You know I last way longer than a second."

The banging started again. "Don't make me stand out here and talk about things that will ruin the mood. I'll do it. You just—"

His voice cut off into a mumble. Ashton opened the door to see Gavin covering Cameron's mouth with his hand.

"Thanks, Gavin."

Gavin smiled at Ashton. "My pleasure."

As I stepped from the room, I stopped when I looked and noticed Derrick on the couch. I patted Ashton's shoulder. "I'll be down in a moment."

I sat next to Derrick. "Hey. Where's MJ?"

He took a swig from the beer bottle in his hand. "She left."

I turned to face him, pulling my leg up beneath me. "You want to talk about it?"

He took another drink. "Not much to say. She wants to follow her dreams and said that it's the obvious choice because she isn't in love with me."

I sighed. "You know that isn't true."

He sneered, "Do I? She made it pretty clear to me that she doesn't feel anything for me. She said she is attracted to me and we had fun, but it wasn't going anywhere."

"She lied, doofus. She's trying to protect you so that you move on."

He sighed. "I know. I can't make her stay though and give up everything she's worked for, and I can't make her tell me that she's falling for me too."

I patted his shoulder. "Come downstairs and hang out with everyone."

When we made it downstairs, Ashton and Cameron were playing an intense game of pool. The moment my feet reached the bottom step, the doorbell rang. I figured it was Mary Jane coming back. "You go enjoy yourself, Derrick. I'm going to see who that is."

On my way to the door, I had no idea of the next revelation I would discover. Standing at the door was a well-groomed older gentleman holding an accordion folder.

"Are you Gracie Walker?" Holding up his hand, he flashed a badge with a detective number on it.

Before answering him, I lifted my cell phone and dialed Ashton. "I need you up here now."

Within less than a minute, Ashton was beside me. "Can I help you?" he asked the man in front of me.

"My name is Jackson Simms. I'm one of the officers who worked Gracie's case against Hudson James."

Ashton extended his hand. "Ashton Collins, Gracie's fiancé. Come in please." He motioned the man to the couch. Following them silently, I hoped this would be the last time I had to hear Hudson's name on anyone's lips.

"I came by today to let you know we're closing the file on this case." Preparing for the worst, I took a seat placing my hands underneath my thighs to hide the tremble of fear.

Jackson went on to say, "We found files on his computer where he had taped you. There werc hundreds of pictures of you at your workplace, school, clubs, your home."

My chest tightened and I sat forward abruptly. "What... how... why?" Ashton tried to soothe me but I pushed him away and stood up. Pacing the room, I tried to take calming breaths, shaking my hands at my sides in a nervous fidget.

Jackson continued, "It's classic stalker behavior." His focus turned to Ashton. "He even had pictures of you." As he spoke, my head began to spin with how far Hudson had gone.

"We have determined Hudson was a danger to you and your family based on the information gathered. No charges will be pursued against you for the supposed trespassing he accused you of, nor will they be pursued against Derrick Collins."

Bile rose in my throat, threatening to spill forth. "Were there any pictures, any videos of...." I couldn't finish the thought of the compromising positions he may have captured.

Jackson understood my concern. "No, there was nothing sexual that I saw. I'm sorry to drop all of this on you. We wanted to give you closure on the matter."

I stepped forward and extended my hand to him. He shook it as I said, "Thank you. I don't mean to be rude, but I would really like you to leave my house now." I needed the space and distance before a stranger would see me break down. I was too close to the edge of losing it.

Ashton stood up and escorted him to the door. Just when I thought it couldn't get any worse, I had to relive everything Hudson did to me. Thinking back to determine what moments he might have captured, what sick twisted things he did with those pictures.

Ashton closed the door and stood there waiting to see what I needed. Emotionally exhausted, I collapsed to the floor in tears. He slid beside me and wrapped his arms tightly around my body. Finding shelter in his arms, I let myself release raw pain. He pulled my head into his chest, comforting me silently as I sobbed. It seemed that every time it felt like I could move on, something else made the world crash down around me. Knowing that Hudson had been watching my every move, taping moments of solitude, it felt like being raped all over again.

"If you two are engaging in happy naked fun time again, I'm going to have to bust in there and end this madness once and for all! For freak's sake, you have friends in the house!" Cameron yelled into the bedroom.

He didn't notice us on the living room floor until Gavin said, "Ash... what happened?"

Cameron ran over and bent next to me. "What's wrong, baby girl?"

I shook my head, not sure I would ever be able to share all I'd discovered. "Ash, please, can you tell them?" Ashton went downstairs to fill everyone in at once. It was more than I could handle and I went to lie down. Downy comfort welcomed me in its arms as I slid under the blanket. Closing my eyes, I wished the world would disappear for a little while until I was ready to face it again. As much as I needed the closure, it was hard to stomach the extreme nature of Hudson's obsession with me.

I was drifting to sleep when a familiar smell filled my nose and I felt the bed sink with his weight. He pulled me close and kissed my head. I grinned. "How'd you know I needed you right now more than anyone else?"

His head leaned against mine. "Because practically from birth, it's been you and me, baby girl, against the world."

I turned to face Cameron. He kept his arms around me, and I sighed deeply. "When do I get to be happy, Cam? When do Ash and I get to move on and enjoy our lives?"

Cameron kissed my head. "Soon. Your time is right around the corner." He lifted my chin to look at him. "You can't let every obstacle that gets in your way stop you from going after what you want. You're about to marry the man of your dreams. Hudson is gone. I can't imagine anything else will come out regarding that. I know it hurts, but you have closure today. You now know everything that was going on and you know that Hudson was a sick man."

"Tell me you and Gavin are planning on living in Nashville. Please, I beg you." I placed my palms together, the way we were taught to pray in church.

Cameron scoffed, "You can't get rid of me, you know that." The thought of losing all my friends at once made my stomach ache with apprehension. Angel and Mary Jane were the two closest girlfriends I had ever had and soon they would be hundreds of miles away.

The bedroom door opened, and Ashton walked in. He sat on the edge of the bed next to me and reached for my hand. Cameron glanced up. "You wanna join us in bed, Ash? You can cuddle with me if you'd like." He batted his eyes at Ashton playfully. I giggled as Ashton shook his head. Cameron's skill at lightening the mood was unmatchable.

He brushed my hair aside. "I may need to move you in with us, Cam, so you can keep that smile on her face."

I sat up instantly, worried that I had made him feel inadequate. "You make me smile too."

Cameron sat up. "I'm going to go round up the gang to head home and give you two some alone time."

I stood up and hugged Cameron. "Call me later?"

He kissed my cheek. "You know I will. I'll need to hear all the dirty details of the dirty deeds you're about to take care of."

I smacked his butt as he walked out of the room. He howled and stuck his hips out toward me. "Do it again, baby!" I shoved him through the doorway, laughing as I followed behind him to say goodnight to my friends.

Once we had the house to ourselves again, I settled next to Ashton on the couch. "You know you've brought out my smile many times."

Lips lingering against my forehead, he mumbled, "You make me happy, too."

Chapter Thirty-Two

The next two weeks went by incredibly fast. Mary Jane, Angel, and I tried to spend as much time together as we could by running errands to get them ready for their move. Packing the house got in the way of that, a lot.

Ashton was helping me pack my room. I had gone down the hall to Angel's room so that we could switch back the clothes we had borrowed from each other. When I returned a few minutes later, he was sitting on the bed with his back to me.

"Oh no, you found my senior scrapbook," I said, groaning and taking the seat next to him.

He smiled. "These pictures are awesome. I had no clue you went to private school."

I sighed. "Yep, not just private school, a catholic private school. Don't ask if I still have the uniform."

He snickered. "What? Why would I ask that?"

Rolling my eyes, I responded. "Every time a guy finds out I went to Catholic school, his next question is always 'Do you still have the uniform?'"

He flipped through the album remaining quiet. I watched his face as he fought with the urge to ask.

Finally, he grinned and looked up. "So... do you?" I tackled him to the bed. He guffawed with laughter as I rolled around on the bed with him.

After we settled down, he flipped through the book some more. "Oh, what's up with Cameron's hair in this one?" It was striped with purple and pink.

"He was going through a phase, trying something new. It lasted maybe a week before he grew bored with it. I snapped the picture as a reminder in case he got the idea again. A definite don't."

There was a knock on the door, and Mary Jane entered. "Ash, can you help Cameron and Gavin with loading the van for Angel and me?"

Ashton handed me the scrapbook and jumped up. "Absolutely." He left and Angel came in behind Mary Jane.

"We got you something," Mary Jane said as she sat next to me on the bed. She handed me a small velvet bag that was tightened with rope to hold it closed. "We wanted you to have something that you could carry with you to remind you of us." I opened the pouch and out dropped two charms.

Mary Jane lifted one from my hand. "High heels seemed appropriate for both of us. These look like the ones you borrowed from Angel the night you met Ash." She lifted the other charm, which was a pea pod with three peas inside. "This charm is to represent how we are three peas in a pod."

Together they held up their wrists to show matching bracelets with the same two charms. My emotions got the better of me. Three sets of arms entwined in a huddle as our bodies shook with sobs.

Cameron pushed open the door and exclaimed, "What the hell is all this crying about?" When we showed him the bracelets, he stepped back, placed one hand on his hip and stuck the other out palm up. "Where's mine?"

Mary Jane reached into her pocket and pulled out a velvet bag that matched mine. "We didn't forget about you." Cameron pulled out his charms that were attached to a key ring. He had two charms as well, one was a princess crown and the other was a tree symbol.

Mary Jane took the keychain from him and said, "The princess crown is obvious. The tree is the Celtic symbol for guardian or protector. You're our protector and we'll never forget that."

He stepped back and fell to the bed covering his mouth. He cursed, "I am so pissed at you, bitches." His face screwed up as he began to cry.

The three of us embraced him. "We love you, Cam."

He sniffed and whimpered out in a high-pitched voice, "I can't believe you made me do the ugly-cry today. I freaking hate good-byes and you know that crying totally makes my face puffy and gross looking." We tried to laugh through the tears. The tears won.

Ashton opened the door and said, "Cars all packed and... what did I miss?"

Cameron stood up and threw his arms around Ashton. "Hold me." Ashton hugged Cameron tightly. I loved how he would appease him no matter what.

Displaying my wrist, I said, "Check out what MJ and Angel gave me, more charms for my bracelet."

Ashton smiled at them. "I have one for you as well." He pulled a small silver charm out of his pocket and it was a tree that matched Cam's. "They told me about the idea and I went with them. This is a matching charm to Cam's, to represent him as your protector on your bracelet. That way, you have all of us on there now."

From behind Ashton, Cameron shouted, "Son of a bitch!" I moved to see what was wrong. His hands were tangled in his shirt as he used it to blot the tears from his eyes. "That's it! I need out of this cryfest!" He stomped out of the room and down the stairs.

Angel snickered. "He's such a drama queen."

From down the hall, Cameron's voice yelled out, "I'm a drama *princess*! Gah! Get it right!"

The last of the boxes were packed. The house was emptier than I ever remembered it being. I remembered the day I moved in and it wasn't this empty. Angel had moved in the day before and her things were strewn everywhere. Mary Jane and I gave her a hard time for staking her claim on her bedroom before we ever had the chance.

Everyone had moved outside where they were standing around, desperately trying to avoid saying good-bye. I stood in the doorway and as I looked in the living room, I could see all of us sitting around the table playing cards. The laughter, the music blaring, the drinks sloshing, it was a constant party in this house at one time.

Angel came up behind me and put her arm across my shoulders. "You ready to go, chica?"

I sighed. "I'm going to miss this place."

She leaned her head against mine. "Me too. We had a lot of good times here." We left the spare keys on the stairs in an envelope for the landlord, along with a nice gift of thanks for always being good to us.

Mary Jane, Angel, Cam and I stood in a group hug, not wanting to let go. After more tears, we broke apart.

Angel turned to me one last time. "I'll be hopping on a plane to New York soon! Next time I see you, you'll be getting married!"

I smiled excitedly. "Can't wait. Love you, guys! Be careful, please! Call me as soon as you get to Florida."

Mary Jane hugged me tightly. "I love you. I'm so sorry I'll miss the wedding." She pointed a finger in Cameron's face. "You'd better get a great video of it for me!"

He raised his hands. "Yes, ma'am! When did you become Ms. Bossy Britches?" She tugged him into her embrace and gave him a kiss. As they were saying their good-byes, a car pulled into the driveway.

Derrick stepped out and I looked to Mary Jane for her reaction. She hadn't seen him yet. Holding a gift box, he ran to her. "MJ!" She turned and smiled as he ran straight for her. "I know you didn't want me to see you again. I had to get this to you though." She opened it up and found a painted coffee mug. It had a handprint painted on the mug in pink with "I love you" in black; the background of the mug was baby blue. "Katelyn painted it for you. She wanted you to have something to remember her by," Derrick said.

She glanced inside and pulled out movie stubs, a pink carnation and some tokens from Chuck E. Cheese's. "I added those to remind you of me. I won't forget our time together and I hope you won't either."

I clung to Ashton as I watched the immense joy and heartache roll over Mary Jane, all at once. With his index finger, Derrick lifted Mary Jane's chin to look at him. "Are you mad I came by with it?" Instead of answering, she pulled him forward into a very passionate kiss. His hands tangled in her hair as her hands went around his waist and pulled at his shirt as though she couldn't bring him close enough to her.

Cameron, in true Cam fashion, interrupted with, "Whew, honey—" But before he could finish, Gavin and I both slapped our hands over his mouth to muffle him. We stood watching them lose themselves in each other. Their good-bye gave me mixed emotions. I was elated at how close they'd become, but sad that they may be over before they even had a chance to begin. When the moment ended, they stood smiling, foreheads pressed together. "I'll call you when I get to Florida?" she asked, not sure how Derrick would feel about it. Crossing my fingers, eyes closed, I hoped they would decide on giving a long distance romance a try.

His grin widened. "I'd love that. Be careful, sweetheart." He kissed her forehead, took her hand and walked her to the car. Nudging Ashton with my elbow, I flashed him a goofy grin of excitement over the sweet couple.

We waved good-bye as they drove away. I couldn't stop waving until they were completely out of sight. Again, my emotions were at war as I felt happy for Mary Jane's success, yet heartbroken as my friends moved hundreds of miles away. Shoulders slumped, I turned back toward the house one last time. Ashton put his arm around me. "Come on, let's go home."

CHAPTER THIRTY-THREE

When the plane landed in New York, Cameron broke out into song. He walked through the airport singing "New York, New York" as he kicked his legs up Rockette style.

Once inside the city, he was elated about everything. "This is just how it looks in the movies! I love this town! Look!" He pointed at a group of people that were all same-sex couples. "I'm in gay heaven." He turned to Gavin, grabbing his hand. "We may need to move here!"

My heart clenched at those words. He turned to me and winked. I relaxed, knowing he was teasing me. With everything we'd been through, I was unsure I could handle Cameron living more than a short drive away. It'd been hard enough getting used to my girls being gone.

Angel would arrive later that evening. They had been gone for two weeks. Though we spoke every other day, I missed them immensely. Mary Jane and Derrick decided to be friends, as hard as that might be. In two years, when her program was complete, they would revisit the idea of a relationship if they both felt the same.

Arriving at the hotel, Ashton checked us in, and then Cameron and I shopped in the boutiques while he took our bags upstairs.

After an hour, we headed to the room. Ashton and Gavin would share a room tonight and I would be with Cameron. This was to keep up the tradition of not seeing the bride the night before the wedding.

I opened the door to the suite and stepped inside. The suite seemed to be bigger than my house. I flopped down on the plush white couch, propping my feet on the coffee table. Ashton smiled. "Go check out the bathroom. You can have your *Pretty Woman* bath moment in there."

I jumped up and ran to see. The tub was humongous and I couldn't wait to use it. I ran across the living room to the bedroom and flopped on the bed, bouncing as I landed. I smiled at myself and the thought I had. I slipped my shoes off and pulled myself up on the bed. I began to hop up and down, using the bed as a trampoline.

"Can't take you anywhere, can we?" a female voice rang out. I screamed and fell to the bed as I was tackled by Angel. We rolled around, hugging. "Come help me with my damn bags." Angel's sparky attitude is one of the things I've missed most about her.

For the next few hours, we explored the city. We didn't have a lot of time to go to all the museums and shows that we would've wanted to. We visited the Statue of Liberty and the Empire State Building. Those places were fun, and we took crazy pictures to send to Mary Jane. Cameron wanted a picture of himself as he went up, inside the Statue of Liberty.

He posted it on Facebook with the caption of, "The one and only time I'll ever be inside a woman."

We texted that to Mary Jane with the same caption, and she texted back immediately with as many LOLs as she could type.

We headed back to the hotel for the evening. Cameron and Gavin said their goodnights while Angel went to set up some drinks for our evening of girl time. The day reminded me of old times—before Hudson. Even though it reminded me of the past, this trip in itself was a new beginning.

"This time tomorrow, you'll be Mrs. Ashton Collins."

My heart fluttered at those words. "I can't wait." He pulled me forward and pressed his lips to mine. His tongue ran across my lips lightly, pressing me to open and invite him in. If I felt even half the love for him in fifty years that I feel on this day, I knew it'd be an amazing marriage.

"Ahem!" Cameron interrupted.

I giggled, pulling away from Ashton. "Uh-oh, it's the make-out police again."

Cameron smacked my bottom. "Get to your room, young lady. It is getting close to midnight and you cannot afford any bad mojo for tomorrow!"

One last kiss from Ashton and I reluctantly left him to go to my own room. Angel had a couple of cold beers waiting for us. She turned on the television and found a movie on for us to watch. We had run ourselves so ragged, that the couple of beers we drank put us straight to sleep.

In the morning, I woke up smiling. I bounced on the bed to wake Angel. Cameron wasn't in his bed to annoy, so I assumed he'd woken up earlier.

"I'm getting married today!" I exclaimed.

She reached back to slap me and pulled a pillow over her face as she mumbled something in Spanish that didn't sound like a nice word.

I ran to get in the shower and my phone beeped. It was a text from Ashton.

Ashton: We can't talk or see each other, but we can text. I missed you last night. Walk to the door. Place your hand in the center, right over the peephole.

I texted him back, one handed.

Me: Done.

Ashton: Now press your body against the door and press your lips to it. I'll do the same on this side.

I did as he asked. I heard snickering from behind me and saw Cameron texting and laughing.

I stood with my hands on my hips. "What the hell are you doing?"

He snickered. "Making you look like an asshat as you molest the door. Ash left his phone here last night, and I couldn't resist! Shit, you'll do anything he tells you to do." He made the motion of a whip with his hand and made a sound to accompany it, "Wi-kssh."

I rolled my eyes. "As if Gavin doesn't have you whipped as well."

He grinned. "Touché." Thinking back to the struggles we both had with men,—for me it was bad decisions, for Cameron it was that he loved men in a world where many called it wrong—we'd both come so far in a short time.

The wedding was in Central Park and we had three hours until we were supposed to be there to meet everyone. Ashton's parents were meeting us there with Katelyn. They flew in the night before and kept watch over her so that Derrick and Ashton could spend time together.

Angel fixed my hair. In awe of her talent, I admired her work as she curled the edges and pulled one side back with a beautiful comb edged in diamonds. "The comb is your something new. Mary Jane and I bought it for you. As for your something old,"—she reached in her purse and pulled out a pair of thunderbolt rainbow earrings— "remember these?"

I doubled over in laughter. "I wore them every day of high school! They were my favorite earrings until I lost them when we went camping. Where did you find them?" Words escaped me for how perfect they had done in upholding this long-time wedding tradition.

She smiled. "I found them when I was packing the house. Now for your something borrowed." She reached into her pocket and pulled out a necklace.

"That's MJ's mother's necklace," I said as I reached for it. Desperately fighting back tears, I gazed up at the ceiling as though trying to make them roll back into my eyes instead of down my cheeks.

Angel nodded. "She sent it for you to wear today as

your something borrowed and as a piece of her with you." Closing my hand around it I held it next to my heart. Mary Jane had rarely been seen without this necklace on. I knew it took great strength for her to part from it.

"Last but not least, your something blue." She held up a blue garter belt and wiggled her eyebrows at me. I grinned and stuck my leg up for her to slide it on.

Once we were all dressed and ready to go, we stepped outside to hail a cab. Angel gasped as she saw a horse drawn carriage approach. "Dang, girl, that's the ride you need! Let me ask how much it would cost. Maybe we can get it for you!"

Before she could move, the man on the carriage yelled out, "Ms. Gracie Walker, Mr. Cameron McIntosh, your carriage awaits."

Ashton and Gavin must have arranged the carriage for us. Angel, Cameron, and I squealed with delight as we climbed up into the coach. We were on our way to the park in style. I felt like a true princess in my beautiful gown. Everyone on the street waved and took pictures of us. Angel looked stunning in her red satin dress with thin diamond belt. Cameron was dashing in his white tuxedo with his red rose boutonniere.

When we arrived at the park, I saw Ashton and Gavin standing together under a flower archway. Ashton's gaze met mine as I was helped out of the carriage. His face illustrated the joy that I felt. We both sucked in our bottom lips to keep from crying.

Katelyn ran up to me with her basket of flowers. She stepped in front and led the way by scattering the petals. She was thrilled at the opportunity. Before Angel started her walk, she whispered, "Don't ruin your makeup or Cameron will kill you." I laughed and gave her a thumbs-up. She moved down the carpeted walkway to stand beside Ashton. Cameron stuck his arm out to me.

My family had wanted to come, but they were overseas on business for my stepfather. They made a family trip of it and had planned it long before I knew I was getting married. Disappointment wouldn't cloud my day. Most of my family was with me today, the family I chose. We decided it was poetic for Cameron and me to walk each other down the aisle.

"I love you, baby girl," Cameron whispered as he kissed my cheek. Practically perfect in every way, that's how I would describe this moment. Nothing could ruin it for me, and I didn't even worry about jinxing things by having the thought.

"I love you more, Cam." He handed me over to Ashton and we joined hands before Cameron stepped over to Gavin and held his hand. The minister would perform both ceremonies at once.

When it came time for the vows, I began, "Ashton Collins, you are my very best friend." Cameron cleared his throat, loudly. I chuckled. "My very best *straight* friend."

Cameron gave a curt nod. "Much better."

A wave of laughter erupted. "From the first moment

I met you, I knew I loved you. When you met me I was incomplete, like an unfinished painting. You came into my life as a friend and opened my eyes to the beauty and the goodness in this world. When my world became dark again, you brightened it with your love for me. You took me in and you protected me and loved me unconditionally. Your love saved my life."

Ashton had tears in his eyes as he smiled at me. It was his turn. He sniffed back his tears and took a deep breath. I gave his hand a squeeze. "You say I saved your life, but you saved mine. I never thought I could love someone as much as I love you. The night I met you, my life started over. You make me laugh. You amaze me with your strength and loyalty. I knew that first night that I wanted to know you for the rest of my life. No matter what role I played in your life, I wanted to be part of it. You've brought me more joy than I ever thought I could feel again. You're my best friend, the love of my life, my Gracie-bug."

Everyone around gave a resounding "Aww." I laughed through my tears of bliss while Ashton winked at me, squeezing my hand.

Epilogue

Ashton and I had been married for two years and I kept waiting for the day I'd wake up from this fabulous dream. Each day, I came home from school expecting that he wouldn't be there because I had imagined the whole thing.

After a long day of classes, I wanted to curl up on the couch with Ashton and relax with a glass of wine. As I opened the door, my heart stopped at the sight in front of me.

Ashton was holding her in his arms, gazing into her eyes, and telling her how beautiful she was and how he never thought he could love someone as much as he loved me.

A tear fell from my cheek as he glanced up and said, "Uh-oh, Autumn, Mommy's crying again."

Autumn was five months old and I still hadn't gotten

used to the sight of her with Ashton. He was the best father that any woman could want for her daughter.

"They're happy tears, though." He grinned and patted the seat next to him.

"What have you and our princess been up to all day?"

Her chubby cheeks shifted as her little plump lips formed into a grin at seeing my face. Ashton passed her to me to cuddle.

She giggled as I pressed kisses against her chubby cheeks and spoke in my cartoon voice to tell her that I'd missed them both so much.

Once I had hit my last trimester of pregnancy, I took the next semester of school off so I could spend time with the baby after she was born. I then started back once she turned four months and it was almost time for me to graduate.

Ashton spent the day with her while I went to school. He ran his business mostly from home now. We set up an office for him to meet with clients in the third bedroom. When they couldn't meet at the house, he could meet them at their clubs at night, so it worked out that one of us was always with Autumn.

Her name was easy to choose; it was the time of year when we met and our favorite season. Soft silky jet-black hair fell in curls around her chubby face. The happiest baby I'd ever seen with a smile like her daddy's that could melt my heart. Everyone loved her and she loved any attention. She rarely cried and, of course, she was the most beautiful little girl in the world.

Even at such a young age, it was plain to see that she adored Ashton as much as I did. Cameron and Gavin had a baby girl via surrogate, shortly after we found out we were pregnant. They named her Addison Grace, which meant the world to Ashton and me. Cameron spoiled her rotten.

I thought, between Autumn and Addison, he would go broke in no time. He dubbed himself Uncle of the Year, but I had to say, I agreed with the title.

"How was school?" Ashton asked.

I was working on my doctorate in psychology. If it all worked out, in a year, I would complete my studies.

"Not bad. We start our internships soon. I spoke to my counselor and she has agreed to let me intern at her practice. She is going to give me a few of her patients after she speaks with them first. She asked if it would be all right to tell them about my experience, to make them more comfortable. Of course, I told her it was fine."

Ashton nodded. "I'm so proud of you, bug."

Life was good. I could say that now without a doubt. The first few months without Angel and Mary Jane were difficult. We soon discovered, though that we talked as much as we ever did. It was still hard not to see each other every day, but we had been down to visit twice now, and they'd visited to meet Autumn.

Though the journey had been a long one with many curves and complications, it was worth the ride. Everything Ashton and I have been through brought us to where we are now and I wouldn't trade a minute with him. At last I could find peace with what happened to me and be proud of the woman I've become.

THE END

If you or someone you know has been the victim of rape or abuse find a crisis center close to you for help by logging on to <u>WWW.CENTERS.RAINN.ORG</u> or you can reach your local crisis center at any time by calling National Sexual Assault Hotline at 1.800.656.HOPE (4673).

No one is ever alone.
There is always someone out there willing to help.

Acknowledgments

For the inspiration of Gracie's friends in this book, I'd like to acknowledge my "Looza" buddies. We created the Looza events four years ago, and those are some of the best memories I have. We may not see each other every day, but you're all very special to me. Without you, there wouldn't be crazy card games, wacky shots, stories of immense TMI nature, pirate talk ("Argh, where's me cup?") and nights of good-natured debauchery.

Thank you to the wonderful Hot Tree Publishing for helping me relive this book all over again and taking so much time to help make it great!

I've been very lucky and made many amazing friends in the book community. We share a love of books, we boost each other's confidence, we "pimp" each other out, sometimes we even inspire each other. It's an amazing community!

Some of my biggest supporters have been right here at home. My mom "pimps" me out to everyone she knows. She has sold more books for me than I have sold for myself! Both of my parents have been fantastic in supporting me in this endeavor in my life.

Last, but in no way least, my husband. He was the inspiration for Ashton in this book. He is my Prince Charming, my saving grace. He may not read my "mushy" books, but he supports me in every facet of my writing. He encourages me to keep going, even when I'm ready to give up. He helps me with technical support, allows me to bounce ideas off him, even helps keep my Facebook pages running. Without him, I'd be a mess. Daniel, my best friend, my love, my everything... thank you!

I enjoy making new friends to share my love of books with. Feel free to come join me on my Facebook pages:

www.facebook.com/AmyKMcclung is my author page on Facebook where I share information about my writing. I also pimp other authors, do lots of giveaways, and just post random thoughts at times.

www.facebook.com/CascadesOfMoonlight is the book page for my first set of books, a YA paranormal romance, The Parker Harris series. I'd love for you to get to know Parker and her friends. My next YA series will be a spinoff of Parker Harris with a character introduced in the second book.

About the Publisher

Hot Tree Publishing opened its doors in 2015 with an aspiration to bring quality fiction to the world of readers. With the initial focus on romance and a wide spread of romance sub-genres, we envision opening up to alternative genres in the near future.

Firmly seated in the industry as a leading editing provider to independent authors and small publishing houses, Hot Tree Publishing is the sister company to Hot Tree Editing, founded in 2012. Having established in-house editing and promotions, plus having a well-respected market presence, Hot Tree Publishing endeavors to be a leader in bringing quality stories to the world of readers.

Interested in discovering more amazing reads brought to you by Hot Tree Publishing or perhaps you're interested in submitting a manuscript and joining the HTPubs family? Either way, head over to the website for information:

WWW.HOTTREEPUBLISHING.COM